The Sermon & Other Stories

Haim Hazaz

THE SERMON
& OTHER STORIES

INTRODUCTION BY

Dan Miron

The Toby Press

The Toby Press *LLC*

First Edition, 2005

POB 8531, New Milford, CT 06776–8531, USA &
POB 2455, London W1A 5WY, England

www.tobypress.com

Introduction copyright © 2005 by Dan Miron

The Toby Press thanks Aviva Hazaz and Gil Weissblei of The
Haim Hazaz Memorial Foundation for their kind assistance
in the preparation of this revised edition. All translations
are © The Haim Hazaz Memorial Foundation.

ISBN 1 59264 121 0, *paperback*

A CIP catalogue record for this title is
available from the British Library

Typeset in Garamond by Jerusalem Typesetting

Printed and bound in the United States
by Thomson-Shore Inc., Michigan

Contents

Dan Miron

Introduction

*Eppur si muove**

Haim Hazaz burst in Hebrew literature in the 1920s as an innovative, revolutionary writer. His innovation appeared to flow directly from the tempestuous times and from the content of his first stories, which fixed his image in his readers' eyes for a generation: Jewish *shtetls* in the Ukraine, overthrown in the pangs of the revolution, the horrors of the civil war, with constant pogroms, and the oppression of the Bolshevik regime. It was already clear to Hazaz at that time, in the early 1920s, before pretending to settle a general account with the revolution, that it would bring utter disaster down upon the historical life and identity of the Jewish people, as they had taken shape over generations in Eastern Europe.

This reality—agitated, shaken, tragic, and apocalyptic in its essence—required a literary transmission that was no less agitated: a transmission full of sharp twists, breaks and fragmentation, dialogues spoken as though by people who are meeting one another on the run, and their brief words said as though between gasping breaths. The

* An address given at the President's House at a conference to mark the thirtieth anniversary of the author's death (July 21, 2003).

I

characters, the landscape, the world of the shtetl, the snowstorms of its winters and the glow of its summers had to be transmitted all at once, with no lingering embroidery of characterization or description, with the shortcuts of bold metaphors, with compressed and grinding alliterations, like the sound of snow pressed under boots, which Hazaz compared to the sound of a radish crying while a knife cut it.

Those who read stories have felt how the upheavals of the period and its horrors reached them, tangibly and directly—though out of the pages of the heavy volumes of the period. All at once, ponderousness and respectability were laid aside, and those tomes became light and vibrant. For years, many readers would recall descriptive passages such as this one:

> Wrapped up and dark stood the shtetl, and against its will bitter, plaintive rains washed it. From above—wet gloom, and from below—a fallen, quartered, sunken, prone land, screeching with its thousand mouths of mud.
>
>   ("Shmuel Frankfurter," *Ha'tekuphah*[1] 23, p. 91).

Or:

> Suns overlapped with moons. Moons overlapped with suns. Stars shone in daytime and squeaked underfoot. The heavenly hosts, bandaged, rested on the tops of houses and trees, and, dully, over the street—flew the winds. Suns, moons, stars, fires of candles of Yom Kippur eve, lights of Havdalah wicks.
>
>   (Ibid., p. 119)

Or sentences like this one:

---

1.   *Ha'tekuphah* (Heb. "The Age") Hebrew quarterly appearing 1918-50, published chronologically from Moscow, and then from Warsaw, Berlin, Tel Aviv and New York. Besides original contributions, both literary and scientific, it contained translations of major works of world literature.

Like a white-haired ram the first snow suddenly battered the darkened houses (Ibid., p. 95).

The evening twilight ended. The twilight was tangibly yellow, physical. Above, above, up to the sky, the evening rose.

("From This and From This," *Ha'tekuphah* 21, p. 20)

There are many similar examples.

It quickly became clear, at any event, that the shock and sense of dislocation, which perhaps really came to the stories from the times and from the subject (although in the literature of the time, there were also works, like the novel *1919* by Abraham Freiman, which processed the same background and the very same subjects in broad, leisurely, epic scope), extended far beyond them. At the start of his career, the stories of Hazaz seemed to want to break out of any narrow thematic boundary: to go beyond the landscape of the besieged shtetl to reach other landscapes and areas: to the Constantinople and Paris of Russian-Jewish immigrants, to mythical, biblical antiquity, in which Bible stories take place as though in an ancient version prior to the biblical one, to Ashkenazi Jewry in the days of Shabetai Zvi. In all of these, Hazaz remained faithful to the new principles of literary transmission that he applied in his stories of the revolution.

The distance between the stormy, snowy landscape of the shtetl and the ancient desert landscape was not great, as was evident from reading the first, unforgettable lines of the story, "Bridegroom of Blood," a masterpiece of the young writer:

The desert wastes rested, spread out. Flattened, flattened and wave upon wave—sometimes brush, sometimes rocks and ravine, the desert's body extended: depth within depth and light-crevice within light-crevice—from close, close by to far, far off. The beginning of the world, glowing, is measured, its extent obeys the firmament and is equal to the barrenness: the sky borrows its desolation, and the desolation borrows from the sky—and they suit each other.

(*Seething Stones*, p. 7)

3

Thus, we find that Hazaz not only brought a new subject or tone to Hebrew literature but also a new narrative principle, and his artistic mission, which is essentially revolutionary, was embodied in that principle.

⅋

What was that principle? It may be said simply, without getting involved in various literary "-isms," as respectable as they may be, such as expressionism or imagism: the principle was the principle of movement—total, energetic, constant movement, action, motion (so much so, that sometimes you wonder whether that was the source of his nom de plume—since "Hazaz" could be read as meaning: the "one who moves")—and with the movement, the interpenetration, as well: everything penetrates everything and mingles with it—earth and sky, cosmos and man, one person and another.

The literary transmission of reality is determined according to this principle, the essence of which is not the solid object and also not the subject possessing consciousness and emotions, but rather something more comprehensive and general, a kind of cosmic inter-leaving that mixes space and time, nature and history, that sweeps both the object and the subject into it, merging them and making them into a single dynamic entity.

In 1930, when Hazaz published the first two volumes of his first large novel (which was never completed), *In the Forest Settlement*, it turned out, to the consternation of quite a few readers, that he had decided not to part with the principle of feverish movement even when he told a leisurely and seemingly calm story, dealing with what appeared to be reality distant from any focus of tension and danger: a dense forest in the Ukraine in the early twentieth century. There Ukrainian woodsmen chop down the trees, a Jewish "*kassir*" (cashier) lives in a house in the forest and supervises them, and a young Jewish intellectual, who recalls the deracinated heroes of Gnessin and Y.R. Berkovitz, is brought to his house to serve as tutor to his sons. The atmosphere of the forest in the spring, which might have aroused another author to paint a static, ideal picture of nature, is described in the following way:

4

Curled up and closed green, painted brown, broken up with opening after opening, break after break to the sky, the forest stood, friendly and singing, and it raised its convoluted folds on high, to between the upper and lower worlds. Murmurs in tendrils of sun and shade, bright and gay, gladdened by the cheery art of chirps and chirping and song. Rutted paths stretched into one another. Long blue shadows flitted like madmen in the grass from one tree to another, meanwhile making the air all green like the sun, a new and clear brilliance.

(*In the Forest Settlement*, 1)

The essence of this description, which begins by presenting the forest as a static object, brown and green, closed and blockaded, is its breaking into the object, making holes in it, making it move increasingly both upward, toward the space between earth and heaven, and also downward, toward the earth, where long shadows spread like "madmen," spoiling the order, mixing tree with tree and blue with green. What appears to begin as a complex and heavy sentence rapidly becomes a syntactic bacchanalia, full of movement, voices and hues that intermingle, become a single ecstatic experience.

If we place this description alongside prominent descriptions that preceded it in modern Hebrew literature, we sense that Hazaz took a third step after the two steps that had been taken before him. First the literature taught itself how to describe what was, reality, as a static, well constructed object, with weight and fullness (Mendele and his school). After that, in the work of Berdichevsky, Brenner, and especially Uri Nissan Gnessin, it learned to present reality, what is, as movement taking place within the subject—movement of the mind, consciousness, and emotions, which is usually movement around a point, moving in repeated circles. Hazaz took another step. As noted, he discovered the cosmic movement that rules both the object and the subject, like the discovery of the movement of electrons, which continues in the prison of the atoms, from which the objects, which appear to be stable and static, are composed: a mountain, a boulder, a knotty tree trunk, the shtetl houses, wealthy Reb Zundele, who sits at his table with all his weight and enjoys the ringing of pots—none of these is truly at rest or in its place. The mountain stands with all its weight but also floats in the air. The houses of the shtetl Otshratnya in *Dorot Harishonim* ("Previous Generations") appear to be the faces of people burdened with heavy hats, abundantly bearded, lying on their sides, collapsing, raising themselves, sinking, rising. The wealthy Reb Zundele and the poor husband-author, invited to his table, are swept into a quarrel that shakes them out of their tranquillity. Their story in itself becomes part of a polemical, vigorous sermon, full of repetitions and sharp arguments, about the tranquillity and good-ness—true or imaginary—of the previous generations. In that sermon, even detailed descriptions of kinds of foods become a series of argu-ments and counter-arguments, interpreted in one way or another. In brief, in the works of Hazaz, even the stones boil.

⅔

Movement always takes place within a given arena; in the stories of Hazaz, it takes place in several areas, four in particular: the arena of the cosmos, the arena of language, the Jewish domain, and the geographical and historical arenas. There are also the arenas of movement between the earth and the sky, between the bodily and the transcendental, between the visible and the hidden. The move-ment in the cosmic arena has already been demonstrated as much as possible within the narrow framework of the present remarks. The movement in the area of language is, of course, a topic for extensive research, both linguistic and stylistic, which will reveal, among other things, how Hazaz made the Hebrew dictionary dance, in all its strata, including its most esoteric and neglected parts. He tangled together biblical and rabbinical Hebrew, the medieval philosophical language of the Tibbonim with the language of rabbinical responsa, and the language of the Kabbalah, with words of Ukrainian, Yiddishisms and the clumsy Hebrew speech of Palestine, turning all of that into a single lively, dynamic, virtuoso display. That said, it would be a matter for examples and detailed research, which cannot be entered into here. However, one cannot refrain from saying something about the language of Hazaz, whose soul is constant motion. Thus, we must turn from detailed analysis to a summary comparison: if Hazaz had been a painter, we would not find a single straight line in his paintings. Rather, all the lines would be twisted, both rounded and sharp, pouring down and leaping up. In short, lines recalling the display on a monitor when it gives graphic presence to a heartbeat. Moving from the simile to the thing itself, it should be pointed out that there are four basic characteristics in the clumps of sentences or clauses that are typical of Hazaz (whose basic syntactical unit is, indeed, the cluster of sentences, or the paragraph, and not the isolated sentence): repetition; fragmentation; intensification of the semantic message by winged metaphors, and focused alliteration; rising or falling from the average, realistic line to positive elevation or plunging to negative descent, to the heights of heaven or to the depths of the abyss. Such a generalization would really require an illustration from every period of the author's work, but let it suffice to give a single one, from "Bridegroom of Blood":

> Burn-burn, blaze-blaze, flame of the desert space. Rivers of sand pour down like streams of fire. To the rivers of the scrub. Silence reigns all around, yellow silence, as though carved from the wheel of the sun, preserved by the desolation of noon.
>
> *(Seething Stones,* p. 19)

Repetition and fragmentation are the mother and father of the syntax here. The fragmentary sentences, short though they may be, are composed symmetrically, making each part of them a repetition of what preceded it. The metaphors, which include oxymora ("streams of fire"), synesthesia ("yellow silence") and alliteration (in the original Hebrew) produce increasing power, as though he kept on turning up the volume of his voice, until it reaches the heights: "the wheel of the sun," above, and "desolation of noon," which embraces the entire universe.

The drive to repetition and the need to constantly raise the volume bring Hazaz to use the richest and most esoteric lexicon that we find in Modern Hebrew prose. The author employs rare words and forms, marvelous and strange in their sounds, just as certain composers feel the need to add antique string and wind instruments, which are no longer used, cow bells, church bells, women's, men's, and children's choruses, the sound of glass, the noise of sheets of tin, shaken and moved, to those commonly found in the orchestra. In his language, Hazaz is the Gustav Mahler of the orchestra of Hebrew, the one who has given voice to Hebrew by means of it to the "Symphony of a Thousand." His language is that of the apocalypse. Therefore, it must be the opposite of the economical story, which brings forward a narrative movement from point to point along the shortest lines. Not coincidentally, Hazaz drew most of his biblical linguistic inspiration not from Bible stories, the language of which underlies the stories of Agnon, despite the rabbinical language and the patterns that are usually accumulated above it—but rather from the poetry of the Bible, with its repetitions and parallelisms. In his rich use of rabbinical Hebrew and the language of Midrashim, he is not close to the foundation of Aggadah, upon which Agnon built, but to the foundation of the sermon or to the language of midrashic vision, such as the Midrashim of redemption, which describe the pangs of the Messiah's advent. Hazaz is also close to the language of the apocalyptic books (even if they were not originally written in Hebrew) such as the Book of Enoch, whose influence on some of the works of Hazaz is particularly great, and also to the language of the Zohar and that of the Tibbonim, the language of medieval philosophical discussion, used extensively by quite a few of his protagonists.

This topic leads us to fluidity of Hazaz' movement within the Jewish geographical, ethnic, and historical arena. It has already been said that as soon as Hazaz raised his head from the dark and drizzly world of the declining Ukrainian shtetl, he rushed off to Constantinople; from there to a settlement in a Ukrainian forest a generation earlier; from there to the Paris, then to the tents of the pioneers in Palestine, and from there to the tranquil streets of Rehavia (the Jerusalem neighborhood inhabited by German Jews, such as the Hirschfeld family in "Muddy Barrel" and "World's Birth.") From Rehavia he meandered to the Yemenite neighborhoods in the Jerusalem of "Thou That Dwellest in Gardens", and from there, in "Ya'ish," to distant Sana'a, the expanses of Yemen, and the paths of its villages, where Ya'ish and Hamudi made their way on their donkeys, like Jewish avatars of Don Quixote and Sancho Panza. From Yemen he returned to Palestine, to the fields of the Lachish region in *Ofek Natui* ("Stretched Horizon"), and the cellars of the prison in Jerusalem, where members of the Jewish underground who have been condemned prepare themselves for death in "Gallows." From there, he returned to the Ukrainian shtetl at the time of the revolution, to the Haredi neighborhoods of Jerusalem, and to modern Paris in "And He Commanded," from *Pa'amon Ve'rimon* ("Bell and Pomegranate") and "Fan and Amulet" from *Even Natui* ("The Sun Dial"). Everywhere, he was immersed in Jewish geography, wandering on the path of the legions and travels of his people, and describing them on the road and in their dwellings. However, nowhere did he content himself with a static description of the entire region and domain for itself and in its place, but he always saw the entire Jewish map, all at once, as it swirled about in a kind of whirlpool, drawing everything found within it into one sunken center, the missing center, or the center that was already to be found in the redeemed Land of Israel.

Much has already been said about Hazaz as a pioneering writer, who included all the Jewish ethnic groups in the scope of his gaze, presenting a kind of general picture of the Jewish people or, as people say, a "Jewish Comedy," along the lines of Balzac's *Human Comedy*, with its many characters and life situations. To this statement, whose truth is evident, one must in any event add that Hazaz not only expanded the scope of the social vision of Hebrew literature but also presented many encounters, mixtures, and collisions in it, which had not been present hitherto.

For him, the Jewish Diaspora was not merely a series of landscapes of life, each one of which demanded its own description. Rather, it was a single, broad arena, where the figures move, tossed from one side of it to the other, and constantly encountering people they had not expected to encounter. This is already true of the encounters between the young Bolsheviks who meet the elders of the shtetl in "From This and From This," and in "Shmuel Frankfurter," and even more pronouncedly in the encounter of Rabbi Pinchas, the refugee from the Ukraine, with Papa, the fat and easygoing Jewish merchant in Istanbul in "Rich and Poor Meet." It is also true of dozens of other encounters, full of both pathos and comedy: Menashke Bofrozovny, the depressed pioneer, who has lost his way, and Rahamim the Kurdish porter; the meetings of Moroshke, the voluble and tireless Russian Zionist, with Macht and Hans Hirschfeld, the inarticulate German Jews; Ya'ish, the Kabbalist and visionary of Sana'a, with the coarse and earthy Hamudi, on the one hand, and, on the other hand, with Joseph Makhov, of Jerusalem, that wanderer who could be the emissary of the Messiah or an adulterous charlatan. Similarly, there are the meetings, against the background of the fields of Lachish, between the Moroccan woman Rachela and Benjamin Oppenheim, a wandering Jew, born in Germany and raised in America, perhaps a Jewish scholar who has studied in a rabbinical seminary or perhaps a communist who has changed his mind.

In each of these encounters, which both bring together and confront the extremes of the nation, Hazaz performed the act of setting these Jews in motion and mingling them. Each of them is moved from his place and native haunts by the sweeping power of a single mighty, shaking, uprooting, ruinous, destructive movement, which uproots and builds—the movement of redemption. That movement is revealed in the arena of national life, but the parallels of these movements are revealed in nature and the language. All of them together confirm and maintain the principle of vigorous mobility, the perpetuum mobile, which is the main thematic principle of Hazaz' work and the axis of the poetical system built into it.

ॐ

What appears in the arena of national geography and ethnography is even more evident in the arena of national history. Here, too, Hazaz flies from one extreme to another: from the time of the Russian Revolution to ancient Israel in the desert; from Palestine at the time of Jesus and the revolt against the Romans in the unfinished novel about the life of Jesus to the period of Shabetai Zvi in the play, *At the End of Days*; from Otshratnya in *Dorot Harishonim* ("Previous Generations") to the days preceding the crises of the modern age in the kibbutzim of the Jezrael Valley in the very heart of that crisis; from the ostensibly Kabbalistic-mystic Safed of "The Great Traveler," to the time of the underground war against the British in, "Gallows"; from the time of the Russo-Japanese War in *In the Forest Settlement* to the time of the settlement of the Lachish Region in *Ofek Natui* ("Stretched Horizon"); from Tuscany and her painters at the time of Dante in the story, "Ecce Homo" to the painters of Bezalel in Jerusalem of the early twentieth century in "Until Afterward." Here, too, Hazaz does not present the various historical strata only in order to juxtapose them, each in its respective nature and form. Rather, he does so mainly to mingle them. He shakes up heavy Jewish history, which emits only those kernels that are meta-historical or pan-historical. He discovers the distant in the nearby and the nearby in the distant, the crisis of redemption of the present in the Sabbatean crisis of redemption. He finds the British occupation in the Roman occupation at the end of the Second Temple period, and so on.

Hazaz reveals not only the present that is reflected in the face of the past, as in all historical fiction and drama, but also the past reflected beneath the surface of the present. Just as the Zionist and revolutionary present and the destruction of the Diaspora are reflected in the historical drama, "The End of Days," this very play reveals the Sabbatean underpinnings of the Zionist present, nihilism and "Canaanite" anti-Jewish antimonianism, it may be said, are enfolded in it, as expressed famously in the story, "The Sermon," just as the Russian Revolution is reflected in the rage of the desert in "Groom of Blood." In that very story, Zipporah's love and jealousy for Moses, who has fenced himself off from her and deprived her of the masculinity upon which her femininity depends, a difficult and cruel struggle, apparently sexual, a kind of warfare between woman and man, which takes place throughout Jewish history between the earthly heavenly elements, between a lustful, masculine God, who wants to mate with Zipporah instead of Moses, and between a spiritual, severe, hidden God, whom Moses seeks on Mount Sinai. The compromise that Zipporah finds—circumcising her son with a flint knife and thereby attaining "mastery" over her husband by virtue of making him a "groom of blood"—heralds several historical episodes among the elements that vie with one another in the heart of the nation; compromises, most of which led to bloodshed in general and the shedding of the blood of young sons in particular, many of which took place long after Hazaz' story was written and published in 1929. It was, however, written before the tragic events of that year—the massacre of the Jewish residents of Hebron and general rioting by Palestinian Arabs; events which are still unfolding before our very eyes on the stage of Jewish history.

Above all, Hazaz relates to history as a field for leaping (if I may be permitted to use an expression coined by Dov Sadan regarding a different author)—from period to period, from crisis to crisis, from the Diaspora to Palestine, from servitude to redemption. He makes these leaps by both hidden and visible analogy, which in order to uncover and place it in the foreground of his stories, he had populated his work with various embodiments of a unique figure, which seems to appear only in his work: the figure of the ardent, historical preacher, the "Reader of the Generations" from the present backward, the man who embodies the thought of his times—not cold, scientific thought, but blazing-personal-visionary thought. Among these are Yudke in "The Sermon," Maroshke, in "Muddy Barrel", Drabkin in the eponymous story, and "Aristotle," the educated man in the later reworking of the revolutionary stories. Indeed, the narrator of the story, *Dorot Harishonim* ("Previous Generations"), also belongs to this group of protagonists. The special contribution of the members of this group is embodied not only in the content of their thought, but in the tonality of the implicit or visible controversy that they wage, in the rapid, bitter sometimes quarrelsome flow of their speech, in the logic-chopping of their formulations. This tonality often presents them in a comic light, such as that which illuminates the figure of Maroshke, while he gives a sermon to the German-Jewish members of the Hirschfeld family on the subject of Jewish history, while they are entirely given over to the shocking influence of the heat of the Jerusalem summer, to which they are unused. At other times, the figure is flooded with tragic light, as in the case of Drabkin and especially that of Yudke, the sentences of whose "sermon" all flow from a painful and wounded source, like the blood dribbling from a wound. In either case, all of these embody the rhythm of shocked history, which throbs throughout the work of Hazaz.

⁊⟡

Central to the words of these protagonists, "who understand the times," is the essential duality of the life of the Jewish people—which imposes an obligation, even as it is in constant motion—a kind of pendulum-swing between the earthly and the heavenly, between the homeland and the Diaspora, between the petty cunning of merchants and pathetic innocence, between this world and the world of spirits, between the most bodily, instinctual, sexual and the most abstract, the world of angels, where there is no sex and no sin (therefore, Hazaz' protagonists, starting with Ya'ish, discover that it is also empty and barren, despite its exalted décor). This is the most essential movement, which shakes up the reality described in Hazaz' fiction, from the early stories of the Revolution all the way up to stories such as *Even Natui* ("The Sun Dial") and *Pa'amon Ve'rimon* ("Bell and Pomegranate"). We find it everywhere. Every description of space, every landscape section opens the way to heaven and digs deeply into the depths of the earth. The land of Israel is:

> Abstract and abundant nature, located and shackled, and broken open. Nature tyrannical and cruel. Coddling and spoiling until exhaustion of the soul, and it has ways equal to lewdness and wantonness, ways that are equal to the ills of profanity and moody physicality—and ways equal to mystery and to visions and dreams and all that which is above people and this world, and here there is nothing between the good impulse and the evil impulse except a hairsbreadth.
>
> ("Muddy Barrel," in *Seething Stones*, p. 150).

The Yemenite neighborhoods of Jerusalem in *Thou That Dwellest in Gardens* and in "Those with Shutters," and even Yemen itself in *Ya'ish* are no more than arenas for the almost heretical encounters between those ill with secularity and the mystery. It would be not be incorrect to state that the continued and extensive referring of Haim Hazaz to the world of Yemenite Jewry did not derive solely from the exotic charm, with which that Yemenite folklore and the colorful figures of the ethnic group, who appeared to him to be purely Jewish, flooded him.

> Chosen from among all [the Jewish ethnic groups], well recognizable, and finely special—they are swift and sharp, clever and witty. They are all sinews and bones, and there is no meat on them. They have done away with the superfluous and only maintained the main thing.
>
> (*Thou That Dwellest in Gardens*)

No less important than these traits, and perhaps more important, was the marginal attitude, special in its sensitivity, that Hazaz attributed to the Yemenites when he presented them as very earthy people, sensuous and cunning, on the one hand, and innocent and holy, ascetic and visionaries and kabbalists, on the other. Hazaz chose a Jewish tribe that seemed to him as if it had narrowed the Jewish moral expanse and brought closer the boundaries of pollution and purity, sexuality and celibacy, the here and there, one within the other, so that it was possible for its members to leap lightly from real to realm, and perhaps also to stand with one foot in one realm and the other in the opposing realm.

In *Thou That Dwellest in Gardens*, this duality appears in the confrontation between members of different generations. Hence this is a story of generations, fathers and sons, and the struggles between them. In contrast, in *Ya'ish,* that duality is not in the conflict of the hero with his brother Salem or with his partner, the Hamudi. Rather, it is primarily within himself, in his soul. For that reason, *Thou That Dwellest in Gardens* is primarily a social novel, whereas *Ya'ish* is a novel about consciousness (though not of stream of consciousness) and of incessant spiritual doubt.

Ya'ish, young and poor, embodies Hazaz' principle of movement in its most internalized form, in a series of mental crises and repeated ascendencies to heaven and then falling back down to earth. At the same time, he embodies this principle in his artistic form, as ecstatic and pure as possible, in his dancing, which is a bodily, mystical interpretation of the hymns of Rabbi Shalom Shabazi, and in which the soul's constant effort is revealed, always a failure but also always aroused anew, to raise itself on high and take the body with it. Ya'ish is neither the only nor the first figure in Hazaz' work to embody this ascending and descending motion, a movement of physical and spiritual dance. That figure already appears in the early stories about the Revolution, in a protagonist such as Motl Pribesker in "Revolutionary Chapters," and in other characters, who constantly skip between instinct and the creator and between matter and non-matter. However, in *Ya'ish*, a giant novel, Hazaz spread out the character's inner world, which is treated against an incomparably grandiose background.

Only superficially is this gigantic story an epic novel, full of episodes and colorful folklore. Actually, there is very little of the epic in this work. The epic quality and the folklore at most serve as a thin icing on the cake, the interior of which is entirely lyrical tempest—this is true of Hazaz' work in general and of *Ya'ish* even more so. This is the story of a person who was born full of earthly instincts and desires. However, under the pressure of hunger, the body breaks down, poverty oppresses the soul, and by virtue of absolute spiritual concentration, he attains a degree of elevation that is almost like that of an abstract spirit, of someone whose place is in heaven, among the angels, more natural to him than his place in the family home on earth. The angel to which he gives birth with his mystical intentions and ascetic practices is more his progeny than the son that he and Giné produce after an extended period of infertility, and the spirit of the dead man, Yihia Tairi, which enters him for an entire year, is more earthly and less abstract than his own soul, that of a living man. This is a story of incessant vacillation between life and death (the very name "Ya'ish," which means, "he will live," expresses a desire rather than confidence), between the realistic and the imaginary, between Jewish Sana'a and the fantastic reality of journeys among the Temples of heaven and the mountains of fire in them, in the spirit of the heavenly journeys in the Book of Enoch and the mystical Merkavah and Hekhalot literature. However, the story, as it turns out, leads to closure that immobilizes this vacillation once and for all. Ya'ish's last ascent is not to heaven but to Palestine, in the Zionist meaning of the term. While Ya'ish himself imagines that the Land of Israel, above which the gates of heaven are always open, will allow him easier access than ever to the upper worlds, upon his arrival there, he is suddenly cut off from heaven: or, as the closing sentences of the novel state, with categorical vigor:

> Despite all the labor that he labored and all the effort that he applied, heaven was locked before him and never opened to him all his life, forever.
>
> (*Ya'ish* 4, p. 231)

※

This highly meaningful conclusion allows us to bring our own remarks to a conclusion, with two not terribly happy thoughts about the place of Hazaz' work in our time and place. The first thought, a matter of principle, with a truly tragic character: the entire body of Hazaz' work identifies the mighty movement with the Diaspora—a movement that dislocates this work—on the one hand, and with the pangs of redemption, on the other. Only the Diaspora situation requires constant movement in space and time; only the situation of being on the eve of redemption or on the brink of destruction justifies vacillation that knows no repose. However, the situation of a nation that lives on its own land, that is planted securely in its place, a nation that maintains an intimate and self-evident bond with its surroundings and does not think at all about distant and strange experiences, is essentially static, and the poetics that it create is necessarily a static poetics or one of cyclical motion, the movement of the cycle of seasons in nature, the cycle of life from womb to tomb, and so on. The poetics of movement and penetration, upheaval and admixture, does not suit such a situation at all. At most, it can suit an early stage in it, such as the stage of the ingathering of exiles and the mingling of ethnic groups. However, over time, it necessarily becomes unsuited and will appear increasingly irrelevant, belonging to a spiritual world that has faded away and to emotions that formerly existed but are no more.

Hazaz himself was entirely aware of this tragic character of his work, which, as it were, prepares for the state of redemption, in which it will not be heard. More than once, he allowed one of his sermonizing characters, especially Moroshke and Drabkin, to speak at length about the obtuseness of the coarse nations who dwell in immobility, set in their places, especially the Jewish people in its land, while at the same time singing the praises of exile, whose constant upheavals prepare those who live in it for spiritual existence in time and not in a place. Even Yudke from "The Sermon," an almost "Canaanite" hero, who speaks from the direction of place and against the orientation of time, from the Land of Israel, against the exilic nature of Judaism, understands the hearts of the Diaspora Jews, who did not want to be redeemed and who created the myth of redemption that cannot be accomplished, at any rate not in their time, not within the horizon of the reality of their lives. He even argues that exile and Judaism are the same thing, and that Zionism is the end of Judaism, which has fallen from the heights of time to the deep pit of place. One may not conclude simplistically from this that Hazaz agrees with these protagonists. All of Hazaz' historiosophical characters express aspects of his world, but none of them expresses his world in its entirety. Hazaz accepts the verdict of redemption or its judgment, just as Ya'ish accepts the verdict of the closing of heaven to him. However, Hazaz knows the price of redemption, and it is no coincidence that he used the word "decree" in the words cited, as a kind of motto, at the beginning of his book of speeches and articles, *The Right of Redemption*: "A decree was issued against this generation, to stand up for redemption." He knows that the right of redemption is also fraught with tension, and he and his work are among those judged.

The second thought is of a lower character: Hazaz, assuming that critics know how to measure the "presence" of authors and intellectuals from the past in the field of the present, is a forgotten author, and, perhaps worse than that, he is a author who has been spurned, and there is a difference between the two. Most classical Hebrew authors have been "forgotten" in the usual sense of the word (they have few readers, young people are indifferent to them, and so on). However, not many of them, while they are forgotten, also arouse inexplicable but visceral and querulous opposition, something which is apparently bidirectional and nevertheless its existence is certain (like the existence of anti-Semitism in countries whose Jews have gone).

Hazaz appears both to arouse revulsion and, paradoxically, to leave readers indifferent.

As that were not enough, not only does the public avoid buying his books, but commentators on literature also do not work at deciphering his works. In academic circles, the dissertation industry has ceased making use of him.

Recently, a clever but unwise person, highly regarded at present on the literary journalism scene, publicly demanded removing the entire body of Hazaz' "monstrous" work from the high school curriculum. Although neither he nor the other opponents of Hazaz were prepared to spell out to themselves or to anyone else the reason for their bitter antagonism, the reason is clear. Hazaz is an author of a world in fateful delirium, and we, although our world is as far from tranquility as east is from west, have lost the ability for delirium, that capacity for spiritual and nervous movement, and for immediate emotional response to the deep tremor of reality.

What have we in common with Hazaz? Who can meet his demands—his unique language that's so full of flourishes and upheavals, which, as already noted, does not allow for the tracing of a straight, simple narrative line? Who can meet the demands of his lexicon, which requires knowledge that is not even available to experts today? And his plots, full of twists and turns, ruptures and repetitions? And the prolonged doubts that his protagonists indulge in…repeatedly, and with such gusto? Today, all of these aspects seems "baroque"; wearisome, and distant, they seem to represent qualities we no longer need.

Hazaz' work, along with a few other gigantic literary projects, dwells not far from the literary tenements of today, like a strange castle with towers and dungeons, walls and moats, banners flapping madly in a wind that we no longer feel. Who would want to enter this castle and wander about in it? Or else Hazaz' work looms like a high ridge, jagged and rocky, barren and thorny, with contorted features and a mad outline, visible from the plain, where simple, straight roads take our cars from place to place. Would any of us care to abandon the car and the highway to climb that ridge? The answer to those questions is: there is certainly someone who would. If not today, then tomorrow or the day after. And not only because the ridge "is there," as one famous climber said when asked why he had climbed to the peak of Mount Everest. But also because what is rejected by today's arbiters of taste may be accepted by tomorrow's arbiters of taste.

Those famous words were spoken by British climber George Mallory in 1924 when he was asked why he wanted to climb Mount Everest. In August of that year Mallory and his partner Andrew Irvine disappeared on the way to the summit. The large scope of public grief over their demise marked the beginning of Everest's allure and fascination.

Nowhere has Hebrew literature given such powerful, intelligent expression to the experience of beforehand, of almost, of wavering on the threshold, of the movement between being and nothingness—as in the wide-ranging work of Hazaz. The time will come when this plangent experience will be seen anew as the substance of being, as the essence of existence. Then new poets and novelists will be found, who will give expression in a way that is attuned to their time and place. Then he will certainly find readers, including the poets and novelists and those who hear their voices. They will return to the work of Hazaz and lend their ears to it, as in "Thou that dwellest in the gardens, the companions hearken to thy voice: cause me to hear [it]" (Song of Songs 8:13). They will return to the spring to drink in that feeling of essential existential shock from its deep source, as recorded by one whose every bone spoke of an enormous Jewish and worldwide historical upheaval.

In truth, the pangs of redemption and the torments of the Messiah are not a passing human condition. Only our obtuseness and perhaps also the desperate need for repose are what conceal from us, sometimes, the flimsiness of what appears to be solid to us. At every step we are treading at the brink of the abyss, and every day that passes for us might be the Last Day, but also the last day of servitude and the first of redemption.

Translated by Jeffrey Green

Revolutionary Chapters

T he war went on and would not be stopped. On the contrary. It proved futile to hold it to any schedule or limit. At no prearranged time would the land be quiet, not at harvest time, not near winter, and not in the spring. At harvest time, and near winter, and also in the spring it was as if the war had just begun setting to work in earnest. Like a pot left on the fire: it was like when the water starts simmering and is about to come to a boil.

In short, all the filth and noxious scum rose to the surface. Rasputin, secret spies, a wireless hidden in a Holy Ark in the House of Study, alas; a windmill somehow waving its sails and transmitting signals to the Germans, Jews driven out, old Jews hanged on trees as spies...

And the whole country, from one end to the other, seemed full of war, darkness, poverty and the fear of sudden death.

Man and all his generations perished!

Sons called to the army shortened their years as much as possible, violating their faces and shaving their whiskers very, very close every day, to remain boys, absolute youngsters, while the fathers added on years and grew older and older—

But to no avail!

The war visited fathers and sons together, old man and youth—no one was exempt.

Old and young, fathers and sons, all together joined the army! Everyone in the world took up a gun, shaking arms and legs, walking from the barracks to the bathhouse, humming tunes.

"No end to her, damn her!" men shouted to themselves and to their comrades. "What's to be done about the bitch?"

Eventually, but not necessarily at the appointed time, when the Revolution occurred, the dream came true at last. Then everyone was like a dreamer[1]: joyful, surprised, a bit apprehensive, as one is sometimes surprised and apprehensive after a dream.

Even the heavens and earth seemed to have been created only to assist the dream: blue skies, sparkling and fresh.... The snow melted outside, and the heavens were planted in their waters, the roofs were scoured and dripped bright drops of water. A cool breeze blew. And people were drawn outside, walking in crowds, bright, glowing, like throngs of blind men, singing, raising their voices, shouting, and yelling—they truly withdrew their souls from their bodies! Weeping, they hugged and kissed each other, red flags fluttered in the breeze above their heads and the wheel of the sun shone and rolled above them, and it seemed as though the throngs led the wheel of the sun wherever their spirit happened to take them...

War had not yet fallen silent in the land. But now it was of another degree, another degree and a different flag.

"War with no annexation or confiscation," the formula passed from mouth to mouth.

"War to the final victory!" some said.[2]

School children learned how to deliver those proclamations and spread them throughout the world.

The deserters, who had hidden in corners all during the war, became human again and emerged into daylight.

---

1. Psalm 126:1.
2. This was the motto of Kerensky, who headed the provisional government.

A huge mass of people marched through the streets toward the railroad station, all of them bearing rifles with a song on their lips,

"Arise, ye workers of the people!..."

The deserters made a great name for themselves in town.....

Nevertheless, the benefit proved to be flawed. How is that?

The reason is, to borrow from Torah cantillation, that *darga*, the rising note, precedes *tevir*, the falling one.

Thus said Reb Simcha Horowitz.

Reb Simcha was an expert Torah reader, a true connoisseur of notes and signs.

Then the word got out: the soldiers have mutinied.... They've had their fill of war.... Impossible to keep them in the trenches...

"Of course! They aren't laying hens, and who could get them to hatch these?"

Conspirators pressed and insinuated themselves into the crowds, grumbling, "An end to the war! True liberty!"[3]

Even Henya Horowitz, Reb Simcha's daughter, had plenty of demands, "An end to the war! Enough!"

"Everyone will immediately stop what he's doing and listen to you," Reb Simcha chided his daughter. "Don't mix into other people's business!"

"Let them put an end to the imperialist war!" Henya spoke in denunciation.

That was precisely the phrase she used, "the imperialist war!"

Henya had an infernal spirit, a rotten pest, not a maiden, an agent of destruction! Since the confusion of tongues,[4] no tongue was ever found like Henya's.

"Do you really think," Reb Simcha asked her, "that since I never studied geography and Sherlock Holmes, I lack all understanding?"

Why, she couldn't see the strength of his position at all!...

Round and round revolved the wheel. Events took a bad turn and sprouted up like weeds in the land. The front collapsed and sol-

---

3. This was Lenin's position.
4. After the Tower of Babel.

diers flowed up out of all the fields and the paths over the mountain crests, they and all their hordes—horror! The whole land rumbled before them.

As though through an open door, they passed through the town.

Generally speaking: the war was abandoned.

"It must be because the town is situated in the center of the earth," says Reb Simcha, "right in the middle, and that's why those passing through here are so numerous they cannot be reckoned up in real numbers, with no end to them...And perhaps the soldiers have lost their course, and they go back and forth, back and forth, because the earth is round, and since those marchers have no set and determined longitude, they come back again and again."

Yes, that brigade had already been through once, like a rat trapped in a maze, without officers or military equipment, with only a large cooking pot, on their way to their home country somewhere.... Then, the first time around, they had stood, perishing with empty bellies. They broke into all the ovens and removed the *cholent* and all the Sabbath food, without the tiniest leftover, cleaning everything out spotlessly, and they sat in the center of the marketplace and ate away their hunger and pain, even dancing and celebrating. Now the brigade came back, the very same one with the same quality—as borne out by their looks, without officers and without military equipment, with only a large cooking pot....

"What's this?" the townsmen explain to them. "We are of the opinion that you have already gone through here once."

"No, no, not us," the answer. "That is, we have not yet gone through. We are considered another brigade, so to speak."

As it seemed, they spoke the truth. Since they left without breaking into the ovens.

Such righteousness!

"Happy are we and happy our lot," says Reb Simcha, "that surveyors are not commonly found amongst us. For if that were not so, those splendid orators and all the public speakers who have risen up over us would propose and demand miles upon miles and plots of land…. Now, since we have only storekeepers, those speakers will offer up their deceitful arguments and claims and all their imaginary assurances according to the length of their own yardstick.

"They have one title—Bolshevik! Such a sect. Jewish sinners. Blast their souls for having studied the Revolution with Rashi's commentary! Not the literal meaning, but the homiletic meaning: what's mine is yours, and what's yours is mine…. And their ulterior evil intention is visible to everyone who is at all knowledgeable about them."

In one swoop, like the tail of a comet, in the wink of a single eye, the plague spread through the world: bolshevism.

"The world is holding a memorial service," says Reb Simcha, "and so all the minors with parents still living have been set loose!"[5]

All the young people and boors had usurped their birthrights and begun ruling, even Henya has been made a commissar. A regular commissar.

The worms in the earth would wreak less destruction than they!

"Absolute redemption!" Henya girded her loins against Reb Simcha and mixed things up. "Now redemption has come to the proletariat!…The rule of workers and peasants…Wars will cease, poverty and slavery will be no more; there'll be no oppressors and no oppressed."

In short, the whole world is grace, mercy and peace. And the wolf shall dwell with the lamb…[6]

A rotten pest, not a maiden! The spirit of redemption throbs in her breast! Just get a load of her theories and doctrines! Try and plead a case against her!

Bad, bitter, helpless. There is no restoration in the world, no one setting things right. What has come to pass!…

"Where are you going, comrades?" Reb Simcha shouts, con-

---

5. According to custom, those with parents still living exit the synagogue during Yizkor, the memorial service for the dead.
6. Isaiah 11:6.

fused and distraught. "What are you doing for the bitter sorrows of our soul?"

The comrades, armed to the teeth, reply, "Remember this, old age, and pay heed, the whole land is in the hands of the people—who are all aroused. Don't you wish to go along with the people in their uprising?"

"Have pity and mercy, comrades, for you are murderers, armed robbers, O Lord of the universe."

"Spare us your poetry, comrade Reb Simcha, your Lord of the universe has created a new spirit within us—to raise the edifice, to give it an upper story."

Those are the words of Henikh the carpenter to Reb Simcha, and as he speaks, he raises his hand aloft and calls out,

"True, comrade!…We agree!"

"The Holy One, blessed-be-He, created a will in us, to submit our will to His blessed will!" Reb Simcha shouts to Henikh.

"Look, look!" Henikh thrusts his callused, soiled hands in Reb Simcha's face. "Did you see? We don't know how to study the Mishnah! Since the start of this imperialist war, I haven't set eyes on a book. Understand?"

Another "sinner" like that went up to Reb Simcha, stared at him with murderous, robber's eyes, as though to slay him, "You old dog's nose, where are you sticking yourself, eh? If I step on your foot, you'll be lame. If I crush you in my closed fist, you'll no longer exist. Old louse!"

A second sinner walked up to Reb Simcha, yawned in his face as if he were a dog, took his hand and pushed him to the side, saying, "Get out of here."

To be sure, Reb Simcha left. By the skin of his teeth, you could say, he slipped away from the murderers and hid in a cellar beneath his house.

Nothing restrains those heretics! All who are compassionate have compassion for Israel. All dwellers in the dust will beg for mercy.[7]

---

7. Cf. Isaiah 26:19

The next Sabbath Reb Simcha was called to the Torah and said the blessing for one who has escaped death.

II

The world has gone mad; the world is satanical, torn to shreds. Band after band, piled up and confused, quarrel with each other, speaking in floods of words. Life is engulfed in hunger and blood, dread and darkness. And the mainstay, scattering hunger and blood and dread and darkness from one end to the other, is comrade Polyishuk.

The winds snatched up that fine comrade and brought him to the town!

"Authorization," people reported. "He has one in his pocket from Petrograd itself, to put things right.

And people actually found it amazing that a young man of such short stature, mere skin and bones, tattered and worn, should set out to conquer towns and cities—what at man! People tried to avoid encounters with him. They knew that he had an authorization from Petrograd itself and that he came swooping down in a train bearing a sign in red letters, "Death to the Bourgeoisie!"

Comrade Polyishuk took up residence in the home of Reb Simcha. Henya herself brought him.

Reb Simcha was secretly fuming, grumbling to himself about the comrades, men and women, and their evil seed. Finally he became reconciled, "Very well, let him stay. What can we do? Eventually he'll probably go away. Perhaps a spirit from on high will be aroused in him, and he'll go. Perhaps the blessed Lord will grant that his days be short."

So he stayed. He stayed in the large *zal.* He slept on the old sofa. He folded his coat beneath his head and slept. At his head, on the wall, hung his rifle, and on the table the pistol and several deadly cartridges were scattered about.

"I wouldn't make room for anyone else in the *zal,*" says Reb Simcha. "Only for you."

Comrade Polyishuk smiled as if to say, "As though it depended only upon you and your wishes."

It was evident right away: fine fruit! A vicious foe, inside and out!

"What is the main reason for your coming here?" asks Reb Simcha.

Reb Simcha wants clear and straightforward information.

"To put things in order," Polyishuk answers vaguely.

"Well," Reb Simcha offers advice, "put things in order so those bastards won't be bastards!"

"That's not my job," Polyishuk says with a sneer, the words trickling drop by drop, even freezing.

It looks as though he himself is quite a bastard. If only the house would vomit him forth forever. Thus thought Reb Simcha, putting his hand over his mouth.

But what comrade Polyishuk left obscure during the day, he clarified at night. His sleep told the story. Night, darkness and silence—suddenly he was hauled from his bed as though a fire had broken out in the house, perish the thought, and he paced irregularly back and forth in the room looking for some kind of bomb.

"It's me...me," Henya takes him by the hand every now and then. "It's me, comrade Polyishuk!"

"Happiness at last!" Reb Simcha was annoyed at his daughter. "It's me, it's me! Do leave him alone, won't you."

In short, that was the only telltale sign of who that person really was.

Day after day the town went downhill, oppressed in low spirits and heavy with melancholy and mute silence, like a deserter.

"No doubt," says Reb Simcha, "like a deserter, like a number of deserters all in the same place.

"Now these are the three categories essential to a person's needs: children, life and food. None is quite in the shape it ought to be; quite to the contrary.

"The children are bastards, criminals, sinners, Amalekites...not children. Life is nothingness, absolute zero, inimical to the heart and soul. And as for food, it's extremely dear when it's to be found at all!

"But it is known to those who know, and the truth is, as it is written: behold the eye of the Lord is upon those who fear him....[8]

"Only the problem is known too: where did those Jewish sinners come from, who at first were neither seen nor known at all?

"Since the souls of all the Jews come from the same place, and things taken from the same place are a single entity through and through, it follows that every Jew is implicated in his fellow Jew's sin, for they are a single building. Like the body, for example, if the feet rush off to do evil, isn't the evil in the whole bodily frame?

"But here was the difficulty: where had all those cruel, evil bastards and sinners come from—if the whole nation was righteous?[9]

"*Gevald!*"[10] Reb Simcha shouts to himself. "Robbers, murderers! Yet all of Israel are responsible for one another,[11] so what are you going to do?"

Daily they came to the town. Some in sheepskins and others in great-coats and still others in leather jackets. What they all had in common was that they were all bastards....

Daily they came to the big stores owned by Brilliant and by Margolin and that of Hayyim Zelig the blacksmith, and they loaded wagons full of goods. Then they went on their way.

"Anarchy! The world is lawless! Liberty is abroad in the world," grumbled Reb Simcha. "Only there's no freedom from robbery and theft, only there's no freedom from the enemies of the Jews, from 'thou shalt murder,' and from 'thou shall steal,' and from 'bear false witness against thy neighbor.'"

"Are things good this way?" Reb Simcha challenged Polyishuk. "How does it seem to you, comrade Polyishuk, is it good this way?"

"Thank God," answered Polyishuk. "Nothing's wrong. One could even say it's good...a Bolshevik doesn't know how to complain."

Reb Simcha cannot bear it any longer. His heart is hot within

8. Psalm 33:18.
9. Isaiah 60:21
10. Yiddish for "Help!"
11. Shevuot 39a and elsewhere

him. He cannot simply stand there because of his anger and the coursing blood.

"Good? Good? Get out of my house! Right away! Get out! This is my house! Mine! M-i-n-e."

Polyishuk measured Reb Simcha with his eyes, at his own pace, slowly, with his eyelids and eyebrows, slowly, as though wishing to root him out of his sight and remove him seven cubits from the face of the earth. Then he looked at Henya and gave another glance at Reb Simcha, turned his back, and left.

"You get out too, you hussy!" Reb Simcha was boiling with angry rage. "Bolshevik! I won't stand for it!...Not for a single minute!...get out!...May your names and memories be blotted out, sinners, boors, carpenters' and shoemakers' apprentices!"

That very day Polyishuk returned, took up his rifle and went to live in the bathhouse.

Fear then seized Reb Simcha to hear about such a person—a madman like that, God in heaven!—going to live in the bathhouse! Then Reb Simcha even regretted the whole affair. But regret is not the stuff of a merchant. "Let him break his skull and neck! To the bathhouse—the bathhouse, the devil take him! And may everyone else from his abode[12] be equally blessed!"

A good man is comrade Polyishuk, and a better one is comrade Soroka—so similar looking!

With the town like a wide open door, if you please! Some leave, some enter: disturbers of the peace, ruffians, their unsavory faces as if skinned, their eyes mad and evil...

On foot came comrade Soroka on the road leading up from the woods. Walking, sheepskins on his head, a military coat hanging on his back and dragging a small machine-gun behind him by a rope held in his hand...

That very night, in the stillness of the dark, came a shriek from the steam power station in the village of Svirodovka, and on all sides the sky turned fiery red.

Dread and fearful silence spread through the whole town.

---

12. Liturgical appropriation of Ezek. 3:12

From mouth to mouth, "What happened? What happened? What happened?"

From mouth to mouth, "Fire in Czupowski's manor."

"Fire in Kowalewski's manor."

"Fire in Count Branicki's manor."

The whole town was surrounded by fire on all sides and stood hiding with its face covered as though by a crow's wings.

The steam power station shrieks. The church bells strike with a great din. Dogs howl at their masters' heads, and a storm rolls through the air, raising itself ever higher and piling up like a huge mountain, flying and passing by with a howl, pulling the treetops after it…. And suddenly, in the meanwhile, an oppressive silence, like the peace of death….

Now the sky was bright and clouds of smoke and flames wander and roam. Comrade Polyishuk went down on his knees before the snowy plain, stretched his arms before him and cried out,

"Revolution, behold, *ha-ha-ha*!"

"Revolution, *ha-ha-ha*!" Henya repeated after him.

They looked at each other and leaped into each other's arms.

Night after night the sky burned around the town. Night after night the sky was red, flaming and smoky, without stars or constellations.

It was as though comrade Soroka wished to uproot not only the stars and constellations, but also all the angels, as it were, the seraphim and heavenly host.

For nights and weeks the sky was wrapped in flame.

All those weeks Soroka was never seen in town. Until once he came and went through the street: sheepskins on his head, a military coat hanging on his back, and his fingers were reddish blue as though uprooted, pulling behind him a small machine-gun on a rope, and so he walked, clanging with an iron key,

"Arise, ye workers of the people!"

Of all the huge quantity of booty stolen by the peasants from the noblemen's estates, Soroka took for himself only an iron key that had fallen from a smashed door.

Soroka's voice was heard from the street. Immediately all

the comrades, men and women, leaped up and went out, shouting, "Hoorah!" "Long live the rule of the workers and peasants!" With a waving of hats and hands in the air, they raised their voices in the "Internationale."

At the sound of the song, comrade Soroka stood at attention, stretching his whole body upward, turned his stern face to the side and raised his hand in a salute...

The crowd took hold of comrade Soroka by his arms and legs, picked him up in the air, carried him in their hands, bearing him to the council building.

A mass of men pressed at the entrance, and Jews from everywhere were drawn after them as though to a circumcision or bar mitzvah.

Soroka stood in the middle of the room, extended his hands to all present and spoke,

"Ha, shake my hand, but hard!...Even though you're no Bolshevik, as I can see, and not at all different from a bourgeois, nevertheless, shake, as I am a Jew."

That evening, in comrade Polyishuk's residence, in the bathhouse, there were festivities and celebration. The whole band of comrades from the town, men and women, gathered at the bathhouse. Polyishuk did not falter in the commandment that hospitality be offered in the proper fashion. Nothing necessary for a celebration was lacking, neither food nor drink.

By candlelight all the comrades, men and women, sat in a circle on logs and inverted tubs, indulging themselves with lard, pickles, brandy and tea. They drank tea in famous fashion: wrapped in towels till the seventh degree of sweat[13]—one slurping from a cup, another from a soldier's mess tin and yet another from a plate with Hebrew writing in red letters on a white background, "Bread and salt shalt thou eat, and reap the truth."

At midnight, when their hearts were gladdened with eating and drinking, they shook the benches and beams of the bathhouse with their mighty dancing, as much as their legs could dance.

---

13. A Russian custom, to order a towel along with the tea.

From the hole in the oven, flames reached out and licked the sooty bricks. The stones heaped up around the boiler turned black, and splinters of flame flickered. Above the boiler a thick column of steam rose to the beams of the black ceiling and veiled the benches. Heels pounded. The bodies were linked in a single chain, spinning, rocking, a chain of whirling skins, red shirts and gun-belts, boots, wild hair, shouted song, whistles, sudden outcries and guttural, throaty sounds.... Everything in the bathhouse danced dizzily: the boiler and the stones, the ritual bath and the regular bathtub, old bundles of twigs, piles of full sacks and even comrade Gedalia hopped on his crutch.

Then the poor bathhouse, torn in roof and ribs, saw joy, a joy great enough for all the days to come! The homes of rich landlords and officials in their glory were never honored with even a sixtieth of that honor from the time that the temple—the temple of the bathhouse—was a bathhouse. Truly that was a happy occasion!

But what was even more marvelous was the end, the end of the celebration!

The festivities, the singing and dancing were like the air all around, invisibly filling up space, like something not properly understood.

At the end of the night, when everyone was acting in his own way and dancing according to his own nature: one prancing on an upper bench and another hopping inside the empty, steaming bathtub, someone shouting, "Help! Help!" and someone else had made himself into a wagon and rolled along the floor on his belly—comrade Polyishuk fled outside as though mad with worry and anger. He ran to the river and plunged in through a crack in the ice.

The other comrades noticed immediately and raised a panicked outcry. The women wept and wailed, the men ran with iron tools, laboring to crack the ice, some hastily smashing it, others peering into the black water.... Shouts all around, then suddenly a dreadful silence, the howl of the snowstorm, fear and dread and the sound of breaking ice. Suddenly Polyishuk's head gleamed on the rushing water....What a hubbub, what racing about, shouting, shoving.... Polyishuk was stuck between chunks of ice. Looking about him, supported by the arms reaching down to him, he jumped up out of the river, healthy and strong, running to the bathhouse on his own feet with the whole crowd behind him—in a noisy, rushing tangle.

In the bathhouse all the comrades pressed around the one standing there, trembling in all his limbs, everyone astonished and enjoying the sight.

Soroka stood above him, gave him brandy to drink, hugged him and kissed him on his blue lips, asking how he felt,

"Is your soul restored? Is your soul restored, tell me, hey!"

Henya cried and laughed, wrung her hands, cried and laughed, and all the others hastened to do something, making loud noises to each other.

"*Mazal tov! Mazal tov!*" cried out Polyishuk, his enthusiasm animating his blue face as he leaped into the steam room with Henya after him. Henya was nearly crushed between the door and the frame.

The whole crowd wandered around the room in little groups, everyone by himself, but all together in a single mass, dark, moving, singing in joy and enthusism,

"*Mazal tov! Mazal tov! Mazal tov!*"

Nothing like it had ever been heard.

Only Soroka stood at the door of the steam room and shook his head from side to side, clapping to the sound of the singing and shouting,

"To kill the lion in the well on a snowy day!"[14]

Such a high level of devotion.

III

Deeds that make the heart soar, not sermons or clever speech and the like, truly inspiring actions, at the sight of which a person might even forget to rub his own flesh—such were Soroka's. Fire!—Here it

14. Apparently the lyrics to a Russian song.

is, ho! Fiery flames and the sight of torches…. The noise of war—that too is good, you might say!

But Soroka's spirit fell, and he sat in front of his machine-gun, ripped a page from a Menshevik[15] pamphlet and rolled himself cigarette after cigarette.

"In this world every dog is stuck to his own tail," Soroka argued with the machine-gun. "In this world every dog is stuck to his own tail."

For a few days the little machine-gun listened to that general observation, which was spoken and reiterated a hundred times or more, until Soroka stood up, shook his head as though shaking a heavy burden from his shoulders, spat in his palm, and said, "May the seven spirits be in your navel!"

He girded his loins with his pistol, left the bathhouse, and went out into the street. He passed by as though to say, "I am a king and worthy of it!"

People saw him walking in the street that way and cursed him roundly,

"President, stones in his guts! Look how he's walking! A parade like that…. Lord, may such a presidency collapse, ha? *Nu?*…Is there still any reason to live in this world?"

Where did Soroka go that way, standing erect and taking straight steps? Impossible to say he knew clearly where he was going, in any case, not to the council building, certainly not….

In the council building they're always giving speeches, scheming in speeches; a plague on them! Quickly get yourself a pair of ears and stand and listen…. Soroka avoided speeches like poison!

Nevertheless, Soroka did go to the council building. An important reason brought him there. He came with something to say,

"Yes, comrades, there will be a union of Jewish soldiers—that's all there is to it!"

No words, no arguments, no putting off were of any avail.

15. A Social Democrat who, after November 1917, was officially opposed to the policies and methods of the Bolshevik Party.

Soroka was not one to scatter his words to the winds.

"Yes, comrades, there will be a union of Jewish soldiers, and not only that! This is how...."

Councils of counselors met to take counsel, discussed, argued, pondered and debated, squabbled with each other in good order.

"Well, comrades!" Soroka stood at their head. "Have you decided yet? Yes? I want to be allotted five hundred rifles immediately, twenty machine-guns, three hundred hand grenades and five hundred pistols!...Is it signed yet? Comrade Polyishuk, it seems to me you have all the qualities needed to become a clearminded Bolshevik. Is it signed yet? Comrade Polyishuk, don't tell me stories from when your grandmother was a bride. Is it signed yet?"

The mandate was written out and signed and delivered to Soroka.

The union was established.

A staff and duties and sergeants were appointed.

The head of the union, comrade Soroka, rode like a hero, as is proper, mounted on a fiery steed.

The assistant to the head of the union was comrade Gedalia, the man with the crutch, and like comrade Soroka he rode on a tall horse, tied into the saddle with ropes, proud and glorious, edifying the entire assembled crowd with looks from his black eyes.

In vain the astonished people wondered, "Who made an army out of the Jews?"

Not only that, Motl Privisker, the teacher, instructed Reb Simcha that Shamgar Ben-Anath, who smote six hundred Philistines, had done so with an oxgoad,[16] and was redeemed through him. Motl Privisker, the teacher of young boys. For the word "oxgoad," *malmad habakkar,* can also mean a *melamed,* a teacher of young oxen, who hits his pupils to make them learn. And those six hundred were an esoteric reference to the six Orders of the Mishnah...

But when that force of Jewish soldiers passes through the street, ordinary mortals had better pay up in good coin and regard that pleasurable spectacle—

16. Judg. 3:31

That is what Motl Privisker himself says.

"Comrades," Soroka spoke to his army. "Take heed: Like a drum major, look! This is how you should march!

"One two, one two!"

After much labor and effort the job was finished and Soroka was idle again.

Soroka had only to sit and wait for coming events.

But such conduct was completely foreign to Soroka's nature.

And events did not tarry.

One snowy and sunny day, the market was stunned. The Jews laid aside their business and fled: they were prepared, anticipating a pogrom.

"Because of the flour," they reported, "because they supposedly give the Jew the finest, and the Gentiles get only dura flour."

The council members arose and tried to address the Gentiles who had surrounded the cooperative store, using soft language,

"Comrades! Comrades!"

In response, there came the roar of the mob,

"Can't we eat bread fit for humans?…The Jews get fine flour!…A Jewish kingdom!…Clobber him, that dwarf!…He's a bourgeois, you can tell by his pockets…."

"Comrades!…Comrades!"

Then Soroka went through the market with his band. Not to make war against the goyim, but just to show them how soldiers march in good order and how they sing….

The goyim immediately noticed it and fell silent. At the same time everyone was made to comprehend perfectly well, visibly and palpably, the yellow dura bread that the Jewish women brought out of their houses for proof.

"Dura bread too…so what do you have to say?" The goyim kneaded the crusts of bread with their hands and put it in their heavily bearded mouths, milling it between their molars.

Go remove Balaam from their mouths,[17] a thorn in their sides!

17. A reference to the curse that turned into a blessing. Num. 22-24.

IV

Wrapped in their cloaks, Reb Simcha in a tattered fox-skin coat and Motl Privisker in a balding cat-skin coat, the pair of them tried to make a place for themselves at the side of the oven and warm up.

They were both heavy in years, having completely forgotten how they had once been their fathers' and mothers' little boys, yet they still remembered the Garden of Eden well, the angels singing, the Tree of Life in the garden,[18] and the incorporeity of the Holy-One-blessed-be-He. For all that, neither of them knew what "the end of days" might bring.

Motl Privisker sat and crossed his booted legs, placing one foot on the other, flourishing a bottle of brandy now and then, squinting at it, pouring some into his cup, and from there into his mouth, wiping the remnant from his black beard with his sleeve.

The brandy goes down into him like a fiery torch, till it reaches his very heart, making a hot conspiracy with his stomach. A sprite, not brandy!

Reb Simcha likes to sit with Motl Privisker, and each time he honors Motl with these words, "May the blessed Lord help us, may every man take pity on his fellow and may we all be saved soon, amen."

Good taste and discernment has Motl, weighty teachings and wonderfully wise sayings, interpretations of the Bible that delight the listener…. A mighty lion in Hasidic wisdom! A rose of esoteric learning!

When Motl Privisker opens his mouth, Reb Simcha can sit and listen to him day and night. All of Israel, the holy nation, each according to his capacity and virtue, will then stand before the eyes of Reb Simcha.

"The Master of the Universe and the Divine Presence are in exile, right and left, flushed and pale with judgment and mercy, the wings of the dove, the wings of the commandments, the matron and the bird's nest, the Jews lie in prayer shawls and phylacteries in exile,

---

18. Based on the folk belief that the unborn soul resides in Paradise.

and Jannes and Jambres the sons of Balaam,[19] Remus and Romulus,[20] the tortuous serpent, the piercing serpent,[21] and the two lips that are called flames, and the two apples between which the spirit of the Messiah emerges, and the king bound in stocks...."

"Now, Reb Simcha, lay aside the worries that concern you.... Lay them aside, I tell you.... For when I reflect, Reb Simcha, that I never committed adultery nor murdered, nor did I steal from my fellow, I put on my prayer shawl and phylacteries every day and wash my hands and behave according to the laws of the Torah as ordained by our rabbis of blessed memory and the earlier and later halakhic authorities, and have even exceeded the requirements, no matter what, I am happy with my lot! What do you have to say, hmm?...*Lehayim.* Reb Simcha...."

"*Ech!... E-ech!...*" Motl Privisker shuts his eyes, stretches his jaws and wags his head. "A sprite, not brandy!"

"A *Tsavele,*[22] fine, fine, delightful.... It truly gives wings to the soul, *eh!...*"

Reb Simcha rubs his shoulders against the stove and says nothing.

Motl Privisker puts the tail of a salted fish in his mouth, chews and slowly pours another cup,

"Fish like to swim.

"Reb Simcha, why? Why are you so down in the dumps?" he continued, "Speak up, foolish man!...Vanity of vanities, mud of mud...Have a drink and don't let your wings stink! Hmm?...A glass of brandy is a weighty matter, a matter of ritual purity.... It cleanses the filth, the ugliness from the heart, very much so, oy, very much so!...Drink a *lekhayim,* I tell you, and return to your proper state."

Motl Privisker empties the cup into his mouth, wipes his mustache with his sleeve, raises a crust of bread up in his hand, leans over to Reb Simcha and whispers in his face,

19. In rabbinic legend, magicians who opposed Moses and fashioned the Golden Calf.
20. Mythical founders of Rome.
21. Names of the Leviathan in Isaiah 27:1.
22. Tsav in Hasidic usage is brandy with 96 percent alcohol.

"'An evil, behold an evil is coming....²³ The end is coming, the end is at hand, putting an end to you.... It's coming.... The designated hour.... The time is come.... The day is close.... Turmoil and not the echoes of mountains.... Let the buyer not be glad nor the seller grieve....' Choice words, Reb Simcha, precious words, deep, deep... They should be kissed with great kisses.... The whole matter...Drink a *lehayim*, I tell you, and don't be a fool. Ezekiel—brother and friend, I shall make thee learned and wise—is the most remarkable of the twenty-four books of the Bible.... Ezekiel is the soul of the twenty-four....²⁴ Drink a *Lehayim* and don't let your body dry out!"

From time to time Motl Privisker empties the cup into his mouth, turns around and hums in Aramaic, "Children, life, food."

Inside, darkness rotted in the dreariness and silence. Outside the wail of the embittered wind could be heard. All of a sudden the winds fell from on high. The house groaned with the crash of the wind, and the howling snow pounded the windows.

"Henya, Henya!" shouted Motl Privisker. "Another piece of bread!"

"Henya! Give me a piece of bread."

"Henya, a maiden reaching those years, an evil spirit in your bones!"

Motl Privisker walks through the room on his soft boots, walks to the window, and stands still.

Outside the window, there's a deep, broad night, full of drunkenness and turgid whiteness.

"Henya, may a pig gnaw you."

Outside the window—a white orchard, stormy and spinning dizzily in rage, moons and planets, with spirits and angels...

"True is it, ha?" Motl Privisker leaps and stands as an adversary to Henya, who has entered with a piece of bread in her hand. "That the world is on the path of truth, hmm?"

"Go away, go, you Hasid, you drunken Jew!"

---

23. Motl is quoting bits and pieces from Ezek. 7:5–12.
24. The twenty-four books of the Hebrew Bible.

"Hold your tongue, hussy!" Reb Simcha sits upright. "You'll talk yet!"

"In truth, ha, a maiden reaching those years, an evil spirit in your bones!…The truth, eh, is it yours? Does it belong to you?…The truth belongs to the Holy One blessed be he. Stu—pid!…The Lord's seal, youuu shrewww! Ri—ight!…*She* discovered the truth!…. And you are unaware of your foolishness, that you only found the pudendum of truth!…And who sent you this face eh?…The shape of your mouth and forehead and cheeks, eh?—a maiden reaching those years, an evil spirit in your face!

"My soul is tossing within me," Motl Privisker cries out to Reb Simcha, waving his arms and making a strange motion, "the whole of my inner being!"

He paces back and forth in the room, fumbling in his trouser pockets and talking to himself,

"The pupil of the eye is a mirror… a mirror… even though it's black,…When it disappears, it's an impenetrable thought…. And when it appears—at the same time the heavens open and I see divine sights!"

Motl Privisker paces back and forth, returns to his seat, sits next to Reb Simcha, lowers his head and speaks, saying he very much wanted to travel to Ger to see the Rebbe.[25]

Then he says, "If I had a violin in my hands and could play now…I would play such a melody, gathered from running brooks and set with precious stones!"

And then he empties the bottle into his mouth, sitting and speaking incomprehensible words, sketches, drawings, shades of color, toward which he is headed, as it were….

"By way of secret," he speaks "Adam…Adam of *beriah*[26] rode on a lion…. Turning to the right he sketched roads; and paths—

"And to the left, Adam of Assiryia rides on an ox and takes fire from his mouth and draws pictures—

---

25. Travel to Ger (Gora Kalwarja) in western Poland was impossible at that time.
26. *Beriah* (creation), *yetsira* (creativity) and *assiya* (action) are Kabbalistic terms.

"Adam of Assiryia rides on an eagle, and the spirit in his mouth makes shades of color."

Motl places his hand over his eyes and sits in silence, then he speaks again for a moment,

"Lord of the universe. Lord of the universe!...Give my heart wisdom and knowledge to persevere!.... On what path shall I start upon and persevere? Where shall I begin my effort? What can I do with my soul? Lord, Lord, Lord of the universe, I don't know the meaning at all!"

"Forget it, Motl, forget that confusion," said Reb Simcha. "Leave it be!...You've imbibed and gotten drunk like a goy...You'll only dishonor yourself, feh!,.. Tell me, why don't you go back to your wife and children?"

"Leave me be, leave me be.... I'm doing something great for the whole Jewish people, and this isn't the time to deal with personal matters."

"Motl, now nothing's stopping you from going home. They aren't conscripting men for the army any more."

"Simcha, Simcha, Simcha! Why are you mixing me up?...*Gevald,* why are you disrupting my train of thought!"

Motl Privisker leaps to his feet and starts staggering drunkenly, circling the room.

Then he lies on the hard, narrow bench, speaking to himself.

With an old, shaking hand Reb Simcha pulls down his hat and covers all his gray hair. For long moments they plunged into the depths of oblivion.

Covered with crushing layers of snow, the town stands: veiled, sinking.

Snow—infinite in breadth and height...

All around the winds race in brotherhood and friendship, singing in wails.

Above, the empty space of the world hangs like a silver lamp, and a storm comes flying and lights up stars and fiery flames in it....

A hairy beast, frightfully white, walks to and fro in the air, grasping the town the way a man might take a nut in his hand, screaming, terrifying with its voice.

44

No bird flies above, no man walks below.[27] The wind comes and picks up the snow like a curtain above, and there, shot through with silver and carried along were given at by the storm, are Polyishuk and Soraka on street.

"Hey, hey, snowstorm! Here we are! Come out, comrade Henya!—*Yoo hoo!*"

Winnowing storm winds blow, hills are thrown up, white darknesses are flattened.

"Hey, hey, hey!"

White darkness blocks the eyes. Frost plucks at faces.

"First, where to?"

"There's no first, comrade Henya, and no last!"

"Comrade Henya, the heart exults, the heart is happy, bursting in fiery sparks, hey, hey!" Jumbles of wind whip out and pound from face to face.

"Comrade Henya," Soraka calls from within the storm, "Comrade Henya, tell me: Who am I?"

"You are married!" Henya laughs.

"Comrade Henya, I can't sleep…. Do you love me?…Do you love me?…Tell me!"

"Whom?"

"Me, *nu!*"

"No…"

"*Nu* love someone, it's all the same, all the same!"

Henya's eyes, in their coquetry and their laughter, glowed over the field of snow and looked lovingly. Like white columns of smoke the snow flurries rise above Henya's head.

"And the Revolution, eh?"

"Ah—my daughter!"

"Hey, hey!…Revolution…*A-ho-ho!*"

The storm rises up and hangs over them.

Pulling each other by the hand, the three of them race into the eye of the storm, in the brilliant wheels of snow, between white, winged fires.

---

27. As when the Ten Commandments were given at Sinai.

"Hey, hey, hey, my white darkness!"

Henya throws her hands up in the air on both sides.

"Hey, hey—he-hey!…"

Roaming towers formed in the air, white sleds raced, sheaves of wind flew about and whacked one's face, sharp black things rocked in the whiteness of the opaque space; the storm was set dancing wildly, the one that put eternal generations to sleep, the order of creation, emperors' and kings' sons, houses of study, beards, the Torah, the commandments, and the King of kings, and which raised white tablets between heaven and earth….

"Listen, listen—until the soul is lit with pain and light!"

"Hey, hey, as fierce as the revolution."

And from the heart and soul, "Henya!"

With a loving voice, melting the heart, "Polyishuk!"

"Not that way, I don't want it at all!" cried out Soroka, turning his shoulder and leaving.

"Why are you acting that way, comrade Soroka?" called Henya, and stood in anticipation.

Polyishuk began to chuckle.

"What happened to him?" asked Henya.

The white storm whirls and whirls, scattering flames in every wind. The world leaps, screams.

From within the turning storm,

"A third part of thee shall fall by the sword round about thee—and I shall scatter a third to every wind—the evil arrows of hunger—and plague and blood—and I shall bring a sword upon you—."

"Hey, who's there?"

Polyishuk and Henya stand stock still, their bodies inclined toward the darkness; they look hard, look and see: staggering through the snow, a single man, falling and rising, waving his hands, walking, and on his shoulders something like the starry sky all poured out.

"Who's there?"

"It's I, have no fear, I!…. Wait!"

The wanderer drew near them. It was Motl Privisker.

"Where are you coming from, comrade Motl?"

"From where?...From the prophet Ezekiel...Yyess!"

They didn't understand what he was talking about.

"From whom?"

"Didn't I tell you? He was here just now.... You didn't recognize him, ha-ha-ha. I'd never seen Ezekiel in my life.... He came and asked, 'Who are you, my son?' 'I', I answered, 'I'm a certain Reb Motl....' 'Give me an interpretation of my verse, "A third part of thee shall fall by the sword."' Then I understood right away."

"*Nu?*" asked Polyishuk.

"Nothing at all. I said..."

"*Nu?*" Polyishuk asked again.

"*Nu?*...Nothing at all."

"Ezekiel, Ezekiel," laughed Henya. "For the extra glass of brandy he took."

"You, don't laugh!" Motl turned to her. "You, don't laugh! You would do better to go home. Your father doesn't know what to do. He's sitting and crying, crying."

V

It was a bright morning, rough, bristling with frost and snow.

The trees stood drawn like Sukkot palm branches—decorated and veiled with marvelous playthings and ornaments—of pure silver.

The houses were sunk in snow and the bright glow.

With joy and song like sharpened knives the snow creaked underfoot.

The frost burned with flames and searing.

On an upturned tub, without raising his head from the ground, sat Soroka before the flaming hole in the furnace.

He had returned to his seclusion with his little machine-gun.

He passed several days just in thought and cogitation.

That day Polyishuk transferred his residence from the bathhouse to a room he rented for himself. It was a fine room in every respect. A room that was a house in itself, amid a large courtyard, peaceful and quiet.

"Join me," Polyishuk spoke to Soroka. "The room's big, and there's only Henya who'll come and live with us."

Soroka delayed his answer, as though weighing his words very very carefully before speaking.

Hardly was the crunch of the snow under Polyishuk's feet heard as he went away from the bathhouse, before Soroka sat down and repeated his motto,

"In this world every dog is attached to his own tail."

Soroka hadn't managed to repeat that saying a hundred times before going out and heading for the staff courtyard.

In the staff courtyard Soroka reviewed his men, went out before them, strutted and paced back and forth, stood, and with his second in command, comrade Gedalia at his side, he called out,

"Comrades! At this moment I still have the power to give you orders! Therefore, first: drum major!…Second—always remember this: the force of the union of Jewish soldiers has no right not to be hanged, not to be shot, not to be burned and not to be buried alive!…Now, friends, as you have heeded me, so shall you heed the head of the union, comrade Gedalia."

The troops were bewildered. A secret voice of complaint passed from one end to the other.

"Comrades!" Soroka made a circle in the air with his arm, "Obey the order! Now your chief will be comrade Gedalia, and I leave you to go to my work and my activities, and the like…. I thank you, comrades, for your work and your assistance, may you all be well."

"*Kru-gom marsh!*"[28] comrade Gedalia spoke out after Soroka.

Soroka turned his back and left.

Soroka disappeared, he and his machine-gun together, as though the wind had taken him away, a silent wind, and no one knew where he went.

---

28. In Russian, "About face!"

VI

In Reb Simcha's house, silence and barrenness—enough to make you burst!

Reb Simcha angrily paces about his house, wandering here and there like a colt blasted with rain and wind. Conversation between him and Henya has ceased. He but sees her and turns his head away so as not to look at her impure face.

Sometimes Motl Privisker comes and has a heart-to-heart talk with Reb Simcha,

"If the blessed Lord can sit and see the troubles of the world and keep silent, then we, Reb Simcha, can suffer in silence. Anyway…"

He also spoke to Henya,

"Tell me, Henya, wouldn't you ever think, 'What's happening to me?' You're stuck far away, absolutely distant!"

As for Henya; nothing touches her soul, and today passes like yesterday: beautiful as though drafted with a compass, her mouth reddish and her cheeks white. Beauty and splendor.

Grief, grief. Reb Simcha restrains himself. He sits with his feet up in front of the oven, burning logs, and sighing to the oven,

"*Oy-oy-oy.*"

If only Motl Privisker could stifle that grief of his! If he could but be silent or pour his heart out like water in a humble voice and spirit submissive to the very center of his heart! Tears flow from both his eyes without cease.

"You're stuck far away, absolutely distant!"

"Henya, tell me what in the world you're doing?…Do you know what in the world you're doing!"

Motl Privisker spoke, giving Henya a look, a look of Reb Motl Privisker's sort, till Henya became completely ill at ease and didn't know where to turn or what to say.

"I ask you, what are you actually doing?"

Motl took large steps and walked across the room, sitting in his chair, putting his head on the table, then raising his head and putting it down again.

"The world is destroyed…. The world is destroyed…. Oh Lord,

Oh Lord…The world has gone mad, mad.What can we do? What can we d-o-o?"

He stood up and shouted,

"Henya! Henya!"

Then he went back and resumed where he had stopped,

"The world has gone mad, mad…. And I'm mad…completely…."

"Motl, I am very surprised at you," Reb Simcha broke in. "I'm astonished! What idea have you fixed in your mind?"

"That I shall cut them to pieces!" Motl put a hand over his mouth and turned away from Reb Simcha.

"Motl," Reb Simcha spoke sternly. "I don't understand. What do you expect? Why won't you return to your home and your wife?"

"Not me, not me, teach your *daughter!*" shouted Motl, and his eyes glowed like fire. "There you have someone to instruct!"

Reb Simcha fell silent. He gave up. Motl's eyes almost turned white, but Reb Simcha would not say what should be said at such a moment.

The logs didn't burn. Reb Simcha sighed. He mumbled the first words of the afternoon prayers and dealt with the furnace.

A bluish light surrounded the room.

Motl Privisker stood in the corner, swaying and moaning a weepy chant, saying his afternoon prayers. During the central portion of the prayers, when he reached, "Forgive us, our father, for we have sinned," he secretly wept, and tears flowed ceaselessly from both his eyes.

VII

The storms spread out—long, dangling, crooked, smooth and round—and they blasted and blew about freedom on earth and about the end of redemption; about Amens once answered with voices loud and joyous that had since grown silent; about the trilling song and psalm with which congregants, once upon a time, backed up their leader of prayer; about festival feasts that had been disrupted; about grooms and marital honors that had been abrogated—about the Jewish pulse that had gone dead.

The heavens and the earth whistled evening prayers with all the vowels and points of the Torah, but slightly obscure: Je-ho-va-ha—ha-ha!. .. And answering with a "Jee-hee-vee-hee—He! He!" Others echoed, "Jo-ho-vo-ho—Glo-o-ory!"

And this at the door,

"Knock knock!"

"Who's there?"

"I, Reb Simcha. Open up!"

And before Reb Simcha could close the door,

"Close the door! Close it!"

Reb Simcha closed the door.

"That?" Reb Simcha pointed to a small, loaded sled.

"Where's the ax?"

"Right away, right away."

Motl Privisker's lips were twisted, and his face was pale. His ears were full of the trumpeting and fanfare.

"What are you looking at? Rip up the floor, Reb Simcha!"

"Is everything there?"

"Everything except the *Handful* and *The Devil's Skin.*"[29]

"Shh…Shh."

In the large *zal*, where the tiniest memory of the goodness and grace of broad, peaceful life still remained, the floorboards were ripped open.

A cold, wet smell wafted up from the bared earth.

Motl Privisker and Reb Simcha bent down over the bared earth like hungry wolves during a storm.

Outside a kind of wolves' howl was heard.

The ax struck softly like teeth.

It was as though they, Motl Privisker and Reb Simcha, were sitting and howling and gnashing their teeth.

Boxes of textiles well wrapped up were buried.

The work was finished.

29. Cryptic use of Hebrew titles to describe the contraband.

The floor was repaired, once more becoming what it was.

"How will it be found? eh, Reb Simcha? How, I ask you, will it be found? No! It will never be found."

Reb Simcha hurried over to the furnace, sat and struggled to make the fire blaze up in the wood in the oven, to heat the house, which had become chilled.

Motl Privisker roamed about the room, briskly moving his legs and body.

"The famine years are over, over.... What hunger have we, hmm? What hunger, I ask you, have we? What is the wickedness of the evildoers for us? Nothing, we shall bear it and suffer!...It's nothing...."

The furnace blazed. The wind sent little fiery candles flying.

The fire burned higher and higher.

"Ah, what has been done? What has been done! Tell me, Reb Simcha!...What is the Revolution like?...Seven times a revolution, and seven times a malignancy!...Have no fear, Reb Simcha, my friend, my brother. You have great plenty, great plenty. We'll lack for nothing—Motl is no liar, eh?"

The fire of the furnace lit the wall. On the splinters of wood rose budding flowers, braided Havdalah candles,[30] and above them all—a single flame like a large golden censer. Below the wood, on the bottom, coals glowing like bars of pure gold.

"Ah, what has happened!" crowed Motl Privisker and grasped Reb Simcha's belt. "It is not in the heaven...nor over the sea...not the entente, and not world capital...but close, close... beneath our feet!"

From outside the snowy window the storm howled about the entente, about world capital, about the worldwide revolution and about the Internationale.

In the howl of the storm could be heard the sound of Henya's triumphant laughter.

"Did you hear? Oh-oh, a girl who's come of age!...Ah, why's she laughing, that evil thing."

---

30. A candle with multiple wicks used at the conclusion of the Sabbath.

"*Nu-nu*?!" Henya's voice came from outside. "Ha-ha-ha."

"Are you coming?...Come!" Polyishuk's voice.

"Ye-he—he, he!" the sound of the storm.

Reb Simcha was bewildered. He didn't know what to do. He ran about the room, back and forth, sat down again in front of the stove, ran about again.

"Ye-he—he! he!" the sound of the storm at the window.

VIII

By the window, near the place where the wind raged, dresses and shawls floated up, old rags, and felt boots and threadbare, hairy coats, fur caps wandered on the whiteness. The snow gleamed with the cleanliness of teeth, Reb Simcha sat with his white beard falling down over his blue hands, and his spectacles, fixed with strings and iron wires from old "Fialka" bottles,[31] mounted on his nose.

The wind trumpeted and whistled outside about freedom in the world and the end of redemption, loudly about the silenced response of "Blessed is He and blessed be His name, amen," about Sabbath hymns and *cholent* and *kugel* that had been put away, about the study of Torah, which had completely ceased, about the reciting of psalms, which the old men nevertheless continued, the remaining old men, each one in the bitterness of his heart, and his torn voice, and especially about the twelve psalms one says for a sick person.... [32]

Motl Privisker wandered about the room like an angel of destruction, not as was his wont, but with frightfully big steps such as were never seen, standing before Reb Simcha like a tree pleasant to look at, with the secrets of the Torah, from which wise teachings flourish, for a few moments he stood still before Reb Simcha like that, as though planted there, looking him over with his eyes, and

---

31. Perfume derived from flowers.
32. E.g., Psalms 6, 20, 25, 30, 32, 38, 41, 51, 86, 91, 102, 103. Traditions vary among Ashkenazic communities.

in that too—the likes of which had not been seen, with those eyes in Motl Privisker's famous fashion, saying,

"What is it, Reb Simcha, that Rabbi Akiba said to his disciples? 'When you reach the place of the pure marble plates, do not say, "Water, water," lest you endanger yourselves'—ha?"[33]

Afterward Motl sent his legs, may the all-merciful preserve us, all over the room—and that was an affair in its own right!—Revolving around a pole wondrous to heart and soul, when we see him with our own eyes, turning and talking to himself secretly with a soft, crestfallen voice, weakening the mind,

"That is a high secret, more elevated than can be borne...a high secret...high...."

With enthusiasm and ardor and waving his hands upward,

"Ex-al-ted!"

Reb Simcha already heard disturbing noises outside, hu-ha and hu-ha, the sound of people pursuing and running.

Outside there was also order in its own right.

Dr. Yukel the Bundist crawled, beaten and wounded, on hands and knees through the snow.... A red flag that proclaimed, "Long Live the Constituent Assembly" spreading in the wind and rolling...The student, Cahan, and Reb Aharon Shapira's son fleeing, and Polyishuk and his people running after him and crying and shouting out loud....

Motl still paced about the room, not seeing or hearing anything, turning around and around and talking,

"*Bereishit,* the beginning...in the beginning...Listen, daughter, and see...listen, daughter, and see.... In the beginning, there in that passage—there—*bat* 'daughter,' there—*re'i* 'see'...'Listen'—the same letters as in 'the beginning,' 'daughter'—there it is, the same word. And here is the word in the middle...."

"Motl, Motl!" shouted Reb Simcha in a voice not his own.

---

33. B. Hagigah 146. In Merkavah mysticism, refers to the dangers confronting the mystic in his ascent through the seven palaces of the seventh heaven.

"Murderers…. Murderers…What are they doing! What for! Motl, Motl, go tell them…. Motl! They'll slay him…."

Motl turned about preoccupied with his own thoughts and spoke to himself, "Listen, daughter, and see…. Listen, daughter, and see…."

Outside the wind caught up with the sun and the sun with the wind. Lights interwoven flew up. Veils. Handfuls and handfuls of pure white curls.

On the windowpanes, decorated with scepters and palm branches, rainbows stuck each other in all their colors.

Bearing a day like a copper column and wind.

IX

Like a green wave, pushed back and leaning into the distance, lay greenish the layers of snow, and the crimson of the sunset was on and around them.

Among the columns of smoke rising from the chimneys of the houses the wind hung as though among the masts and shrouds of ships in the heart of foamy seas.

Suddenly a rumor was heard, noise, a tangle of voices, massive and fearful,

"They're coming."

"The murderers."

"Murderers."

Polyishuk flashes through the street garbed in the flames of the sunset and, with his right hand, drawing the pistol at his side,

"Toward the enemy!…. Toward the enemy!"

Like a spirit he went by the House of Study, contemplated the three old men who had come to say their afternoon and evening prayers,

"And even to defend," he shouted from his throat, "this House of Study!"

Outside, flight and hubbub.

They ran away from Polyishuk to the right and left, hopping and running and limping and groaning.

No two were left together.

Silence blanketed the street and houses.

Sky blue and white.

As though no human soul had been there for many days.

The snowy wasteland, an abandoned salt mine…

Red the sun sets. The snow soaks up its dark blood.

Leaving the courtyard in front of the Union of Jewish Soldiers' headquarters, at an hour when the eye can no longer distinguish between one thing and another, on his horse, bound to the saddle by ropes in pride and glory, was comrade Gedalia, and behind him, like a river, flowed the files of armed men.

The snow gleamed.

Chill and darkness floated up into one's eyes.

The footsteps whistled in the dark blue of the snow.

Row upon row, two by two, in good order, the armed and silent men went up.

They all passed under Polyishuk's critical eye, as he stood at the side, supporting and fortifying them with his voice,

"One two, one two!"

"Who brought you here?" Polyishuk raised his voice against a few of the men coming up. "Wh-who took you out? I order you to stay behind and guard the town!"

"Comrade Polyishuk, are we one-armed or one-legged cripples, that we must sit in the rear?"

"Wh-what?…Are you still arguing with me?…Follow my orders!…On the double, march!"

"Ah, may his guts collapse!" the ones left behind muttered, wrinkling their noses and turning to the side like whipped dogs.

In a moment they lifted their feet and raced after the camp.

The files moved over the snow like black stains.

From a distance they were visible, near the old cemetery, which they passed with loud singing, the new and carefree life disturbing the ancient dream of those lying in the earth.

Then they were swallowed up in the darkness.

In the town life stopped.

The silence of death.

Darkness.

All night the dead town was silent.

In the morning the soldiers returned, with the sound of singing and joy they returned.

"It's a brigade of soldiers on their way back from the front, not murderers!" the returnees announced.

The town came back to life.

In the afternoon the soldiers entered the town. They went to the council building and began speaking,

"Comrades, regarding the Jewish brigade with you in the town, let them lay down their arms, comrades."

"What's this? Comrades, you…"

"Now, do as we said: Lay down your arms, that's enough!"

"How can you say that, comrades?" Polyishuk negotiated with them out loud. "They are in favor of the rule of soldiers and workers."

"Don't argue with us, shorty! See this?" They waved grenades in the air.

As ashamed as a jilted bride removing her jewels, the members of the Jewish brigade were humiliated, walking with their heads down, quietly cursing and swearing, each man to himself, with filthy and vile curses, returning their weapons to the armory.

Actually only a few returned them. Most hid them in the bathhouse, in the poor-house and in potato pits.

They returned their weapons, and they were all summoned, all the members of the union, to the courtyard of the council building and ordered to stand against the wall.

Their faces turned black, their eyes went dark, as when the stars come out.

"Low, low," they whispered quietly.

"We have failed."

Ten soldiers with angry faces, silent, stony, looking and waiting, stood in the middle of the courtyard. Every one of their movements, every blink evoked the fear of death.

The courtyard was barren, full of snow piled up, pink and blue.

Silence fell. Then Polyishuk appeared at the gate, with his hair and eyes wild, running into the courtyard with a single breath and stood at the wall among the rest.

The soldiers went up to each of the men standing at the wall, searching him.

No weapons were found.

The men standing there moved away from the walls.

To the sound of laughter and cries of contempt the fighters were dismissed and sent away.

Near the fence stood one of them, dressed in black, weeping.

That was a day of utter defeat, of humiliation. Every heart burned like fire. Every heart cried out against the injustice.

That night the soldiers left the town.

X

Every house is heavy with melancholy and worry.

Every eye expects enmity. All the lips are bluish—you mustn't speak out, only curse and cry out against injustice silently.

Driven from the house is every favorable sign, all cheerful expressions and grace.

Oblivion and expiration whisper, fasting and cold rustle about... Gone is the woman of valor who nurtured and raised her children as commanded by the blessed Lord. No more is the active householder with his sharp eye and quiet pace, searching here and pecking there, dragging a grain and bearing a bundle, urgently rushing, reading the cantillation marks vigorously and gloriously like a rooster, disagreeing with God...

No more are the maidens, preparing dowries with skillful hands and waiting for bridegrooms.

The women of valor lie still, exhausted, like sick goats, mourning, with dried dugs.

The sons die untimely.

The solid citizens race about like roosters with their throats extended, slaughtered, dripping blood....

And the maidens—

"May you know a good year!"

The world has gone mad. Heartbreak!...Heartbreak...And the blessed Lord knows! There is nothing left to do but "get up and lie in the street and laugh!"

In the month of Shevat,[34] the name of which is related to the word for severe judgment according to Motl Privisker, Henya left her father's house and went to live in Polyishuk's room.

That made no impression in the town. The town had seen so much lawlessness and wild living that it had become used to it.

The town was silent. It saw and was silent.

Not her alone, but another one too,

For comrade Polyishuk also opened his room to Nechama, the daughter of Reb Meyer the slaughterer, and Leyzer Potashnik's Shprintsa, also to comrade Gedalia and comrade Henikh the carpenter, and they all lived there together,

"A commune!"

"They strung up a rope," it was whispered in town, "from one wall to another across the room: dividing the women's beds from the men's!"

The town looks for similarities between Sodom before it was destroyed and Polyishuk's "commune." The deeds of the former are like those of the latter....

"The daughters of such righteous men, ah? Will you split their bellies, Lord of the universe!"

"Reb Simcha," people whispered about him, "has gone completely mad!"

That seemed quite likely.... True, one could go mad.

"Reb Simcha," they whispered, "is sitting in mourning, nodding his head ceaselessly and whispering, 'I have no daughter.... I have no daughter.... I have no daughter!'—nothing more."

---

34. The fifth month in the Jewish calendar, usually coinciding with parts of January and February.

On Friday Motl Privisker visited Reb Simcha and told him an interpretation of the verse, "Because thou hast forgotten me and cast me behind thy back."[35]

"I have no daughter…. I have no daughter…." Reb Simcha sat on the floor and nodded his head.

Motl Privisker turned his face away from him and remained standing there.

"Reb Simcha, Reb Simcha!…You are a father, are you not?… shouted Motl in a tearful voice. "Are you not a father?…Are you not a Jew, and the Lord is in heaven?…Why are you silent?!…Why are you silent and doing nothing?"

"I have no daughter…. I have no daughter…."

"Why are you silent!" cried Motl in tears. "Lord, Lord of the world, why are you silent, oy, oy!… Why don't you watch over your children, for they are in great misery."

"I have no daughter…. I have no daughter…."

"Simcha!" Motl Privisker jumped, raising his head and hands in the air. "I want to break the law!…I want to curse…To violate the Sabbath in public!…I want to be an adulterer!…I will transcend my nature!…Master of the whole world, master of the whole world." He grasped both his earlocks, "May I not be given a Jewish burial!…I'm a Bolshevik!" He pounded the table with his hand till the windows rattled. "Now, now the time has come…. Enough! I want to be a Bolshevik!"

"I have no daughter…. I have no daughter…." Reb Simcha's desolate voice was heard.

Motl leaped up onto his long legs. The hem of his jacket fluttered in Reb Simcha's face, as he sat and whispered, "I have no daughter…. I have no daughter…." And as though stones were being split, the door slammed against the doorpost, and the corners of the room shuddered—Motl was gone!

35. Ezek. 23:35.

XI

Lying in the snow, shoved and pressed together, the humiliated houses crouched. The winds wept bitterly over them. The barren, red sun set over them.

On the surface of the snow runs a purplish shadow.

Silence outside.

No one is to be seen. No one greets his friend, no one wishes anyone well. Silence and snow. As though the snow had covered the towns and settlements forever. Neither good nor evil will ever find that place.

Just one man, who appeared drunken in the full, pure whiteness of the snows, was Motl Privisker. He too was like a soul that had already died, whirling and wandering in the world of chaos.

Nightfall in the silence and snow. An encrusted city preserved in the sinking red sun…

The snow whistles and whistles beneath one's feet, making a sound like a radish being sliced. Spread before one's eyes is snow, near and far, sparkling on the ground like a bridegroom's prayer shawl.

Is this a dream or reality? Is it Motl Privisker there in the snow or some lone, forgotten, derelict out after the curfew? Who is it? Is it a poor teacher who lost his way, or some crazy man whose brains have been addled? Is that silence only apparent? Or are they voices, calling loudly, and after them the silence came? He is not clever enough to understand….

The snow sparkles and sparkles like crates and crates of candles lit all at once to make a great light!…

No matter, for he is weary unto death! No matter, for he has been beaten into silence! No matter, for he is bereft of kindness or joy, of motive or interest….

He walked slowly and heard a kind of silence, voices calling. Slowly he walked and looked at the moonlit snow, glowing under his feet.

Motl Privisker walked slowly by himself, until the voices of nearby people overtook him, real voices. They were Polyishuk and his bunch, who appeared in the street. As if they had come outside just to rule over the silent snows. Motl Privisker was alarmed. He looked at Henya walking, dressed in a leather coat, a pistol belted around her waist, booted, and his heart wept within him. In a moment his heart returned and was joyous. Motl spoke to himself,

"I was meant to suffer, and I have suffered already."

He looked again at her reddish mouth, her cheeks and fore-head, and he said again, "I was meant to receive suffering, and I have received it already."

"Ah, comrade Reb Motl," Polyishuk greeted him. "Where are you going?"

The people crowded around him, standing there and stamping their feet.

"Comrade Motl," Polyishuk continued. "Come with us! Be a Bolshevik, ha-ha...."

Motl Privisker raised his eyes toward Henya, who was standing at the side, and he said,

"If I am destined to go to hell, I wish to do so as a kosher Jew!"

"Ha-ha-ha!...Ha-ha!" people raised their voices in laughter.

The silence returned to what it was. No one was visible. No one greeted his friend.

Silence. A silvery round moon overhead. A long shadow on the snow below.

"I was meant to suffer, and I have suffered already."

And sometimes, "For it is forbidden to look her in the face, forbidden, forbidden!"

XII

Time passed, bringing other skies to rise over the town. A young sun with lovely rays melted the snow and opened spots of light outside. The winds chewed up the snow by the mouthful, and with every bite they wandered on, full of thoughts and melodies of spring.

The houses shed the white pie crusts from their shoulders and stood warming themselves in the sun, dark, old and a little distant from each other.

The roofs wept before the glowing sun like little children.

Bit by bit the snow yellowed and fell into its own water.

Puddles spread in the street like big clouds spread in the heavens.

Before the gates calves jumped, wild-eyed with tails erect.

Crows moved in the boughs of the trees, calling "krak-rak."

Motl Privisker was covered with his prayer shawl and phylacteries—and lo: there was no oppression or injustice in the world, no evil and malicious joy, but everything was as in earlier times,

"The Lord is one...."

Then, during prayer, while he was standing and acknowledging the Creator as King, proclaiming "The Lord is one!" in came two soldiers and shouted,

"Citizen Mordukh Karasyk, in the name of the Soviet Socialist Republic of Russia, you are under arrest!"

As though preparing himself to study it very thoroughly, Motl Privisker took the paper that was handed to him, and all his eyes saw that on the paper was the signature, Henya Horowitz.

Afterward Motl Privisker turned to face the soldiers and said, "That's how it is."

"That's the way it is. Come with us!"

They didn't offer to allow him to finish his prayer.

Motl Privisker removed his phylacteries, took off his prayer shawl, draped himself in his balding cat-skin coat and went. All the time he was walking in the street between the two armed soldiers, the image of Reb Simcha, with his floorboards ripped up, and Henya never left his eyes.... His throat was warm with the heat of sated thirst, and his heart beat within him as at a time of arousal and desire.

Many days passed, days and weeks.

But, could it be that many days passed, and yet comrade Soroka is walking down the street!

The days that passed were not many—many were the deeds done by comrade Soroka! Many are the nests he burned and many the fires he lit in the country he went through!

From the end of the street, which was darkened with gunpowder, went forth Soroka.

It was a debilitating spring evening.

Saturated silence, thick and dark, as it is sometimes in the depths of one's heart.

Swallowed in a gullet, the berry of a blue night is seen.

The town crouched in its mud like a sick, mourning goat with dried dugs.

Following footsteps stamped in the mud, large and small footprints of men and women, Soroka walked till he reached Polyishuk's house.

When he opened the door and went in, his eyes saw a rope before him, stretched from wall to wall, and two beds on either side of the walls, full of bodies, bodies like cadavers.

Soroka placed himself in the center of the room and shouted,

"You're still sleeping, you devils! Get up: the Germans are coming!"

Translated by Jeffrey M. Green

Bridegroom of Blood

And it came to pass on the way at the lodging-place, that the Lord met him, and sought to kill him. Then Zipporah took a flint, and cut off the foreskin of her son, and cast it at his feet; and she said, "Surely a bridegroom of blood art thou to me...."

Exodus *4: 24–25*

The desolation of the wilderness couched wideflung.

Waste upon waste, billow upon billow lay the heavy pallid sand, sown with scattered black stones; feverishly flaming and sparkling, sparks of silver and of gold—

Into the deep which God had cast off, and which stood frozen with wrath...

Hewn in the sun's cycle, giant boulders and everlasting hills, herbage and barrenness of the brookbed; the sunstricken body of the wilderness went wavering on like the air of untold furnaces; depth within depth, solidity upon solidity, light entangled in tangles of light—

To ultimate horizons, to beyond all distance....

Most ancient of the Universe, the arid firmament stretched glowing and gasping above, measuring itself against the desolation. They were twain as one, heavens borrowing from desolation and desolation from heavens—and twin they continued. Flaming stillness faced in every direction; stillness petrified and burdened with drought and aridity—as a secret of mighty gods.

Entire in her beauty and adornments, Zipporah sat upon the camel mat.

Bold in the glittering light, her swarthy face shone strong.

Her tresses, tress upon blue-black tress, nestled upon her head like heavy serpents and were gathered in a crest above her forehead; a long black veil was cast behind from the tip of the horn, and rested by her.

Sparks upon sparks, the leaden earrings gleamed pale. The sun squeezed flames upon flames from the nose-ring and its links and from the bronze-inlaid copper bangles on her arms. Great heavy necklaces were on her neck, and rows of stones like those upon the throats of camels; stone upon rounded stone they hung. Fringe upon fringe, woven a third white, a third black, and a third tawny-yellow, descended across her broad blue robes. The boy, eyelids swollen, belly shining copper-yellow, slept between her knees.

The swaying camel of Zipporah paced midway between the other two.

He stretched his throat in the air, toning into the mighty hues. Crowned with tufts of green wool, red madder-threads and plaited gray bark, threads oven-black and indigo, his small snakelike head gazed lofty and cold over the desolation.

His hump reared, highpiled. The scarlet carpet of woven buck wool, rise from the mat like two decorated walls. Steadily swaying, pace after pace, pace upon swaying pace, the three camels rocked on, following one another.

Shriveling in the heat, neither asleep nor awake, gazing around and drowsing, gazing anew and drowsing, Zipporah hovered disconsolate, her seat swaying hither and thither....

Harsh is the desert.

An evil home—

Verily an evil home!

Her spirit desired not to go, nor her heart to descend.

Yet she descended and went.

Nay. Her heart went not....

Wherefore was his path to Egypt, that his feet went down through the wilderness?

Lusting in flame for Egypt as a serpent for garlic.

Wherefore was his path to Egypt, that his feet went down through the wilderness?

Without compassion for her; what spurred him that he should go?

Her soul did not wish to go, nor her heart to descend.

Nay. Her heart did not go....

She had indeed inquired of the wise, and of such as know the future times.

And of the prophet had she asked;

With one voice all had spoken good alone.

They studied the stars and gazed at the liver. Lots had they also cast for her; and such as had skill therein divined by the flight of birds.

Each one, each one spoke, and with one voice all of them had said but good.

Thus had one said,

—Turn to the path, go straight in the way; as they hear thee shall they answer thee. Thy bread is given, thy waters are faithful; be it so with thee!

And one had spoken thus,

—By the path wherein thou goest, shalt thou return. The mountain of God be in thy borders. Let all the bald hillsides be a highway. Thou shalt go and thou shalt prevail. May my end be like to thee!

And one had rushed around the tamarisk and clapping his two hands had cried,

—Thou shalt indeed run; so let me run!

Then had she descended and gone.

Nay. Her heart went not.

The skies breathed flames of fire. The desert flared, flared, flared. Awesome rest, rest of ages and eternity, had enclosed the width of all the distances around.

Languidly, leisurely, pace swaying on pace, swaying pace on pace, the three camels lagged rocking on—

From watercourse to cleft watercourse and from mount to mountain....

Gazing and drowsing, gazing anew and drowsing, Zipporah rocked. Her disconsolate heart mused, all of her murmured sorrow.

From how great rest was she removed, woe to her that she wandered!

She had been still and now was cast about; blessed in the tent and now—set awandering; woe to her that she wandered!...

Long is the day of the desert, a day ever prolonged.

The soul could not bear it....

Deep the sea of light, deeper than depth.

The soul wearied therein.

Than the brightness of the full Universe there is nought more lovely, save the mire of the rills and rivulets which are by the fountains....

Sick with dejection, grief and much yearning, stealthily, her heart amoan, she began to hum a song.

Solitary, low voiced as the sweetness of distant weeping, she rocked weeping hither and thither. Lilting and tender, her voice hovered, quivering the most lilting and sweet of songs, "Pitcher by the bubbling spring...."

The song was already still; but it bubbled yet in her heart, filling her soul with bitter gushing trilling tears.

Tears smarted her eyes and hung sparkling, heavy. She gazed through them as into a glistening mirror at Sela her birthplace, blazing and shining....

Zipporah gazed,

And Sela her birthplace was seen broad and lofty.

Square black tents sloping down at the back were set here and there amid the rocks. Her mother who had borne her, blessed above women in the tent, was sitting behind the tent, between the figtree and the heaped-up droppings of the herd, and wove ram's hair for the tent-curtains.

"Where is Zipporah?" asked her mother who had borne her, blessed above women of the tent. "Where, O daughter exiled from me? Secure was my daughter and is exiled, most restful of the maidens—and is driven forth. Zipporah, why dost thou not sit at the weaving-beam, my daughter, at the entrance to the tent? My daughter kept her home clean as a bird, her babe at her bosom like a fledgeling; at her feet he played, he crawled...."

Silent tears trembled in her eyes. Silent she restrained them, while the full vision of Sela her birthplace hardened—till they fell.

Her eyelids quivered a moment. Charm of grief suffered but restrained from tears was molded over her twisting, trembling mouth....

Zipporah sighed from her heart and breathed deep.

Her mother's mother, the old grandam, sat on the goathair rug within the tent grinding barley to meal for food. Around were set the iron flails, the iron ingots, the lances and the cauldron; the camel-saddles, the "bird" and the spindle; the fleeces of the goats, of the ewe-lambs, of the rams; and the camel-wool. "Where is my daughter's daughter?" wept the old woman as she gripped the quern-handle. "Why doth her camel delay its coming?"...

Zipporah wiped her eyes with the veil, and her lips trembled in whisper:

—Why doth her camel delay its coming?

And before the tents, in the caves, in the clefts and crannies of the rocks, coal pans were kindled. The men to their work; each to his labor, to all manner of artifice in iron or in burnished copper. Iron to iron and copper to copper; they hammered. The muscles of their frames swelled in toil; sinews of flint and rounded pebbles. Their faces flamed; their hands hammered heavily. Their iron sleds clanged upon the iron; the iron picks rose and fell and clanged, clanged once more, clanged anew. All the hills answered after them, giving voice; and the rifts in the rock made echo.

"Where is Zipporah?" they were all saying. "Zipporah is not in her home, but is gone into the wilderness afar!"

And the iron picks rose, fell and clanged; clanging anew, clang-ing once more. All the mountains answered, giving voice; and the rifts in the rock made echo....

And they clanged; and again; and they bent the iron upon the stone, and they fashioned of the iron a bow. And they whitened the burnish to the keenness of a lance; and they forged the copper and polished it with files....

II

The night was at an end.

It was yet dark when the camels began to straggle onward anew....

Light illumined the waste.

Dim; umber; greenish-rusting; ashy-gray and grayish-white; the spindle peaks of the rocks and the fangs of the boulders projected.

Gilded and burnished, flashing and glancing, the wastes of sand caught fire.

Heavily dragged the wheel of the sun through the Universe—a bruised, drear desolation.

Desolate and empty the spaces of morning dragged on; were lost in the light and lonely stillness of the Universe....

Ponderously, leisurely, the three camels lagged, rocking on, winding and twisting in frigid restfulness through the borders of the wasteland.

Zipporah rocked in a daze.

Hardened her grief, as a root dried up to its depths.

An evil habitation—

Verily an evil habitation!

She turned her face back toward Sela her birthplace and cried in the uprush of her yearnings and grief,

—Sela, Sela, Sela, pasture of copper!

Quietude of desert silence all round....

Bonny as burning coals, his visage as the copper of the furnace, his belly a sparkling mirror, all of him like copper from the rocks and the river-diggings, the boy lay sleeping at her feet....

Zipporah gazed long, and her eyes grew light:

At her feet shone the rock and the brook of copper!

The boy seemed to her as a boulder set fast together, and as the brook of copper in the dale....

Rejoicing and exultant she bowed herself, bending over him.

Silent she passed her hand over his belly; silent she kissed him on the lips and lapped his face with her tongue; caressing and fondling his little frame, she dropped her face to either side and sat choked with joy and laughter....

As she sat face lowered, the boy stretched his legs, rubbed his cracked lips together and stirred, undecided whether to wake.

Pressing silent finger to lips, Zipporah started back and sat crouching on the mat, guarding herself against noise.

Scarcely a moment passed ere the boy slept again....

Her lips guarding the silence, her face grave, full of holy awe she bowed again, swaying hither and thither; she charmed in whisper, her lips moving silently:

—From the starting and the evening side, from the hidden north and the right hand side, and evermore.

—As the rock of the watercourse, as the eternal sandstorm, may thy light be great as the world.

—From the seven portals of Earth, from the nine bars of Earth, may thy years be many generations.

—Upon thee may there be no evil eye! No evil speech concerning thee! No evil tongue be upon thee! Nought lead thee astray.

—No ill of pain in thy head, no halting in thy gait, no bleeding of thy heart, neither burden nor breaking, no plague nor falling of hair, no bright pustules; leprosy nor scabbiness; may the signs thereof never be seen!

—Cramp, lameness and strife—mayst thou never know their signs. I order thee indeed. Mayst thou never recognize the signs thereof!

—Zefi, Shefi and Madan the ravaging tribes—mayst thou never know their spoor! I bid thee so—mayst thou never see their spoor!...

The camels ambled on.

The wilderness flared and flashed; deep within deep, solidity within solidity, light entangled in tangles of light.

To infinite horizons, to beyond all distance....

The way turned by the watercourse and descended.

The lagging camels grew lower....

Zipporah gazed sighing about her.

Another, new spirit, seemed to hover above the far end of the watercourse ahead.

Hues upon hues fluttered in the middle, flying thence to the sides....

Wondering, Zipporah shaded her eyes to look. And behold— In the watercourse before her, filling the vision, was the likeness of a builded town; saffron houses, houses crocus, blue-green, aquamarine and peacock-green...towers, bastions, curtains secured by silver ring-clasps; pillars, rows of pillars, burdened with pediments and capitals—

Citrus and red, grape-black, anthraconite-black and hyacinth....

Trembling and distraught, she clapped both her hands in joy,

—Water! Water!

Rills of water spouting from the middle and the sides.

Water, running water, fructifying, irrigating, thirst-quenching water.... Water amid the buildings, in the soil and in the vessels; deep water; shallow, spreading water...splashing and dripping, spreading and springing from spot to spot; spreading by ways many as the feet of a centipede, crawling hither and thither and flowing....

Quaking and panting, with bounding heart, Zipporah tottered on her seat,

—Water! Water!

She would spring from the mat, rush to the water, and drink, drink without stay or end till her belly was full.... And the water would trickle over her mouth, would spill over her neck and her bosom! And it would overflow and pass down over her breasts and belly....

—Water! Water!

The wilderness cast its spells and flashed.

The vision flickered and trembled, blurred and rose on high, wavered and secured itself once more, fluttered in the middle and flowed away to the sides....

Frantic, her throat parched as though filled with gravel and sand, her bowels charring, her bemused senses forsaking her, Zipporah seethed, prostrate and faint, her body hanging over the camel's side; and her lips murmured in the weak, torn, broken cry of her stupefied heart,

—Water! Water!...

The more she gazed, the more her flesh became fire upon her; as though she were surrounded by crackling vineshoots. Her eyes were swollen; her bowels seethed and her spirit was near departing from her. Until she fell wearied, no breath in her....

Her hands were lax, her eyes hidden, her mouth foamed and her head was awhirl with twisting and turning, winding and circling....

Lost in heart and perplexed in spirit, her mien ailing and her eyes a question, a search, Zipporah roused herself and whispered again,

—Water!...

And behold—

The sight was finished, the vision was ended—

The wilderness had returned, was become a desolation....

She leaped agonized from her place,

—Water!...

⋇

The camels came out of the watercourse.

The desert stretched flaring and flashing on; depth within depth, solidity within solidity, light entangled in tangled light—

To furthest horizons, to beyond all distance....

Her spirit returned to her little by little.

Weak-kneed and dry as a shard she swayed hither and thither and sat desolate and confounded....

An evil home—

Verily; an evil habitation!

For what sin had she been set here?

She meditated, mused on many things, her spirit bitter.

Writhing and wringing her hands she swayed from side to side, moving ever.

Suddenly she raised her head, her eyes wide with wonder,

Had she not but now seen the chosen land; which a man sees—and it is not; he gazes—and it melts away?...

She remembered the man of the caravan speaking in the ears

of the people, he sitting in the entrance of the tent when the sun had set on him in Sela; and he had spoken thus:—

—It is true; we having tested it, know it to be so. The chosen land, grown of the desert, is hidden in distance unknown, and man has no dominion over it nor dwelling in the midst thereof.

—For Man vieweth it—and it is not; he gazeth—and it melts away.

—For it is of the very oldest of old time, from the beginning of the creation of the Universe, from the day when the father of the world went forth from before God....

The boy roused from his sleep.

He stretched his legs out on the mat, set his hand on the fox-tooth hanging from a thread about his neck, and opened his eyes—

As a gloomy cistern watching for the sun.

Naked, asweat, glistening in the sun, the boy stood on all fours, then straightened and rose erect, gazing in astonishment over the desolation.

As though seeking her counsel he turned his head to his mother, laughed over all his copper face, and gaped about him in surprise.

Darting after his father who sat the foremost camel, he stretched out his tiny hands and laughed and chattered and called,

—Father! Father!

Zipporah drew the boy to her by his foot, he resisting like a stubborn ram. She pushed down the hands stretched after his father and pressed him to her bosom. She touched anew the tooth upon his neck; from the tooth of the dead fox to the tooth of the live fox.

She took the roll of pressed figs from beneath the mat and severed pieces with the hatchet; she took the cheese and grated it with a grater.

The boy rolled and gobbled away at the bits, large and small—even like a yearling ram.

He ate to repletion, his face exulting; and his gross belly shone like the flux of copper.

Gabbling and meditating he preyed hither and thither, hopping and crawling or walking hunched like a kid or lambkin; he stood on all fours like an ass of the smiths, swinging on the sumpter-saddle, hanging thence and standing up; setting his feet amid the vessels, hanging from his mother's neck by his hands, gripping with his feet and climbing aloft....

It was as though a cover of gloom had been removed from Zipporah's face. She pressed him to her heart with all her strength; the boy bore with her in silence and as though he felt nothing.

She pressed a plethora of kisses upon his cracked lips and on his entire little frame; putting his foot into her mouth, she kissed it with all her passion; she seized his wire-like, nailbitten fingers with her teeth; he freed them; she turned him back to front in wanton and bright happiness, as he hung swinging in the air; he kicked the right foot and the left, crowing at the top of his voice; she played to him on the tympanum and he set his little feet and danced the "iron dance" as it is danced in assembly at Sela and the brook of copper.

Then, taking counsel with herself, she set herself to perform nine and thirty labors with him; all the adjustments of the world and its needs.

She kneaded him like dough, set him in a dish, shaped him, and baked him in the sun.

Then she bent him, and tore, beat and combed him to a flake of wool, spun him and wound him into hanks. And with him she performed every detail that the world needs....

The boy screeched and laughed, frolicked and rejoiced; and her delight and happiness of heart increased.

Until he wearied and lay sweating and glistening in the sun, panting and gasping like a bellows wheezing at a fire.

Zipporah sat radiant with pleasure and goodwill, her spirit fragrant within her; she took her tympanum in hand and set her voice to song.

Hushed, in proud praise, as in exceeding storm, she quavered song, her hand tapping the tympanum as she continued.

Mournful and lilting her voice; swelling as a pipe; hushed, secret, gaining pride and rising, growing stronger and more passionate; she uttered the stanzas of the song as the sons of iron have uttered them in Sela and the brook of copper since time untold.

Feats of Cain, father of all who labor land and field; feats of

Jubal, father of all who pluck lute or puff the flute; Tubal-Cain, artificer of all implements of copper and of iron; the battles of the sons of Cain with Seth when they did battle together; and the feats of the sons of God who took the comely daughters of men....

Sweet the drum and trembling; she smites with power and her song ascends. She raises her utterance and continues, strengthening to thunder and hurricane, to warfare and to battle. Blow up, fire, blow! Hoofbeats, hoofbeats of fire, thunders and flame and shoutings, torches be flashing and quick! Let the rocks around be aroar and the boulders cry out in shoutings; let the widths of the wilderness clamor and mountain smite mountain, beating in time!

Her stretched mouth flecked with foam, her eyes tight-closed, her swarthy face as lightning and all of her ashout, Zipporah raised her voice on high, beat the tympanum with her palm—

Breach of a mountain fallen in the desert and shattering with a mighty outcry; the sound of thunder in the cycle of the sky, thundering,

Pass ye the call through Sela,
The drum through the seat of old;
When the Almighty set Cain aside,
And wandering, he dwelt in the land!

III

The basin of the wilderness caught fire, flamed, flared; filled with God's flaring fires and the spirit of His wrath.

The heavens hid their deeps and puffed at their mighty fire.

Drought-stripped, rusted, leprous and eternally waste, rocks of dread mien quivered in the sands and spattered sparks of fire and light....

As from huge streams of fire overflowing and gushing now hither, now thither, pools of sand were poured forth and led downward to the arid watercourses.

Glancing and drowsing, glancing anew and drowsing, Zipporah rocked, her heart wormwood.

An ancient tradition the mothers announced, the fathers related to such as hearkened; deeds from the oldest of time, from the fashioning of the world....

She sat in judgment upon herself.

Had then God done thus and thus with her, visiting upon her the sins of the first fathers? Cain, father of the world, had been a wanderer and a vagabond; and now she strayed in the dread and mighty desert....

God had visited the sin of the first fathers upon her; as is related in full assembly, as is sung thus in song,

Visiting the sins of the fathers upon the children....

Zipporah swayed from course to course, wandering vagabond, her heart shivered and crushed,

Visiting the sins of the fathers upon the children....

Hallowed with divine dread, the wilderness rushed swelling and untamed aloft, looming awesome and terrific; awe was round about and stillness; the wilderness hearkened, hearkened....

Sooty-black, sapphirine and dim, dank with curling wisps of mist, the mountains pressed and the crags crowded; boulders circled in heavy desolation.

In the distance rose Mount Horeb, the mountain of God....

The path became one of clefts, stones and pebbles.

As ordered by the All-puissant, the stillness pressed down, haughty in its awe and pride.

Pressure of aeons, of ages on ages.

Every hoofbeat of the camels noised through the stillness.

Thundering and quaking the hills responded to the clatter of each hoof, glowering and wroth that they dared disturb sanctity.

Fearful, her flesh as softboiled turnip heads upon her, her spirit fluttering from her in tiny starts of dread, Zipporah sat neither dead nor alive.

Lest God gaze from His habitation, appear—and she sleep in death.

Lest He rouse at the sound of the camels, stare at the land and it tremble, stride on the hills—and they shake....

From deep to depth, from thence to thither and from end to

end rushed the untamed desert, and the dread of God and His awesome glory increased.....

The steps of the camels grew short.

Hill cried to hill at the sound of their hoof-clatter.

Crags rose, grew high, and were low.

Shameless rocks shifted, veered, and strayed.

Murk-burdened, unshaped; stoneheaps faded red and brown; foothills of glinting beaten copper, and mounts of dissolving crystal; peaks upon peaks of sparkles, mists and cloud—hills by the thousand; hundreds and hundreds and many hundreds; smashing, forcing their way; rushing and gushing aloft.

Ringing and wrath, the wilderness leaped in its fury and bided its time.

The camel rasped in its throat and stood. Its terrifying bray rasped in its gullet.

Her soul slipping for dread, fearful and uncomprehending, Zipporah blinked her eyes all round and saw Moses descend from the camel, face the mountain and stride away from them.

Astounded she gazed after him. Her face was pale and her eyes big with dread.

The camels went on their way once again.

Trembling, her knees aquiver, her senses dizzy; and Moses afar on the mountain, the mountain set opposite, awesome and dread with God; Zipporah fell on the mat, kneeled and prostrated herself.... Knelt and whispered spells, not knowing which—and as a sudden thought, a cry was uprooted and thrust aloft as though borne upon the wings of the wind....

—Father! My father! she cried in a voice of dread and fell in a heap, no breath within her.

The rocks clamored round about, and the boulders scolded and yelled. And all the hills hissed and thundered, piping and thunder and quaking and breaking of rocks, fearful as darkness....

Startled, unguided and rasping from rock to rock and from way to way, the crazed camels chased, leaped and brayed in fearful voice, making Earth tremble—

Heaven and Earth trembled, mountains trembled, all the foundations of the wilderness....

IV

The silent wilderness arched and went on; deep within deep, density within density, light entangled in tangles of light—

To infinite vision, to beyond all distance.

Slowly swaying, pace upon pace, rocked the camels....

Her flesh aching, her bones numb, as though a roaring lion had passed her by and closed her path, Zipporah roused herself and breathed deep.

Astounded by the sun, without trust in her life, she gazed around.

She remembered, and sat quaking and quivering.

She trembled, awe of Sinai in her heart, the dread voice of God roaring from His habitation. From His holy dwelling place He gazed and watched her....

All agog she mused, rejoicing within her,

—Joy, my soul!

Her soul was escaped from flame, her flesh was whole from death,

—Joy, my soul!

Now might she extol God, proclaim His valor in assembly!

Riding through the wilderness, when she rode down through the desert, bless ye God!

But an instant between her and death; God had shewn lovingkindness that she might not perish; bless ye God!

That which God saith—is already done; that which God saith—is long prepared.

Mountains quake before Him, the foundations of Earth are stirred, thunders and plentiful lightnings, bless ye God!

Even through the days and years of wandering the wilderness and Egypt, until the third evening, unto the seventh morrow, let Him be blest evermore; bless ye God!...

Lauding and praising, Zipporah rocked to and fro till sleep fell on her and she slumbered....

In a little while she sprang up confused and amazed and sat staring in all directions. She spoke,

—What is this dream which I have dreamed?

In her dream she sat at the entrance to the tent spinning goat-hair. And behold Moses returning from the wilderness. She ran toward him to greet him. And behold God appeared in the likeness of a man of war, clothed and robed in pride, glory and majesty, and came toward her. Moses hastened, passed across and came toward her. God strode, showed Himself and neared her. Thus they contended, each striving to pass in front of the other; now God and now Moses, clamoring after her and drawing closer.

Fearing for herself, she leaped to her feet and hid in the barley heap....

She forgot the dream little by little. She said the charm,

—Buck of my home! Old baldhead buck!

She had had nowhere to hide save in the heap of barley—

—Buck of my father's house! Old baldybuck!

Sitting in the center of the carpet, Zipporah basked in the sun.

She stretched herself, straightened her knees, tossed her head, her countenance directed aloft, her fresh, strong, sparkling beauty blossoming, all of her dipping in the depths of eternal light, light burnished and extolled. Relaxing, she lay with fluttering heart; her heart pale and languishing for Moses, her soul longing to give him joy and to rejoice with him in her beauty and allure.

Fire flashed in her heart; her spirit flamed as the ardent day, as a heath and the weary Earth; all of her fire, hewn of fire, made entire by fire....

Meditating, not knowing her soul, she was aflame, her soul thrilling; her eyes were sealed by love delayed and allure; her form was abandoned to the sun, which sent fire and desire from on high throughout the widths of the desert; her arms were slack; her bosom swelled and heaved; her strength ebbed from her; she lay watching, like a man thirsting for water, for the power of his awesome hand; that it might rest upon her in delight, strengthen and refresh her soul. Forward and back; the face of Moses flickered before her closed eyes as in the dream. Forward and back wavered his face; she could neither focus nor control it. Now he seemed as a mighty warrior, tightlipped, his eyes scattering fire; now as a needy pauper, as a rock alone upon a hill, as a rock about to fall; his head subdued and his face concealed. Now he seemed of great height, of double height, his appearance awesome; now a man's height, stalwart, and broad as any man, dumb as though he passed on the way and gazed toward her from afar.

How greatly her heart desired to gaze upon his face!

But Moses warded himself from her. These many many days he warded himself from her, guarded his path from drawing near to her, and did not approach her nor touch her. He had made her desolate as the wilderness; as a widow, a woman in her courses; let God account it for grace in His eyes, for the lovingkindness of God is eternal....

Swerving after her heart, she lay in flickering black flame, her soul dazed by love battened down, her heart dripping away in melting drops like wax before a fire....

She remembered her dream, and pondered:

Had not God approached her, a man of war robed and trapped in pride?

Let God make her find favor in the eyes of her husband, for the lovingkindness of God is eternal!

Surely God had appeared to her in a dream, had made Himself known in vision; mighty and a warrior, a man of battles, swathed in grandeur and glory....

Not knowing; her spirit fluttered, flashed and kindled. Her eyes were sealed fast, her face was black, radiant, bubbling in flame; as though the sun were inrooted, shed light from within. Her teeth gleamed white with the fragrance of flaring allure. She lay until sleep seized her and she slumbered.

V

Vivid in the sun, tangible in the wilderness and lovely as noontide, Zipporah opened her eyes and lay, dazed with the delight of her sweet slumber; the horn base hung askew above her brow, and her finery glittered in the sun, glared in fire.

She was brilliant with her dream; joy and radiance rose tendril-wise from the visions of her mind.

She had dreamed a dream once again, and pleasant had been this dream which she had dreamed.

In her dream God had appeared from Sinai, had darted down like a winged creature and had hovered over her bosom...she could yet feel on her bosom the heavy burden of light, like the sun which illumines the noon-hour with its vigor; it had passed over her heart and scorched, had overflowed and oppressed her with flame and ardent pain....

The searing fire still trembled upon her lips; she was bowed down in her inmost self; fire had kissed her fusing expiring soul.

She could still sense flames stroking her face; the portions of her body groped as in a dark night, straying as drunken, bawling and fearstricken, the spirit not returning....

Brilliant, radiant and exquisite she lay where she was, dipping in a brook of delights.

They had desired her; the lofty ones of Heaven had made her their mate; the sun had aspired to her and had panted and gasped to her in ardor. The desert waste had puffed at her in his heat, cleaving and splitting to the roots of the heart; they had deceived her and given her over to impure thoughts.

She was bright, pleasant and lovely.

The lofty heavens sparkled with the radiance of God's visage, with the fiery radiance of the Awe of Sinai; the place of His abode was Sinai, the ends of the heavens; and His supports were at their ends. As though God concealed Himself within the Universe and peered around, watched, lusted for, enticed His love from the fullness of the heavens, from right to left, from dawning to sea....

Her twin breasts like a half-coulter, the camels shambling ever on, Zipporah raised her head:

—What was this thing that befell me?

Bemused and quaking she gazed hither and thither as seeking refuge from a foe.

—What was it that befell me here?

Her hands failed, powerless and withered.

Dread fell upon her and fear, panic of death.

—I shall indeed die, for I have seen God.

Knees trembling she prostrated herself, fell on her face.

—I shall perish indeed, for I have seen God.

Kneeling, she moaned in dread.

Until she raised her head and said to herself,

—Did God desire to slay me He would not have left His habitation these two times. Nor would He now have shown me all these!

She clapped her hands in joy,

She sprang up, dancing hither and thither, the stones and fringes clashing together from her throat,

—If God wished to slay me He would not have left His home twice. Nor would He have vouchsafed me all these but now!

She butted with the horn on her brow, butted right and left, saying again,

—Did God desire to slay me He would not have forsaken His habitation these two times. Nor would He have vouchsafed me all these but now!

Turbulent as a day of storm; her heart fluttered convulsively like a bird in the air, and her flesh was radiant with joy. Nay, indeed she would not perish!

For had God desired to destroy her He would not have forsaken His habitation these two times, nor would He have shown her all these but now.

She gazed radiant over the waste, turned her eyes straight ahead, saw Moses seated on his camel foremost of all.

Cloud-bound her visage, and she sat crushed of neck and heart confounded.

She bowed her head, said,

—Be still....

And she sat crushed of neck and heart confounded.

She said,

—Hush....

And she sat crushed of neck and heart confounded.

For now the matter would be heard thus in the ears of her lord.

Thy wife hath strayed from thee, hath faithlessly deceived....

And she sat crushed of neck and heart confounded.

And her good man would hearken and his wrath would glow against her....

And she sat crushed of neck and heart confounded.

And he would blot her name from beneath the heavens....

And she sat crushed of neck and heart confounded—

Joyless at heart, no light in the eye. The flush of her face was gone, her neck was crushed, she was silent as a desolate mound. Her heart was sore confounded, her spirit feared, feared without rest.

—*Ai hoo*, time and troubles, *ai hoo*!

Stumbling by reason of the transgression of her strength; no man near her, no man near her, yet woe that her strength had stumbled.

—*Ai hoo*, time and mischance, *ai hoo*!

God had wronged and abused her, had no mercy, but wished to destroy her wantonly, had led her astray from the path, forced her.

—*Ai hoo*, tune and mischance, *ai hoo*!

She dragged her keen, prolonged and dragged it, squeezed her head between her knees and sat sickening, weeping, sighing, her loathing on her face, her heart bitter and her spirit shamed.

Moses would gaze, his ire kindling; would press his lips together, his eyes scattering dread; his visage would grow as storm, as flame flashes on rock...

Verily he would stone her till she perish, till death drop upon her lids!

Her soul had not desired to go, nor her heart to descend.

Yet she had descended and gone.

Nay. Her heart had not gone.

—*Ai hoo*, time and troubles, *ai hoo*...

Why did he wend to Egypt, his feet in the wilderness?...

She raised her head a moment, moved to numbness and perplexity of heart.

—Would Moses go down to Egypt for nought?...

Her bewildered eyes strayed hither and thither and she sank down upon the mattress; her face was fallen and her thought confused, wavering and restless....

Suddenly she was ripped as by fire from heaven; her eyes grew and filled with flame; her face glowed lurid, the hair of her head rose, and a screech of despair lodged in her throat.

—Would Moses go down to Egypt for nought?...

What indeed could be within his inmost heart! He sought another Zipporah and for that he went to Egypt, went away!

Her eyes flared, her face blazed as a flame puffed-at, fed and crackling. She was all of her afire.

She knew now why he held aloof from her, now she knew indeed! He sought another Zipporah.

Was she then such, and so grievous a burden, that he need change her for another? Or was she of the house-parings, or perchance come of blemished stock?

Or mayhap her visage was wan, her eyes blear, her nostrils pinched, her ears heavy; or was she squat or green hued? Or mayhap a barren mule, putting forth no branch and bearing no fruit, neither building nor builded, that he should do this thing sinfully and with deceit!

Now indeed she knew why he held aloof from her, making her as a wilderness, as a widow, as a woman in her courses; now she knew in sooth....

She passed an hour somber as night.

All of her was gloom, confused and tumultuous; her hands gripped her plaits; her breath soughed heavily through her nostrils, stopped again and again, as though to force a great bitter cry from her. A howl and wail of destruction whereat would tremble wilderness and the bases of the world....

Twisting like a blazing strip of bark, she threw herself down, writhing, kicking, tearing at her hair; she struck her face, her flaring fury increasing.

—Another Zipporah! Another Zipporah!

Screeches were uprooted from her lips as flames are torn from the coalpan and mount aloft.

—Another Zipporah!

Now let him see and know!

Nay in sooth; but now let him see and know!

The Lord is God, nor is there other, beside Him there is no God! The Lord is God, nor is there other, beside Him there is no God!...

Swaying hither and thither in eagerness, she burrowed amid the vessels in agitation, took her ornaments and began to deck herself in haste.

She set the hairnet on her brow, and the frontlet from ear to ear.

She wound the band round her hair, set the strings upon her cheeks and the necklace on her throat; so that she might seem full in flesh. She hung the chain and the moon-amulets, the drops and the veil; and so with all the rest, four and twenty ornaments; and she sat bedecked as a bride, fashioned of storm and flame; there had been none like unto her for beauty since the days of Naamah sister of Tubal-Cain and those daughters of Adam of goodly mien whom the sons of God had taken to wife.

≀₹

Turbulent and comely, so lovely as to merit her own praise; the fringes lay upon her robes, her necklaces crossing the fringes and stretching from ear to ear and from cheek to cheek; the rows and the nose-ring blazed, the chains and the moon-amulets burned, pressing flashing flames forth into the sun.

She raised her countenance and gazed at the heavens, sat waking her belly and rousing her breasts, turning around with laughter, dragging at love and charming aloft,

—From the summit of Sinai, from the crest of Horeb and the Heights of God!

—Garbed, yea robed in glory, mighty and valiant, a man of war!...

She fell, hiding her face in the mat, choking with suppressed tears....

Sealed-up and brimming with fears and dread, the Land of Egypt flickered before her eyes as a vale where all trees rise, wherein all herbage flourishes, whence every duct of water flows....

Behold the store-cities, the walls shimmering, veiled in mists of purple, scarlet and ivory.

Behold the princes, Uza and Azael; Elah and Eloth and each daughter of divinity....

Behold the wizards garbed in death's-heads, beastskin and birdskin; all possessed of enchantments and weavers of spells; lemans and harlots more than the daughters of Ashtoreth and Milcom; clothed in majesty, burning incense of myrrh....

Zipporah shrank, shrank down, and moaned silently.

—*Ai hoo*, time and mischance, *ai hoo*!

Who would lead her to Sela, to the brook of copper?

Would that she might return to her mother, blest above women of the tent.

—*Ai hoo*, time and mischance, *ai hoo*!

Yea, would that she returned, that she returned from wayfaring, that she went not down to Egypt as she had never yet descended.

Ai hoo, time and mischance, *ai hoo*!

Or that God might seal the way from her; as the day when the heavens had warred, when He had sealed the Deep and barred it, had commanded, Thus far shalt thou come but no farther....

She knew great bitterness and grievous anguish, raising keen and lament in secret, her eyes dripping tears. She sent her eyes across the widths of the wilderness, to the ends of sky and brightness—

Whence would her help come?

She gazed despairing in every direction, and as she lay shrunken, so shrank her soul within her.

It was hushed, hushed her beginning; quietly, quietly she shook hither and thither, her eyes closed and her lips moving in the charm,

—Mountains in the Heavens, mountains! Mountains upon Earth, mountains! Gather unto me and set yourselves around, seat ye here, and be firm set!—For the daughter ye have strengthened, set yourselves! For the daughter ye have nourished, set yourselves! Lest mine enemy be glad, yea, she that troubleth me, set yourselves firm!

—Mountains of the Heavens, I call you! Pillars of the Universe, I beseech you! Ascend and subdue the land from end unto end; that the traveler may return, the wayfarer before you!

—Yea conspire against the plain and the path, and send forth the lowland and the stream, and smite ye, yea smite the dale and the desert. Where there is desert let the mountain-heights be, and where the stream—the flanks of the mountains; where there is flat-land—hills; till my good man return, return to his tents.

—Ye pallid mountains, fence us about! Mountains of secrecy, stand over us! Mountains in the skies, surround us! Mountains black and red and white! Mountains in your height, mountains in your thickness of cloud and every lofty hill! Ye doubly lofty mountains, ye mountains thousandfold exalted! Mountains twin and folded, mountains united, mountain chains! Mountains East and West! yea mountains of prey, be stalwart together, stand erect and take God's countenance captive; till my goodman return, return to his tents....

Mourning, dumb in her sighing, she sat swaying hither and thither, nodding her head....

The Land of Egypt appeared to her open as a meadow; and she trembled and shook.

Many, many maidens adorned and scented, all their garments perfumed with cassia, merrily dancing in market and road; the whole land filled with them from end to end....

She tore at her throat, oppressed by its necklace, as though freeing herself from the slave's neck-band, and stared confusedly around, without path or refuge.

Her eyes grew large, were kindled with flame; and the breath of her nostrils swelled within her, seething, puffing, writhing as snake-venom.

Suddenly she raised her head and cried out, her upflung hands clutching at the air.

And in that instant—

The wilderness quaked, cast itself prostrate and cried out bitterly; and the sound of the roar, roar of a wounded beast, burst out and passed from end to end; fear, dread round about, terrors and desolation....

VI

And it came to pass on the way at a lodge.

The shade above the lodge stretched heavy and thick.

Rank within rank the slight, erect palmstems raised their dome of leaves on high.

More wood than leaf, tall acacias stood with their multitude of sharp white thorns like elders set over the congregation.

Warped, crooked terebinths, terebinths the wood of which is meet for the bows and bulwarks of the rowboats on the Nile, stood wedged in their mighty piles of greenery.

Here and there, amid the thickets of tangled clutching mint, of bending fig and of untrimmed sycamores, the broom flickered white and emitted the savor of its bitter balsam.

Figtrees cleft a way amid the rocks, tenting and canopying the ground; their fallen leaves bathed in the broken ducts whence the water flowed scurrying over the herbage and amid the trees, giddy, frigid and clear; and moistened the air, fragrant as a perfumers' mart....

The tent loomed black in a snow-white brake of lofty flowering broom.

A small fire burned beside it; a thin pallid plume of smoke rose palmwise and slowly spread on high.

The three camels grazed, freed of their burdens.

By the waterduct opposite the tent sat Zipporah solitary,

decked and arrayed like a bride. Zipporah was burdened with suffering as with a pair of millstones, and her heart was sore bitter....

The boy crawled at her feet, crawled in the grass, and cooed and gurgled to his heart's content....

From time to time Zipporah roused from her reverie; watched the boy to guard him from snake, from hoofed beast, from the thorns and from the pool of water lest he fall therein....

She mused to force upon herself forgetfulness of the pain and anguish that had befallen her. But the thoughts of misfortune rose of themselves and were pounded in her heart like spices in a mortar.

Could she restrain her heart in its dungeon, by cedar-wool, or by mullein, the wick of the desert?

For gladness had ceased in her heart and was no more; it had taken wing like a bird and vanished.

Her heart had been filled with precious stones, but now—with charcoal embers. Her heart had been a light of day, but now—was gloom; rejoicing and glad—to nought and nothingness.

There had been a diadem in her hand; it had been taken from her. The grace of earth was lacking in her eyes, her heart was ill in all. Her good man had betrayed her as a vision of the night, her husband—as a morning cloud; she was as a wilderness....

Thoughts of misfortune rose of themselves, wedged themselves in like cow-wheat among canes, like iron nails.

What indeed could she do now?—

Though her spirit might depart, she knew not.

Should she wend homeward, return to her mother's tent. Should she sit here for ever, till her appointed days be finished and her memory gone from the earth....

Though her soul might depart, she knew not; no word, no counsel, nought.

Would that she had wings, pinions like a dove; then she would soar and return to Sela, the brook of copper!

Would that she had a mighty voice; then she would summon her mother to aid her in her straits!

Would that she were strong of heart; then she would come

before her spouse and her words would make him abhorrent unto himself.

Would that she had strength of arm; then would she go down to Egypt and smite every woman in the Land of Egypt, from the princess seated upon her throne down to the girl-slave at the quern; and there would rise a great outcry such as hath never been nor ever will be more....

At her wits' end she gazed around. She looked to the right and saw a palm tree with a long shadow. She said,

—As the shadow of this palm stretches afar, so is rest far from my soul. She looked left, saw the stump of a hewn-down palm and said,

—As this hewn palm will not grow, so is my generation cut down and will never renew.

She gazed before her and watched her son crawling in the grass; and her ruth for him arose. She charmed,

—My son is a sheep alone, a youngling kid strayed from his flock.... Zipporah stretched out to the child and beckoned him with her finger,

—Son, son...

And the boy—was a boy.

He sat on his behind, turned his curly head toward her and sat hesitating as though considering a matter. Then he winked his eyes thrice, and stretched his mouth in wide laughter....

Zipporah caught him by the foot and took his little body in her arms; and she stood rocking and caressing him, kissing his face, cooing and weeping and uttering every affectionate expression....

She charmed,

—Laden in the belly, borne in the womb.

She kissed his tiny hands and wept.

She charmed,

—Thy hand is full of comfort, many handfuls of comfort, my son! Thy fingers are rolls of gold, thine arm—a swordsheath!

She lifted him on high and swung him from side to side.

She charmed,

—My son is a winged bird, of happy singing wings! A young-ling kid, choicest of the flock, fat and every portion good! She pressed his full belly to her face. She charmed,

—Unpruned of flesh is my son, eight days and upward yet hath not witnessed the blood of the covenant!

She wept on his neck, wept bitterly, and told him all her heart's bitterness.

His father had acquired another mother; another mother—he who had given him being; therefore had he forsaken them to the wilderness, to a desert land, to Egypt, the plains of Zoan....

Thus and thus did she tell, and thus and thus she wept; and with her wept the boy.

They would weep bitterly, one with the other in bitter mourn-ing, till the lad waxed big....

Sobbing, she bent over the boy, quieted him, appeased him with her words. No, she would not go down to Egypt. Ten plagues have the Egyptians. Blood, frogs and lice have the Egyptians. Rats snatch the newborn of the Egyptians; the first born of Death would consume their falsehoods, the Lord of Terrors—the falsehood of their skins, and the killing spirits—their beasts....

Thus and thus she spoke to soothe him, weeping as she spoke, and the boy wept with her.

So would they bitterly weep with each other, in bitter mourn-ing till the lad waxed big....

She bent sobbing over the boy and quieted him, soothed him with her words. The Lord would be wroth with the Egyptians and destroy them, each woman known of man and every child among the women! Burning and salt all their land, seedless as salt; they would sow no seed and bear no fruit; they, their sons, their daughters, their flocks, their herds and all their cattle; as though eternally dead, an everlasting reproach till sun and moon were gone....

Thus and thus she spoke to still him, weeping as she spoke; and with her wept the boy.

So would they weep with each other bitterly, in bitter mourn-ing till the boy waxed big....

She took him and riding him on her shoulder she turned and

walked in the shade of the lodge to near the trees and the founts of water.

Ripping her way through the cane-brake, hidden to her neck in grass and growth, she emerged and went on, her soul moaning within her but her tongue a song.

She came to the fount, a fountain dwelling in stones, concealed from the sun and overhung with green; two rivulets fled from it, leaping stone to stone they fled, scurrying giddily, bright as gold; hid in the herbage and vanished.

Zipporah bent low by the fountain, dipped her hands, scattered water on her head, and recited a charm under her breath.

She rose and went on weeping; and with her wept the boy....

She turned and passed through the shade of the lodge to approach the trees and the fountains.

She came to the thicket, the terebinth thicket, the holy terebinths in whose shade the titan Rephaim came to rest. She stood with straightened palms and whispered a charm under her breath.

She rose to go and went on weeping, and with her wept the boy.

She turned and passed through the thickness of the lodge to approach the trees and the fountains....

She came to the wood, the tamarisk wood, the warlocks' tamarisk in whose shade the warlocks delight to sit, their spells in their hands.

She stood with flattened palms and raised a charm beneath her breath. She rose to go and went on weeping; and with her wept the boy.

She turned and passed the depth of the lodge to approach the trees and the fountains.

She came to the brake, the brake of figtrees, the restful figtree in whose shade the old women delight to sit and drowse and dream.

She stood with hands held straight, reciting a charm beneath her breath.

She rose to go and went on weeping, and with her wept the boy.

She turned to pace the depth of the lodge to near the trees and the fountains.

She came to the wood, the wood of date palms, most graceful of trees, most choice of the forest; in whose shade the maidens delight to rest, swart and comely.

She stood with outstretched arms and repeated a charm beneath her breath, speaking thus,

As the sun in eastern skies
Is the palm amid the trees.

Awesome 'mid the warriors, so the palm
Rears in might;
Thy youth is age on age,
And thy glory on thy visage;
For as the sun in eastern skies is the palm amid the trees;
For as the sun in eastern skies, does the palm
Establish the world.
As rays the clusters haste to meet mine eyes.
As rays the clusters haste to meet my face. Rays and clusters both
      shed light for me.
Thy praise is sweet for me, thy goodwill with me;
Thy good feats which
are with thee.
Sixty are they and three hundred.
Yea three hundred are they and eke sixty.
I have blessed ye, all your number.
In assembly tall I sing you nor shall bend,
Sixty and three hundred years and evermore.

VII

Zipporah sat solitary, her face lowering and black as the lowering mouth of a kiln.

She had shed tears in the sun, she had shed tears in the shade, amid the trees, beside the founts of water—like a fish within a net.

The songbird of her spirit had been blinded; her heart clamored, drooled venom like a serpent.

Obscene thoughts fluttered about her like flying creatures, like defiling black flying creatures....

In assiduous grief she bettered her face, gazing deep into the fountain.

—Thou hast beauty, Zipporah! Thou hast beauty, Zipporah!

The fountain whispered to her, the heavens peering thence.

In assiduous grief she went and passed before her goodman.

She was thinking,

Mayhap she would find favor before him.

She passed in front, returned, and sat solitary.

Her tears were sun to her, her tears were shade, trees, founts of water—as a fish within a net.

The bird of her soul was pierced, her heart made outcry, the venom twisted like a snake.

Evil thoughts fluttered about her like birds, like polluting black birds....

She bettered her face in assiduous grief, gazing deep into the fountain.

—Thou'rt beautiful, Zipporah! Thou'rt beautiful, Zipporah!

The fountain whispered to her, the heavens peering thence.

In assiduous grief she passed before her husband.

She was thinking,

Perchance he would turn his mind to her.

She paced and passed, paced and returned, sat solitary....

Tears her lot in sun, tears her lot in shade, mid trees and by the fountain—as a fish within a net.

Malign thoughts fluttered above her like birds, like unclean black birds...

She set her hands on her head and her eyes welled tears.

—Ah woe, Lord God....

And her eyes trickled tears.

—Ah woe, Lord God....

And her eyes trickled tears.

—Ah woe, Lord God, gaze from Thy mountain and see....

So she entreated and spake, then rose from her words.

She remembered God, a man of war, robed and garbed in pride, might and glory, who had turned toward her....

Perturbed she gazed around as men stare and peer in thick murk and black night....

She suddenly she sprang to her feet confused of soul and bewildered as though one had set an ambush for her, seized the boy in her arms, rushed and sat on the other side.

She set her hands on her head and her eyes welled tears.

—Ah woe, Lord God....

And her eyes trickled tears.

—Ah woe, Lord God....

And her eyes trickled tears.

—Ah woe, Lord God, my goodman hath forsaken me, both me and my seed...

So she spake beseeching, and ceased from her words.

She remembered God, a man of war, robed and garbed in pride, might and glory, had lain in her bosom....

Perturbed she gazed around as men stare who peer through black murk and deep night.

She suddenly leaped to her feet, bewildered of soul and mazed as one surprised by an ambush, seized the boy in her arms and ran and sat by the fountain.

She set her hands on her head and her eyes welled tears.

—Ah woe, Lord God....

And her eyes trickled tears.

—Ah woe, Lord God, he hath made nought of the covenant between Thee and his seed, and hath not guarded it!

Perturbed she gazed around as men stare and peer through the gloom and murk of midnight.

Suddenly she leaped to her feet, astounded of spirit and mazed as one surprised in an ambush, and seized the boy in her arms, her face to heaven.

Her heart was hot within her, tender as a fresh-green plot; her eyes flamed and her visage was a newkindled fire; fiery wrath and flaming zeal.

—He hath made nought of the covenant between Thee and his seed, and hath not kept it!

The soles of her feet were loosed and she began a supple walk, fanning herself with her robe, lustworthy in her grace, embellished in her finery.

—He hath made nought of the covenant between Thee and his seed, and hath not kept it!

Fringes clashed on stones, earrings blazed together with nose-ring and links, rings, bracelet and cloak.

—He hath made nought of the covenant between Thee and his seed; he hath not kept it!

She clapped her hands, stamped her feet and burst into a joyful dance, her breasts leaping, song on her tongue.

—He hath made nought of the covenant between Thee and his seed; He hath not kept it!

And behold a mighty wind come from across the desert; tempest, whirlwind and hoary cloud. The trees shook and whistled and bowed their tops to earth.

Terrified, Zipporah clutched the boy and leaped up to flee, sprang bemused and distraught, rushing from side to side like a blind man, shrieking in distraction.

And darkness and earthquake came from the desert; the Earth trembled and the mighty mountains.

Her path reeled and pitched; Zipporah staggered, ran, fell, rose, swayed, was tossed like a girl's playball. She shrieked and screeched, the boy screeching after her, writhing and twisting as though stung by a scorpion.

Then there was silence round about, heavy silence bearing down on the fullness of the wilderness.

And the Lord came from Sinai, from Mount Horeb, from Mount Paran; His glory covered the Heavens and His light filled the wilderness.

—God is in the midst of us!...

Zipporah whispered in dread and terror and hid her face.

It seemed to her a spirit of zeal had passed over God; therefore had he roused her jealously against Moses....

Trembling, terrified she gazed at the tent, and behold—
Moses falling on his face...
"God is exceeding wroth and would destroy him!"
The thought flashed through her heart as lightning glares
through thick cloud.

Terror-stricken and bemused, she tore the veil from her face
and uprooted from her place she screeched. Her scream passed from
end to end of the lodge.

Speedier than a young cow, her voice like the howl of the wind
in Sela, she stood a moment confused and undecided, cast a distraught
eye about her, gasped and breathed deep together.

And she suddenly smote the boy to the ground, and roaring
distraught like a wild beast strangling its prey, she pounced upon him,
fell on him, seized the rock and cut off the foreskin...

The boy had no chance to cry out—

And hushed around was the desert, seized by listening
silence—

Gleaming like six talents of copper, gory and awesome in
her beauty and finery, she sprang up, cleft between God and Moses,
stretching her hands aloft toward God—and the wilderness vibrated
and shook with awe and majesty—and cried,

—Bridegroom of blood! Yea, bridegroom of blood art Thou
to me!

Translated by I.M. Lask

The Incarnation

Among the folk of the Jerusalem quarter where she lived the Old Woman went to and fro like a legend that is passed on from one to the other, like a wondrous tale of something that does not happen to every man nor in every age. There was about her something verging on the mystical; the glow of some occult state of existence emanated from her, together with a rare integrity and considerateness; these were hers and within her, in her bent frame, her seamed face and the whole of her.

A dwarfed Old Woman, she was bowed down like a fine ear of wheat that is laden with grains. Her mouth was sunken, her lips quivered and her eyes rolled. Her face was lined and soft like a baked apple. Its dimming radiance was not, it almost seemed, that of flesh and blood but something different; reminiscent, maybe, of old parchment illumined from within by a light; something hinted at, more or less, in the whispered recitation of the *Tehinoth,* the Yiddish prayers for women, or in the soft sweet chanting of a worthy, Godfearing leader of prayer.

The folk of her quarter treated her with great respect, esteeming her highly as befits people who love a marvelous legend just because it is marvelous. When the women saw her coming they would set a chair for her in the street and stand surrounding her, tall and upright, their faces bright with pleasure. If she did not wish to sit down they would form a retinue about her, setting her between them and pacing along as though they were proceeding together to perform some righteous deed. They greatly desired to be in her immediate vicinity, to talk to her and hear what she had to tell; as though she might inform them of things hidden and unseen, or relate some distant rumor going back maybe to the days of their great-grandmothers or forward to their grandchildren, unto the third and fourth generation. Even the men, when they caught sight of her, would stop whatever they were doing and stand looking after her with affectionate humility, wonder and astonishment. At such times they seemed not to know whether they had lost track of the things of which they were certain or those they doubted, and could do nothing but stand wondering and meditating on hints of mystical intents and things concealed in the underlying, non-manifest sources of being; each according to his own degree of insight and after his own nature.

People never called her by name, nor yet by surname, by her town of origin or her family. One felt that all these adjuncts were transitory, immaterial, casual and superfluous, neither bearing witness nor giving information; they had already departed from her, vanished out of the world. Folk merely used to call her "The Old Woman", simply the Old Woman. The very simplicity served as commentary and contained in itself more than any commentary in the world. There are such things, to which human beings never give a name since they cannot really be gauged by human standards. Thus, for instance, men do not say that a vast height is so much, an abysmal depth so much, a distance so much or that there was such and such a considerable time of a century. Instead they talk simply of the height, the depth, the distance and the time of a century; and similarly with other extra-human units which lie beyond the standards of men. The Old Woman was one of these. For the seven and ninety years of her life were far more than was the whole of her, and contained far more than her entire vestigial frame and body. They were the essential thing and she was just an adjunct. She was not, so to say, like all folk nor to be classed with other people, but was beyond the boundary of the normal world and to be regarded as a creature unique: as "The Old Woman".

Solitary and alone was she before the Lord, alone and isolated, all by herself. Her offspring were not with her; neither sons nor sons' sons, neither brother nor kinsman; there was no support whatsoever upon which she could depend. Yet in times gone by she had had a numerous family, heavy, so to say, with sons and daughters, bride-grooms and brides, grandsons and granddaughters, brothers and sisters, inlaws, kinsfolk and the kin of kinsfolk. All the Houses of Study had been filled with them. All the market places had been filled with them, all the Societies for the Study of Gemara, of Talmud, of Mishna, for the saying of Psalms and so on and so forth. Now the bundle had fallen apart. There were those who had departed this life, some in their due time and some out of their due time. Some had scattered over the seven seas. Some had fallen martyred in pogroms to hallow the Holy Name; and nobody had lamented them, nor inscribed them in the records for the commemoration of their souls as an everlasting memorial. And there were some still left, starving and poverty-stricken, under the rule of the Bolsheviks, in prison or in exile, gradually and surely vanishing out of the world. The bundle had fallen apart. Not through the decree of Exile nor by the Black Death, not through the revolts of the peasants and lepers and the "threshers" of the Jews, nor any such disasters and calamities, had that befallen her family, which has befallen families in Israel since generations untold. The way of the world is the same; the Shadow of the Kingdoms is the one shadow, whether it be that of past or present.

Seven and ninety years! No trifle that. Who was left with her of that generation? Who beside her could remember the tales and happenings, the sorrow, joy, and suffering of a hundred years? Not even one. And indeed not even a single grain of buckwheat, not a single half-pea remained of yonder days, let alone a human being. She could still remember when serfdom had been in force, the days of the evil Nikolai the First and the "snatchers" who in his days used to kidnap Jewish children and hand them over to the Government. Close to her indeed had been that communal fast with weeping and wailing and the sound of bitter mourning because of the decree regarding the "recruits"; when the rabbis and leaders of the congregation had risen and placed in the hands of one who had just died a scroll of their sufferings to be brought before the Glory Seat! And few years away from her had been Reb Leib Sarah's, who could travel vast distances at a single bound, as was generally known; and who came secretly, seeing yet unseen, to Vienna the capital and to the palace of His Majesty the Kaiser to whom he said, "If you annul your decree against the Jews all is well, but if not this will be your grave!" And she was barely a stride away from that man Napoleon and the great dispute between the Saints of Riminov and Rophchitz, may their saintly memories be blessed, regarding Napoleon and the Tzar, Alexander, the Kings of Gog and Magog, and the victory of which of them might be preferable for Israel. And she was just a tiny step from that famed festival of Tabernacles when the saints of Lublin and Riminov and the Preacher of Koznets, of blessed memory all of them, had risen and veritably stormed the Kingdom of Heaven in order, for His Name's sake, to bring Messiah in that very year. And by reason of our many sins the wiles of Satan had prevailed and Heaven itself had prevented it; and the angels had overcome the mortals, and in that very year all three of the saints were summoned to the Upper Assembly…. All those times had gone by, and other times, bitter and headlong, had come; and still at every hour, the Messiah was on the verge of appearing!

Oh, how great the hopes had been in those bygone days; they had been like a flame leaping up in everyone's heart, fervent sparks of a mighty yearning the like of which has not been seen again; a tremendous hope and a spirit of goodness prevailing wherever Israel was scattered, suffusing all the Holy Congregations and passing on like a great broad river that is full to its very banks. Neither man nor woman could express in human tongue how great the expectation and longing had been; there could not be the slightest comparison between those days and our own times…

Yet that is not so. It would be an exaggeration to claim that there could be no comparison. For she, the Old Woman, used to watch for the coming of the Redeemer just as her mother and grandmother had done; nay, she watched even more. Her entire essence was nothing but one steady waiting, rooted, fixed and set incomparably firm in hope. In her universe nothing existed but the Footsteps of Messiah; and her heart had room for naught but him. In her heart she knew that she would not depart this life despite her old age ere he came. That was something certain, the most obvious thing in the world, and its sole basic fact. Neither wonder nor fervor nor things mystical, deep hid, secret and concealed were needed. It was quite a simple business; he would come! There you were! And while her fire still smouldered he would be here. For it was generally to be accepted that we were all but at the finish; already very near the End of Days. Assuredly he would not be long delayed. And then we would merit to see the Revival of the Dead, when all the old folk renew their youth like children, and it will be the final wonder and the renewal of the world, that end which is better than the beginning...

Her faith in the coming of the Redeemer could be recognized in all the commandments she fulfilled, all the good deeds she did, and even in her faith in His Blessed Name. She performed all the commandments according to prescription as a matter of course, yet merely as her duty and without any special sense of devotion; even with a measure of the absent-mindedness that comes with habit, doing things because it is so written and the "Verse" demands it.

As a matter of habit and without any particular sense of devotion she went day by day to the little houses of prayer, wept for the destruction of the Temple, recited Psalms and prayers of entreaty, fulfilled the commandment of visiting the sick, accompanying the dead on their last journey, and so on and so forth. Equally without any particular sense of devotion she would call attention to anything not quite as it should be among the residents of her neighborhood; any sign of heresy, any casting-off of the yoke of the Torah, the shaving of a beard or of earlocks, the wearing of "un-Jewish" clothes or a maiden behaving without becoming modesty, and similar regrettable occasions and improper goings-on. She would behave as though she were very particular, but she was not really so. After all, it was not really important. In any case the Messiah would be coming speedily and in our days and would not be delayed; neither by rain nor snow, neither by bad roads nor bad behavior, nor yet by a shameless wench strolling about with her breasts semi-exposed, or her legs bared, "going down to naked death," may the Merciful One deliver us. At that time, please God, there would be great signs and wonders that would not be according to the ways of nature. And then, likewise not according to the ways of nature, the wicked would change and become wondrous saints, and everything would become as it ought to be.

This coming of the Redeemer was what bound her to the Land of Israel; she did not regard the resettlement of the Land of Israel as in itself of much importance. For when the Messiah comes all the seed of Israel will in any case come to the Holy Land, flying upon the wings of eagles, young and old, to the very last and least and most worthless.

For this reason she did not sorrow at all when the Holy and Blessed One compelled her to go from door to door and resort to the charity of flesh and blood. Vanity of vanities. Let no man esteem himself on his wisdom, for the wisdom of man is naught against the Lord, nor is there aught in the might of the mighty, who blossom in the morning and then pass away; nor in the wealth of the wealthy wherewith to fashion him wings. Remember Ahitophel and his counsel and Korah and his pride...Pah! Vanity of vanities, the troubles and vanities of treacherous Time!

Only a few years, no more than four in fact, had gone by since first she had had to fall back upon the mercies of human beings. At first her great-grandson had made all arrangements for her and did everything for her that had to be done, providing her with food and clothing and lodging. He had given her all this with much honor and boundless affection, their two souls being as close as though they were one. It was on his account that she had come to the Land of Israel. The Revolution had uprooted them, both her and this great-grandson who supported her, and flung them from one spot to another, till finally they had found themselves in Berlin. The great-grandson was intelligent and lucky. Before he had been in Berlin any length of time he had become quite a wealthy man. Almost absent-mindedly, by way of laughter and trifles, he had become wealthy. And almost absent-mindedly as well, by way of laughter and trifles, he had become

a success and acquired houses and property and money and goods
without any particular effort.

And those would have been good times, were it not for the
unhappy rumors and reports which reached them from their kin
who were still in Russia in the hands of the Bolsheviks. Theirs was
one endless scroll of calamities, a scroll of poverty and starvation,
vicissitudes and terrors and physical and mental suffering. But worst
of all were the sufferings of one of her great-granddaughters, a girl
of eighteen or so who had been arrested because of her love of the
Land of Israel, and who was shifted round from one prison to the
next, being finally sentenced with the full severity of the law and
exiled to some desolate, godforsaken spot in the wastes of Siberia.
It was for this great-grandchild that she, the Old Woman, sorrowed
more than for all the rest of her offspring, staying awake by night
as by day, weeping and shaking her head and constantly whispering,
like somebody who is not quite right in her head, "My chick, my
little baby…"

And in the middle of all this grief of hers, her great-grandson,
a widower in the prime of life, took himself a wife. The woman he
married was good-looking and had been divorced; and all the trouble
came from her. She had taken a dislike to the Old Woman from the
first moment, kept wrathful eyes on her and would vex her, play all
sorts of nasty tricks, and continually bring all kinds of charges against
her, each one more strange than the other. The husband, who loved
his wife very much and submitted to her and endeavored to do her
will, grieved in secret but remained silent.

Days passed, one after the other, and matters went on and on
and do not need to be told in detail. But, after the habit of women
in our days, people began coming and visiting her, sometimes in her
husband's presence and sometimes otherwise; the door swung to and
fro without closing, and things began moving to and fro like that
selfsame door and even more, and there was gladness and rejoicing
all day and all night. Until at last she went wrong with one of the
young fellows who were always hanging round her, and she rebelled
against her husband and went her way.

For a long time he tried to win her over and finally persuaded her to return. Then they decided that they would go to Paris. In vain did the Old Woman entreat them to take her with them, and not leave her grieving among strangers and Gentiles. Nothing helped; they paid no attention to her and would not do as she requested. They told her that Paris was no place for her as it had no Jewish cemetery, and the townfolk had the custom of burning their dead instead of burying them...Thereupon she became silent, folded her aged arms across her bosom and wept. And the great-grandson wished to bid her farewell and could not do so for grief and yearning, but kissed her and embraced her, gazing at her and weeping; and the tears fell from his eyes upon her face.

So the Old Woman was cast away in a pension, lonely and forsaken. And many months passed, months of grief, until at last her great-grandson sent her money for her fare to the Holy Land; and her eyes grew bright. And by the grace of God she met a family that was also going up to the Holy Land; and she accompanied them and arrived safely, thanks to His Name, with all that group of beloved and merciful people, brethren and friends who were joining the Lord.

So they came unto our City of Strength, Jerusalem the Holy may it be rebuilt and established, Amen, all in peace, living and in peace, and all of them gave thanks to the Lord who is good, at the completion and rounding-off of this commandment. Every month the great-grandson used to send her enough for her requirements in Jerusalem, with all honor and boundless affection. He even proposed to come to the Land of Israel and dwell therein. But meanwhile his luck turned and he lost all his wealth; and evil and bitter days came when he could no longer aid her as he desired in the goodness of his heart.

Then in those evil and bitter days he sought and found wealthy kinsfolk in America, who undertook to send her a small sum in accordance with her modest outlay and requirements. While as for him, the waters had reached his very soul and he kept on going down; and at last he insured himself for a considerable sum, and immediately went and strangled himeslf in order that his wife might receive the insurance. And thus he died, well before his time and in an outlandish fashion, her great-grandson, that precious and choice man, who deserved to have said of him "happy was she who bore him"; one of the last of that great and numerous family of times gone by…

From that time forward the rich relations in America (she could neither remember who they were, nor the sons of whom nor the degree of their kinship nor even their pedigree) began to send her small sums now and again. But at length things went badly for them as well, and they lost all their wealth. And thereupon there was nothing left for her save to go from door to door and be maintained at the high table of the All-Present.

Without regrets, without shame or any diminution of self-respect, like a House of Study that has been converted into a shop or a house or any other thing, she put aside her honor and made herself one with low creatures. It did not affect her that never in her life before had she broken bread that was not her own or that of kin. What place was there for shame here, and why should a human being be grieved, seeing that the Messiah would come on the morrow? On the contrary, this was an adorning and great honor for her! His Name be praised for giving her strength in her old age to go from door to door and receive lovingkindness and mercy, love and brotherhood and friendship, thanks to the good and precious qualities wrapped up and hidden in the souls of Israel, may the Lord have mercy upon them according to the multitude of His mercies; and in his love of them may He redeem them and raise them on high for ever and ever…

As she grew older and older she began to forget things and not be troubled by them. Once again it was not the wealth and splendor of her bygone greatness and the honor of her house and the deeds she had done and sights she had seen. Nor was it the sons who had come forth from her, fine big handsome creatures like flourishing trees, nor healthy daughters radiant as great lights, nor grandchildren manifold and murmurous as a field of wheat with the ears swaying and whispering in the sun in the heat of the day. She had forgotten them all; as though they had never existed and were a mirage. She seemed like a little girl who has not tasted love and grief and is not burdened with things remembered and forgotten, but remains calm and content in body and soul…

The relations between her and others, the normal relations of a man and his surroundings, grew weaker and weaker, more and more cloudy, like mist that is blown apart in rags and tatters. She grew ever more distant from the affairs of the world, divesting herself of them and sinking into the state of being that is within the here and now, where present becomes one with what has already vanished from the world; sinking into the void of that distant and misty past until she was once more a little girl in the presence of her mother, an infant in her cradle and, if one may say so, until she had not yet appeared in the world...

Pleasant for her were those sunny Jerusalem days that take away the light of a man's eyes and the mood and emotions within him, making him forget himself, his soul and the whole of his world. At such times, on sunny days, she would sit alone at the door of her lodging facing the spacious courtyard that lay open to the sun, her face bent slightly down yet seeming to be raised aloft. Something like the rustling of a long dry field would ring in her ears, her two hands would quiver on her knees like the very tips of the treetops at the commencement of Spring; and her lips would move as though she were tasting the flavor of the sun in her mouth. The sun rested on the whole world, scratching her wrinkled cheeks, contending with the stones arranged as a wall and with the piles of stones lying heaped together on the earthenware-dry ground. The stones flickered and sparkled, spattering sparks like a man hammering an anvil and sending the sparks in every direction. The day flashed and flamed. It seemed to be made of jewels, a solid mass of jewels, of tremendous colors harsh as metal utensils; of lights and all the laughing interplay of hues and shades to be found in light. In the vastness of space the mountains wove a gilded, desolate blue. The earth and sky snatched from each other till all bounds were blurred, till all limitations and distinctions between them had vanished; they uncoiled and stretched as one, without boundary and restriction, above space and beyond time, sinking into a deep radiant state of being in which all the universes seemed to be united, the animal with the vegetable and mineral kingdoms, past, present and future; all stricken with dream and forgetfulness, with one measure in sixty of death; bearing the semblance of bygone generations...

At such times she seemed to be forgotten by everything as everything was forgotten by her. She needed nothing and lacked for nothing and was removed from the world and the fullness thereof, and had no dealings with it. It was almost as though she found herself in empty space, skies around her, sun part of her and she part of the sun; and diminishing, her senses failing and her limbs passing away in the light of this world which was warm and pleasant as the love of her spouse in times gone by when he had been a lad and ardent. The world seemed to be melting and vanishing away; it was hard for her to say whether it existed in actuality or only in imagination, whether it was dream or truth; whether it was the truth that is in dream and all those occult and doubtful matters, or the most vivid and definite of them all: namely, Messiah the king in all his glory and brightness...

Sometimes, before she came to sit down as was her habit at the entrance to her lodging, she would stand awhile gazing abstractedly and in surprise, as though she recollected something but could not remember what it was. At such times the whole spacious courtyard seemed to her like a vineyard destroyed or a barren, overturned field lying open in all directions with the sun shining rather too strongly into it; as the sun always shines in places of desolation and destruction. She, the old woman herself, was like a tree whose branches have been lopped and whose top has been cut away, and all the shoots that came forth from it have been removed as well, so that it is left stripped, lonely and unwanted. As through a mist she would gaze on small towns with dwindling populations, houses where the dwellers were few in number, sons and grandsons whom the nations and their governments had cut off with their decrees and terrors. She would remember and forget, half-remember and forget, having no complaint at heart against the peoples and their governments, neither hatred, jealousy nor anger nor anything else whatsoever. For such has been the order of the world since time untold...

But, God willing, those bitter days will pass from the world, the evil will come to an end like smoke and good will follow; and the future contains within itself an atonement for all things, in the hour when the Righteous Redeemer comes, may it be speedily and in our own times...

Far more than her memory dwelt on family affairs, sons and daughters, it would dwell on trifles of all sorts. Blurred, indistinct reminiscences would return and mingle in confusion, a trifle from here and an oddment from there; the memory of the old graveyard in her town with the seven great giants who lay therein, seven graves that were long and broad beyond measure; the memory of the great synagogue and its Holy Ark with the leviathan and the lions and the deer carved thereon, as well as the "Calendar" prepared until the year Six Thousand, corresponding to 2,240 of the Gentile era, showing all the new moons in order; the memory of Zlata the bath-woman, and her two sons-in-law, the expensive one and the bargain as they had been called, because one had demanded a large dowry and the other took a small dowry and was a dear fellow, tall and wonderfully handsome. The memory of festive Reb Abraham Joshua who used to dance on the tables in his socks at every wedding and at the Rejoicing of the Torah; the memory of Reb Asher the cantor who was so popular with the womenfolk because of his sweet voice, and they used to peep at him from behind the curtain until the Holy and Blessed One took him, he being drowned one Passover Eve when he dipped the vessels in the river and the ice broke under his feet; and countless more trifles of the kind, snips and tatters and odds and ends. Sometimes she would confuse one thing with another, recent with long ago, first with last, so that those bitter times of Nikolai the First would seem to her identical with present, and the misfortunes and evil decrees of yonder days identical with those of the Bolsheviks now; as though the world had remained just as it had always been.

Thus when she heard folk talking of the Jewish Communists who were oppressing the ordinary Jews in Russia she began confusing them with the "snatchers" of Jewish children for the Russian army and the like informers and converts of bygone days. And she remembered and told the tale of Borushke the informer who was executed by the members of the community in the House of Study on the Sabbath day itself; and all the trouble caused by him. Likewise when she heard that the Bolsheviks were persecuting the Zionists in the cruelest manner possible, and were giving the Jews land in Siberia, she mixed it up with the incident in the days of Nikolai the wicked who wished to attract the Jews to the tilling of the soil and gave them lands in Siberia and afterward went and brought all kinds of trouble upon them. And she would shake her head and blink her old eyes and say: the works of Satan do not prosper, and His Blessed Name would not permit that evildoer to succeed and separate His Holy People from their faith and Holy Torah, God forbid.

And similarly when she heard folk telling how the Bolsheviks were persecuting religion and faith in His Blessed Name, and were closing synagogues and taking away scrolls of the Torah from Jewish houses, she remembered the days of Nikolai the First when they used to steal Torah scrolls from Jewish houses and take them down in waggon-loads to the authorities at Kiev in order to put them on the fire. "And are they still taking them to be burnt?" she would ask in astonishment.

Once she received a letter from one of her kinsfolk in Russia, who entreated her in every way possible to "make his soul precious in the sight of our brethren the Children of Israel in the Holy City, who are merciful and the sons of those who show lovingkindness so that they might remember the soul of their unfortunate and suffering brother who was perishing of starvation with his household", and send him two or three dollars for food for the little ones, infants who asked for bread, dear and outstanding children but they asked for bread; and so on and so forth. Then she went from house to house to ask for money for the *gildia,* just as Jewish folk in those times gone by had gone from door to door and asked charity for the purpose of the *gildia,* in order to acquire guild certificates and exempt their little ones from the evil decree of the recruits, as was the case with the proud possessors of guild certificates…

"Give me guild money!" she would say, holding out her hand. "Merciful ones and sons of merciful ones, give guild money for a poor Jew of good stock. Please God, when Messiah comes I shall return you double, I shall support you for six full years, and give you as much as you can hold."

Another time it happened that a Jerusalem woman wished to bring her old mother from Russia, but the Bolsheviks would not permit it unless she paid a considerable sum as ransom. And the old woman heard about it and as in a dream remembered a similar incident which had happened ever so long ago. This story told how a certain great man came to the country, an ambassador sent by Rothschild to Nikolai in order to take out the Jews to some distant broad land which was in the hands of the French; and the evildoer and troubler of Israel agreed, but made a condition that they should pay him a considerable sum as ransom for every Jew whom he permitted to go.

"I can't understand it," the old woman turned her tiny seamed face this way and that in astonishment. "Is that old evildoer still alive? Why, when I was only a tiny little girl he was already at the height of his strength! And he's still alive!..."

Many such incidents happened to her; and she would refer them to bygone events and wonder over them and not know how to understand them. The one she found most difficult to understand was the case of her great-granddaughter, who had been arrested by the authorities because of her love for the Land of Israel. For she could not make out why such girls were put under arrest. She had never heard of such a thing. True, it seemed to her that once upon a time two women had been arrested on account of the Blood Libel...So this must be a Blood Libel! Did the like of such things happen nowadays, such a dreadful heart-shaking thing, that they came and made the same old false charges against her great-grandchild and arrested her and sent her into Siberian exile, where she would be slain to hallow the Holy Name? Or maybe, after all, these latter ages were like those timeold generations; maybe a new king had arisen who was even worse than that old sinner and was reestablishing recruiting-centers and paragraphs and decrees far more savage and wicked than those of former times. And had he now introduced a center not only for the boys but for the girls as well?...

But what was the reason people told her it was for the love of the Land of Israel? What special and specific love of the Land of Israel was there? What new charge was this of loving the Land of Israel? And what did that have to do with a girl anyway? Wasn't it her duty to sit waiting until Messiah came, when as a matter of course she would come to the Holy Land along with all the rest?

Although she heard no more at first than that her great-grand-daughter had been exiled to Siberia, she took it for granted that the girl had been slain to hallow the Holy Name. And thus, of itself and unconsciously, the matter cleared itself up in her mind; partly because of her confusion of facts, her memory having grown weak so that she could not remember things as they had actually occurred, and partly because of the course of nature, it being in the course of nature that any man in Israel may be slain to hallow the Holy Name; but most of all because this had been her favorite great-grandchild…

And sure enough her heart had not spoken falsely. For in the end the girl perished in the hospital of some faraway desolate village lost in the north of Siberia, and hallowed the name of the Land of Israel among five or six other suffering hopeless lifelong exiles…

The trouble of her great-granddaughter brought old age leaping upon her. And so she herself used to say, "Old age has leaped upon me." For she feared the evil eye and always refrained from revealing her real years, pretending that she was not at all old and the total of her years was small, no more than eighty or eighty-two in all…It being generally known that folk are jealous and want to know everything, particularly the years of an old person, as though they had deposited something with him and now wished to see his accounts; and as though they were the trustees over the lives of other people!

From time to time women of the quarter would come to visit her, and would sit with her in her lodging, a gloomy room, long and deep as a cranny in the rocks, littered up with rusty old boxes and cases, with white curtains that had blue ribbons running through them, and with all kinds of dresses in piles on the walls. The visitors were elderly women who were already tending toward the shadow of death. When they used to sit in her company they seemed, after the many vicissitudes and seas, winds and tempests through which they had passed, to have entered a port; and there they sat with one another, calmly and quietly. One might suppose that the sea had ceased raging and its billows and vast combers lay far behind them and could be seen by them only at a distance, gleaming and then lightless, lightless and then gleaming…

There was one of them, Granny Meide, seventy years old,

with a face yellow as wax or as a shriveled leaf shining in the sun all alone on its twig; her face seemed to hide the secrets of earliest Autumn with its clear and withered calm, translucent and spacious. A second was deaf Leahle, whose visage had in it something of the vapor that rises from a *tzimmes* (dessert dish) of old shriveled carrots, and something of a man who sits out in the open on a fine spring evening between the afternoon and evening prayers, with the sun setting behind him when scents, bitter, sharp and fragrant, fill the air while the gentle coolness of evening approaches. Then there was a third, the rabbiness of Krivoplis, a short thin old woman, full of the mood of Sabbath eves and festivals, and pale as silver grown tarnished with age. And then there was a fourth, Yucha of Safed, a woman of seventy-three, big-limbed and bony, with a dry, sickish face, narrow and crisscrossed with countless fine wrinkles, and all of her clearly moving to Heaven.

It was to these that the old woman would tell the praises of her great-granddaughter, saying, "The little one was such a fine housewife, so clever, with such a golden heart, and graceful and a beauty as well, an innocent dove, bright and shimmering, like the early Spring days before the Passover.

"And," she would add, "God willing, when the dead revive you will see with your own eyes how lovely she was. With your own eyes you will see her beauty! She hasn't got her like anywhere, from one end of the Tzar's Empire to the other!"

And she would go on recounting her praises, listening and recapitulating until suddenly her face would change—as though a wing descended and covered her face. Her eyes would stare ahead of her into the room, and like an ailing chicken clucking to itself in its sickness, she would begin dolefully and tunelessly chanting:

The decree came out to make soldiers of Jews,
So we all ran away to the lonely woods…
To the forests and woods we all ran away,
And in empty ditches we all hid away…
Woe is me, woe is me…

Heads bent and sorrowful the women sat before her, at such times, bowed one next to the other, like ears of grain on a stalk or branches by neighboring branches, shaking their heads with mingled awe and melancholy.

The only one to scold her or rebuke her was Yucha of Safed, who was a tiresome irritable old woman with a nasty tongue and temperament. In earlier times when she had been in her own town, they had called, her "Bitter Yucha"; but the change of place had led to that name being forgotten, and now folk called her the Safed woman. They called her so because, at first she had dwelt for a little while in the almshouses at Safed. And the reason she had left the place was the dreadful things she had seen done in those almshouses. Fearsome and dread! For it was the habit of the wardens there to put poison in the food and help the old folk out of the world. If an old man came there and had money—for sure he would not live! Scarcely would he have time to turn this way and that ere he would depart this world. Murderers! And it is a pious deed to say the truth, to proclaim and keep on proclaiming it; they were absolute definite murderers! She herself had escaped from them safely, because unlike the usual custom she did not give them all her money at once but paid them out month by month only…That and nothing else had saved her. And she had already made this thing generally known in all the quarters of Jerusalem, in full and even excessive detail, each detail after its own fashion, with much use of curses and oaths beyond the power of the ordinary person even to repeat. And not of the Old Age Home alone did she tell her tale; but of every individual, of each local committee and every institution in Jerusalem did she also have her evil tale to tell; of Jerusalem wardens and trustees and emissaries and students and instructors at the Talmudical colleges; not a single one passed muster. She injected her gall into all of them, investigating their behavior and telling scandal beyond all hearing.

Her charge against the Old Woman was that she didn't know what she was talking about. Her ears were just about falling off and her reins dulled beyond measure. For what was this decree she was talking about? That was something that had happened in ancient times, when her own grandmother was a maiden child, while what was happening now was different and beyond all human bearing, what was being done by the Bolsheviks…

Then she began telling how numerous her own household had been of yore, the calmness and security, the wealth and splendor they had known, her many sons and daughters, precious and learned, wealthy and well known. But the Bolsheviks had come along and had taken away everything, all the property and all the goods and all the money, all the jewels and the silver and the gold and the garments, and had not left as much as a single pinch of sawdust. They had left nothing, nothing at all for her old age. And she went on to tell of her children who had no food and suffered from starvation and writhed in sickness; never seeing even a little flour, a few potatoes or bread for the children...Further she would tell of her grandchildren who had to labor to exhaustion for the Bolsheviks, and supported themselves and their parents very sparsely indeed; until finally the Bolsheviks had come and visited the sins of the fathers upon the children and took away their source of livelihood and their right to work, so that they were just dying away...

"The Bolsheviks lowered them from their own degree to the lowest level of harmful and unnecessary people," she said, beating her heart with her hands, shaking and lamenting, while her eyes ran tears, "and they aren't even classed as human beings and the Bolsheviks don't want to suffer them or keep them alive or let them make a living or let them get near anything that might help them make a living, seeing that they belong to this declassed former bourgeoisie and there's nothing lower..."

"Woe's me," the Old Woman quivered, bowed and weak, shaking this way and that, with nodding head and quivering lips, her face twitching and twisting. It seemed that she had remembered something distant and forgotten, something which may or may not have existed. She had suddenly remembered the "declassing" of the days of Nikolai the First, when the greater part of the Jews had been subjected to this degrading law, all the hawkers and the peddlers and the commission agents and the merchants. And the Government had brought all sorts of savage laws to bear upon them, oppressing them and badgering them and worrying the very lives out of them, so that they could not even breathe...So one story led to another told by the Old Woman to the grief and sorrow of the whole group; as though all those troubles and distresses had happened to them and about them; and the more they spoke the more they found to speak about.

And apart from this, Yucha found many ways of annoying or trying to annoy her. Even the great respect everybody showed the old woman seemed like a needle piercing her own flesh; even the additional years she had lived above the usual measure, and her mighty patience in awaiting the coming of the Messiah at any time and at any hour, set Yucha fuming.

She herself was quite different from all the old women with their faith in the coming of the Redeemer and their readiness for long lives, those two things that seemed to go together. Her faith in the coming of the Redeemer was weak and questionable, a mixture of sheer imagination and of the reflection of a reflection, without any great vitality to it or anything dependable and trustworthy. What was more, she did not wish for length of days, only two or three more years in all, at the most three years. Thereafter, if one might say so, she was prepared to die. Enough! Be done with it! And in this she did indeed differ from all the other old women.

"How many more years have I to live? Very few. In another two or three years the days will come, long and short, long and short, long, long," she used to say to the Old Woman, her eyes glaring at her while her slack lips seemed to smile. "After I'm gone I'll leave you all the dresses I have, and the warm kerchief. You'll be my heir."

For it was the Old Woman's habit to collect dresses, whole piles of dresses from various folk; dresses left by women who had died, dresses which sick women had vowed away during illness, and archaic dresses which charitable women had given her as gifts. She put the dresses together, adding those she herself had left from bygone days, with bustles and double pelerines and capes, and all kinds of other worn-out garments that were so old as to be coming apart. All her boxes were full of them, all her trunks and drawers and the full depth of her cupboard, the empty space under the bed and all the walls; whole piles and heaps of dresses, peacock-green, yellow as waves in the sunlight, pinkish-white like the flowers of the broom, blue and glittering like lightning on the flat rocks on a cloudy day; and many others. Naturally it was not for herself that she kept all these, but for the days of Messiah, for the time when the dead would rise from their sleep, so that they would find everything ready to wear and cover themselves...

One year passed, a second and a third, and she was already a hundred years old. Another three years passed, and there she still was, most of her gone but a small part of her still left. Those old women who had been accustomed to visit her had died, and she had taken all their dresses as far as she could save them from the trustees.

Grannie Meida had died. It had happened after midnight one night, while the doctor was standing by her and saying the things it becomes a doctor to say as he set the "cups" on her thigh; and while he spoke she passed away.

The deaf Hayya Leahle had also died. One Thursday morning the neighbors had summoned the doctor to her. He came and found her standing by the window, praying out of the great *Korban Minha* prayerbook. He sat and waited for her to finish her prayers, for what else is to be done with an old woman standing praying? Then he examined her, said nothing, wrote what he had to write, again said nothing, and looked round and saw a piece of meat lying on a bench.

"Whom is this meat for?" he asked wisely.

"Whom should it be for? It's for me!" she said.

"I think, for instance, that it ought to be thrown to the dogs," he answered and went his way.

And she had gone and listened to the crazy fellow! On Friday they had made her a fine Sabbath pudding and on the Sabbath she had eaten her fill with enjoyment; and on Sunday morning the neighbors had found her lying on her bed as cold as ice, as cold as ice...

And the rabbiness of Krivoplis had already gone the way of the world. At the last hour she had moaned like a dove and had entreated,

"Mister doctor, Mister doctor, save me! I still have much work to do. I haven't done anything yet, nothing at all yet..."

Only Yucha of Safed was still alive, but she had grown feeble-minded with age and used to go down into the quarter and curse anybody who came along; the men for being ruffians and the women for being shameless and wanton. Finally people set a sort of wicket-gate inside her dwelling so that she should not fall from the steps nor descend into the quarter. But it did not help them at all, for she broke the wicket gate and came down; so they sent her to the hostel for such in the Old City, to stay there for the rest of her life.

The Old Woman had not apparently changed much, except that her face had grown still smaller and more like a squeezed lemon. The doctor who frequently visited her testified that she was hale and hearty, with sound heart and lungs and kidneys and all her other organs intact; he doubted whether she would ever die, since he saw nothing about her that was liable to lead to her death.

"It doesn't look as if she's likely to perish," he would say, shrugging his shoulders.

She was very pleased to receive him, and whenever he called she showed her pleasure, as though she had sudden cause for satisfaction, becoming lively and cheerful in his presence like a child. No sooner would he arrive than she would offer him her pulse and uncover her chest for him to put his ear to. She enjoyed having him examine her, having him touch her body with his hands; and she used to find all sorts of excuses so that he should prolong his examination. When he examined her it seemed as though some light had been lit within her, like a candle coming into a dark entry; and there was a permeating, cloudy warmth, distant offspring as it were of the fire of love and privy matters and their like, and things like the like of them, all filling her heart, which stirred while her bowels warmed and moved as in yonder faroff days when the child had stirred within them. He would prepare to go, but she would be holding his hand between her own as long as she possibly could.

As before, she used to beg from door to door, toddling into the quarter and moving slowly along. And as before the womenfolk used to put out a chair for her in the street, talk to her affectionately, wait for her to speak and repeat every word of hers to each other in wonder and astonishment, their faces glad and bright. Not that she knew who they were or what they were doing round about her, nor what they asked and what they wanted of her. They all floated before her eyes like clouds or shadows of the twilight. The world and all that is therein seemed to her to be a twilit place functioning in a sort of pinkish gloom, viewed as through the eye of a needle and growing ever more blurred and dim.

Her intelligence also grew less, and sank like the declining of the day. The last odds and ends of her memories dispersed and became extinguished. She no longer remembered either far or near, neither her days of content nor her suffering and toil; neither the children she had borne nor the weddings at her house nor yet the deaths in her home. The mirror had become blurred beyond use.

As through a mist she seemed to glimpse uncertain, doubtful things from her past but she could not glimpse what they were nor could she explain their character. Something or other…Once upon a time…Grownups and children, children, children…Dead, yes they were dead…The All-Present would soon bring them back: today, tomorrow, in the dark, or maybe while it is still day.

The only memory she retained, confused and distant, was that of her great-granddaughter, who had been imprisoned by the Russian Bolsheviks because of her love for the Land of Israel. It was less than a memory, the memory of a memory, a sort of faded image or forgotten dream of which nothing was left but the general mood and impression. Without yearnings and without grief, but just casually and, as it were, in passing she would remember her, with complete indifference if one might say so…

Of the dresses she collected for the Rising of the Dead she carefully set aside the best and prettiest for her great-granddaughter; all dresses of silk or velvet, or of pretty colors. She would sit in front of a great heap of dresses, matching one against the other and whispering to herself, "This one is made for her, that one is kept for her, yonder one suits her, and she will deck herself in this other one for the Palace of Messiah…" She would go on whispering, forgetting herself and then waking up and sinking again in the vast gaps between thought and thought, till finally she would fall asleep. At such times it seemed to her as though a corpse were seated on the chair protecting all that great pile…

Once she went down to the market and found a pigeon for sale. She paid for it and took it, telling herself that it would serve for the

Sabbath dinner. On the Sabbath Eve she took it to the slaughterer. The pigeon hid its head against the Old Woman's bosom, heaving to and fro and cooing as though begging for its life. She held it in both hands and went on. Then the pigeon began beating with its wings, beating at her hands with its beak, spreading its wings over its head and quivering and thrusting and twisting to escape, until it suddenly broke loose from her hands and flew up into the air. The Old Woman remained standing with her head raised aloft, gazing behind her, not knowing what to do. Finally the pigeon vanished from sight, while she still stood wondering at the understanding which the Holy and Blessed One had set in the heart of so slight a creature that had nevertheless known how to deliver itself.

"Like human being," she breathed to herself.

And then it occurred to her that this could be nothing but metempsychosis, an incarnation of her great-granddaughter...

The women of the quarter noticed her standing in the middle of the street and immediately gathered round her from all sides. She sat among them like a child, worn and weary, on the chair they set for her, and in a heavy sorrowful whisper told what had happened to her. They all agreed with her, saying,

"Yes, that was an incarnation, your great-granddaughter took flesh as that pigeon!"

There was one young woman among them who did not have too much experience of life; and she said, affectionately teasing,

"And so the pigeon defeated you, grannie?"

The Old Woman remained silent and did not answer. But later, when she returned home and went to bed, being very tired and feeling as though all her strength had vanished and her body was broken to bits, as though her organs were beginning to pass away within her, the words of the young woman came back to her; and she lay looking upward, her eyes closed and her lips whispering, "She defeated me, she defeated me."

That Sabbath day she kept to her bed. At the close of the Sabbath, when the doctor came to visit her, she did not recognize him.

"Who are you?" she turned her startled weary eyes on him.

"I'm a Jew. Don't be afraid, granny. I'm a Jew."

"And if you're a Jew, what are you feeling round here for?" she set her hand on her heart and started back.

"I'm the doctor. Don't you recognize me?"

No, she did not recognise him and was afraid. The more she looked at him the more frightened she became, for she said he wanted to give her "the weakness of age" to drink.

"I don't want to...I don't want to! The weakness of age," she complained to the neighbors standing at her bedside. Then she wept and said, "Let that Angel of Death get away...I don't want to...In a little while. Just a little while...For Salvation is very close..."

It was useless for the neighbors to try and persuade her to let the doctor see her. It did not help. She would not let him see her and would take no medicine from him.

"Send the Angel of Death away..."

After the doctor had gone and the neighbors had left her room, she found the strength to leave the bed. Dragging herself along, bowed and bent of knees, she reached the door and locked it against the doctors and all the other evil spirits and Angels of Retribution in the world. Then she went back to bed, lay down and paid no attention to the neighbors knocking at her door. She lay with eyes turned toward the great heap of dresses, whispering,

"Just a little while...only a little while longer...Only a little while longer, my dove, my tender chick...For Salvation is very close..."

Early next morning Reb Nahumche the milkman, known to all and sundry as "the milky initiate", came riding into the quarter on his donkey. His yellow beard shone in the sun like gold, gold plentiful and pure. His laughing eyes were bright with happiness and goodness. His milk cans sloped down on either side and his donkey ambled under him, stretching its throat and braying for all it was worth.

Reb Nahumche the milkman met the idiot of the quarter and immediately burst into his usual greeting, offered as ever from a joyful heart,

"May gladness and rejoicing reach thee!"

The idiot of the quarter stood with his long coat gleaming like bronze, his beard and earlocks shaggy and fibrous as threads of wick, his face the color of the inside of a dried pumpkin. He placed his two pale hands on the head of the donkey, which was shaking with its prolonged braying, and responded,

"Donkey, donkey! When will he come, that poor man riding upon an ass!"

"He comes, he comes!" cried Reb Nahumche the milkman from his seat between the milk cans. "May gladness and rejoicing reach thee!"

The weeping of women sounded in the distance. Nahumche the milkman turned his head.

"The Old Woman has died…" said the idiot, patting the head of the donkey. "Donkey, donkey! You run off and tell that poor man riding upon an ass that the Old Woman has died…"

The quarter lay empty, deserted and forsaken as though following an earthquake. The houses projected above like desolate battlements. Files and platoons of buildings stood crowded together and tottering, poured on top of one another and thrust elbowing one against the other with their party-walls and washing-ropes and attics; a patchwork of colors and stones, of wooden boards and flat pieces of rusty tin and all the other odds and ends of an exiled, forsaken people. There was a dry heat all about, heavy, oppressive and still. The light was weary and excessive, like the light reflected by sands baking under the sun. And there was desolation round about, neglect and stupor and apathy. There was no sound and no live person; nothing but the weeping of the women in the distance, and the idiot who stood dancing in front of the donkey.

Translated by I.M. Lask

The Account

All the praises and laudatory epithets with which Jewry so dexterously adorns philanthropists were monopolized by four or five rich men in that large town outside the Pale of Settlement. They seemed to have become strange, outlandish creatures, if one might be permitted to say so; no more or less than chimaeric adjectives. Like that species of vegetable which consists of nothing more than skins one within another and neither food nor satisfaction of any other kind as its center, since its skins are their own reason for being. But Baruch Yalover was an everyday fellow, whom folk did not credit with thousands and million in coin; there was no particular praise accruing to him, no special adjective, nor was he renowned; he was just a plain straightforward common noun, like potato or black bread or loaf.

He did not belong to the class of the well-to-do, and what was seen and heard on all sides must be stated; so everyday was he as to be the acme of everydayness. Just the sort of man to dismiss with a snap of the fingers. Rabbi Doctor Spitz, the one who was neither a rabbi nor a doctor but who was a rabbi because he was a doctor and a doctor in order to be a rabbi, used to say of him that he was an ignoramus by the grace of God. Nevertheless he had adopted the exalted merit of doing more charity and opening his hand wide to scatter more money than could be expected, like one of the great philanthropists. Well, his fame did not spread abroad, neither in his town nor in the world at large. He was not doing charity for the sake of that. Those who knew him knew him: communal workers, wardens, treasurers, patrons and all who were in charge of charitable institutions. He was known best of all by Rabbi Doctor Spitz, who called on him at any hour and under any circumstances when funds were required for the poor and needy in Israel, no matter for what reason.

He never permitted himself to join the philanthropists and well-to-do when they assembled in meetings. Where would he fit with his shabby, creased clothes, his unimpressive height, full belly and bent back, which made him look like something pleated over and over, with his gross everyday face was red as a fine piece of meat fresh from the butcher's, his nose fleshy and ruddy as the comb of an old cock, and lined with fine blue veins like a kind of spleen. The others were all such fine wealthy folk! Important and respected individuals of good stock, of fine appearance and plentiful knowledge and the gift of the gab and the manners of the great. They were artists, artists! They were not like all other folk nor even like themselves; they did not look like Jews nor did they speak like Jews; they did not have the same movements nor the same twists nor the same habits. You could almost say that everything about them was borrowed from other folk, such as counts and dukes. And you could almost say that they were always acting out some drama or another, nobody could say whether for themselves or for other people, maybe as a joke, maybe in earnest; they spoke as though they whispered from on high, and made themselves far bigger than was in the power of any ordinary man who goes his own way.

They went according to their standards and he according to his. They were important and well known, and he was a simple fellow; they seemed to wear masks, and behaved like spoiled, lightheaded boys, while he was like an experienced and firmly established old man. They did what they did out of pride and competition and so that folk should have something to speak about, while he did it for the real reason and the necessity of his deed.

Requirement, necessity and the work which had to be accomplished—these were the outstanding principles by which he had guided himself since he came to know his own mind. According to them he did business, according to them he built his house and according to them he expended his money in charity. His house was a basic requirement, and his money was like his house and the love of the people of Israel like his money and the Awe of the Name was as the love of Israel; and all were intertwined and united within him in a single uninterrupted strand.

But in this bitter generation of ours, in which peace has been taken from the faithful houses of Israel, a man's house is not a house and his security is not security, he has no actual strength and power, and all principles have been effaced save the principle of suffering alone. First Baruch Yalover's daughter tore his world to shreds about him by marrying a Gentile, a public prosecutor in one of the towns along the Volga. And it was not long thereafter that his son went on the long journey, for he rebelled against the Government and was sent to Siberia. Now there was nothing left for him but charity and the fear of Heaven. As before, he feared God and served him without excessive fervor and without excessive dread; he neither increased nor diminished, but served God at heart in his usual, quiet way, which kept the scales evenly balanced between the two sides as always; but he began to do even more charitable deeds than before, and though all the poor folk of Israel had become his sons, all their needs and troubles were left to him to satisfy and put right, and he had to support them with his labor as if they were so many infants.

When the Bolsheviks came and deprived him of rights and took away everything he had, they did not find in his house, as they had found in the homes of the philanthropists and the well-to-do, either salons or boudoirs, either bedrooms or tearooms with frescoes and paintings by renowned artists; either Karelian birch or furniture of black oak or white oak; either Abramtziva majolicas or the porcelain of Sèvres and Copenhagen; there was no collection of tom-toms or idols brought from South Africa, nor yet fine pictures of Monet, Cézanne, Degas, Gaugin and all the other ultra-moderns. They found no more than a flat of four rooms with stout plain utensils, his wife lying sick with all the suffering she had endured, and twenty thousand roubles to his credit in the bank. His wife did not remain sick long but departed from this world, which is so much worse than all the Curses written in the Fifth Book of the Torah, and from this life which is more bitter than death. When he was robbed and despoiled and flung from his house and his wife died in his arms, everything vanished and he was left a lonely, forsaken old man, possessing neither goods nor needs of the body. Submissively, silently, without knowing what had befallen him, he bowed his head before every wave that passed over it and accepted the judgment; it was decreed from Heaven and no human being had any power or dominion over it. For only if it were all decreed from Heaven was there any sense in the sufferings; and only then could he have the strength to suffer patiently, and only then were all recriminations prevented; he had no place to enquire, and all accusations and remonstrances were vain. It had been decreed from Heaven that he must be imprisoned and imprisoned over and over again, and that he should be pursued and driven from pillar to post and oppressed, and all the rest of those sufferings and afflictions. It had been decreed from the Heavens even when he went to entreat his daughter to repent and found her killed by the authorities, both she and her husband, the former public prosecutor. And the hardest decree of all to bear was when they arrested his son who had returned from exile, and imprisoned him for being a social revolutionary.

After they arrested his son he used to wander about as though bemused and dazed, his mind in a whirl, his heart rent and weeping within him and his eyes weeping on their own, silently and secretly. It seemed as though he had reached the end of the road. Old age leaped upon him. His face grew lined, dark as pitch; his belly, which had already disburdened itself, drew inward, and he seemed to lose height. The whole of him seemed like a mushroom that had shriveled with age. Day by day his strength diminished and his spirit recoiled, since what was it all for? The world was a gloomy Gehenna; some men were led out to be killed and others came to their end by starvation; the malevolence of humankind was hardest of all to bear; justice and mercy, freedom and equality and all the promised good were not to be found; and why should the streets and the houses remain standing in rows with this sun and these skies...? He felt like a child, and everything about him began to seem childlike; his height, his appearance, his tiny toddling steps and the thoughts he was thinking; and all the world round him was mysterious and unclear. He felt just like a little baby. Sometimes his heart would be soothed by fine hopes which had no foundation in reality, and weird fantasies, almost an entire mythology, went round in his mind and fashioned of all kinds of hopeful tidings; wonderful things were done to him and his son and they were miraculously delivered. Thus he once happened to cross a bridge. He stood staring at the water, his thoughts running on as though he and his son were transformed into fishes that swam side by side through the water till they reached a second river, and from that second river to a third, and from the third river the sea, and from the sea they came out on the coast of some other country and were delivered.... But it was not always with fantasies that his mind was occupied. Sometimes he conjectured on actualities, and every fresh thought then seemed more likely and more probable; such and such reasons under such and such circumstances would finally lead the Cheka to free him and his son from suspicion, and thenceforward they would be considered full citizens, and they would apply themselves to making a living and would live quietly; and so on and so forth.

Weary and hopeless, he would wander through the streets and markets looking for enough to give him his daily food, any sort of living. Fearful and quivering, startled and quick as a broken hare pursued by relentless dogs, his bowels were taut and clutched with hunger, and his spirit would all but leave him before all authority or the shadow of authority or the shadow of that shadow. The whole atmosphere seemed to be suffused with a spirit of tumult and dread, as a forest is steeped in the scent of greenery. The windows of houses opening on the street were dangerous, the pavements, the terrifying posters, the crowds of the street, the public thoroughfares when they swarmed with men; and even more when they had emptied and stood weirdly broad and vaguely frightening....

There was fear round about. Fear and dread. All life was fear and dread. A freezing dread, as though all had frozen into immobility and history no longer occurred, and the world were an empty void and there was nothing—"His Blessed Name alone knows what it all is and why."

...And nonetheless all would end well. Or was it possible that things would never be well any more? Was it possible that the world would not return to its former conditions, to a beauty greater than it had formerly possessed? Impossible, it would have to go back! The heart demanded its own; everything would be all right in the world. It was of no account that for the moment everything was evil and bitter. And it did not matter that he derived no benefit whatsoever from all his devoted running hither and thither, to the associates and associates of associates of the authorities, to plead mercy for his son. Salvation must come at last! No one can take an oath that improvements will never be brought about. For if indeed truth will grow out of the earth, then out of the world which is deeper now than the earth, it will certainly grow. And when truth will grow from the earth justice will be seen from Heaven and the Lord will also give that which is good....

When he came out of the prison gate he walked strangely, as though walking were a craft he had never been trained in. The ground swayed beneath his feet, his head whirled and all sorts of rainbows revolved in confusion before his eyes. The city heaved about him as through a gilded veil; its restless streets, its mixed motley crowds, the glaring posters which menaced the passersby at every street corner, the height of the dusty, weedy-looking neglected trees—what were all these here for?...It was a hot summer's day when there is no escape from the heat and it is impossible to breathe. He did not know whither he should go and what he should do. Just as though he had been transferred from one prison to another which was even more severe.

A few days after he came out of prison he visited Rabbi Doctor Spitz, finding him in one of the two rooms of his former dwelling, to which the authorities had limited him. The room was small and dirty, crowded with all kinds of different things tumbled together, blankets and cushions and pillows tossed about, plates, cups, piles of books standing crazily on the floor in a corner, pairs of shoes, his top hat in all its shine and glory, and a good deal more of the like. The room contained elements which made it equally resemble the shop of a dealer in old junk, the temporary lodging of a man whose house has been burnt, and the abode of an emigrant to whom something has happened on his way to America.

It was with an important request that Baruch Yalover came to Rabbi Doctor Spitz; to ask him to make an account of the charity he had done in his lifetime; since his own head felt heavy and his mind was confused and he could not think. To begin with Doctor Spitz treated the thing like a sort of joke. When he saw it was not a joke he tried to divert his attention to other matters in one way or another. Since he did not succeed, he began to argue, to mock and to make him look silly. Finally he saw he would not get rid of him, since the old man insisted on his account as though he were a monomaniac; so he gave in despite himself and against his will.

"You've done your full share of charity, I know. More than your full share!" he said with annoyance, his face angry. "How much money you've laid out through my hands alone! Treasures!"

He rose, brought some paper, armed himself with a pencil, sat down at his disordered table and took down by dictation the details of Baruch Yalover's account.

"For the Society for Providing Cheap Meals for the Needy," he dictated in a weak and shaky voice, "membership dues for twenty-seven years, in all, eighty roubles."

"Eighty-one roubles," noted Doctor Spitz in annoyance on the paper, and sat back to hear more.

"Shoes for a hundred and fifty lads of the orphanage at six and a half roubles a pair, every year, amounting to nine hundred and seventy-five roubles a year; and then for six years—it amounts—it amounts—it seems to me it amounts to five thousand eight hundred and fifty roubles. I think that's right. Please go over it and see…."

"And fifty roubles," concluded Doctor Spitz, holding the pencil loosely in his hand.

"Clothes and linen for the orphanage, nine hundred and nine roubles, ninety-eight kopeks a year. How much in six years?"

"Five thousand four hundred and fifty-nine roubles and eighty-eight kopeks," reckoned Doctor Spitz and noted it down.

"Right. Now note down, one thousand and six kosher meals for prisons; if I do not err I remember paying in all one thousand nine hundred and seventy-three roubles."

"I've noted it," nodded Rabbi Doctor Spitz in boredom and impatience.

"Now seven thousand five hundred eggs for the hospital to commemorate my silver wedding, amounting in all to one hundred and sixteen roubles and sixty-one kopeks."

"And sixty-one kopeks. Noted! Go on...."

"Wood for fuel in the hospital, thirty-one wagonloads, amounting in all to three hundred and seventy-five roubles and twenty-two kopeks."

"Twenty-two kopeks. Go on...."

"To Jewish soldiers for Sabbaths and festivals seventeen thousand one hundred and four kosher meals, amounting in all to three thousand three hundred and eighty roubles and forty-five kopeks."

"You have a memory!" laughed Doctor Spitz ironically.

"Now one hundred head of cattle for the kitchen, and I don't remember any longer how much I paid...."

"How shall we enter it?" Rabbi Doctor Spitz stared at him with a mixture of laughter, astonishment and simple perplexity how to enter it.

Baruch Yalover closed his eyes, thought it over a moment, while his face grew soft and as dark as a crack in a tub.

"Note them down as they are: a hundred of cattle!" he said.

"A hundred head of cattle!" responded Rabbi Doctor Spitz with a laugh, "and may the Holy and Blessed One reckon them as though they were a hundred offerings."

"Passover flour for the hospital: sixteen roubles and sixty-seven and a half kopeks a year, and I donated it for four years, how much is it?"

"Here you are. Audited and found correct. Sixty-seven kopeks and a half, ha! ha! ha!"

"Yes. And another four thousand roubles I gave anonymously for the site of the handicrafts school...."

"So that was you?" Rabbi Doctor Spitz turned his sharp, surprised eyes on him.

"Note it, note it.... Small disbursements for writing books, pens, ink, etcetera, for the orphanage on the day of the confirmation of my son, may he be granted a long life..." his voice trembled and broke, but he controlled himself at once and continued whispering, "three hundred and thirty-seven roubles and ninety-eight kopeks."

"I've noted it," responded Rabbi Doctor Spitz in a low voice. "I've noted it, Boris Yakovlevitz."

"Now an account for the war refugees," Baruch Yalover returned to his theme. "Write: one thousand five hundred and eighty-six sacks of flour which are in all..."

He continued dictating an account of all the disbursements he had made, each disbursement on its own, a long list which seemed to have no end or limit.... Rabbi Doctor Spitz grew weary with the toil, sweat already covered him, and still the other sat there and went on enumerating.

When he finished Rabbi Doctor Spitz's face grew bright, he stood up, straightened his back and stretched himself.

"Bless be He who has freed me!" he said jokingly and began to total up the account and see how much it all amounted to.

While he prepared the account Baruch Yalover fell asleep, for his weariness and hunger had sapped his strength. But he had not been sleeping long before Rabbi Doctor Spitz awoke him.

"Boris Yakovlevitz! Boris Yakovlevitz!" he shook him by the shoulder.

He wearily opened his eyes and looked at the rabbi as though he did not know what the other was doing there.

He spent a moment collecting his thoughts, wrinkled up his deeply furrowed brow and said,

"Rabbi, what will happen when we come over yonder? Immediately, the first moment we come over there yonder?..."

Doctor Spitz was startled and surprised at his words. Although he knew that the other's words referred to the World to Come, he pretended not to understand.

"Yonder where?" he asked in astonishment. "Were you dreaming or what?"

"Just asking, just asking...."

"Here's the account. One hundred and nineteen thousand roubles and forty-three kopeks in gold coin... gold!" he said with a smile. "You did plenty of charity. Would that there had been many like you in Israel! How much were you worth, Boris Yakovlevitz?"

"All I had was forty thousand roubles. Neither more nor less, but exactly forty thousand roubles."

"Forty thousand? Only forty thousand!" exclaimed Doctor Spitz in a low astonished voice as though he had been suddenly reduced from his glory.

Boris Yalover took the paper and studied it, while it shook in his hot hand.

"A good balance," said he after a moment. "A fine balance.... Only I myself am worth nothing, whatever there is of me doesn't get entered into the world's accounts among the lists of the creatures of the Holy and Blessed...."

"A great sum!" said Rabbi Doctor Spitz, waiting for him to go. "The Holy and Blessed One owes you a great deal, a great deal, Boris Yakovlevitz. Keep your mouth covered and say nothing—you mustn't tell how much He owes you...."

Baruch Yalover, who felt that the other wanted to be rid of him, wished to rise and go, but his legs paid no attention; weariness was creeping over him and he could not move.

"Just a few minutes," he excused himself. "I'm tired."

"By all means, Boris Yakovlevitz! The pleasure's mine," answered Rabbi Doctor Spitz politely with secret annoyance, and returned to his desk.

Baruch Yalover sat weary and weak, his face sunken and sickish, his head resting on his palm and his eyes staring afar, as though he might be thinking or listening to an answer to the problem that had been gnawing at his brain: what would happen *there,* the very first moment he would arrive *there,* just at that very first moment?

Rabbi Doctor Spitz sat in annoyance thinking: here he comes troubling you three hours on end, and you have to go sitting with him, Devil knows why! An ignoramus like him....

"You did plenty of charity while you had the opportunity!" he turned to him. "Blessed be the hands that donate so!"

Baruch Yalover turned his head toward him, dropping his eyes at once in uninterested weariness. Slowly he stretched out his hand, took a Bible that was lying on the table, and began glancing at it. In a few moments he raised his eyes from the Bible, put his hand in his pocket and took out two bundles of Soviet paper money.

"Rabbi..." he began slowly and calmly, his face growing still paler, "I am leaving four hundred thousand roubles with you.... And I ask you to do me the last true kindness and bring me to a Jewish grave.... And my son—long life to him...if the hour does not come..."

His voice broke and he stopped.

"Already he's..." he dropped his head, his voice quivering and sinking, "he's been eight days already neither eating nor drinking, on hunger strike...the eighth day...."

He rose, put the paper money on the desk, patted the bundles two or three times and urged his limbs to move. Rabbi Doctor Spitz hastily began to try and comfort him with the encouragement suitable for such a moment and such a subject. But the words did not enter his ears. He bent over the Bible for a while. Presently he turned aside, looked across the room, placed his finger on the open text and said,

"How strange this people is! They saw clearly...eye to eye they saw...and all the same, 'And he did that which was evil,' and 'they did that which was evil'..."

There was silence in the room, that difficult silence which sounds excessive and high-pitched, like an essence of the whole of life, all things and all paths.

"Good-bye, Rabbi." He took the hand of Rabbi Doctor Spitz in his own and retained it a long while. "Good-bye...."

Vainly did Doctor Spitz hasten from one side of him to the other, trying to comfort him and raise hopes in the aid of His Blessed Name. Slowly he shifted himself, walking heavily and with difficulty as though his feet were being sucked down by the floor. And Rabbi Doctor Spitz stood stock-still looking after him, his mouth twitching, his eyes big, his face wonder-struck, with nothing whatever to say.

Translated by I.M. Lask

Rahamim

One sunny day Menashke Bezprozvani, lean as a pole, wandered through the streets of Jerusalem, his face seamed and sickly-looking, his mouth unusually fleshy and red, his eyes discontented and disparaging.

Bitterness gnawed at his heart, piercing through him like some venom—a bitterness of heart which was unconscious rather than clearly expressed, arising from the years he had spent without achieving anything, neither contentment for himself, nor property, nor a family; the bitter, gloomy quintessence of fever and hunger, of unsettled wandering from one agricultural commune to another, of vexations and suffering and troubles enough to drive a man out of his mind and drain all his strength, and all the other effects of his past experiences, his lack of employment, and his present sickness.

His despair put him in a fury. All sorts of evil thoughts possessed him, recriminations and accusations directed against the Labor Federation and Zionism, against "the domination of the Zionist Imperialism"; against everything in the world, it seemed. As though one might claim that everything was fine and bright, he would have had a job, his spirit would be refreshed, he might have everything he desired and the whole of life could be brilliant, were it not for worthless leaders and the Zionist imperialism that hindered things.

All these were the complaints of a dejected, despairing person who, more than he wanted comfort, wished to torture himself, to cry out aloud and rebel and remonstrate against the whole state of affairs. But his complaints were only half-hearted. Like it or not, he possessed a great love for the land and a great love of the Hebrew language; a strong, deep, irrational, obstinate love that went beyond all theories and views, and led beyond all personal advantage. And since his complaints were no more than half-hearted, he complained all the more, denying everything and destroying everything in thought without getting anywhere, and just making himself uncomfortable.

Apart from all his bitterness, the excessive heat exhausted him. It was the middle of July. The heat was like that of an oven stoked with glowing coals, and the white light dazzled to blindness and distraction. The roadway quivered uncertainly in the light as though in a dream; it might have been so much barren soil or else a field left fallow because of drought; or it might have been anything you like in the world. The sun quarreled with the stones and the windows. The slopes of the mountains on the horizon shone yellow-brown through the dryness, while the skies in their purity of blue called eternity and worlds-without-end to mind.

A yell stopped him as he walked. A dozen or so Arabs dashed excitedly among the crowd in the street, yelling at the top of their voices as though attacked by robbers,

"*Barud! Barud!*" (Blasting going on!)

Menashke Bezprozvani stood among the group of folk who stood pressed together, until the road echoed to a loud explosion and stones flung aloft scattered around and fell here and there in confusion. When he began to resume his walk he found himself accompanied by a man riding a donkey.

"Noise, eh!" said this stranger, turning his face to him with a smile of satisfaction and wonder.

He was a short fellow with thick black eyebrows, a beard like a thicket, his face bright as a copper pot and his chest uncommonly virile and broad. He was dressed in rags and tatters, rent upon rent and patch upon patch, a rope girded round his loins, and a basket of reeds in front of him on the donkey"s back.

Menashke Bezprozvani glanced at him and made no answer, but the stranger entered into conversation and eventually he replied.

"Got a missus?" the man swivelled on the donkey's back to ask.

"What do you want to know for?"

"Ain't got one, a missus?" wondered the man on the donkey.

"No, I haven't, I haven't!"

"Not good," the owner of the donkey commiserated with him, as though he saw something strange and impossible before his eyes. "Take yourself a missus!"

"I'm poor and I have nothing. How shall I keep a wife?" Menashke Bezprozvani answered, half-mocking, half-protesting.

"God is merciful!"

"How's God merciful? I'm an old bachelor already and so far He hasn't shown me any mercy!"

"God is merciful!" maintained the owner of the donkey. "Him, everything He knows. Me, got nothing and His Name never forsook me."

"That's you and this is me."

"What's the matter, huh? Must be everything all right. I had sense and got missus! Plenty all right."

He lowered his head between his two shoulders and closed his eyes tight with satisfaction and contentment.

"Plenty all right, His Name be blessed!" He opened his eyes and went on speaking. "Plenty all right...one day was in shop, I brought boxes. I saw there's one missus there...first, long, long before men gave me a missus and wasn't luck. His Name never give... I heard they told me, it is a missus come from Babylon, that's as now calls it Iraq, who wants to marry. Goes to Kiryat Shaul—and that's the missus from the shop...From heaven, eh! No money I had—not got money what'll you do! Look, look, took six pound in bank and did business. At Muharram I made five pound also—and married! His Name be blessed, plenty all right...take you a missus, a worker, a fat one, be all right. His Name is merciful..."

He rapped his two soft sandals on the belly of the donkey which was plodding slowly under him; while his face expanded and broadened till it beamed like two copper pans.

"Never get on, no man, without a missus!" He moved from where he was sitting toward the donkey's crupper, speaking in a tone of absolute and assured finality. "No mountain without top, no belly without belly button, no man get on without a missus!"

"And how many wives have you?" asked Menashke Bezprozvani, looking at him from the corner of his eye. "Two? Three?"

"Two is two." He raised his outstretched palms aloft as though saying, Come and see, I have no more than two...

"Do they live at peace?"

"Eh! Mountain looks at mountain and valley between them." He turned a mouthful of strong white teeth toward him. "If there's a young one in house, old one always... brrr, brrr.... "

"And how much do you earn? Are you a porter or what?"

"Yes, mister."

And having found himself a comfortable part of the donkey"s back to sit on and having settled himself firmly there, he began telling him all his affairs. To begin with, he said, he had been a plain porter, and now he was porter with a donkey! This donkey under him was already his eighth, and from now on, nobody swindles him anymore. He was already a big expert on donkeys, an experienced and well-versed donkey-doctor! Through a bad donkey and a bad wife, said he, old age comes leaping on a man, but a good donkey and a good wife, nothing better than they in the world. Like a fat pilaf to eat, or the hot pot on the Sabbath! And His Name be blessed, he earned his daily bread, His Name is merciful! Sometimes one shilling a day, sometimes two shilling a day, and sometimes one mil.... All sorts of days, all sorts of days!

"Then was all right, long before," he passed his hand over the back of his neck as he spoke, "earned four shilling a day also! Then was all right."

He put his hand into the reed basket before him and took out a few dirty eggs.

"Take the ecks." He held them out to his companion. "Take, mister. Fresh as the Cooperative!"

Menashke Bezprozvani did not wish to take them.

"Have you a chicken run?" he asked, in a better humor.

"His Name be blessed! Got seven hens!" replied the other contentedly and with pride. "All make ecks, eck a day, eck a day…take, mister! Please, like the Cooperative…chickens all right, His Name be blessed!"

Were it not, said he, for the money he needed, he himself would eat the eggs his hens laid, so all right were those eggs! But his little daughter lay sick in Hadassah and not a farthing did he have. Yesterday he had bought her bananas for half a piastre and she ate….

"Eating already!" he said as one who announces great tidings, while his face lit up in a smile of good nature and happiness. "Eating already, blessed be His Name!"

While he put the eggs back in the basket, Menashke Bezprozvani noticed that he wore two rings on his fingers, two copper rings set with thick projecting colored stones. He asked,

"What are these?"

"This? Rings. And you haven't got?"

"Haven't got."

"That's it," he smiled into his beard. "I'll tell you saying they tell by us in Babylon…"

And he began telling him the story of a certain man who loved a beautiful woman. "Once it happened he had to go a long journey. He said to her, to that beauty: Lady! because that I love you much, you give me your ring, and as long as I see it on my finger I remember you and long for you. And that beauty who was sharp, never wish to give him her ring but said to him: Nat so, only every time you look at your finger and see my ring not there, you remember me because I never give you ring, and you long for me…"

Ending his tale, he burst into a peal of laughter.

"Ha-ha-ha!" He threw his head back and filled the whole road with his powerful, noisy laughter. "And so you also, ha-ha-ha!"

His laughter and the yarn he had spun turned Menashke

Bezprozvani's mind in a different direction. Despite himself, he began to think of his own girl—her merits, her strangeness and the whole of that chapter.

The donkey, left to its own devices, was proceeding lazily and heavily while the porter sat shaking on its back, his face ruddy as copper and glinting, his beard spread in his satisfied smile, and his mood as beneficent as though he found everything in the whole world satisfactory. Menashke Bezprozvani turned his eyes to him and observed the way in which he sat on the donkey's back among his wooden vessels and ropes and pieces of metal; short and broad, a sort of doubled-over and redoubled-over man. It looked almost as though his height had been doubled over into breadth, bis backbone was double, and the teeth in his mouth were double echoing from one end of the road to the other, his laugh—which had the merriment of childhood in it—scattered itself throughout the universe; and the Holy and Blessed One was with him, near him, at home with him among his children and his wives, His chickens and his donkey...

Menashke walked slowly beside him and pictured the other at home. Here, his thoughts gradually emerged in clear pictures; the porter sits at the entrance to his home of an evening in the closed courtyard beside the cistern built over with stones. The children—a sundry heap of children—hang round him and tumble over him from every side, squalling and yelling. The womenfolk are busy at the fire. They cook the evening meal and curse. Both are heavy and solid as two blossoming garden plots, and he makes peace between them, looking at one with affection and at the other with even more; every glance of his falls like rain upon thirsty soil. At the side lies his sick father, a heap of rags in a corner—an old man, his days drawing near to their close: The fire crackles, cheerfully and brightly, the pot boils, and one of the wives begins singing, rolling her voice toward the stars and drawing out her song...

"How did you come to the land of Israel?" he interrupted his reverie to ask.

"With the help of His Name!"

And before a moment had elapsed he was telling him all his wanderings. Thus and thus, he was a Kurd from Zacho. Did he know

Zacho? One day he heard there's a legion in the land of Israel, warriors of the Children of Israel. He said: wish to be a Jewish warrior—that's what! He rose and went from Zacho to Mosul and from Mosul to Baghdad and from Baghdad to Basra. And already in Basra he is a servant to a Jew who has a shop to wear clothes, a rich man, plenty blessing he has, His Name be blessed. He made bread, he made food, everything, everything…because a man is better fit for work than a missus, fit much more...and then from Basra he went to Bombay, as the way to Damascus was then—long, long before—closed because of the war with the Turk. He stayed in Bombay two months, and every day, every day walked in the garden of Señor Sassoon, eating and drinking and walking…until at last he went to the land of Israel. Did he know Haifa?…As yet then in Haifa the Commercial Center wasn't, 'eh! The lads told him there in Haifa: stay with us, Rahamim! But he didn't want—to Jerusalem; to the Jewish Legion! So he came to Jerusalem and the Legion wasn't…

"None there!" He clapped his hands together, speaking in a downcast, long drawn-out voice.

For a while he was silent, shifting on his saddle. He turned his eyes and casually glanced at Menashke Bezprozvani, and his face changed. It was as though something astonishing had occurred to him just then.

"What for you're so sad?" he asked in a slow, soft voice.

Since Menashke Bezprozvani did not answer, he scratched the back of his neck two or three times and stirred himself.

"Late already," he said, raising his head aloft.

He kicked his heels into the donkey's belly and tugged at the reins in his hand. The donkey tossed its head, put its feet one here and one there, and began kicking up its heels and galloping.

"Take a missus! His Name is merciful!" he turned his head and shouted back to Menashke. "Farewell! Peace to Israel!"

The donkey changed its gait, began to move with a delicate clipping, and its tiny hoofs tapped in the roadway like castanets.

Menashke Bezprozvani remained alone and walked on, his body heavy and his spirit worn-down and weary. Strange feelings were pricking at his heart, chop and change, piecemeal, in turn, then all tossing within him in confusion; dim recollections of his childhood, the affairs and misadventures of his girl, and all his suffering and distractions. For some reason he remembered the days at Migdal, the baths at Tiberias, Ras al Ain and Kfar Gileadi; and the rhythm of a tune which was still indistinct began to trouble him, half-remembered, half-forgotten-half-forgotten, half-remembered; he could not bring it fully to mind....

Until he heard the sound of a donkey's hoofs clacking on the road-way like castanets. He raised his eyes and saw that the porter had turned back toward him. He stood in surprise, blinking his eyes in the sun, and stared.

When the porter reached him, he pulled up his donkey, and stopped.

"Mister! Mister!...Listen!" He lowered his head to him with a wayward smile, his face strangely affectionate and humble. "Mister!...Don't be sad! By my life!...Be all right! By my life! His name is merciful!"

"His name's merciful...." he explained again, with a modest, almost maternal, smile. "Don't be sad! Upon my life! On my head and eyes! It'll be all right!"

Menashke Brezprozvani stood astonished with nothing to say. His heart leaped within him, and the beginnings of a confused smile were caught frozen at the corners of his mouth. The other had already left him and vanished along the road, but he still stood where he was as though fixed in the ground, his heart leaping and his spirit in a protracted, dark turmoil, like a distant echo caught and hanging all but still of an evening. And he could not understand it. It was as though something had happened within him, something big, but he did not know what. As though—as though—the guilty and soothing smile of that porter and his face which had been bright with love and humility did not disappear from his thoughts, but soothed him, comforting him and raising his spirits above all the errors and mistakes and recriminations and bitterness.

After a while he moved and turned and stirred to go. He descended into an open space covered with dry thorns, with many sunken stones in it, and a few twisted old olive trees. Under one of the trees stood five or six sheep pushing their heads one under the other and standing as though bewitched.

Menashke Bezprozvani sat himself down on a stone. He looked up at the Mountains of Moab—-desolate in their blue, indistinct in outline—as though they had been swallowed by the sky or, perhaps, as though the sky had been swallowed by them. Before his eyes stood the likeness of the porter with his smile; his spirits rising within him, his thoughts divided. He sighed, almost tearful, then began to hum to himself the words of the song which the children had used to sing at Kfar Gileadi in those days of hardship and hunger:

> In Kfar Gileadi,
> In the upper court,
> Next to the runnel,
> Within the big butt
> There's never a drop of water…

Translated by I.M. Lask

The Hidden Puddle

T here are many Eliahs in the marketplace but none so down-and-out as Eliah Kotlik. Some people don't own a house but have a store. Some people don't own a store but have a goat, but Eliah Kotlik has neither house, nor store, nor goat. He has nothing. As folks say: No goat, no coat, not even a snip of wool. He was stripped like a peeled onion. So what can you do? If you go to the bathhouse, you might as well work up a sweat!

And how he toils, how he chases around…. From sunrise to sunset, he storms and bustles, buzzes and rumbles, jostling and elbowing his way into business like a swirling sea wave. Grabbing a deal here and taking a plunge as a day jobber there. Here he takes up an option and there he turns one down. Here he says "Ah," there he drops a "bah", twists and turns with every wind combining three or four deals into one. Not that any of them would have a leg to stand on, if the good Lord did not perform miracles on his behalf at every turn. That he, his wife and his children have not starved to death until now is proof that the ways of our Lord are mighty indeed.

The truth of the matter is that only a trifle makes a difference between a full table and an empty one. Vanity of vanities, all is vanity, the world and all its tumult. Except that there's still some hope in this world for the world to come.

His wife is different. All she knows is how to make demands. Give! Give her the world: bread and potatoes, wheaten bread and meat for the Sabbath and all kinds of things to eat. Every day she metes him out his full measure, a hundred times, whining in a sort of whimpering, ranting, cursing sing-song. If the curses she utters were ever fulfilled, the world would fall apart.

Oh well, a woman can't get on without her tongue. A woman's a woman for all that and particularly since a woman's aches and pains are worse than a man's. But what can he do? What does she want him to do, put himself up for sale? In all likelihood God will have mercy. He will, surely, have mercy. After all, from where, if not from His open hand, could he get anything for her now that the market lies buried seven fathoms in the earth. Many men, more capable than he, have fallen flat on their faces—merchants who, if luck would have it, were competent enough. Because business is dead. Business is like the days of the *Sephira*[1], the more you count, the less is left.

Between transactions, the market being dead, Eliah dashes home, despondent and distraught, to be greeted by his wife with a grand "Well, how's it going?" He pretends not to hear her. She begins to dum him with words unfit to be heard. He ignores them in silence. She starts to goad him into a quarrel. Working herself up into a fury, she cuts through to his very bones and claws at his liver and his lungs. He grabs his cane and flees the house. Greatly agitated, he takes giant strides, his face flushed and his eyes aflame, looking like a man whose luck is with him, as if he were another Eliah altogether.

"My staff, my bread-winner!" Her voice still sputters in his ears.

Little by little he calmed down and was himself again. His face paled and assumed various masks—the "All right, then" look and the "Oh, well" look. His eyes squint and glare like the eyes of a man emerging from the dark into the light. The tip of his beard glistens in

---

1. Seven weeks counted from Passover to Pentecost (Shavuot—"weeks"—which occurs on the 50th day) hence the name, in keeping with Leviticus 23:15 *et al.*

the sunlight and his moustache droops over his mouth in a diffident, and almost furtive, smile. His cane hangs loosely from the neck of his worn and faded caftan which has the color of the water in a bathhouse, swinging back and forth and knocking against his knees.

Once again he returns to the market. He passes the many shops and the stalls where tradeswomen sat selling cherries, mulberries, raspberries and other wild fruit. Turning in every direction, half chasing and half chased, he hobbles between the wagons of the country-folk. He comes across a straggle of peasant women and calls out to them, "How much for the wax?" He plunges his hand into a bunch of stiff bristles. He bend over a goose lying on the ground beside the wheel of a wagon, its neck plucked and its wing spread. Although his pockets were empty he stopped to haggle over a hen. Earlier, before he had gone home, he had had no luck with that hen, since he had tried to buy it without a cent to his name. All the same, he squeezed it once more, blew into its feathers, examined it under its neck and weighed it in his palm.

Turning about, he noticed Reb Yitzhak Simha standing in the doorway of his shop. Reb Yitzhak Simha had a powerful stance: fleshy and tall, proud features, nose protruding like an onion out of his abundant beard, belly round as a cask, *yarmulke* down over the back of his neck, shirt-sleeves glistening white in the sunlight. The years had obviously been good to him and he held the world in the palm of his hand.

Eliah Kotlik sighed and lowered his head. Jokingly he reasoned closely, "If Reb Yitzhak Simha, who has many expenses, is able to make a living for himself, certainly I, who require little food, ought to be able to do so."

Reb Yitzhak winked to him as if to say to him, "I've got something on you."

With both his hands, he lifted the tire of his belly, wheeled about heavily, as one does after reading the sixth Sabbath portion,[2] and disappeared into his store.

2. The *Parsha,* the weekly portion of the Pentateuch read during the Sabbath morning service, is subdivided into seven sections.

Eliah stood as if some mishap had befallen him: slack, odd-faced, limp-armed. And standing there, he closed one eye and wrinkled his nose.

"If only I had the cash," he smiled like a man who has lost most of his teeth, "of what that man has already sunk in his belly."

And because he had nothing to do and did not know what to do with himself, he began to walk.

The houses were bathed in the sunshine, the street opened out to the sky, which slanted toward the edge of the field at the opposite side of the river. Here and there a gate cast its shadow, drawing a long line of nettle, mallow, ox-tongue and a wild assortment of thorns. From Isaac the carpenter's house rang the pounding of a hammer. The dull, incessant pulse of the grist-maker's mill rose from the end of the street. An old woman sat at her doorway sifting peas. Nissel the carder sat beside his house, under the awning, and shaped an ox-horn over the pile of shavings that lay at his feet.

"A *shofar?*"[3] asked Eliah.

"What do you mean a *shofar*," answered the carder. "It's a hair-comb."

"Oh," replied Eliah, like someone proved wrong.

Lyuba, Isaac's son, a boy of about seventeen, handsomely dressed in an embroidered shirt, with pince-nez on his nose and a shiny visor on his cap, came toward him reading a book. Minna, Nissel's daughter, began to sing. She stuck her head out the window and looked at Lyubka.

"Prepare the dowry," said Eliah to Nissel smiling wanly, "I've got a proper vessel for you, a good thing."

He walked about in this fashion until he reached the Odessa Hotel. On the bench beside the entrance, sat Velvel the Plague, Cross-eyed Benzel, and Yossel Kreike. They greeted him and made room for him. He sat down. One began to josh him, another to pull his leg, while the third heaved a sigh in his behalf. They took up the conversation where they had left off. They had been talking about Yehiel Michael Zayedni, who had hung a new sign over the

---

3. Ram's horn used for ritual purposes.

store. Velvel Swerdlik, nicknamed "the Plague," said, as his wrinkled face shone like a chicken-leg in mustard, "A new sign is sure proof of bankruptcy—that's a first principle."

"It's self evident," confirmed Cross-eyed Benzel. His head shook and his eyes took off in opposite directions, one toward Egypt and the other toward the graveyard, as the saying goes, while he sat smiling, so to speak, at all the world.

Kreike then said, "How many times did he go bankrupt?"

The talk was pointless, the banter of dawdlers.

Eliah wanted to go home for he was hungry, but he was afraid of his wife. She might be hard on him. He sat reluctantly, brooding over his fate. He turned his eyes toward a flock of swallows pecking away along the curb at some oats which had survived. He was, at that moment, like a truant boy who had fled the schoolroom for fear of his master's wrath. Looking at the birds and seeing how industrious and how noisy they were, he recalled his childhood. Now, wherever he cast his eyes, he would discern some facet of this period in his life. The row of shops in the marketplace, the fence of the inn which had blackened with age, three hens pecking in the refuse, the broad street opening to the luster of the fields—there was something of his childhood in each of them. The heat of day was also part of it, so was the filtered, yellowing dampness whose very essence derived from childhood and so was the sky, colored like the Havdala candle,[4] just at it had been in his youth,—forty years ago.

They—Velvel the Plague, Cross-eyed Benzel and Yossel Kreike—were still talking about Yehiel Michael Zayedni and about his father, the late Jacob Meir, who was a miser.

"Folks are different. Fathers and sons are different. Just as one may be a miser, the other may be a spendthrift. One lent his money with interest, the other borrowed on interest," they said.

"The wheel of fortune turns," ruled Velvel the Plague, as his face lit up like a citron ripening in the sunlight.

They recalled Jacob Meir's mannerisms and his deeds, telling whatever anecdotes there were to tell.

4. Candle lit at the ritual which marks the end of the Sabbath.

Their remarks impressed Eliah and helped him remember what had been forgotten. Many people had already gone to a better world and many matters were now consigned to oblivion.

Velvel the Plague recounted,

"They tell a story about him. When he was in his death throes, the squire came calling upon him in order to borrow some money at interest. Jacob Meir recovered his strength momentarily and managed to mutter 'two'—that is to say 'two percent per week,' but did not go on for his soul had expired."

Cross-eyed Benzel then said, "Reb Itzikel, of blessed memory, said about him that Reb Jacob Meir was greater than Rabbi Akiva, for Rabbi Akiva's soul expired as he uttered 'one'[5] but Reb Jacob's when he uttered 'two.'"

The stories were well known but they laughed all the same and Eliah laughed with them. And he recalled that once when he was still a schoolboy, his father, distraught because he was not making ends meet, had beaten him and driven him out of the house. It seemed to him that this incident had taken place the very day on which Jacob Meir had died.

Memories seized him: his relationship with his father as a boy, as a young man, as a bridegroom and as the head of a family—and he was filled with pity for his father and the life wasted in poverty, in suffering and in bitterness of soul.

So that his companions might not sense his anguish, he began to explain why Jacob Meir bore a grudge against him.

"Subtraction is proof of addition, and a full belly is proof of thievery."

"But his Shmulik is a scholar," said Velvel the Plague.

"He *was*," Cross-eyed Benzel squinted both his eyes.

"To this day, they say, he studies Talmud," Yossel Kreike defended him.

---

5. A reference to the martyr's death suffered by Rabbi Akiva, whose soul expired as he finished the recitation of: 'Hear O Israel, the Lord our God, the Lord is One.'

"He studies the Holy Torah with defiled eyes," retorted Cross-eyed Benzel. "There are no pious men in Odessa."[6]

"He's a Zionist, one of the important ones."

At this they plunged into Zionism and from Zionism to the Land of Israel.

"God made too many promises," said Cross-eyed Benzel, "and carried out too few. He promised the Land to Abraham and his seed, but in the end Abraham had to buy a burial place for his wife at full price. And Isaac was a *ger,* a sojourner. He had to drag himself to the river Gerar, in the land of Philistia. A long and pretty story."

Just then Velvel the Plague looked up and saw the Rabbi walking in the marketplace. He whispered,

"The Rabbi—take off!"

They raised their eyes and saw their Rabbi walking past in short, hurried steps. Face to the ground, one shoulder raised and the other drooping, his back bent as if it had been under a rolling pin for thirteen successive Passover eves.[7]

He looked as if he were walking between Mahoza and Pumbedita,[8] preoccupied with talmudic matters. They followed him with their looks in silence until he turned off into an alleyway and disappeared.

Then Yossel Kreike said, "He's probably going to perform a pious act. A dear Jew."

Cross-eyed Benzel's two eyes glistened in the sun and he let a syllable fall from his lips.

"Pure…"

Velvel the Plague joked, "Such is the way of world. If a man's enterprising he's a thief, but if he's a saint he's a *shlemiel.*"

"An absolute saint," Eliah sighed deeply, "and in addition an absolute pauper, almost as poor as a corpse, the Lord preserve us."

---

6. Cultural capital in South Russia, the seat of Jewish secularism in the late nineteenth century.
7. The Passover rolling pin not only flattens the dough but also perforates it.
8. Two academy towns in talmudic Babylonia.

"How could he be anything but poor as a corpse," said Velvel the Plague, putting his hand to his beard, "if we pay for his groceries."

"An absolute saint, an absolute saint," Eliah shook his head into the void.

"And all the same he, too, will be bankrupt," argued Velvel the Plague. "After a long life, he will still owe the baker for two or three loaves."

"Because of our many sins," asserted Eliah, "he starves to death a hundred times from Sabbath to Sabbath."

"Think nothing of it," Velvel the Plague assured him. "It's simply the general rule: all the nanny-goats are for milking, all the chickens for slaughtering, and all the Rabbis for contempt."

A few minutes later they halted. Cross-eyed Benzel's eyes glistened as he said,

"Doesn't add up to a living."

A sigh shook Yossel Kreike's very bones.

"Yes, it doesn't add up to a living, *oy, oy.*"

And Velvel the Plague also groaned,

"Oy, our Father in heaven!"

He scowled in all directions and said again, partly to sum up, partly in despair, "Such is the way of the Torah."

They took leave of each other, each to his home. Eliah sensed that it was too early to return home. His wife had not yet calmed down.

He went wherever his legs led him. His ears caught the sound of a pony whinnying in the meadow—a clear, cheerful sound in harmony with the sun, the green fields and a world radiant with June. Of course, the days between Pessah and Shavuot! Days whose luster is new and young. The fields are green with wheat, the meadows spangled with flowers as with stars and suns, the trees adorned with blossoms as with heavenly lamps and the skies spread like a bridal canopy—each like a guest at a wedding. And mirth, song and the joy of wedlock fill the earth from end to end.

Eliah glanced sideways standing like a man who suddenly finds that the streets of his city are altered and he does not know where his own home is. He raised his eyes toward the sky. His beard was flooded with light, his lips opened and appeared as if he were smiling. As he looked toward the sky, he remembered that these were the days of *Sephira*, in which one may not be joyous, and he sighed deeply. He began to meditate upon the forty-nine days of the *Sephira* which parallel the forty-nine gates of repentance,[9] gate within gate, until the Feast of Shavuot which is the fiftieth gate. None of them open, except at the recitation of "Out of the Depths."[10]

It would be a good thing if he were to enter the Beth Midrash[11] right now, recite Psalms and occupy himself with a bit of Torah. He would be immediately transformed, he imagined, into a new being, like this field so to speak, which was watered from above and now grows green in the sun, or like that tree which buds and sprouts blossoms. But he was unable to do as he wished—time was too short.

It occurred to him that he might go to the *heder* and check on his little son's achievements in Torah. His eyes lit up, his body straightened as if he had gained dignity in his own eyes and in the eyes of all men.

"Rascal," he shook his head as his face wrinkled with smiles of affection, "you big rascal."

He strode on, basking in sheer delight. The sun shone down on his face, the earth was soft to the touch of his feet and the charm of the day was upon him. The charm of the day was unique, lovely and bathed in brilliance. It was like a goodly portion in the world to come.

But a few moments later, he once again recalled what these days were, the days of *Sephira,* and was troubled. Then he forgot Rabbi Akiva and his disciples as his limbs hurried him along. He was walking: head high, face illumined, beard askew and his cap on the nape of his neck.

From that moment on, the day split into two days: a day of joy and a day of mourning and they intermingled, one part joyous, the

---

9. According to a talmudic legend one must pass through forty-nine gates of repentance to reach the fiftieth gate of redemption.
10. Psalm 130.
11. The study hall attached to the synagogue and used for both prayer and study.

other somber, one part viewing him with favor, the other eyeing him askance. And he would stand upright or slouch alternately. Finally, both days merged and became one and the same, as if woven out of the same cloth—out of sunlight and Psalms—as if made up of yearnings and moments of solitary communion of man with his Maker, and of a sorrow whose pain has been spent, and is fragile and distant like a dream that was once seen, but is now, in the main, forgotten.

Every man was like a boy; every man, so to speak, had a fine and worthy woman, and all the world is washed with tears and glistens.

But luster once departed does not return. His soul being stirred, it remained stirred. Again childhood took hold of him, rising from the strip of grass which grew along the sides of the houses and stretched out like a shining road, from the imprint of horse-shoes and wagon wheels in the sand, from the flowering shrub tangling with the leaning fence, from the weeds which grew on the roof, from the expanse which rose above the fields opposite him. Even those dark, huddled houses built of aging wood and straw, which were about to collapse, were it not that they supported each other (some sunken, for the most part, into the earth, their slanted roofs touching their windows and their windows eating into the ground, others askew—doors unhinged and windows crooked), even those houses seemed to him, at that very hour, to be beautiful. Beautiful, precious—ah, God's world!

No, really—he was not he—not the same Eliah Kotlik, but someone else: a little boy running away from school or a visitor from another country. He hummed a hassidic tune and walked away smiling with delight. He saw Zipkin's Pharmacy opposite him, in an alley rendered impassable by a large puddle of water that filled it from end to end. He came to a halt, stopped singing, shook his head and said, using a turn of phrase which his father, of blessed memory, had often used when in a merry mood, "Not all that glitters is gold. For example—the pharmacist's bald pate, ha, ha, ha!"

He had something else to say about him, "Why does he need his pate, if he has no head?"

Folks hated Zipkin, the old pharmacist and the sole rationalist[12] in town. They hated him, not because he looked like a "German"[13] and spoke the language of the Czar, but because of his foolish ways. He was commonly held to be a fool. Jewish folk are clever; they forgave him his heresy but not his foolishness. They elaborated upon it, probed into it over and over again, with relish. It is impossible to relate all the things which they said, as folks generally do, behind his back—things which he did and things which he did not do.

But he did have the habit of screwing up his expressionless face into a scowl whenever he ran into a Jew, and of screaming so loudly in his high-pitched voice that the spectacles on his nose trembled, and his bald pate turned red as blood,

"*Wo Polk Yeva! Wo Rutu!*" Which is to say, "Draft that Jew for the army and make a civilized man out of him."

He also had another characteristic: He was critical of all Jews and of their ways. He would reprimand them severely and try to win them over to "civilized ways." They should become like the Gentiles, as he, Zipkin the pharmacist, had done,

"Let's put an end to Volozhin and Medzhibozh![14] he would fume and sweat, waving his arms above his head as if stirred by the wind.

When that happened, anyone who saw him, if he were level-headed or even somber could not but burst out laughing.

"A farce!"

Eliah Kotlik stood in front of the pharmacist's alley and its puddle of mud and enjoyed himself. He felt good. His mouth broaded into a sneering smile, his eyes grew bold and his hat slid down on his sidelocks. Standing as he did, gay at heart, he lifted his fist and shook it at the pharmacist, "You just wait," he called out in a brave whisper, "We'll show you civilized ways."

12. Hebrew *maskil*—enlightened one, modernist.
13. He wore European dress and not the caftan.
14. Volozhin, seat of a talmudic academy in Lithuania; Medzhibozh, a hassidic center.

He was not satisfied until he said in an acid whisper,

"Hey, you fool with a diploma, you certified fool. Strong enough to stand up without prayer only after you've eaten your breakfast."

Having said this, he turned on his heels and went merrily on his way, his heart as gay as a psalm of victory.

He took step after step chuckling in calm delight. "Ho, ho, ho—fool until judgment day."

Then he raised his eyes and saw Reb Kamatzel in the distance coming toward him and he was seized with panic.

This Reb Kamatzel was called Reb Kamatzel because of his shape.[15] He was a short man, as tall as he was broad—his neck sunken, he was apple-faced, with eyes of heavy, faded blue. He owed Eliah half a rouble. He owed him the money since before Hanuka[16] and had not yet repaid him. Obviously not all who wish to pay off a debt are able to do so.

Eliah, who knew that he was hard pressed and simply had nothing, tried to avoid him so that he would not appear as if he was deliberately going to meet him. His eyes measured the street for possible alternatives. He dashed from side to side, backtracked and turned into the pharmacist's alley. In his panic he jumped into the stagnant puddle which had been contemplating the heavens and stringing together celestial clouds row on row. Noisily, he pushed aside the ball of the sun, kicked the edge of a faded cloud, bent over and stood in water up to his knees with his back toward the street and saw the reflection of his eyes in the glow of the heavens.

At that very moment, the priest's wagon arrived on the scene quite by chance. The priest was on his way back from a sick call in the country, and sat on a straw mat in the back of the wagon dozing contentedly. Kyrilla, his servant, sat up in front in the driver's seat just behind the horses. When the horses reached the middle of the puddle, they lowered their heads to drink some water.

Kyrilla leaned toward the puddle and shouted, "Look, father, take a look at what's inside the puddle!" The priest opened his eyes,

---

15. The *kametz*, a Hebrew vowel-sign, is shaped like half a cross.
16. A holiday which falls in December.

looked, and, lifting the full breadth of his beard to the sun, burst into a loud, raucous laugh, "Ho, ho, ho." Again he looked down, placed his two plump hands on his knees and shouted, "Ho, ho, ho, what are you doing, man, sitting in the puddle like an unclean animal, God forgive my word, ho, ho, ho!"

Eliah ran his eyes back and forth, glancing hurriedly to the side.

"Drive on, Batyushke," he motioned to the priest with his wan hand. "Drive on."

"Abram Bernardovich," the priest turned his face toward the pharmacy, bellowing like an ox. "Please take a look, Abram Bernardovich, at this!"

Zipkin emerged at the sound of the priest's voice, shaded his spectacles and stood like a manikin, his face small and circumscribed, bald pate running down in every direction and teeth beaming in a smile which was at once flattering, stupid and amazed.

"So what's wrong with him, Abram Bernardovich, sitting in the muck, ho, ho, ho!" The priest threw his head back in a great spasm of laughter.

The horses relieved themselves in the water.

"Ho, ho, ho, man, man…" the priest laughed directly into Eliah' face.

"Drive on, Batyushka," Eliah repeated his earlier remarks in a low voice and with a faint movement of his hand.

Kyrilla took up the reins, let his hat slip backward, turned his chin to the side and his rump to the driver's seat. He beat the horses several times until the wagon rolled up out of the puddle in a clatter, splattering Eliah's clothes with the filthy water.

Eliah pulled himself out, churning the water with his feet.

Zipkin stormed and poured a stream of invective and abuse upon him.

"You're a fool," Eliah heckled him in a whisper and muttered to himself, "You doctors and pharmacists, every one of you 'Germans,' you discover all sorts of sciences but you, yourselves, remain absolute fools!"

When he reached dry land, he stopped, shook out his shoes

which were dripping with water, and bent over to wring the cuffs of his trousers.

"An end to Volozhin and Medzhibozh," he heard the pharmacist angrily shouting behind him.

"Wait," said Eliah to himself as he scraped away the mire which stuck to his legs with a piece of wood, "Wait, I'll show you civilized ways."

After he had cleaned himself up a bit, he retraced his steps. He had changed his mind about going to the *heder*; he said to himself, "It's late and the children will have gone home for lunch." He also surmised that by now his wife had calmed down and was worrying about him. Besides he was hungry, for he had not eaten a thing all day long.

He walked on, musing to himself, somewhat peeved but at the same time somehow pleased,

"Oh Reb Kamatzel, the evil ones blew you in my direction!"

As he was immersed in these thoughts, the Rabbi, who was on his way home, ran into him, swaying like a boat groping its way through a fog. He was thin and self-effacing like a small religious tract. The gray hairs of his beard in disarray, like a jumble of type, flew about in the sun. His eyes sparkled with mysterious glosses on the sacred texts, and his sickly face was aglow with the light of the Talmud and its Commentaries. One of his shoulders slouched downwards, the other was raised upward, like the two pans of a scale, and as if he were holding his holy congregation and the whole of the house of Israel in the balance.

Lifting his eyes, he became aware of Eliah and saw that he was filthy with mud. He stood amazed and asked him,

"Where did you get so dirty?"

Ashamed, Eliah did not reply.

The Rabbi repeated, "What happened to you? You look like you've been walking in a pond for three miles. Have you turned fisherman?"

Eliah fixed his eyes to the ground and stammered,

"Uh, uh, a debtor, I saw,...uh...uh...I was a little frightened

lest I should be seen as a harassing creditor and violate a severe commandment," and he told him the whole story.

The Rabbi bent over and began to clean the cuffs of Eliah's
trousers. Eliah looked down and seeing what the Rabbi was doing
became alarmed. He quickly pulled one leg away, hopped and then
pulled away the other leg and began to stammer in confusion,

"Rabbi...Rabbi..."

The Rabbi grabbed his legs and stopped him,

"Stand still, stand still...not a scholar to be sure, but yet...A
man should be careful about his dress."

So he stood, bending over him and shaking out his clothes,
scraping, rubbing and sighing from the very depths of his heart,

"*Oy! Oy!* And I shall throw holy waters upon ye and ye shall
be pure...holy waters...and ye shall be pure."

Translated by Ezra Spicehandler

Scenes from
the Holy City

An excerpt from a novel

1. The Case of Nissim

In a little while Moroshka left the barber, his face bright, shining and with all unnecessary adjuncts removed, his eyebrows bristling like ears of corn and his nose darting about like a kid run away from the pasture. Hardly had he taken more than two or three steps when the shoe-shiner from Urfa began banging his brushes on the box and ringing his bell to gain his attention, his teeth white, his eyes smiling and his face all lit up as though the sun of righteousness shone upon him.

"Shalom, mister!" he greeted him joyfully.

"Shalom, Nissim, Shalom," Moroshka turned toward him and responded as affably.

"How are you?" Nissim asked him affectionately, taking pleasure in his question.

"So-so…" responded Moroshka with the classical response of inhabitants of the Land of Israel.

"'Everything will be fine!" Nissim forcefully informed him.

"'Everything will be fine!" confirmed Moroshka, like a pupil repeating his teacher's lesson. Maybe you'd polish me my shoes,

Nissim?" "And why not?" Nissim flashed white teeth at him. "I shall see the work of His Name and His deeds…"

"Well, what's the news?" Moroshka set his foot before him on the box. "How is business?"

"The Name will show mercy…" Nissim reassured him.

"Have you paid the rent yet?" asked Moroshka.

"How can I pay, mister?" Nissim took his implements in hand and sat staring up at him. "How can I pay?"

"And what will the end of it be?" Moroshka asked one of those questions to which there can be no reply.

"Do I know?" answered Nissim, then added, "His Name will show mercy."

"And the landlord keeps quiet?"

"Blast his name and memory, but he makes me trouble! You see this?" Nissim pointed to a bruise on his head.

"What's that?" asked Moroshka, peering at it.

"What's that?" smiled Nissim, busy with Moroshka's shoe. "That's where the landlord gave me a hit over the head, blast his name and memory! Every day he beats the living daylights out of me…"

"He has no right to hit you!" Moroshka grew stern, his face becoming dark and the knot between his eyes twitching and twisting.

"What would you do, my dear?" Nissim turned his eyes on him smiling, his hands busy at their work and the brushes flying hither and thither.

"He has no right to hit you!" Moroshka boiled over, half-standing half-hopping upon one foot. "He's entitled to take you to court, but not to hit you!"

"And the court's better?" Nissim studied the shoe carefully, rubbed and massaged and smoothed away, then set his brushes flying joyfully and skillfully once again. "He wants to bring a case…"

"Who is that landlord of yours?" Moroshka raged, all prepared to slay, destroy and annihilate.

"Who knows what pest he comes from…" Nissim beat his brushes on the box as a sign that he should shift to his other foot. "I think he's a Mugrabi. After all he's a poor unfortunate devil too. I sit

176

in his house, his own house, and don't pay. It's not as if he doesn't have the right...!"

"And your wife?" Moroshka shifted from one foot to the other as he skipped from subject to subject.

"May God show mercy..." Nissim looked down at the shoe on which he was engaged.

"Sick?" Moroshka lowered his voice and face.

"Passes blood, mister," Nissim stated apologetically.

"And the children don't go to school!" remarked Moroshka as of something obvious.

"I have raised children and brought them up and they have transgressed against me," quoted Nissim, energetically waving his two brushes hither and thither. "Hadassah hospital wants money, the school wants money, they all want money.... What can I do?"

"Have you been to the Social Welfare?" Moroshka sighed from the bottom of his heart.

'And what?" Nissim beat against the box as a sign that the work was completed, and replied with cheerful face. "They don't want to help. They got a bed and mattress from an old woman who died and that's all."

"Ah Nissim, Nissim..." Moroshka gazed at his double reflection in the pair of polished hammerheads on his feet.

"What, mister?" Nissim was strangely satisfied.

"Ah Nissim, Nissim, how will it all turn out for you?" Moroshka asked simply.

"I should know?" Nissim turned his eyes on him and smiled. "God knows, mister. It'll be fine. His Name will show mercy..."

11. *Jewish Ethics*

No sooner was he done with that Nissim than all manner of cripples and sufferers came along; those sons-in-law of All Israel who depend upon the table of the latter for their sustenance; the men of the Wailing Wall and the Houses of Study and the Cemeteries, who bear the service of Heaven in their hands and Jewish ethics on their tongues.

They began crowding round, thrusting each other out of the way, plucking at his sleeves and coat-tails and gurgling and murmuring and whistling and roaring and waving their hands about. An old man with the stench of a billygoat twitched his lips and moaned and groaned, "Healing, injunction, alms," and an older woman fell upon him cackling, "*Haham, haham.*" Here some bundle of rags, a warped and crooked image-of-God, bound in rags and wound in rags and crowned with rags with nothing but beard and earlocks alone sticking out and separating the nether rags from the higher rags, complained and lamented and keened, "charity, charity." There a dumb woman braying like a blocked ram's horn howled and sobbed oddments of sound; yonder a lame man went dancing before him on his crutch, whistling to him and calling out, "Mister! Mister!"; while a blind man wobbled in front of him declaring the praises of Israel, who are "merciful and the children of merciful ones." An old beldame laden with charms against the evil eye, her face like a squashed pancake, her nostrils dripping and her eyes red and running, raged and started and quivered and made her demands with mouth and hand; while another, complete with all defects and wrapped up like a twilight cloud, wheedled and pleaded and begged, calling down upon him not a single strand but a whole frayed rag-end of grace. The crowd grew larger from moment to moment. One pulled at his right arm, another at his left; one thrust against him and kept on thrusting as though he were trying to dodge payment for a due note of hand, while another went chasing him, dashing after him as though he were keeping his inheritance from him; one pushed against him from behind, while another ran along beside him.

Moroska turned round among them as though in a wheel, dealing with each of their troubles in turn. He knew them all from beginning to end, the one who jumped and the one in rags; he could tell the poor from the needy, was versed in their accounts and bookkeeping, and gave each one the charity which was his due. One received a small gift, someone else a larger and a fourth nothing at all; and he had his reason each time.

"I gave you yesterday," he said as he proceeded to one bundle of rags.

"Charity delivers from death…" the bundle writhed like a woman in birthpangs, and through the rags peered a face like a mole.

"You got something from me as well yesterday," he looked at a squashed, mashed fellow, one of those mighty intercessors between Israel and their Father in Heaven.

"What! Me?" The mighty intercessor stared in astonishment, as though such things had never happened, as though he had not been in the whole country the day before, his face wondering and squashed like a dried mushroom, his eyes looking askance, his nose dripping on his thin beard and his mouth twisted toward the corner of his left nostril.

"Leave me alone!" he turned his face away from a dried-up ancient who had fastened on him and would not move away.

"Charity…charity…" repeated the ancient in a dying voice.

"Please leave me alone! You have two houses and still you go abegging!" He threw the houses in the other's face.

"In the hour of a man's demise," chanted the ancient as though he were studying Torah, "a man is not lent either silver or gold or jewels or precious stones…Mister! Charity…One mil, one single mil…"

Gradually the crowd of beggars decreased and scattered till at last Moroshka stood alone, and began walking on, looking about him from side to side. Suddenly he heard a man yelling behind him. Moroshka turned his head and saw a tiny fellow, quick and nimble and trim, running as fast as he could and waving his hand at him and yelling,

"Hallo! Hallo!"

Whereupon Moroshka stood waiting, wondering meanwhile who that fellow could be who went to the trouble of racing on his behalf.

"Shalom!" The tiny trim fellow burst out in greeting to begin with, cheerfully and in all joyous friendship, his face like the Sabbath eve which also precedes a festival, his eyes swinging to and fro like two little fiery chains, and his pair of eyebrows facing one another like a pair of brackets.

"Shalom, shalom." Moroshka, stared at him in wonder. "What's the matter?"

"Could you perhaps give me alms?" says the other, standing stiff and erect as a ramrod, speaking in one breath and hastily, like a businessman with not a moment to waste, for whom time is money.

Translated by I.M. Lask

The Wanderer

1. *Reb Meshel Yeshel*

In the Holy City of Tiberias there once lived a certain Jew, Reb Meshel, or Reb Meshel Yeshel, as he was called. Folks called him Yeshel maybe just for the rhyme or maybe because "Yesh" means "something," and he was such a little something, or maybe from the acrostic "Yehi Shmo Leolam," which means "Let God's Name be forever." Now this Reb Meshel Yeshel was a Jew like all other Jews, humble and lowly, active and learned and poverty-stricken, head and shoulders shorter than average, with earlocks down to the collarbone and a beard reaching to the navel, and his fringes flapping against his knees and his coat trailing along the ground, and all such signs of magnificence. He was quite fit to be a chief justice in religious and civil cases or a rabbi equal to the greatest of the giants. Since he had the Torah at the tip of his tongue, and the Mishna ever in his throat, he could expound like Moses speaking the word of the Lord, and was as reliable as Samuel in the laws and as Rav in ritual. And needless to add, he had many children, but not a field or vineyard or olive grove to his name; he never ploughed at ploughing-time nor sowed seed at sowing-time, nor harvested at harvesting-time, nor threshed at threshing-time nor winnowed in the wind. But he was like a bridegroom of a good family living at his father-in-law's table, or like a guest in God's good world, with nothing he could call his own. He ate what was at hand and drank what was prepared and clad himself in what was repaired, and confessed himself to his Father in Heaven continually, pleading that He alter the established order of things for him and grant him signs and wonders not known in Nature; and he awaited the miraculous event until Messiah should come, speedily and in our own days, to speed Redemption. In sum and in fine, a fit and proper Jew with all the qualities required and lacking nothing, and the Holy-One-Blessed-be-He, and the Shekhina rejoiced over him, while the angels envied him: Happy in this world, and well would it be with him in the world to come.

Now since a man cannot live without food and drink whether he be rich or poor, and if poor even less than if rich, since no man is in so much need as a poor man, to say nothing of his wife and children, the wife of a poor man being herself like a poor man twice and doubled; and since that time had not yet come when cake, bread and woolen cloaks are destined to spring from the soil of Eretz Israel, Reb Meshel prayed unto Him to Whom all wealth and riches are that He grant him a clean and easy calling wherewith to provide his necessities in this world. And since he was very well thought of on high, Heaven took pity on him and he became a peddler.

Once become a peddler, he went and took himself a donkey from the market, it being the way of peddlers to be borne on their donkeys. He loaded up this ass of his with goods and climbed on top of them and sat on its back and said, "Lord of the universe, my task is to ride on the donkey, and it is for You to perform the miracles!" He became a visitor in the villages one by one, and the hamlets each in turn, and a wanderer amid the wildernesses of Eretz Israel, trading as he went.

Now the donkey was like all donkeys with all the pleasant and asinine ways of an ass. His hoofs were solid, his belly was white, his ears big and his tail short, while his voice was thick. Obstinate he was, and patient and sensible when he wanted to be, suffering and hauling and climbing up and down. He ate thorns as readily as roses, and thistles and nettles like camphor and nard, going around with his poverty like a philosopher with his system; and his works were greater than his wisdom, and he had all the rest of those qualities to be expected of an ass.

Reb Meshel Yeshel, unlike the ordinary Israelite who has no affection for donkeys nor for the likes of them, was far fonder of his ass than was proper. He made him a theme for his fancy, finding in him qualities he had as well as qualities he had not, and praised him as though he were none other than a choice and select ass of the noBlessed pedigree, no ass but a mass miracle, a lion, bravest of beasts, bold as the leopard and swift as the deer.

And since he was so fond of him, and because the righteous man knoweth the soul of his beast, and also because he was always busy conning his studies by memory and therefore had no time to spare, he did not treat his ass severely, nor bother him, nor was he particular with him nor did he speed him on, nor prod him the way donkey drivers prod their beasts. But he handled him easily and let him go his own way as he saw fit, up hill and down vale and along the paths or where there were no paths, heavily and not easily, through all difficulties, and not in haste.

On the first day after the Sabbath, after saying the morning prayers with the congregation, Reb Meshel Yeshel would pack his goods in his saddlebags and load them on the donkey so that they were properly balanced, and then set out to make the rounds of the villages; and on the eve of the Sabbath he returned home. His goods were few and light, enough for a goatload or a deerload, while he, Reb Meshel Yeshel himself, could hardly be considered much of a weight; and they went along together. One proceeded as befitted him and the other as befitted him, one riding and the other ridden; one feeding on thorns and the other expounding whole heaps and hillocks of legality on each separate thorn. For it was the custom of Reb Meshel Yeshel to sit on his ass like a warrior riding a horse, with his belongings balanced on either side, his limbs pulled up tight like to a babe as yet unborn, with his two upper arms on his two knees and his eyes fixed on the Talmud text, all immersed in Torah. He squatted and lovingly studied, so that his ass became a kind of hostelry of the Torah, and proceeded to the spot that his heart did choose. He would complete a tractate and his ass would make holiday for himself. He opened the text where he happened to be reading it and reviewed the section he happened to be reviewing, while his donkey clicked and pattered onward hoof after hoof, half asleep, half awake, feeding as high as he could and reaping rewards at each pace, so that both alike did satisfy, one Heaven and the other the needs of the Ever-Present. And so they went up and so they went down, ass and rider, bell with clapper in one.

And blessed be His Name that this poor man riding an ass did not forsake his calling or interrupt his study to say, "What a fine tree! What a fine piece of ploughland it is!" For he never saw the air of the Lord, nor did he gaze at the heavens and sun or the clouds and winds, or grasses and trees or beasts and birds, or any suchlike idling matters and trifles which distract a man from Torah. But instead he busied himself and strove with the heavenly Torah, and he transformed this corrupt world into an image of the four ells of the Law, and the Holy Land into a replica of those towns and hamlets that are scattered in the Exile and are blessed in Torah; for he was a scholar, both acute and erudite, a complete man, a sheath for the Torah and an everflowing, overflowing fountain.

Because of this in particular Reb Meshel Yeshel was grateful to his ass and loved him even more and magnified and praised him, saying, "An ass is a suitable vehicle for the Torah!"

Yet the best of asses is only a donkey, starting all ears and ending all tail. He has a stiff neck and crooked reasoning and a block head, he is balky and obstinate and blindly determined, and as tricky as can be, with his voice that can be heard a distance of four Sabbath-day journeys and the other marks and signs that are to be found in donkeys. He changes by the hour. Sometimes dreamy, sometimes silly; sometimes good and decent, sometimes crooked and perverse; sometimes sweet and innocent, sometimes rearing and kicking; doing one nice thing and one nasty thing, and swinging his acts and deeds backward and forward like a door. Sometimes, when the time for him to be crazy came, he would obstinately stand still, and then you could not budge him from the spot even if you were to spread out heaps and heaps of oats or beat him with hammers. And sometimes, on the other hand, he would pick up his feet and soar and fly, his chin to the right and his tail to the left and his flanks on either side, bounding o'er the mountains and leaping the hills and cutting capers and braying at the top of his voice—a living peril!—the dead to die and the slain to be slain while he who escapes to survive may live!

He caused Reb Meshel Yeshel all kinds of trouble, and put him through many bitter experiences. Not a few times did it happen that he would start behaving like a perished corpse; and no matter how Reb Meshel Yeshel tried to get him up and back on the job, he would simply not stand, but lay there with his legs outstretched, and indicated as clear as speech that he would lose his hoofs before ever he stood on his feet again. More than once it happened that he rolled over, throwing Reb Meshel Yeshel off, together with all the goods saddled on him, and began rolling this way and that as much as he felt he needed, and then lay couched in the sun enjoying himself. No matter how much Reb Meshel Yeshel cajoled him and entreated him and took trouble about him and uttered a hundred chapters over him, he did not feel in the least bothered or pay any attention to him, merely cocking an eye as much as to say, "Misbegotten she-mule! What you want is a million miles from my thoughts."

Nor only in one place or even in two places do we find him flinging Reb Meshel Yeshel into the thorns and kicking him as he went by, and trampling him a bit and passing on; and but for the merits of Reb Meshel's forefathers which sustained him, he would never have come away whole.

11. The Burial of an Ass

One day Reb Meshel Yeshel was making his way along a path. It was a day in early summer, one of those long days which continue to be noon all the time, and the longer it lasts the longer it seems to lack for nothing; so that you might almost say that it was one of His own days Who lives forever. The place was a desolate spot without plant or seed, without man or beast or bird; a vacant and empty place, a confusion of heaven and hills and unknown country, as in those early times before the earth was inhabited. Heavy, filling the heavens and the earth, the sun rested on the whole world, glowering, burning and destroying, confusing every tree and plant, fevering every rock and stone, mingling all the ravines and valleys with heat and imposing silence all around; rocky silence, white-hot, with everlasting quiet and mysterious desolation. The near, the faraway and the exceedingly distant, all these faced one another and ran counter to one another and piled one on top of the other. Gray, yellow, rose-pink like the almond, and blue as the sea, the mountains rose up and ranged on, with the stern Biblical face to them. Here and there olive trees ventured up the mountain slopes, low and gray and clearly bounded, looking like Mishna texts. Here and there the fields blossomed like legends of the Agada, all a-murmur with late cyclamen and anemone, with tulip and hyacinth, iris and narcissus, birch and broom. Here and there a fig tree stretched out over a rock, while a carob hung on the height of a mountain, lonely, gloomy and stretching aloft as though it were proclaiming: Even though Rabbi Simeon bar Yohai is no longer here, yet his tree is here…

Reb Meshel Yeshel rode in his fashion on his ass and seatedly studied Torah while the ass grazed his way, gleaning his food as he went. Either one was busy with his own affairs, and Reb Meshel Yeshel was enjoying himself and so was the donkey. Reb Meshel Yeshel was pleased that there was so much Torah in the world, laws and works and purification and pollution and forbidden degrees and *pilpul* and argument and explications and differences of opinion and novel interpretations and keen apperceptions; and all the other methods and techniques used in Torah study. And the donkey was pleased because there are so many plants to nibble from in the world; lucerne and clover, wild oats and wild lupine and wild radish, mustard and cress, sharp sage and fragrant thyme, pink savory and leaves of oaks and myrtles and laurels, and similar herbage and greenstuff that are never hoed over or sown, but all grow by themselves.

In due course Reb Meshel Yeshel grew tired of sitting so long. He got down off the donkey and went strolling along very cheerfully since he had learned much Torah; and he went on feeling pleased, with the whole world good and pleasant, as satisfactory as a subtle "point to be determined" in the comments of Maharsha, or a "point to be considered carefully" in the ellucidations of Maharam Schiff. And since the sun was hard to bear and his limbs too lazy upon him and his legs paid no attention to him, he took himself and sat down under a certain oak, to rest awhile and cool himself off in the shade. He made himself easy and sat down, spread out his legs, took the hat off his head and remained only in the skullcap, and a kind of childishness and youthfulness settled about him. Without first asking his permission, his nose began absorbing the scent of the field and finding it pleasant; and unconsciously his eyes played him false and fixed themselves on those handsome and praiseworthy mountains and flowers with all their hues and shades and colors; and he liked the look of them. The flowers won his heart and gave him pleasure, it being the way of flowers to win a man's heart; and he liked them all the more because they cost no money and did not deprive the pocket of anything. Unlike his usual habits and dignity, he behaved triflingly and stretched out his hand to a flower and picked it and smelled it two or three times and set his eyes on it and gazed at its beauty and radiance, its corona and petals and stamens and pistils. While he was sitting like that, inspecting and cautiously feeling it with astonishment and wonder, the way a man wonders when he sees something he is not used to, and has never handled in all his life, the ass brayed loudly and bitterly, so that all the mountains and the valleys quivered. "What kind of thing is this?" Reb Meshel Yeshel raised his eyes and gazed at him. "He must have heard a jennet at a distance, and wants to get at her…"

Before he had finished speaking to himself, his ass jumped up and began leaping and bounding as though a tempest were hitched to his feet, flinging aloft and braying and booming with a powerful and mighty voice that passed forth and was flung back through all the mountains and was transformed into seven voices which filled the whole universe with distress and rebuke, lamentations and bitter weeping. Reb Meshel Yeshel promptly and hastily rose to his feet and dashed off after him, staring at the tail raised high and dashing along with all his strength, shouting,

"*Whoa*! *Whoa*! *Whoa* there! *Whoa* there!" The ass paid no attention and did not stop, but leaped down the mountainside like a billy goat set loose, and vanished.

Reb Meshel Yeshel reached the slope, paused and stood and puffed and blew and panted and looked round in every direction. But there was no ass and no jennet, no voice or echo, nothing but a silent and hushed world, all as though there had never been any donkey at all.

So Reb Meshel Yeshel began to put himself to the bother of climbing down the steep mountainside at the risk of his neck, clambering from plant to plant and from rock to rock and yelling and calling; and between one call and the next wishing him sixty bereavements and seventy-seven angels of punishment and evil demons. And so he made his way between the plants, gripping and letting go and forcing his way through and flinging himself about and howling all at once. At last, and by chance, he looked down toward the dry watercourse running along under the mountainside and—lo and behold!—the ass was lying there with legs and head all outstretched, like an idler in the bathhouse who has sweated sevenfold when the sun shines on him and all kinds of fine bedding are spread out for him and he feels at ease in the world.

But Reb Meshel Yeshel felt full of fury, fit to murder and slay. "Oh, may your hide be skinned off you!" he burst out cursing. "Ah, may your hoofs go slipping everywhere! Are you still as contrary as ever, playing your tricks on me and lying stretched out like a carcass so that I should tire myself out and lose my breath and life on your account! Get up, you carcass, up onto your feet, blast you and curse you!"

And down to him went Reb Meshel Yeshel to heave him up shamefully, and he got at him from behind and kicked him with his foot, crying in anger and sheer vexation of spirit,

"He's a devil, a very devil! May his skin be wrapped over his face...not like an ass born to a jennet!"

But still the donkey did not stand up, and merely quivered and shuddered.

"Why's he doing this?" Reb Meshel Yeshel did not know what to think but went round and looked at him from the front; and there the poor beast was, quivering and perishing with a broken back and broken legs and dimming eyes and a bloody froth over his mouth.

Reb Meshel Yeshel became alarmed and his very spirit sped from him. He bent over him and raised his head and pulled his tail and shook him and pushed him and pulled at him; and while he was so busily engaged with him and doing his best to get him to stand uptight, the donkey stretched out his legs and made an end of it. After that, do what he liked but there was not a sound to be heard out of him. That ass with all his worthy deeds had departed from the place of action to the place where there is no action, from the place where they load to the place where there is no loading. Henceforward, all the donkeys in the world might come, but they would not be able to raise him to his feet again.....

Alas for the pilot who has lost his boat, and alas for the peddler whose ass is broken! Frightened and confused, with gloomy eyes, limp hands, and a twisted mouth, Reb Meshel Yeshel stood there unable to believe what he was staring at. After a while, having gazed and seen how irrefutable the facts were, he felt full of pity for that great servitor who had departed the world and full of pity for himself left abandoned and orphaned, neither living amid the living nor dead amid the dead, and lacking any idea whence he would eat and drink and how he would study Torah.

"Oh, dear, good and faithful ass!" He moved away from the corpse and began bemoaning it in his bitterness. "For you toiled with all your four legs yet never even had as much as a hoof full of pleasure! For you conquered and subdued all these lofty mountains before me and carried me as you rode over the high places of the land, traveling to and fro about my living and the living of my household! Who can bring me your substitute! Who can bring me an exchange for you! It is hard for me to part from you..."

He placed his goods on his own back and started off, but then he turned and looked back at the ass for the last time; and it seemed as though the earth had taken hold of him and he could not budge from the spot.

"How can I abandon him to the beasts of the field?" said he, grieving at heart.

191

He stood thoughtfully considering, weighing the matter and changing his mind and thinking "yes" and "no" and "maybe," feeling bad at the idea of leaving him lying, yet ashamed at the idea of handling him. But within a few moments he slipped his bundle off his back, clapped his hands together in sorrow, and started attending to his dead; thus he toiled and labored to weariness all that day, but did not depart until he had buried him. And furthermore he placed a pile of stones over him, and set him a sign as an everlasting memorial.

III. *A Holy Confraternity*

In the Holy City of Safed lived a saint whom everybody called the Safed Grandsire. He was a famous saint, one of the greatest of his own times, a Kabbalist and godly man, exceedingly holy and dread. Why, this saintly Grandsire merited the visitations of the Holy Spirit, and Elijah was revealed to him. He could look forth and gaze from one end of the world to the other. He knew the speech of beasts and fowl, the talk of palms and trees and herbage and burning coals. He spoke with spirits and incarnations and the souls of the saints who are in the World of Truth. And he knew the particular root of the soul of each and every person who comes into the world, and how many times each individual one has been enfleshed and wherein he had failed and what he had spoiled in each separate incarnation, and what transgression was rooted in him and which commandment was attached to him. Not a secret passed him by; he knew everything. It was his holy habit to spend his time alone amid the mountains and in the wilderness and the caves, in places that no man sees and no man knows; and he practiced isolation and held firmly to His Blessed Name by a restriction and diminution of all thought and all bodily forces, prostrating himself on the graves of the saints in order that spirit might cleave to spirit; bringing a correction to the souls of those dead who go wandering the world of void, and aiding the holy sparks that had fallen into mineral, vegetable and animal, in order to raise them to their source, the place of the Supernal Sanctity. Indeed, these and all the like great achievements which he brought about by his holy wisdom are beyond imagining or explanation.

Now one day this holy and rare Grandsire went forth together with a small circle of his closest disciples, departing from the city on account of a lofty matter known only to him. And he walked the high mountains like an angel of God, mingling with every pace many an Intention and Unification, and in holy and pure fashion expounding the True Wisdom and revealing secrets and the Highest and Most Holy Mysteries, combinations of words and secret alphabets and numerical equivalents, holy names and angels' names, lights and garbings and visages, the secret of the garbing and the inclusion of one divine Sphere within another, and all the balance of the measurements of the spiritual body of the entire Upper and Nether Universes.

His disciples followed him, hearkening unto his voice. In awe and fear they followed, frightened and fervent, their bodies drawn aloft, almost, it seemed, raised a hand's breadth above the ground so that they hovered in the air. Their faces were lit up and burned like fire, their eyes were dim and their minds seething and heaving, filled with the ultimate Naught, the letters that make the Divine Name, the shapes and forms and Sights of God; all as though they were set in heaven, deep within the very heart of the hidden places of the Upper Worlds. The very essence of the world itself seemed to be purified and exalted, as though it were divested of its materiality and had become a kind of exemplar of that which is aloft, the kingdom of the earth, like to the kingdom of heaven. The spaces of the world flamed away and burned like fire; the stones awakened and quivered and emitted sparks and fires and flashes. The clods of earth shimmered like mirrors of what is on High. Couched in the heavens and set cleaving to the heavens, the mountains quivered in the air like many mansions and palaces on High. Each rock was the offspring of Upper Fire, each thorn a creature of the Light. And there was silence round about, silence heavy and deep, above space and beyond time, the silence of heaven and of world without end.

Moved and seething, the Holy Confraternity went down from the mountains, while that selfsame Holy Grandsire, master of secrets, went before them expounding the secrets of the reincarnation of souls.

In the midst of all this he turned his face toward them and said, "Do you know my quiddity and the root of my soul?"

They all stood silent and answered never a word.

Thereupon the Grandsire began reciting in an olden chant, fervently and with holy joy, "Rabbi Simeon wept and said, 'What of Rav Hamnuna the Grandsire, Light of the Torah, whom you have merited to see face to face while I did not merit the like.' He fell on his face and saw him moving mountains and lighting suns in the mansion of Messiah the King..."

Thereupon a great fear fell upon them and they understood the meaning of his words; namely, that he was a reincarnation of Rav Hamnuna the Grandsire who is referred to in the Holy Zohar.

The holy old man went his way before them and they followed him in awe and love, seeing and sensing that every step he was taking was a lofty Work and a Need of the Universe.

Soon he began to discourse once again on the secret of the Mansion of Changes and all their apartments and passages; and from this he proceeded to the secret of Pairing and Gestation, Suckling and Minuteness and Magnitude; and from that to the secret underlying "Now the days of Israel drew near that he should die"; and from thence to the Unification of the "Hear, O Israel" utterance and the Higher Unification and the Lower Unification. And he went on expounding and adding sanctity and comprehension, his face bright with a strange light, austere and uncanny, while his soul was longing and yearning and desirous for that which is high and higher than high. And in the midst of all this he turned his face to his disciples and said to them, yearningly and with great compassion,

"Go to your homes in peace, for many are the ways before you, and many the deeds before you."

His disciples stood like startled men, stupefied for a little while. He held out his hand and bade each separate one of them peace and blessed each separate one in accordance with his own particular needs and interests; and all that he said was very mysterious, as though it were a kind of Will and Testament regarding each separate matter;

and his face kept on changing and altering, and he began withdrawing from them gradually. One of the holy band started and clapped his hands to his head and wailed and wept,

"Rabbi, Rabbi, light of our eyes and source of our hopes, unto whom do you forsake us?"

The old man gazed at them with a face as pale as death, and said with love and joy,

"My sons, I am not forsaking you, God forbid. I am going no more than four ells away from you, departing from this portal and entering by that one."

When his disciples heard this, they sped unto him in alarm crying, "Rabbi, Rabbi, Holy one of Israel and the light thereof, do not abandon us and do not withdraw from us!"

The old man brought his two hands together and shook his head and moaned and whispered,

"It has been of no avail..."

Heaven and earth shook in that hour, just as though the disciples had caused a flaw and a defect in whatever place it was that they had acted thus lightly, thereby bringing about a great Abasement in all the higher worlds and, God forbid, delaying the hour wherein the cycle reaches that point so familiar to the End of Days and the Coming of the Messiah.

Fearing to walk yet equally fearing to depart, they followed their master at a distance of four ells, like men rebuked and banned, removed from His Blessed Will and polluted with all kinds of flaws and slights, their faces bowed low, their spirits alarmed, and their hearts crying out in their midst. If it were possible to say so, the sufferings of all the Exiles had been hung about their heads, Exile of the Shekhina together with the Exile of Israel; anguish of all the ages and pangs of the very Messiah.

Until the selfsame disciple stood beating himself at his master's feet and weeping grievously,

"Rabbi, Rabbi..."

Then the old man gave a long sigh and said,

"Why do you not rejoice when your will has already been done?"

The disciples gave forth their voices in weeping and wailing and keening and lamenting.

The old man turned his head like one who has lost something valuable, and his lips murmured,

"What can I do for you, my sons, when I am but flying dust and ashes, garbed in this body, and in this world, yet perished more than all the dead in the universe?"

And so he walked on with his lips moving almost noiselessly, his disciples following him and weeping as they went. Finally they reached a certain spot of stones and heaps. The old man stood still in awe and fear, and commenced and said,

"Here is concealed and hidden Rav Hamnuna the Grandsire, and this day is the day of his festivity…"

The Holy Confraternity stood still as though the earth were gripping them fast, startled and shaken and astounded, uncertain whether they were dreaming or awake, whether their minds were clear or whether they could not understand what their master was saying. But before many moments had sped, they were beating themselves on the ground and prostrating themselves upon that holy grave, concentrating on all those Intentions which befit the cleaving of soul to soul and spirit unto spirit; and they wept and shrieked entreaties and requests, and they vowed vows and gifts and recited Psalms and prayers, Mishna and Gemara, passages from the Zohar and that other mystic work, the Tikkunei Zohar. Then, thereafter they rose to their feet and set their hands each on the shoulder of his fellow, and set about a dance with much bustle, the old man at their head, dancing each with all his two hundred and forty-eight members like storm and tempest, shouting for joy in a great and terrible voice, with such fervor and devotion as to do away with being and empty the soul so that it might indeed rise ever higher and higher. That was a dance wherein they went up to the heavens and down to the abysses, and its like has never been seen in any Holy Congregation, neither before nor since.

IV. *Great Festivity and the Way of the World*

All this became known to folk and spread abroad throughout the land, so that the entire people were moved from one end thereof to the other, since a father and patron had been found for them in Heaven, one to defend them and speak on their behalf before the Seat of Glory; so that Israel is not abandoned, God forbid. And the wardens appointed over the charitable funds came and devoted themselves to this good and worthy deed and obtained that field and the grave within it for dear and precious money. They brought craftsmen and made a tomb of big stones, and over it they built a House of Study with a large dome upon it; and they made vaulted colonnades and a courtyard round about, and similar provision and big buildings; and they fixed the day on which the Holy Grave had been revealed, and they made of it a day of Great Festivity.

The whole country promptly hastened to come up to the Festivity of Rav Hamnuna the Grandsire, climbing the mountains and wearying themselves in the wildernesses and making their way thither. Group by group and band by band they were drawn aloft, great sages and ignoramuses, pious doers of righteous deeds and men from the street, rabbis, scholars and saints and those of Israel who are empty of deeds, lazy virgins and nervous widows and pilgrim-faring old women, crowds and crowds beyond all number and masses beyond all computation.

The Festivity was conducted with much pomp and circumstance, with prayer and entreaty, kindlings and beacons, song and melody and joyous dances. Women of bitter heart and bitter soul, who were barren, divorced, or those whose husbands had departed and abandoned them, pressed their faces between the stones and yearned before the Blessed Holy One. Nubile virgins, who were sitting waiting to be betrothed and wed, grasped and embraced and kissed each separate stone, and sought to find favor and grace in the eyes of all who saw them. Poor folk shed tears and begged for ample sustenance;

the sick and suffering besought a healing for all their ills. Pious men of good works danced fervently and devotedly, shouting, "All this by merits of the saint!" And all the people clapped hands and responded, "This and the like by merit of the saint!" Saints and scholars of world renown crawled on all fours and cried, "Whither do I, the abject and contemptible, go?—to a place of fire and flame, the very flame of God, with all the Retinue on High here and all the souls of the saints there!" And there was joy and rejoicing, gladness and song in all the worlds, in the heavens above and on the earth below.

Year by year the Festivity increased and expanded and added sanctity to Israel, faith and belief and strength. Many who were blind came to see, many who were mad grew sane, many barren women came to conceive, many forsaken and divorced women found their heart's desire and many old maids came under the bridal canopy, and Israel was benefited exceedingly.

Yet Israel has no luck, for whatever good gifts are given to Israel by the Blessed Holy One, time after time, the Gentiles come and covet and take away from them.

The Arabs, who can do nothing except idle time away, and who always begrudge and have big demands, who neither toil nor trouble nor grow weary and have only what they take from others; who see a sown field and steal it, who see a planted grove and take it by force of arms, who hear of a leader who once lived in Israel and say, "He is ours," or claim of some first-born son of our father, Jacob, "He is our father," or of a sage or saint, "He is of our people". So when they saw that tomb and all the blessings that ensued therefrom, they envied the Jews and brought a great charge against them. For, said they, that tomb was theirs and one of their own, the tomb of one of their holy men named Nunu, Almarhum Alsheikh Nunu, beloved of Allah and one of the Companions of the Prophets. No sooner was this declared than a vast mob gathered and fell upon the celebrators of the festivities, and stoned them and beat them with swords, and drove them away and scattered them in all directions, and took possession and control of the tomb of the saint, and made the spot holy for themselves together with the holy day.

Thereafter the Arabs began coming from the four corners of the land, going up to the holy grave and conducting their *ziara* with much pomp and circumstance, with prayers and songs, oil and candles and incense, with fighting and bloodshed between tribe and tribe and clan and clan; with the neighing of horses and clashing of swords and all the other far-famed deeds and feats and *fantasias*. And the tomb continued to be holy as before; holy to Israel and holy to the Gentiles; holy to the righteous and to the sinners. Many ill were healed, many deaf came to hear, many blind came to see, many idiots grew sane and many barren women conceived; and the world wagged its way as before.

v. *The Martyr*

During all these years Reb Meshel Yeshel was a hawker in the alleys. He went from place to place with downcast face, like a mole burrowing in the ground, through the alleys and passageways of Tiberias. As he went about he would recite Psalms to himself, while his hand would be held out to offer a bundle of ritual fringes, a taper for the *Havdalah* ceremony which separates the holy Sabbath from the profane week, a *mezuza* for the doorpost, or a calendar, and all the like holy and ritual objects and goods of the world to come, the labor connected with which is far greater than the profit. And during all those years it was his heart's desire that the All-and-Ever-Present might make good his loss and restore him a good donkey fit to make a living from without distress, so that he might be seated upon him engaging in the study of the Torah at his ease as in bygone days. Like a tale and legend those early days now won his heart. The further he withdrew from them the closer his thought approached them; so that they hovered before his eyes in all their golden blue like the Hundred and Fourth Psalm or the mystic immensity of the Akdamot hymn which is recited at the Shavuot Festival.

He remembered them as days that led deep within and far beyond the Veil, pleasant and sweet, bright with the light of Torah and filled with Talmudic and Rabbinical studies and flavored with deep *pilpul* and casuistics. One might suppose that they lay couched on the mountains and hills, directed aloft and facing heaven.

Years passed; old age pounced upon him, and not by reason of his sins. His skin began to shrink, his body grew as dry as a sycamore block, his length grew bowed as the knee of the plough, his house emptied of his sons and daughters, and his wife passed away and went to her own place. Reb Meshel Yeshel was left alone and forsaken, without blessing or anything good. One blow would knock him over for good, and what there was of him was broken down far more than it was standing. Yet what sustained him was the fact that he had been freed of burdens and was now able to take a donkey as he wished, to provide him with sustenance in this world and the World to Come; and his dream was fulfilled in a favorable sense.

The day he mounted his ass, it was as if he became a new creature, happy and pleased, with an open face and lofty eyes and smiling beard. What he looked like at the time was an unpopular woman who has just married. He nimbly placed the sack on the donkey and mounted it and rode off, rolling this way and that, that way and this; and joy welcomed him and went ahead, and happiness was all about him rolling before him; while the Sea of Tiberias was a rare sight and vision, and the whole ample air of the day might have come from the Next World. The blowing breeze seemed to partake of a peace which came to him from the Upper Assembly, and the whole of him belonged to a world of spiritual being, fine, purifying, and not of this world of ours. As soon as he left the settled area behind and entered the mountains, he swiftly and without delay produced the Tractate Sanhedrin of the Talmud. He reached his hand to his back and scratched with keen pleasure in the way that great sages have been scratching their backs since time immemorial; and with his mouth he uttered a strange keen sound which cannot be expressed by tongue or words. And without a moment's delay he bounded into the deeps of the Law like a fervent Hassid into a cold baptismal bath; and he began swaying like a palm frond this way and that, buzzing like a bee with the chant and melody of Torah.

For a long while he swayed and hummed and scooped his

thumb through the air, and twisted and writhed and shifted hither and shifted thither, and dived and brought up a difference of opinion between the rabbis with a most fine and subtle piece of *pilpul,* and raised several difficult questions and provided several outstanding and most acute explanations. And so he went on with his study, devotedly and most keenly, and toiled till he was weary and grew hot and fervent, waged wars of argument and brought them to peaceful conclusion, moved mountains and mountain ranges of debate and ground them one against the other.

Until suddenly he heard the voices of tumultuous people. He raised his eyes and saw crowds and crowds, all celebrating, tents set up and horses neighing and asses braying and camels ruckling and people dancing and singing, and boys brandishing the sword, and women trilling with their voices, while powdery dust rose and hid the light of day.

The astonished Reb Meshel Yeshel asked himself,

"What is the business of all these noisy Arabs?"

He took hold of his beard and blinked and looked and sat wondering, just as though he had struck a difficult contradiction to be settled in the works of the Maharsha. First he started moving on, but then it occurred to him to go among them and in a little while sell all the stock he had with him. At that he no longer delayed but turned his ass and his own intention and purpose that way. Once he arrived in their midst, he met with a group of Arabs who were rejoicing very greatly with one another. He began and said to them,

"*Kif halkum, ya assyadna?*" (How are you, O gentlemen?)

They responded, "*Alhamdulillah !*" (All thanks to Allah!)

Then he said he to them,

"What is it you are doing here, *ya akhwana?*" (O brethren) They answered him,

"Here, *ya hawaja,* is the tomb of Almarhum Alsheikh Nunu, the beloved of Allah, one of the mighty companions of the Prophet."

Reb Meshel Yeshel said in astonishment,

"What you say is a great wonder…"

Surprised at him, they said,

"What is the wonder you find, *ya hawaja?*" Reb Meshel Yeshel felt no apprehensions of the popular saying, "Anybody who tells the truth deserves to be flung to the dogs"; nor did he apprehend the saying, "The tomb and what is below it are not subject to examination"; but he gave precedence to his mouth over his ears, and told them,

"Why, thirteen years ago from this day I buried my donkey here!"

"What, what, O evil one!" Their faces filled with fury and they shrieked, "Would you belittle Islam and make our holy place a thing contemptible?"

And before Reb Meshel Yeshel could utter a sound they knocked him down to the ground and fell upon him with their cudgels. And all the crowds of the festival gathered about him at once, and tore him apart and rent him to pieces, and filled him as full of holes as a sieve. And they did not rest satisfied until they hamstrung him and took off his worn shoes from his feet and thrust them into his belly with similar cruel and bitter methods of slaying that they used, destroying him completely.

Days later, when this became known to folk, they went forth and brought his remains down to Tiberias, and there the whole city was transformed into mourning and lamentation. Rabbis and sages eulogized him in all the synagogues of the city, and expounded their sermons with wondrous acuity and scholarship, and roused and awakened all hearts to vast penitence. All the people burst out weeping, all that multifarious population, those full and entire believing ones of Israel; seeing that they were like him, he and they alike multiplying sanctity in the world, and profaning the sanctities of pollution in the world, and held utterly in the hands of the Gentiles who could do unto them whatever might be their will. It was just as though not Reb Meshel Yeshel alone, but all the congregation, were one great victim, the whole assembly of Israel the one selfsame saint and martyr....

Translated by I.M. Lask

Drabkin

T *An excerpt*

here are two kinds of old folk, the easy-going and the trouble-some. The easy-going are that way willy-nilly, for what else can they do except be as easy-going and gentle as a little kid handled by the butcher, or a victim in the hands of the hangman? As for the trouble-some, they are that way because they are like surplus weight, lost and done for, with none to help them out. The whole world's at ease but they are in distress; everybody's marked for life but they are down for death, they alone, they alone, out of all and sundry. Everybody's happy, keeping busy or being kept busy, making war or breaking war; and there's a why and a wherefore about them alone. Everybody jostles them, inherits from them and takes the world over after them, all this fine bright universe, and they alone are left poor and empty, and full of aches, malice and rage.

Malice, and this is an important principle, is more widespread among the old than the young, though the young are more liable to it. And incidentally I may as well mention here that as far as malice goes there's no difference between old or young. Yet in spite of this, most old folk are nastily malicious, cruel as cruel can be, save that they lack their teeth and claws. Otherwise, if they still had their strength, then when their time arrived to depart from the world, some of them would get up from their beds and go and smash everything to bits, and then go back and fall on their beds and breathe their last...

Drabkin was such an old fellow, just like that; old and bitter, more bitter than rue and gall.

Among the Zionists, and particularly the early ones all of whom, as we know, were excellent folk, lovesome merchants, householders and fine and gentle young men, he had been like a king amid his bodyguard. For he had been the wealthy patron, the firm and very active Man of the Movement, who devoted his very soul to the revival of the nation and the restoration of the fallen tabernacle of David. He had prepared many a statute and many a project, all in accordance with the laws of true and proper "economy". He had sped letters to all the great men of Israel, even to Milostievi Gossudar Mnogo-uvashaimiei Gospodin (Most Gentle and Right Honorable Esquire) Doctor Pinsker, Liev Semionovitch. And he would still have been preparing projects and speeding missives, to the tune of the popular songs of the Movement, all about "Hasten brethren, hasten" and "Start our feet agoing"; and he would still be sitting in committee and preaching sermons and bossing over the charity collection plates on the Eve of Atonement, and suchlike army ordnance for our people and for the cities of our God, if only the Revolution hadn't come along and turned everything upside down.

From the time when, as Moroshka used to put it, this great wonder came about and folk just stood up and turned the ladder upside down so that the top rungs were down below and the bottom ones were up above while the ladder continued to stand as before, and folk were glad and gay at this weird and wondrous day and hour and at all the improvements in this improved world,—from that time forth Drabkin found himself right down below.

From that time forth every kind of imaginable trouble came his way, and he underwent more bad and bitter vicissitudes than ever you can think of. All the suffering and anguish of humankind and heaven were his, what with persecution and robbery and violence and being put in prison and undergoing the griefs and servitudes of the Cheka, and being flung about from country to country and from place to place, being exiled ever afresh; till at last he reached the Land of Israel.

At last, at long last! The Land of Israel, eh! *Eretz Israel*...His very aim and purpose, all his long life's dream, the root and substance of his yearnings, his labors and his toil.... Here he was in his own place, amid his folk and brethren, in the heritage of his father's house. Here they all knew him and he knew them all, everybody loved him and he loved everybody, everybody was close to him and he was close to them, one and all. Here, as one might almost say, here he knew each building and cowshed, each path and stone, the whole of the land and its length and the breadth thereof—from Dan unto Beersheba. Here was Rishon Lezion, which the Patron, namely Baron Edmond de Rothschild, had sheltered under his wing, showing it an ever-greater love from day to day, and an increasing confidence week by week. Here was Ekron, that pleasing, handsome and neat settlement with its well of living water in its center and its houses builded therein so magnificently, sixteen houses fair to view, of equal height and dimensions and with spacious windows on all four sides, and with stables for horses and a barn for the fruit of the fields. And here was Rosh Pina in Galilee, where springs of crystal-clear cold water flow from beneath the lofty hills of Naphtali to water her and make her fruitful, and where there were thirty-three houses built of hewn stone, with stables for horses and asses and mules rising in her midst for very glory and its farmers, onetime Hebrew teachers, shopkeepers and pedlars, diligently engaged in their labors with energetic devotion. Here was Petah Tikva, whose farmers were versed in Torah and God-fearing, honorable men who had come with their money in their purses and tilled the soil by the sweat of their brows. Then here was Gedera of the Biluites, the men of the full thought and deed, who had done so much for the settlement of Eretz Israel, being enthusiastic and free, without any family burdens, and who had brought nothing with them save their thoughts in their hearts and their shirts on their backs. And here was Yesod Hama'aleh, founded by the praiseworthy men of Mezeritch, who had set themselves up a settlement with their own money, asking no gifts of men nor loans of flesh and blood....

The entire country from beginning to end was set out and preserved in his heart, tried and tested; aye, no place more familiar in the whole wide world. And does five and forty years of toil and trouble seem a trifle to you? How often he had grown weary, and how many efforts he had made for its sake! How many sermons he had preached and how many debates had he conducted, and how many wars had he waged and won! Aye, none could deny it; he too had hammered a nail or two in here, most certainly! Yes, that much he could say for himself! Yes, it was generally known, everybody and everything knew it, the maimed, the mute and the minor too…

Yes, when he would have the merit of entering Eretz Israel, the whole country would come dashing to meet him and welcome him with honor and glory and love and much to-do, "So you're Mister Drabkin! Mister Drabkin in person!" And they would take him by his sleeves and coattails and proclaim and shout to all and sundry, "Mister Drabkin! Mister Drabkin! You're that Mister Drabkin, that very one, you yourself…" And he meanwhile would stand there and declare and say, "My people and my brethren! Who am I and what am I? Just a soldier, just a simple soldier…" And then he would have to stop talking while the tears gathered and welled up and rolled down into his beard…

"No!" they would respond. "No, you are Drabkin! Drabkin and none other…" And then they would get hold of him and lift him up and take him in and sit him down and rejoice in his presence and deliver speeches in praise of him and speak in his honor, and everything would be fine and happy, rose-pink and grape-clustered…

But before ever those roses had budded they withered, and as for the clusters, before they could even produce their first fruits they vanished, fallen on the head of a lion and the muzzle of a lioness, as they used to say in days of old.

Nobody came to meet him and nobody tugged at his coat, nor did anybody go heralding him in the streets, nor did he land to the sound of trumpets, and in fact nothing at all happened. He might just as well never have been Drabkin, he, that selfsame Drabkin on whom the public weal had depended, the merits of the whole Yishuv,

of all the colonies; for here he was being treated just like anybody
walking along the street.

Oh well, if they never came out to meet him—they didn't have
to. So instead he went and came to them. As they say in our parts, if
Sam didn't come out, then Sim went in; and they never received him.
Or if they did receive him they never showed him any proper respect.
If they did show him proper respect they never paid him any attention, while if they did pay him some attention they simply wanted
to get rid of him. They didn't have the slightest idea of all his good
deeds, they had never heard anything, neither trumpet blasts nor the
faintest whisper. In vain did he announce himself and declare who
he was and proclaim himself and run off his tales and memories all
the way back to Pinsker and Lilienblum, and his qualities and deeds
even unto the days of Herzl and the First Congress, letting it all run
out as though it came straight from the barrel. Nobody would listen.
Go talk to the trees and the stones. Finally, when he had nobody
else to go to and his granddaughter, a girl of about twenty who was
a day-worker, was no longer able to support him, he began to look
around for some way of making a living on his own. But what way
can an old man walking along the edge of his grave find to make a
living? He pushed himself in here and thrust himself in there and
remained all in the same fix.

"The truth is, we're old," said one of the big bosses to him, an
old ruler with a strong arm and as obstinate as a ram among sheep.
"We're old, Mr. Drabkin, our time has passed. All the good stuff has
passed on and only the dregs have remained…. What kind of work
would you like to have?"

"How should I know? Any kind of work in order that I should
make my bare crust out of it."

"How should I know isn't an answer. I don't know either."

"Of all the jobs that you have, is it so hard for you to charge
me with one?"

"What, for instance? Give me some idea and I'll fetch a ladder
or a long stick and reach it down off the shelf for you."

"How I toiled and sweated for the settlement of Eretz Israel.

How I wore myself out! How many nights I spent without sleep and how much money I sank without profiting as much as my little finger was worth! Yet it has to finish for me like this. Less than anybody, down and out, just fit to be sweepings!"

"What has been has been. What you did, you did for yourself. The reward of fulfilling a precept is another precept to fulfill."

"And the whole wide world is worthy and decent, and I'm the only one who is unworthy?!"

"You're quite worthy, but your sixty or sixty-five years of age are a little bit of an extra. Can you get rid of them?"

"Then what is there for me to do?"

To which the boss in question answered nothing at all, merely shrugging his shoulders as much as to say: it's hopeless.

"I labored and toiled, all my life long I toiled..."

"I've heard it, I've heard. Endives, only not today's but yesterday's, and the customers don't want them. That's the way of the world. We are old, crippled and turned down on sight."

"There are all kinds of old folk. There are old folk who draw a salary and old folk..."

"There certainly are. There's everything to be found. Well, Mr. Drabkin, I'm afraid I'm busy. I'll write you a really good letter of introduction and you can go with it to our national institutions, and maybe they'll fix you up with a post. But make sure you don't rely upon it too much, because they don't listen to me and they pay no attention to the words of an old man like myself. Old folk always have the underhand, and as long as they keep on growing older, folk bother less and less about them..."

So Drabkin took the miserable and commiserating missive, as he himself described it, and began beating about from one institution to another, and being sent backward and forward.

His feet gathered plenty of dust in corridors, and his heels left their mark on the thresholds of offices; and to them, namely those institution people, he opened up that entire case of vermin which he carried along behind him, telling them all about his deeds and toil from beginning to end. The folk in question listened with half an ear, talking to him about tomorrows, and speaking in riddles that meant even less than they seemed to. Not now and not near, not near but a little farther off, not a little farther off and nothing clear or definite to say, but come and go and come back and go again, and go here and go there, from head to tail and from tail to the little button on the top, from this one man of the age, may his like never increase in Israel, to that big fellow who is big neither in Torah nor in wisdom nor in good deeds but is merely a big fellow at the Jewish Agency. Of these and their like, said he, King David may he rest in peace said thanks to the Holy Spirit, "Happy the man who has not gone..."

And so he wandered about and went and came back, went gloomy and came back black and became blacker and blacker, going uselessly from day to day and from week to week—long months of demeaning, weary grief. He did not miss a single notable, neither head nor deputy nor official at his officialdom, Sam of the crossroads and Saul of the ferry as they say in our parts. There wasn't a worthless reprobate or scamp of them all before whom he didn't prostrate himself and abase himself and turn himself to nothing. Until at length he began puffing and panting and felt he had had enough. He got up and raised his voice and began complaining and shouting, "How long am I going to go on suffering! When will you stop dragging me about and bossing me about!"

Whereupon some scamp of an attendant who hung round the upper attendants began to fume at him, drew himself up as straight like a stick and yelled at him,

"What are you shouting here for!"

When Drabkin heard this he began to fume and rage and yelled back: "I'm not shouting but shouted at!"

Whereupon the other jumped up from his place, banged his papers on the desk and yelled at him, "Am I holding your inheritance back from you? What are you yelling for here!"

As soon as Drabkin heard this, he shivered and shook and boiled over and fizzed and flared and yelled back,

"Sure you're keeping back my inheritance! If it wasn't for me and what I've done, you wouldn't be sitting about here at your ease! If I hadn't sowed, then it would be a a fine fever you'd have been reaping! If it wasn't for me that devoted my very soul to begin with, then you, you curs of clerks—to hell with you—you wouldn't all be marching about over the heads of the poor!"

The other jumped about this way and that and yelled,

"Don't you go making a scandal here! I tell you this in good plain Hebrew!"

When Drabkin heard this, he responded with a fine piece of good Russian and yelled back,

"*Naplevat!*" (You make me spit!)

At which the other jumped up all over again and put his hand on the bell and yelled,

"I'm going to order them to throw you out!"

When Drabkin heard that, he put his two hands on his heart, raised his head high and screeched back at him,

"Me you'll chuck out?! Me! Drabkin! Drabkin! One of the best of the surviving early Zionists you'll chuck out? That's all I want to see! I'm all set and ready! Pick me up and chuck me out!"

The fellow took his hand away from the bell at once and began twisting his voice about and lowering his tone, while he stormed and raged and erupted over him more and more, adorning him with any mount of vast praises and titles each queerer than the one before, combining name and honor and specifying fathers and forefathers and angels and principalities till he was bristling with titles all over like an ear of wheat, bristling like an ear of wheat, I'd have you know! And by the time he had dressed him up and down and praised him and whiskered him and bristled him all the others were taking a hand, the notables and the clerks, jabbering at one another and running at the sound of the row, all that vine with its clusters great and small, tooting and tarararing and dashing about and squealing and bleating, and backward and forward and creeping all over again. In due course, when they had emptied out all the breath they had and were still rumbling like the last of the thunder as it goes rolling away down the slopes of the skies, one of the crankiest of the clerks raised his voice and shouted at him:

"*Idiot!*" (which is *much* ruder in Russian than in English.)

At which Drabkin jumped at him and shook him and busted him and stretched him and turned him inside out and dressed him up in crowns and diadems and what you will, and told him exactly what and when and where, and how his like and their clique and the likes of them used to carry his things for him to the bathhouse, and so on and so forth, down to the last detail. Meanwhile a Mizrahi busybody came strolling in, a young fellow who might be mistaken for a somebody, with a well-tended beard and a little skullcap on the tip-top of his head, and stood calming him down and stroking him with sweet words and speaking nicely and charmingly, and saying hard things quietly and nasty things without excitement, and got round his flank and surrounded him and assaulted him with verses from the Bible and sayings of our sages of blessed memory; and in between verse and saying he slipped in an open hint, something vague which was yet very clear, that here he had no prospects of work, that there was work only for boys and young men...

Drabkin looked at him mockingly, shook his head two or three times and said,

"Just like the coin that was struck by Father Abraham: An old man and an old woman on one side and a youth and maiden on the other.... Yet still I don't know which is in front and which behind. Maybe it was just the old man who was in front and the youth who came under..."

That was the way he turned it over and gave it back to that Mizrahi fellow who was such a lovable and delightful fellow, in his own language and style; an open hint which declared more than it concealed. Then he turned about and went on his way bowed and broken, his face downcast and his eyes dark.

That was the start of his voracity against notables and officials, whom he devoured with all his eyes, consuming them as though to fulfill a commandment, and gobbling them up just because he wanted to be greedy and because he enjoyed the taste.

It was a harsh hatred that he felt for them, an acute hatred, obstinate and bubbling like some venomous mixture. It was worse than the hatred he had harbored against Jew-haters or against the Bolsheviks. For those had injured his body and robbed him of his property and wealth, but they had left him with his dreams and high hopes, while these had injured his very soul, robbing him of the dream in his heart, the hope of his life and the last ray of light that had shone for him; and had left him as an empty vessel, as a dry palm frond and a vine sprig without any grapes clustering on it; yes, robbed and violated and left without anything. He had nothing in the whole wide world. Everything was gone from him. Things had not seemed like that in his dream, and he had never thought it would be that way…. How he had toiled! How he had labored! For what had he exhausted himself, and for what had he spent his strength—in order to provide something good for those clerks and officials and busybodies and notables and all the other devils and demons? Where was his reward? Where was his good name? Where his standing…? He was like a stranger in the land, in this land for which he had given all his soul, laboring to ensure that it should be settled and built up. Like an alien in the land, among the sons of another people and different race with whom he had no rights, no permission to make a living from them, and no work to do, and no source of livelihood, nothing whatsoever…

The more he tugged at things, the more he went on tugging and found himself stuck. His heart, which had become as empty as a scoured pot, filled up again day by day, ever fuller of hatred and rage, complaining and accusing and puffing up like a snake. Hatred became the main thing about him, giving him spirit and soul, seething within him. It lit up his face and raised his head over the whole earth. Were it not for the hatred, it seemed as though his legs would not have been able to stand any longer, and he would have passed out of the world.

Little by little, from charge to charge and from jab to stab, his values began to change and this whole business of clerks and functionaries was replaced by Eretz Israel as such, so that he saw things being wrong along the whole line. Since folk would not agree with him in all his wholesale charges about the officials, he would wax wroth and switch over to Eretz Israel, and add all kinds of things in his rage and generally reduce everything to rack and ruin. And although he had had no intention of doing this to begin with, yet the fact remained that, once the occasion arose and the words had left his mouth and folk rounded on him and began to quarrel, the issues grew wider and wider and attached themselves to him and held him tight and established an identity with him, so that he was no longer at liberty to get away from them.

In this way suddenly, without wishing it and without being happy about it, he found himself an anti-Zionist, and would tear officials and Eretz Israel to pieces, destroying fence and fenced, wall and vineyard; just uprooting everything as he went. Well, it was only natural that folk girded up their loins against him to wage war, while he girded up his loins against them and made war in return. They laid into him and he laid into them. They smote him with level-headed words and he responded with dangerous words. They set out with trumpet-blasts of joy and fine loud noises off, while he responded with the full defiance that lies beyond despair. Theirs was the assurance of the established and conventional and his the force and might of doubt and craziness, the strength of denial and rejection of one who had belonged to the generation of Enlightenment back in the early days, those early days which had sniffed at a little of Pisarev, at Lassalle and Marx, and who knew a good deal about Rabbi Meir Lebush Halperin, known for short as the Malbim, to say nothing of Rabbi Joseph Albo's *Ikkarim* (Principles) and Maimonides' *Moreh Nevuchim* (Guide to the Perplexed); and who were entirely at home with the works of Abraham Mapu and the pages of *Hamelitz*, the Hebrew weekly of their generation, and the Hashahar, in which modern Jewish nationalism had come to life; a man who had sent love letters to his betrothed and had written to her: *Bezpodobnaya Pavlina* (Incomparable Pauline). For instance, he would set his sharp tongue pounding the Balfour Declaration, and would start playing tricks with it.

"Well, how is it," he would grate, "That Ba'al Peor Declaration of yours?" Or he would sermonize a bit and say, "On three occasions our enemies entered Jerusalem. The first time it was the wicked Nebuzaradan, the second time it was Titus the wicked, and the third time the wicked English…"

Or else he might expound like this, "What good has Eretz Israel done us? None at all, but on the contrary, it has just added another and a greater to all our other troubles, another place where trouble is bound to come…"

That was the kind of remark he used to pass, any amount you like of the spices and condiments of Hell, voiding and denying and rejecting and isolating himself and stripping himself bare of everything and free from everything, tearing off the paint and the powder and the wigs and the window dressing, just being a Zion-hater, a man of quarrels and disputes, opposing just in order to annoy. If you said sacred he would say profane. You say pure and he would answer polluted. If you said, the wind's blowing, he would answer no, the rain's falling. You spoke of the village and he of the big city; if you spoke of the big city and he would counter with the village.

And he had more to do with Moroshka than with all others put together. At first, when Drabkin began to go wrong, Moroshka would come down on him, as they say in our parts, with blue kohl; and Drabkin would up at him and set him in sapphires. Moroshka would be at him and adorn him with sapphires and emeralds, and Drabkin would up and ornament him from the sole of his feet to the crown of his head with all kinds of pearls and chalcedony in huge plates thirty by thirty, engraved in letters ten wide and twenty high; and they would decorate one another and glorify one another, like two starlings on a single branch. But in the long run Moroshka could not bear the brilliance of all those jewels and withdrew from him, merely growling and grumbling to himself,

"Just because those fools don't behave properly, an old josser like him has to go messing about with all this nonsense!"

To which Drabkin responded,

"I can't understand why it is that of all the fools in Israel you alone haven't been appointed a boss or president somewhere…"

After that Moroshka refrained from arguing with him. Drabkin didn't refrain, though, but would bother him and annoy him and tease him and rub him up the wrong way and bother the life out of him at any time of the day or night, at good times and at bad times.

Once when Moroshka was sitting in the café busy with the toils and troubles of Israel and seething and steaming away after his fashion with all kinds of rebukes and tribulations, Drabkin began mocking him and speaking after his fashion, like a prophet in Israel.

"Aforetime in Israel," he blinked at him with those little eyes of his which sat deep in their sockets, "If you had lived aforetime in Israel, you would undoubtedly have been a prophet, a prophet to the Children of Israel. Yes, a prophet of the Lord…You would cry from your throat and shout and curse and lament, and rebuke in the gates, and your lips would be filled with fury and your tongue like a consuming fire, and at the last it would be written down in the writings of the House of Israel and fixed for future generations, for ever and ever…. While now, by reason of our many transgressions, in these base generations, you are nothing more than just Moroshka…To be sure, even then you wouldn't have been too clever, but the Holy Spirit would have been resting upon you and the Divine Presence would be speaking from out of your throat. Of course, as everybody knows, where there's no wisdom, there's where the Holy and Blessed One shows his signs and wonders…. Hmm, there's no difference between a Prophet and Moroshka except just a hand's breadth, and all the difference between the Chosen People and the most despicable of nations is just the width of three fingers…"

As Moroshka did not answer, he turned his face to the ground and croaked,

"The wise and understanding people…one nation in the earth. *Shein ein mol in der erd!*"

At this, one of the people in the café flew out at him in order to stop that foul mouth that was cursing. A second flew out and said things that burned like fire. A third joined in and cut himself his slice, while a fourth came jumping and took, so to speak, a running kick. Drabkin sat there looking at them, twisting about with his slack mouth like a beast chewing the cud, his moustache going up and down and what was left of his face quivering and twitching this way and that. Until at length one of them jumped up from his place, a lean, long fellow with a long, drooping nose and a long, black face and a lofty head of long hair standing over him like a huge wave, and shrieked at him,

"What are you doing here? Why did you go to the trouble of coming here!"

Drabkin raised his moustache toward him, inspected him once and again from the point of his chin to the tip of the wave on his head and slowly, slowly gave back in a weighed and measured voice,

"I made a mistake...I lost my way...yes."

The other shook the wave on his head at him and shrilled his voice and shrieked:

"Go back to the place where you made your mistake and don't come bothering us!"

Drabkin paid him no attention. Instead he stared vaguely, and said in a low, crestfallen voice as though talking to himself,

"Who among us hasn't erred...while we were on the way we lost it, and when we reached the bourne of our desire we saw just how far astray we had gone..."

"You've got the time wrong, Reb Jew," interjected a fleshy young fellow, turning his fattish face that looked like the sun in its setting, and bursting into a whinnying laugh of pleasure at saying such a clever thing by accident. "You've got the time wrong, Reb Jew, ha ha ha..."

Drabkin turned on him swiftly and freshly, just as though he had said something really important and fundamental; then remained sitting queerly thoughtful, his face full of wonder and his eyebrows raised high. But the fleshy young fellow turned his back on him, and hooked his round face on the mountains growing red in the distance, and complacently and cheerfully sipped the coffee from his cup; as though he was taking pleasure in those Eretz Israel mountains, which were shimmering their gleaming radiance at him and happy with himself because he was sitting in the Land of Israel enjoying the coffee he was drinking.

"That's just it!" Drabkin began after a little while, emerging from the thoughts that had occupied him with himself. "Yes, the time.... we've got mixed up about time and place.... Time is the place in which we live, while place is the place where the other nations live...And that's the whole basic might and power of Judaism, and the difference between Israel and the other peoples...No other nation or tongue has that sense of time in all its full depth, from the beginning of the Creation of the World until the end of all the ages, from the first man to the End of Days and from Father Abraham to little Abie down in the bath-house alley, nowhere is it so potentially and actually existent save in Israel alone...yes! And that's our strength among the Gentiles, the strength of eternal Israel...now we have mistaken time for place, the great entirety for one abject little detail, the world of the spirit for this turbid and troublesome matter, the earthly and everyday with all its trifling physical desires and longings...And thence comes danger to Israel, the peril of decline, of decadence..."

The word decadence seemed to take his liking, for he repeated it again and again with a kind of satisfaction and pride, "Yes, decadence, decadence!"

"Decadence, decadence," mocked the fleshy young fellow through the cake in his mouth. "Decadence, ha ha ha..."

"There..." Drabkin disregarded him as he waved his hand toward the West. "There we were above place, in the depth of time, in ages on ages, in everlasting life...A block of eternity in this passing and changing world, one and only, not of this world, differing from all the evil nations, from the very essence of Europe and all its filth; like a rose among the thorns.... Like the Bible among the books of the Gentiles, among novels of nonsense and fornication and all kinds of trifling tales; full of anguish and grief like the Bible, full of fiery faith and sanctity like the Bible, and maintaining ourselves forever like the Bible.... While here we are nothing but like the Gentiles, like this ugly Europe and its nasty culture, its abject, common and empty culture, its culture of artisans and tradesmen busily building up a world of vanity and void, in the homeland of bloodshed and malice and ideals that are petty, nasty and evil as any little crawling vermin.... Here we are in the Space of the world, in the vicinity of the All-and-Ever-Present, so we no longer need everlasting life...Here there are Zionists without Zionism and Jews without Zionism, stripped and empty, free from the need to know the Torah or fulfill commandments, free from all the heritage of the ages...a world of anarchy! All the permanent possessions are canceled, all the values abandoned, all the fences have been breached and it is a duty and a virtue to behave unethically, a duty and a virtue! For the sake of the Homeland and the Land of Israel, for the sake of the unborn and uncreated Statehood of

Israel! This is a Statehood of Gentiles and not a Statehood of Israel! A Statehood of apostates! Yes, yes, of apostates who have abandoned the unity of Israel, or of mean and miserable proselytes who have joined themselves to Jewry with all the deeds of their fathers about them and their swines'-flesh still between their teeth…"

The folk in the café gaped at him, then shrugged their shoulders, smiled at one another and said nothing. Maybe they were thinking to themselves,

"Oh well, those are just trifles! We also know how to run things down…"

Still, the fleshy young fellow felt that he had to wag his tongue a bit in case it grew rusty; and he began to argue the business with him.

"And where, Reb Jew," said he, "was the Bible written, here in Eretz Israel or there among you in Russia or Poland?"

Drabkin swept the sweat from his forehead with his hand and sat as though on the verge of fainting, his face pale, his shoulders slumped and his hands hanging down.

"What bad stuff this people is made off," he began after a little while, in a faint and quivering voice. "First they kill the best they have, and afterward pride themselves on it….not only murdering, but inheriting as well! What have Israel and the prophets to do with one another? The people of Israel are one thing and the prophets are quite another…The prophets are not the mark of Israel, but those about whom the prophets call on heaven and earth, that sinful people, that nation heavy with iniquity, seed of evildoers, wantonly destructive children…. What have you to do with the Bible? It's none of your affair. It's just another missionary pamphlet…"

"Are you a missionary?" The fleshy young fellow stared at him with the innocent eyes of a baby.

"You're a fool!" Drabkin looked at him furiously: *"Durak svin-yatshi!"* (Swinish fool!)

"Ha ha ha!" The fleshy fellow shook with his loud laughter.

For a while Drabkin fumed and poured over him all the vials he had at his disposal, and he accepted all those vials of his and went on sharing in it and shaking and rolling. At last he grew tired of all the vials of bilge, and the shaking and rolling and everything together, and set out to quiet him down.

"Don't be angry, Reb Jew," said he, wiping away his tears of laughter. "I was just joking...I only meant it for fun, ha ha..."

"*Zhivotnoye!*" Drabkin growled to himself in disgust and nausea. "Arrh, *zhivotnoye*. For fun...what has a stupid beast to do with laughter? He hasn't the scent of wit in him, not a sign of acuteness, not a spark of any kind of humor, and he makes jokes! Goes in for wit and wisdom..."

Here he found ample room to attend to him, and began proceeding from light to heavy and from the particular to the general, turning it about on the entire Jewish People and saying what a people of fools they were, how little sense of humor they had, while as for the humor that they did have, how gross it was, low and ugly...

"Where should they have humor from?" he went on expounding. "A people who gave the world the Bible, the Talmud, Kabbalah and Rabbinical literature can't possibly have any humor. It would be impossible!"

"And our sages of blessed memory weren't people with a sense of humor?" One of the café habitue's interrupted him in a tone of wonder.

"Nonsense!" he said with finality. "Our sages of blessed memory were not greater or pleasanter sages than all the sages and rabbis you'll find in Meah Shearim down the road. All of them the same messers."

"Sssssss..." somebody hissed shrilly between his teeth.

"Well, and Rabbi Yohanan ben Zakkai or Rabbi Meir or some other of those oldtimers?" The fleshy fellow added some flavor of his own.

Drabkin took hold of himself and began reciting with the chanting tune of the Talmud student: "If somebody has two sets of daughters from two different wives and says, I have married off my oldest daughter but do not know whether she is the oldest of the older ones or the oldest of the younger ones, or the youngest of the older ones who is older than the oldest of the younger ones..."

Without bothering to recite the whole of the argument on this point between Rabbi Meir and Rabbi Yosi, he burst into a long, low laugh, sitting and laughing, his shoulders quivering and his hands vibrating over his heart.

"Ha ha ha!" The fleshy fellow burst into a spacious and high-pitched laugh after him. "The oldest of the younger and the youngest of the older, the oldest of the older among the youngest…ha ha ha…what's all that?"

"That's a clear passage of the Mishna and it's been commented on by sages and Rabbis early and late…ha ha…and Jews have studied it and studied it and studied it, and said it over and over again for two thousand years…"

"Ha ha ha…that strikes me as really humorous…"

"Two thousand years!" he raised his voice and said with a didactic and pathetic expression on his face. "Two thousand years…yes! Two thousand, two thousand years!"

"Ha ha ha!"

Drabkin looked at that fleshy fellow who couldn't control his laughing, and shook and twitched, and his face turned all manner of colors as though that laughter were punching him in the face and taking him by the throat. It seemed that when he looked he was cut by this decline and emptiness which had come down on Israel; all the way from that upright and happy Jew who, after two thousand years of exile and servitude under foreign powers, proved to be so empty and worthless as all this; and he seemed to be thinking to himself,

"Where are Torah and Commandments to defend us! What part does Exile play—and where are the sufferings to be our protection!"

Thinking his thoughts, he ran his eyes over all those wisps and rags of men sitting at the tables chatting with one another. It would be better for them, it seemed to him, if they had been in the holy and pestiferous congregations of old times, engaging in the dispute with Rabbi Meir and Rabbi Yosi and similar such abstruse subject of contention…

As he ran his eyes over the fleshy young fellow, with his face that was ample and heavy as the udder of a milch cow, he began to wonder at him and stared at him an unconscionable while, as though he were some kind of freak which had come his way for the first time and about which he couldn't make up his mind. The young fellow felt bothered by Drabkin's look, and began to feel more and more bothered, not knowing what it was all about but feeling uncomfortable and uneasy. He could not restrain himself and at last asked, "What are you staring at me for?"

Drabkin did not reply but pecked at him with his eyes, an edged and evil smile gradually quivering his moustache.

"What are you standing at?" the other repeated uneasily.

"I want to see," said Drabkin, thrusting his eyes deep into him and saying slowly and calmly, at ease, as though he were being paid by the word, "I want to see what kind of face a thing has that hasn't even got a face or a look of any kind…"

At first the young fellow was taken aback, but suddenly he burst out laughing.

"Ha ha ha!" He spread his two hands out and raised his head up and laughed as though he were crazy. "Ha ha ha!"

After a while, when the laughter was over and done with, Drabkin leaned over to him and said with an inquiring face: "Who are you?"

"What do you mean, who am I?" The other asked in wonder.

"Who are you?" Drabkin was at him.

"I'm—me."

"Who are you? What's your work? What do you live on?"

"What business is it of yours?"

"I want to know."

"What do you want to know for?"

"Just curiosity."

"Why do you want to know just for curiosity?"

"Have you a questionable trade, or is there something wrong with your family so that you're ashamed to tell me?"

"On the contrary. I belong to a Bilu family. The grandson of one of the Bilu settlers."

"Is that so?" said Drabkin in astonishment. "The grandson of one of the Bilu settlers?"

"Why are you so astonished at that?"

"If you hadn't told me, I wouldn't have believed it!"

"Really?"

"Really. Well, and what do you do for a living?"

"Nothing."

"Clerk or Official?"

"No."

"Leader of your generation? Engaged in public affairs?"

"Not engaged in public affairs either."

"But what then?"

"Why, nothing."

"It seems to me that you are not without compensations."

"Ha ha ha!" The young fellow's round face shone as he shook with laughter.

"Have you any land?"

"Yes."

"Orange groves?"

"Orange groves."

"Building plots?"

"Uhum…"

"Hmm…Now I know what I toiled and labored for, what it was that I used to go for from door to door, adding farthing to farthing for the settlement of Eretz Israel…"

"He's a bit of a broker in lands," somebody who had been sitting to one side interrupted him, and laughed and went on. "He has money, a car and girls…isn't that right, Gideon?"

"*That* to you!" Gideon snapped his fingers at him cheerfully.

And after a few moments he got to his feet and went out, marching away with erect head and upright face, brave and fine, and boss of the whole wide world.

Drabkin gazed after him with a queer and wondering expression on his face, staring and wondering and sitting until he had vanished from sight. Once he had vanished from sight he sat back in his chair, supporting himself in sheer fatigue of the senses, almost faint with weariness, his eyes sad and his face puckered and pale.

After a while he raised his yes, and a faint twisted smile took hold of his moustache and spread it this way and that.

"Well, well," said he gaspingly. "And what follows?"

Somebody was sitting just then delivering his particular lesson of the day, a level-headed settled fellow who knew all about politics, a heavy-set man with his head deep between his shoulders and a face like a swollen lump of dough, and tiny eyes and thick little fingers. He pretended not to hear anything, and went on calmly and importantly,

"They have not carried out Article Two, which requires the Mandatory Government to establish political, economic and administrative conditions in the country which will ensure the establishment of the Jewish National Home. They have have not carried out Article Six, which requires the Mandatory Government to encourage close settlement of Jews on the land and to allocate for this purpose government lands which are not required for public purposes. The Government has deprived us of our share in public works, in the ports of the country, in the health and educational budgets, in the security forces, in the Civil Service—"

Drabkin straightened himself, shifted, sat still and turned his eyes this way and that like two police agents.

"Let the government alone, hang it all, hang and damn it all!" he cried quickly as though he had an opportunity for being satisfied at something. "The Government has deprived…well, and how do we stand? Don't we deprive one another? How are things run overseas? How many Jewish workers are there in them and how many Arab workers, eh? How do you come making demands of others? And by what right, eh? So adorn yourself before you begin ornamenting others! But none of all this is of the least importance, it's all trifling. Yes! Did you see that fellow who was just here? The Biluites, what! A grandson of a Biluite…That's the sign and the symbol, the example for the coming generations! The fathers are idealists and heroes, pioneers who go before the people to show them the way they should follow and the deeds they should do…Fervent zealots, full of dream and vision, the best and finest, tararara, tararara…flame and fire, scattering sparks…bringing a brave new world into being…and the sons are speculators! Eh, speculators, just plain profiteers! That's the stamp and sample, the end of all the wonders, that's the dream and its fulfillment! Well, and what about their grandchildren? The grandchildren of the farmers and the orange growers? And the grandchildren of our own Biluites, the people of the *kvutzot* and *moshavim*? Can you rely on them? Can you be so sure that they'll stay on the land, that they won't come to fool about with law or medicine, or business agencies or shopkeeping or musicianing or painting or dancing or singing, and other such clean and easy jobs? Are you so sure about it? Are you so certain? I'm not so sure! Not in the least…I know all these qualities which you can find among the Jews, oh I know them well, far too well! What are you turning up your noses for? Is it impossible and beyond the bounds of reason?"

"Absolutely!" Moroshka could not contain himself.

"Absolutely impossible?" Drabkin turned his eyes on him and sat gazing at him, waiting, his moustache quivering as he smiled to annoy. "And why, for example?"

"Just so."

"Just so? Can you see into the future? You don't want it to be so?"

"I don't want it to be so."

"Ah, a satisfactory reason, basic and fundamental…And yet all the same! What's the difference between them; what *is* the difference between these children and those children of their fathers? What's more, I'll go further. What's the difference between you and them? You are fine fellows and they are fine fellows. Is it just that you work in town while they work in the fields? Were your fathers and forefathers *effendis,* while they and their fathers were *fellahin?* Is Tel Aviv good enough for you, with cinemas and cafés and concerts and theaters and libraries and University, all good enough for you, while the cowshed's good enough for them? And what will you do when the time comes and the children revolt, as they do all the world over, against their fathers and mothers, and refuse to agree to remain sunk in ignorance and dig up the fields and do charity and grace and love and kindness with the Jewish People? And what will you do when the time comes that they cut out all the ideals of the fathers and there's an end to all that romanticism of work, to that sanctity of labor and love of labor and philosophy of labor and when they stand up and say, what's all this business of work and labor got to do with us? Just look how near this town is for running away to…It isn't as though I were preaching you my own interpretation of the Bible. I'm telling you actual solid facts, things which go on like that the whole world over. And if it's like that the whole world over, then isn't it certain to happen with us? Why, even now you can already find the children of our farmers strutting about in all the capitals and big cities the world over. I saw them in Berlin and I saw them in Paris and Vienna, and there are plenty in London and New York and Tel Aviv, and in the offices in Jerusalem. Even now if you have to get workers into a village, you won't be able to find them, even though the whole of Tel Aviv may be swarming with idle workers from one end of the town to the other. And is that nothing? Isn't that something which needs to be examined a little more closely? We poor miserable creatures, the early Lovers of Zion, we devoted ourselves to nothing but building up villages, one colony and another colony, one cowshed and another, one field and then another field, a settlement in Upper Galilee and a settlement in Lower Galilee. But as for you, who belong to the National Home and the Jewish State, you build another urban quarter and another fine big walled building, one bank and then another café…What have you done so that the village shouldn't collapse, so that the whole foundation on which this shaky building stands shouldn't crumble, so that the soil shouldn't give way under your feet? How much land have you and how many villages have you? How many people have you in town and how many in the villages? Why, if a mere ten or a dozen villages were to be taken away, all of you might as well be flying in the air, and where would that leave you and the whole of the Jewish National Home?"

That was the kind of bitter thing he said, every phrase worse than what went before.

Moroshka partially agreed with him, but disagreed far more; and disagreeing far more he went for him hammer and tongs. The argument moved from one thing to another, ranging from subject to subject until they had got in one another's hair and were in the middle of a major debate, going butting at each other, sparks flying from Moroshka's mouth to Drabkin's mouth and back again, everything boiling hot.

"Oh nonsense," Drabkin rejected all Moroshka's proofs and all the arguments he brought against him, speaking with his soul weary and worn down inside him. "All the trouble you're going to is useless, just empty and vain…Something you're putting up just for a little while, against our will and wishes…"

"It seems as though the Gentiles didn't beat you enough," the well-balanced fellow who knew so much about politics intervened.

"They beat me, plenty and to spare, and they haven't stopped beating me yet. They beat there and they beat here. Beating Jews is law and justice, international law and order," replied Drabkin as though he were giving him something solid to get along with. And while speaking he raised his eyebrows and went back again to his starting point.

"It's just a waste of energy. In any case the Jews will leave the country and go away. There's nothing more obvious than that finish, it's clear as daylight…I see it happening. I can see it…Fifty years' time, a hundred years' time, when there will already be a majority and the country will be properly built up with all your hearts' desires, they'll just drop everything and scatter themselves everywhere…Not through Nebuchadnezzar nor yet by Titus—it'll be without either of them, just simply happening, of their own sweet wills…"

These perilous and terrifying words, which scorched the ears to hear and which the heart cannot accept nor the mind put up with, made their impression on the folk round about. They all sat jaw-dropped and musing, without a word to say. Unacceptable though they were, they seemed to penetrate. Just as though he had seen right through them and had told them what they had deep, deep at the very bottom of their hearts, those concealed things which go on in the heart in secret, not even being thought too precisely or grasped, having nothing tangible about them, which cannot find clear utterance; not thoughts or feelings but the tremor of thoughts and feelings, the scent and savor of thoughts and feelings, nothing more than their implications and ultimate meanings…

For a while they sat as though they were dumb, as though he had bewitched them. It seemed that matters must have become clear to them, and that they could see by some sixth sense how simple it all was, how obvious and reasonable. There was nothing clearer than this in the whole wide world. They would go…They would drop everything and go away…If a little profit should turn up, they would pack up and go at once…scattering to all the four winds of heaven, from one end of the world to the other…back to Russia, Poland and Germany…back to the hardships of the Exile and the servitude of foreign governments, starting the old, old wheel turning again.

Until Moroshka started out of his own private thoughts, stood up and noisily shoved away the table that was in front of him, crying, "It's false! Nothing of the kind will happen here!"

All the others seemed to wake up after him, crying out in confusion and with much todo, as though they wished to confuse themselves, to do away with those deep-lying thoughts. "We are just at the beginning of things, we are, and not at the end or anywhere near…"

"I can't make out what you're talking about at all…" the level-headed fellow who knew all about politics intervened calmly and level-headedly. "We're having to worry about our political relations with England, and not about ultimate objectives."

He was about to start laying down all that huge tractate of politics in front of them when Drabkin suddenly flung out his hands on either side of him, shaking, and shouted with twisted face and gasping, trembling voice,

"*Dayte mnye metlu! Metlu! Vitchistit avgeievi…*" (Give me a broom! A broom! To sweep the whole mess away!)

And as he cried out he swayed this way and that once and again, slipped from his chair and fell with his face to the ground.

Moroshka bent down over him and shook him. He did not move.

"Doctor, fetch a doctor!" he whispered in alarm.

"Doctor! Doctor!" The word spread on either side. "Is there a doctor anywhere here?"

At this a dozen fellows from Germany, who had been sitting in the café, stood up and hurried over from every corner, thin and fat, long and short, pot-bellied or long-limbed, all of them doctors par excellence, all of them highly skilled specialists; and they gathered in their multitude.

One of them took Drabkin in hand until he revived him. Once he had come to, Moroshka helped him up and into a deep armchair. Drabkin sat confused and at a loss, his beard dishevelled, his eyes turning in all directions, as though he did not understand what had happened to him.

"*Nichts gefressen hat der Mann* (the fellow hasn't had a bite of food)," the doctor said looking round with a gentle, wide smile. "Just give him something to eat and he'll be right as rain."

Moroshka ran to fetch a glass of milk. But Drabkin pushed the glass away, took his hat and got up to go. Moroshka wanted to support him and accompany him, but he refused and went along on his own, weak and pale, his back bent and his eyes cast to the ground.

Translated by I.M. Lask

The Sermon

Yudka didn't talk much. He never spoke in public, never argued at meetings or at conferences, rarely opened his mouth when anyone else was around. He was reputed to be a man of few words. And though he was not what he was reputed to be, his reputation grew on him, so that in the end he quite lost the knack of saying anything coherent out loud, no matter how trivial or important it was. Which was why his comrades in the Haganah were surprised when they heard that he proposed to address a certain committee whose existence was a secret to all but a chosen few—especially since the committee had been convened that day solely to hear him speak.

The committee members, all stout and stalwart men, sat in a single row at a green table on either side of their leader. They stared at Yudka curiously, as though waiting to witness some prodigious event—all of them, that is, except their leader, who looked coolly down at the table, whether distracted or indifferent, it was hard to say.

The Haganah leader said a few perfunctory words of introduction and then fell silent so abruptly that it almost seemed as though he had not spoken at all and were alone by himself in the room.

Yudka sat as stiff as a board, a petrified look on his face. He could not remember what he had meant to say or how he had planned to begin.

It was hard to believe how frightened the man was. This stonemason who could smash a rock with one blow, who was not afraid to encounter the enemy singlehandedly on right patrols, had completely lost his nerve before a gathering of his own friends.

After what seemed a very long pause, the Haganah leader declared again to the green cloth covering the table,

"Comrade Yudka has the floor."

Yudka cringed and rose to his feet. Beads of sweat appeared on his forehead.

"You wished to make an announcement," the Haganah leader reminded him, regarding him crookedly from the side. "Talk. We're listening."

Some of the committee members glanced down or to the side; others stared off into space.

Yudka mopped his brow with a hand and said in the soft drawl of a Jew from southern Russia, "I didn't come here to give a speech. I just wanted to say something important…what I mean is, I really shouldn't say anything at all…do you know what it's like to have to stand up and speak when you shouldn't?"

He looked at the men sitting at the table. An injured smile trembled on his lips.

"But I must!" He stared at the walls of the room and his face clouded over. "I don't understand a thing. I've stopped understanding. I haven't understood for years…"

"What don't you understand?" asked the leader gently, like a judge who is used to all kinds in his court.

"Everything!" cried Yudka excitedly. "Everything! But that's nonsense. Let's not go into it now. What I want to know is: what are we doing here?"

The Haganah leader didn't follow him. "Where?"

"Here! In this place. In Palestine. In general…"

"*You* don't understand?" scoffed the leader, lifting his two hands uncomprehendingly. "I'm afraid *I* don't understand…"

"That's a different kind of misunderstanding," answered Yudka. "You just say that to make fun of me."

One of the committee members smiled broadly and drummed with his fingers on the table. Yudka could feel him snicker, but he stared at the floor and pretended not to see.

"Get to the point," declared the leader. "Stop arguing and say what you have to say."

Yudka roused himself. "I wish to announce," he said in a low voice, "that I object to Jewish history..."

The committee members looked at each other in astonishment. The man who had smiled before, now burst into uncontrolled laughter.

"I don't respect Jewish history!" said Yudka again, as though unable to advance any further. "Except that it's not a question of respect. It's a question of what I said before: I object to it..."

The same man laughed again and this time the others joined in.

Yudka turned to him.

"You're laughing at me," he said, lowering his voice still more until it assumed an almost melodramatic tone, "because you took my wife away from me..."

A catastrophic silence descended on the room. The man who had laughed half-rose to his feet, then fell limply back in his chair and nervously dropped his eyes.

The Haganah leader struck a gong four or five times. Then, too taken aback to know what else to do, he struck it three more times.

Yudka waited for the echo of it to cease. "I imagine that he's that way because...well, if I were in his place I'd laugh every time I saw me also...not straight in my face, but like that...it's simply a different way of doing it. I couldn't help it. I wouldn't dare not to...because he can't simply do and say nothing...that would insult me even more...much more ! To say nothing of trying to talk with me about literature, for example, or having me break down in front of him and cry. I can't explain it any better, but it's perfectly obvious. I've thought it over and that's my conclusion, though it really doesn't matter very much..."

There was absolute silence in this room.

At last the leader raised his brows and said with a brusque, irritable attempt at humor, "Comrade Yudka, I have to call you to order. If you have something to say, please say it quickly and stick to the point. If you want to lecture about history, try the university."

"But it is to the point, it is!" Yudka reassured him with a smile. "I wouldn't know where to begin without history. Believe me, I've thought a great deal about it—all through the nights that I've been out on patrol."

The leader shrugged and gestured unfathomingly with both hands. "Then talk!" he commanded bluntly.

For a moment, as though he were the sudden victim of bad luck, Yudka almost panicked once more, just as he had at the outset. "You already know," he began, coughing an uncertain apology in his throat, "that I object to Jewish history. Have a little patience with me and I'll explain why…. In the first place, I must say that we really don't have a history at all. That's a fact. And that's also…how shall I put it?…in a word, that's where the skeleton tumbles out of the closet. You see, we never made our own history, the Gentiles always made it for us. Just as they turned out the lights for us and lit the stove for us and milked the cow for us on the Sabbath, so they made history for us the way they wanted and we took it whether we liked it or not. But it wasn't ours, it wasn't ours at all! Because we didn't make it—because we would have made it differently—because we never wanted it to be the way it was. Others wanted it, and they forced it down our throats, but that's something else entirely…And in this sense—but in all other senses as well…mark my words: yes, in all other senses—but in all other senses as well…you mark my words: in all other senses—we do not have a history that we can call our own. Does anyone think that we do? That much is clear then. And that's why I object to it, why I refuse to accept it, and why it doesn't exist for me. More than that, I don't respect it. I know that's not the right word…but I don't respect it at all! Above all, I object to it. That is, I don't accept it…"

A burst of emotion made him fidget back and forth like an animal dodging the harness.

"I don't accept it!" he repeated with the obstinacy of a man whose mind is made up. "Not one tiny bit of it...not one! Do you believe me? Do you? You can't begin to imagine how much I object to it, how much I disapprove of it, and how much I...I don't respect it. Look here, think for a minute: what is it about? Well, answer me: *what*? Persecutions, massacres, martyrdoms and progroms. And more persecutions, massacres, martyrdoms and pogroms. And more and more and more of them without end.... That's what it's about, that and nothing else. In the final analysis it...it...it bores one to tears, it simply does! Permit me to bring a small fact to your attention. Everyone knows that children love to read historical novels. Everywhere else, as you know, such books are full of heroes and conquerors and brave warriors and glorious adventures. In short, they're exciting. Whereas here, in Palestine, no child who isn't a little bookworm wants to read such stuff at all. I know what I'm talking about; I've looked into it. That is, they read novels, but ones about Gentiles, not about Jews. Why? You can be sure it's no accident. Jewish history is simply boring, it doesn't interest them. It has no adventures, no conquering heroes, no great rulers or potentates. All it has is a mob of beaten, groaning, weeping, begging Jews. And you'll agree with me that there's nothing interesting about that...nothing! If it were up to me, I wouldn't allow our children to be taught Jewish history at all. Why on earth should we teach them about the shameful life led by their ancestors? I'd simply say to them, 'Look, boys and girls, we don't have any history. We haven't had one since the day we were driven into exile. Class dismissed. You can go outside now and play...'

"But all this is only in passing. I'll come to the point. Only please don't misunderstand me. I know that there has been heroism in our resistance to persecution too. I've taken that into account, but...but I don't approve of such heroism. Don't laugh at me...I simply don't happen to care for it. Had it been up to me, it's not the heroism I would have picked at all. In the first place—I hope you follow me—it's a heroism that was imposed on us. And where there is no freedom of choice, everyone is a hero, and you simply act that way whether you want to or not; it's nothing to make a big fuss over.

And secondly—this heroism of ours turned into our greatest vice in the end. Worse than a vice: a unique talent for abasement. I mean that! Because in the end the hero grew so proud of his 'heroism' that he actually took to boasting of it. Look at me! He began to say. Look at what disaster, at what humiliation, at what disgrace I can bear! Who else in the whole world is as good at it as I am?

"You see, it isn't just that we accept our suffering. It's that we love our suffering, all suffering…we actually want to suffer, we long for it…we can't do without it. Suffering is what protects and preserves us…without it we'd have nothing to live for. Have you ever heard of a group of Jews that didn't suffer? I never have. A Jew who didn't suffer would be a freak of nature, half a Gentile, not a Jew at all…which is why I say that such heroism has been our greatest vice. Suffering, suffering, and more suffering! Everything wallows around it…not in it, mind you, but around it. There's an enormous difference there. Yes, everything wallows around it: Jewish history, Jewish life, Jewish manners, Jewish literature, Jewish culture, Jewish folksong…. Jews taken singly and Jews taken *en masse*…everything! The whole world becomes cramped and narrow and upside-down. A world of darkness, paradox and negation: sorrow replaces happiness as an ideal, pain becomes the norm rather than pleasure, tearing down rather than building up, slavery rather than redemption, dream rather than reality, vague hope rather than real plans, faith rather than common sense—and so on and so forth, one paradox after another…it's simply dreadful! A different psychology comes into being, a psychology of the night…. You see, there is a psychology of the night which differs from that of the day. Not the psychology of a man in the night—that's something else; a psychology of the night itself. Perhaps you've never noticed it, but it's there. I know. I feel it every time I'm out on patrol. The whole world behaves differently than it does during the day. Nature lives a different life. Every stone, every smell, every blade of grass—it's all entirely different…"

"Yudka," the Haganah leader interrupted him in a half-joking, half-begging tone of voice, "what you say is all very interesting, but have pity on us. What did I call a meeting of this committee for?"

"Wait, wait just a minute," Yudka hastily replied. "I haven't come to the main point yet. You still don't know.... I have a plan...you'll see what it is soon enough. Bear with me just a little longer...."

"Let him talk," said one of the committee members. "Give him a chance."

"But..." The leader hesitated and then began to say something—only at that moment Yudka scolded distractedly, addressing no one in particular, "Be quiet!"

The leader bowed his head and reluctantly fell silent.

"I'm not disgressing. I'm getting to the root of things, to brass tacks..."

He stopped and looked bewilderedly about him. He seemed troubled, tired and confused, but there was something that kept driving him on. Soon he resumed, "I've already referred to the fact, and I ask you to keep it in mind, that we have developed a special, paradoxical, fantastical, *nocturnal* psychology, if you will, that is different from that of any other people. We love to suffer. It is suffering that enables us to be Jews, that maintains us and makes us appear strong and heroic, more heroic than anyone else on the face of the earth. And in fact I admit, I can't help it, that we truly are heroic in a sense. Human beings, you know, abuse all kinds of fine words...so that in a certain sense, it does take heroism to suffer...just as in a certain sense it takes heroism to be ugly and abased...which is exactly the kind of people we are. We're not warriors or conquerors or rulers. That's the furthest thing from our minds. No, we prefer to surrender, to suffer endlessly with gratitude and love—while saying, of course: you will never vanquish us, you will never break us, you will never exterminate us! No power on earth can do that...because there is a limit to power, but there is no limit, none at all, to suffering. On the contrary: the more enslaved we are, the more superior we feel; the more we are humiliated, the more highly we think of ourselves; the more we're made to suffer the stronger we become. It's become our second nature; we need it as the air to breathe...how cleverly we've arranged it! It's become our character, our personality—which when you think of it, explains everything: exile, martyrdom, the Messiah...that trinity that's really one, that serves a single purpose.... How does it say in the Bible? 'A threefold cord...'"

"'…is not easily broken,'" One of the committee members supplied the missing part of the quote.

"That's it!" cried Yudka excitedly, seizing upon the verse. "Is not easily broken! Not quickly—which means never, never at all…These three things support each other. They reinforce each other, so that the redemption can never come…so that we keep wandering from country to country and place to place, generation after generation to the end of time…and always with new persecutions, and more suffering, and fresh troubles, and enemies and hatred all around…*oo-of*! How we love it and cling to it! It's our holiest, our most beloved, most intimate possession—holier than Jerusalem, more Jewish than Jerusalem, more fundamentally spiritual, more everything; there's simply no comparison. A paradox? But that's how it is…no, no, don't interrupt me!"

He looked anxiously around him, although in fact no one had made a move to speak.

"Let me tell you how I see it…"

He mopped his face and lips with one hand as though he had just climbed out of a bath, then dropped his voice and whispered confidentially, "The exile is our pyramid whose base is martyrdom and whose apex is the Messiah, and…and the Talmud is our 'Book of the Dead.' We started building this pyramid early in our history, as far back as the time of the Second Temple. That was when we started laying the foundations…exile, martyrdom, the Messiah…do you grasp the full profundity of this feverish, delirious, nocturnal hallucination? Do you? Just think of it, think! Millions of human beings, an entire people, wallowed in it and stayed there for two thousand years!

"They sacrificed their life for it, their natural existence; they welcomed suffering for it, underwent all kinds of torment. You may say that it is preposterous, insane. But as a hallucination, that is, as a dream, it became our ideal…yes, our ideal…what a strange people! What a terrible and wonderful people! Wonderful to the point of total madness! Why, the whole world is not worthy of it; the whole world with all its heroes and warriors and writers and philosophers put together! What horrible darkness! What an immeasurable abyss…no, one could go out of one's mind just thinking about it!"

He mouthed the last words practically inaudibly and stood as though bewitched, his mouth wide open, his eyes staring straight ahead, the color drained from his face.

The Haganah leader invited him to sit.

"Have a seat." He pointed to an empty chair.

"What's that?" asked Yudka confusedly, rousing himself. "But it's not just a fantasy, not just a fantasy at all...that is, it is a fantasy too. But it's a fantasy that we had to have.... Why? for what purpose? but it did, I assure you, it definitely had to have...a fantasy, in fact, that had a very specific purpose, that was calculated and recalculated down to the last detail. Look, there's a very subtle point here, a single anecdote with enormous implications—I'm talking about the belief in the Messiah. What a typical Jewish fantasy, typical to the nth degree...the one myth that lived on after everything else, after the whole great drama of judges and prophets and kings, after the First and Second Temples, after all the wars and heroics and the rest of it...yes, the one thing that remained: an innocent little story, nothing more. It isn't much, you say? Well, you're wrong. On the contrary, it's a great deal. Too much. At first glance it may seem of no importance, a fairytale for children. But it isn't! It isn't for children at all. It has in it, I tell you, all the cunning of the wisest and most well-versed old men, a cunning that is infinitely subtle, tragic and abasing at once. (Oh, I admit, it's a marvelous, ingenious myth too—and one that apart from its symbolism and philosophy has its own bitter brand of Jewish humor...the fact that he is to come riding on an ass. This colossus, this great, universal figure, will arrive in the world not on a splendid steed, but on a jackass, a miserable little beast of burden!) It determined the fate of our people and the path that it would take for centuries, for an eternity, far more than all the scholarly debates in the Talmud. I'm not an expert on these things. In fact, I've never studied the Talmud at all. But it's clear that...that if not for this one myth, everything would have been different. If not for it, we would either have had to return to Palestine right away or to disappear from the world. In either case, we would have had to come to terms with things and do something about them—that is, to put an end to them in one way or another..."

The Haganah leader sought again to interrupt. The subject matter, he was convinced, did not pertain to the committee. Yet when he glanced to either side of him to consult with the others, they signaled him to let Yudka proceed. He deferred to them with a shrug.

Yudka failed to notice this exchange and went on, "Whereas now we no longer had to. There was no need to act or even to think about things in the least. The Messiah would do it all for us, and all that was needed was to sit and wait for him to come. On the contrary: it was forbidden to interfere, forbidden to try to make him come sooner. Incredible!" His voice shook. "Incredible! It became a commandment to remain in exile until God put an end to it. It had nothing to do any more with what Jews did or wanted, only with Providence, with the supernatural, with miracles from above…do you understand?"

He stood there baffled, looking at the committee members.

"Do you understand?" he repeated, in a downcast, puzzled tone of voice. "The Jews did nothing, nothing at all—they simply sat and waited…They imagined the Messiah in heaven—and it's terribly important to realize that this is a myth about the future, not about the past!—and they trusted him to make all the necessary arrangements for redeeming them, so that they themselves had nothing left to do at all…How could they have believed in such a thing? (And believed in it with such a passion! For two thousand years! Two thousand of them!) How do you explain the fact that men who were far from naive, far from fools, who were on the contrary very clever and not a little sceptical about things…in short, men who were thoroughly practical, even a little too practical for their own good…that such men should believe in such a thing…and not just believe in it, but base their whole life on it, their national, historical existence? Honest to God! They believed in it wholeheartedly…they had to, that's the whole point! And yet at the same time, you know, somewhere deep down, in some hidden recess of the heart, they didn't quite believe in it either, not quite—at least not that he was about to come now, right away, in their own lifetime—which was, after all, what mattered…. Can there really be any doubt that they did not believe too, despite the fact that they believed with all their heart? Can there?

"This is also a Jewish trait, very, very Jewish; to believe with all your heart, unwaveringly, with an almost insane passion—and nevertheless to not-believe just a little bit too, a tiny little bit, though it's that tiny bit that's crucial in the end...Perhaps I'm not putting it well. But that's how it is! I know I'm not wrong about it. How complicated everything is.... Redemption is their great hope, their one desire, and yet at the same time they bind themselves, they manacle themselves hand and foot and they themselves sign the verdict, which they then go to all lengths to uphold, that they should never be redeemed until the end of time!

"Or else take.... take this business of.... of what's called the birth pangs of the Messiah. That's a chapter in itself, a very interesting one. Why, according to Jewish belief, do such great catastrophes have to take place before the Messiah can come? Why? Why can't he come without them? He's the Messiah, after all, he can do what he wants.... Why can't he come joyously, bringing peace and all other good things? And get this: the catastrophes aren't going to befall the anti-Semites, or the nations of the world, but they're going to befall the Jews themselves! And they're not even meant for any purpose, such as the encouragement of repentance and such things, but simply for their own catastrophic sake, even though there's no need for them...whole oceans of catastrophes and all kinds of horrible disasters, until the Jews can't stand the grief of them any longer, until they're so crushed that they despair of redemption itself...what for? Is it a matter of theology? Of a realistic grasp of the world? Or is it perhaps something else that we don't dare admit to ourselves: the fear of being redeemed? It's mind-boggling."

He stood there, quite boggled, hardly conscious of where he was.

"I seem to remember having heard," he began again, smiling morbidly at no one in particular, "that some rabbi or saint, I don't recall which, was once quoted as having said about the Messiah, 'When he comes, I don't want to be there,' or something of the sort...Perhaps he was joking, or being cynical, or simply sounding off. But perhaps there's a great truth here, the revelation of a deep, dark secret.... Tell me: how did this myth come to be created in the first place? No, not come to be created…that's not what I mean…because in the beginning it almost certainly expressed nothing more than longing for the return of the House of David. What I mean is, how did it become the classic creation of a nation, the brilliant, immortal masterpiece, as it were, of the Jews? What made it more popular than any of our other myths, more accepted by all strata of our people, by rabbis, Talmudists and simple Jews, by scholars and near illiterates, by men, women and children alike? Why did it become the inner essence, the cardinal dogma of our faith, on which we based our lives through the centuries, our self-image as a nation, our historical perceptions, our political strategies, etcetera, etcetera? But it did! That's a fact. Which means there's some relationship between it and the spirit of the people it pervaded, a very fundamental relationship! A deep congruence, a perfect unity between it and the mentality of the people, between it and the will of the people, its will to live as it pleased…There's no doubt about it. It's perfectly clear."

He stopped for a moment, his face a dark yellow hue, as though it has begun to rust. There was silence in the room, a hushed, forlorn, expectant silence such as that when one waits for the first drop of rain after a lengthy drought.

"And so…so," he drawled, building up to his revelation, "this feverish, delirious, nocturnal fantasy…this fantasy that had a special purpose…I've already said that it was because…that it was because…"

He broke off, as if it were difficult for him to go on. Almost at once, however, he looked at them and blurted in a frightened tone of voice,

"Because they didn't want to be redeemed!" He couldn't get the words out fast enough. He stopped, as though expecting to be challenged, then recovered and repeated,

"Because they didn't want to be redeemed! That's the real meaning of the myth—the practical result of which was that they never *could* be redeemed, never could return to their native land. Mind you, I don't say that it was a continuous thing—although if it wasn't, it's even worse…And I repeat: they believed that redemption would come, they believed in it implicity, prayed for it, dreamed of it—even though they did not really want it. I'm convinced that there was no hypocrisy or duplicity here. You're dealing with something unconscious, deeply repressed.... It's no accident that the Jews so loved this particular myth that they fell under its spell like a band of starry-eyed poets. For two thousand years they warmed themselves by its heat and did nothing, and for two thousand more years they'll go on warming themselves by it and meditating on it and mourning and waiting and being secretly afraid of it without ever tiring of it. All of Judaism, all of Jewish life with its love for the holy land, and for the holy tongue, and for God's kingdom on earth, boils down to no more than that...

"But let's leave all that for now.... What I want to know is: what if there are good reasons for being afraid? What if Judaism can continue to survive as it always has in the Diaspora, while in Palestine...who knows? What if, by taking the place of religion, Palestine is a terrible menace to the future of the Jews, since it shifts their fulcrum of existence from something proven and established to something still transient and terribly unformed? What if Palestine should be the ultimate shipwreck, the final end of the line?"

An odd, weary, unbalanced smiled played lightly over his lips.

"Well?" He looked at them as if waiting for an answer. "Suppose the religious Jews are right? Suppose their instincts are sound? You see for yourselves how even here, in our own homeland, they're against us, all those ordinary, observant Jews who live as Jews always have lived. Right on their faces it's written, 'We are not Zionists, we are God-fearing Jews! We want no part of a Jewish state. All we want is to be left to pray at the Wailing Wall in peace...' It's true, isn't it? Of course there are religious Jews who are Zionists too, but they hardly count; they're simply the pollyannas of the Zionist movement. I'm talking about the observant Jew in the street, the gut-Jew. And do you know what? Let me tell you: if I'm right, *if* I'm right, Zionism and Judaism are not the same thing at all but two entirely differ-ent things, perhaps even two contradictory things. Most certainly two contradictory things! At any rate, they're not the same. A man becomes a Zionist when he can't be a Jew any more.

"No, I'm not exaggerating. The first Zionists to come to this land were very lukewarm Jews. And don't tell me that they came here to escape persecution—that's nonsense. They came because they were already shadows of themselves, because they were ruined, hollow men inside. Zionism begins with the destruction of Judaism, with the people's failure of nerve. That's a fact! The real truth about Zionism has yet to be told. It's much deeper, much more radical in its consequences than anyone thinks. Herzl barely sketched the outlines of it. Ahad Ha'am did even less, for all his grand Jewish thoughts. At most he advised the Jews who came here looking to build a new world not to forget to first found a local Talmud society, or to build a house of study and a Jewish cemetery…what's that?"

He paused to stare at one of the committee members, who seemed about to say something.

"It's nothing," grinned the man. "I just happened to remember something. I had an uncle, a witty, clever Jew. The Bolsheviks killed him. For doing absolutely nothing. He used to say, 'Ahad Ha'am is the secular rabbi of Zionism…'"

The committee members enjoyed the quip. The leader, however, felt called upon to deliver a rebuke. "Don't interrupt!" he said sternly.

Yudka stood there at a good-natured loss. It was impossible to say whether he had heard the interruption at all, or if he had, what he made of it.

"I'll be finished in a minute…" he apologized, smiling uncertainly.

He sought to pick up the thread again and coughed two or three times.

"So…in a minute I'll…what was it that I wanted to say? It was about…about Zionism! In a word, the last word about it has yet to be said…the…the hidden, ultimate truth. No one in the world has yet understood the real depth of it, no one has managed to explain…The things we're told about it, you know, are the most elementary, the most banal, the vaguest and emptiest phraseology…"

"Who says no one in the world has understood it?" jeered a committee member. "What about all those absent-minded, Arab-loving professors at the Hebrew University?"

"Professors don't live in this world," someone else put in.

"Ernest Figg…" The man whose name was thrown out was considered a prime example of such types.

"Ernest is no fig and Figg is not earnest," someone joked.

The Haganah leader rang his gong. "I'll thank you not to interrupt or to engage in private conversation," he declared. "Please continue."

"All right," said Yudka, unsure how to go on. "I certainly can't define Zionism for you. I'm not the man for it, even if my head hurts from thinking about it so much. But that's of no importance…This much is clear: Zionism is not a continuation or a cure for a disease. That's nonsense! It's an act of destruction, a negation of what's come before, an end…It's far from a grass-roots movement. In fact, it's not a popular movement at all, no more popular surely than the Bund, or Communism, or assimilation. On the contrary: it ignores the people, it opposes them, it goes against their inner grain, it seeks to subvert and deflect them to an entirely new path, to a certain faraway goal—it and the men at the head of it, who are the avant-garde of a different people…Please listen closely: not *new*, not *renewed*, but *different*. Whoever doesn't agree with me, I'm sorry to say, is either wrong or self-deluded. What? Suppose I'm wrong? But I believe that what we have in Palestine today is no longer Judaism already, to say nothing of what we will have in the future. After all, we haven't begun to see the end of it. I'm talking about Zionism's inner essence, it's hidden power—yes, I am. At least call it a different Judaism, if you insist on fooling yourselves and clinging to the name…but certainly not that which has existed for two thousand years, most emphatically not that. Which is to say…well, a 'no-thing', if you follow me? And nothing will help change any of this: neither bringing grandmother and grand-father over from Europe, nor a steady diet of Jewish sources fed to us like wheat-bran, nor Hebrew literature if it's still stuck in the past, in the shtetl, which is why it doesn't amount to anything. *Kaput!*

"Permit me to mention one little fact that doesn't bear on the matter directly but that still has circumstantial weight…" His lips cracked in a warped smile. "*Circumstantial*: what a lovely word, isn't it? So round and smooth…Well, it's known that Jews in this country are ashamed to speak Yiddish, as though it were somehow a disgrace. They don't hate it, they're not afraid of it, they don't refuse to speak it, they're simply ashamed. But Hebrew...and oddly enough, with a Sefardic accent, which is foreign to most of them...that they speak with their heads held high, with a kind of self-esteem, even though it's much harder for them than Yiddish and has none of this liveliness, none of the juiciness, none of the fresh, spontaneous earthiness that Yiddish has. What is behind this? Can it be that they prefer to make life more difficult for themselves, just like that? No, it's very simple: Hebrew is not a continuation, it's different, it's a case in itself, there's practically nothing Jewish about it. Practically nothing...And by the same token, ordinary people here are embarrassed to go by ordinary Jewish names. They would rather be called Artsieli and Avnieli or something Hebrew-sounding like that. Haimovitz, you'll admit, is a very Jewish name—far too Jewish...whereas Avnieli—that's something else again, although the devil only knows what. The main thing is that it sounds different, not Jewish, so that they can feel proud of it.

"That's also the reason, of course, that you'll find so many rare biblical names among us: Gideon, Ehud, Yigal, Tirzah.... *what?* You say that there's nothing new about this, that Jews have always changed their names to assimilate? But elsewhere that was self-evident; we lived among strangers, surrounded by enemies, and so we had to hide, to stay out of sight, to pretend to be someone else. But here we're in our own land; there's no one but us, and surely no need to feel ashamed or to hide—and no one, for that matter, to hide from. What is one to make of it then? And yet there you are! Clearly it's the same thing...not a continuation but a break, the opposite of the past, a fresh start...

"I've digressed. I won't keep you any longer. I'm finishing: in a nutshell, the purpose. A different people, one above all that makes its own history by and for itself, rather than having it made for it by others.... a real history, that is, and not some communal ledger in the archives...that's what it's all about! Because a people that does not live in its own land and control its own fate has no history...that's my idea. I've said it once, I'm saying it again, and I'll say it over and over and over. Is that clear? Is it?"

He was muddled from so much speech and emotion. His

voice sounded tattered, and he had the look of a man who has lost his way.

"I've said a mouthful, everything…everything that was on my mind…there isn't any more. I don't want to add another word… enough!"

He noisily pulled out a chair and collapsed heavily into it. He sat flustered and livid, his heart and temples pounding wildly while he wiped the sweat from his face.

There was silence in the room, a silence as after a storm. The committee members sat without a word, feeling strangely ill at ease. There was something quiescent about them, as though they had been whisked away on a long journey and were currently suspended in midair.

At last the Haganah leader looked up and asked in as rough a tone as he could muster,

"Are you done?"

Yudka shuddered and jumped to his feet again.

"In a minute, in a minute…" he hastened to say in his fright. "I've talked too much, much too much…I didn't want to, it wasn't what I had in mind. It just came out by itself. God only knows…what rubbish! All kinds of little, unimportant things about Yiddish and Hebrew names…it was ridiculous, really unnecessary. I can see that myself…although sometimes, you know, it's precisely the little, unimportant details that come first to mind…not that it makes any difference. The main thing is…because that's what I wanted to talk to you about…only how did I want to put it…yes, the crux of it, my plan. I haven't been just wasting…not at all! Well then, the main thing, I'll have to ask you to be patient for just a little longer…"

The Haganah members perked up in their seats as if Yudka just rescued them from some great distress—including their leader, who sat studying his fingernails.

"Say whatever you want," he said. "Just go easy on the philosophy…"

Translated by Hillel Halkin

Ya'ish Meets the Angels

An excerpt

Now Ya'ish knew that God had granted him the power to look into the shining mirror and see visions while awake. A great, overwhelming joy, like a flame of fire in a field of thorns, seized him. All morning long he trembled and recited hymns. His heart melted within him out of abundance of delight.

When he returned home from the bath-house—it was Friday—after he had lunched and slept, he rushed to the synagogue. Ah, thank God, it was empty, not a soul was there. He went in, opened the ark and chanted a Psalm aloud.

"My soul thirsts for the Lord, the living God. When shall I come to see the face of God!"

Immediately afterward, he sat down and recited the story of Isaac's sacrifice, then the penitential prayers and then mystical petitions. These he recited until the people assembled for the Sabbath Eve service.

On that particular Sabbath he rejoiced even more than he had done during his own seven-day wedding feast. He sang many Sabbath hymns, toasted "good healths" and drank beyond measure. He drank in honor of the ministering angels, the moon, Mari Salem

Shabazi, Rabbi Simeon Bar Yochai and all the other saints who dwell in Paradise. In the end he fell, like Sisera in his day, at the feet of his wife and slept.

In the course of days he repeated that which he had done, concentrating upon his mystical intentions. He imagined that he would rise again to where both the sun and moon both graze. Having risen, he found himself standing in a place which he did not recognize. He had never been there before in his life.

This was an eerie place where trees and herbs grew from the sky. The likes of which have no match in our own fields nor was their name known in our parts. They looked as if they were drawn the way the moon and the sun are: all done in heaven's colors. The void was filled with lustrous light: twilight hues, the glow of the heaven's expanse which turned to gold at midday, the brilliance of distant places which opened out toward the sky, the infinite light, the green hue which encompasses the world and the vague, hidden light—bright on the inside but dark on the outside, and similar lights, concealed from the sight of men, which the eye is powerless to sustain and the mouth to describe. Here and there, the grass was strewn with the leaf-fall of the sun, the tatters of sky and rays of light. Green and white lightning fragments and meteor-tails appeared like fallen palm branches. The air was warm, as the heart is warm when it is full of yearning and longing. A deep, total and all-encompassing silence, deeper than the stars in their courses and the ball of the sun, flooded him, and he was washed by it and became oblivious of his self, of his body.

Because the silence was so very heavy, Yai'sh did not sense it at first. He stood bewildered and amazed, his eyes fixed upon these hues and lights. Later, when he came to himself, he grew frightened. The silence terrified him. It seemed that it lay in ambush for him, lay siege to him and hounded his very steps. Everything was stopped. There was no sound, no motion. Time stood still and all the universe had grown as taut like a bow.

Trembling and frightened he froze in his place. His heart pounded, he found it difficult to breathe, and his lips contorted in a pitiful smile as if to assuage the terror within him. Slowly, carefully, secretly, he rolled his eyes sideways but saw nothing. He lowered his head to the earth and closed his eyes as if shutting himself out from the world. He sank into himself. Only he and his soul.

For a long time he stood. Then the white light smote his eyes and he bestirred himself. He opened his eyes and saw band after band of angels walking one after the other. There were young angels of uniform size and gait. They were little, and pretty like white geese, and were wrapped in white wings. They all looked alike.

He wanted to run away from them.

"I have nothing to do with them," he thought.

But before he could do so, the first band of angels had already caught up with him.

He got a grasp on himself, smiled at them and said,

"I don't know your custom, but nevertheless I greet you as the custom is in our parts."

The glanced at him as they walked and asked, "Where are your wings?"

He answered, "In the wash tub."

They immediately passed his words from one to another. "He says in the wash tub. He says in the wash tub."

The first band made its way out and the second came into view. They turned to him and wondered, "Why are you clipped? Why don't you have any wings?"

He summoned up an excess of courage and answered, "His mind is greater than the fowl's."

Immediately they passed on his words one to another, "He says, 'His mind is greater than the fowl's.' He says, 'His mind is greater than the fowl's.'"

The second band made its way out and the third came into view.

They said, "Who are you?"

He answered, "A creature."

They asked again, "What kind of creature?"

He answered, "The righteous man *lives* by his faith!"

For what is called *Ya'ish* in Arabic means *lives* in Hebrew.

The third band made its way out and the fourth came into view.

They said to him as did their predecessors, "Who are you, clipped-winged one?"

He said, "A Jew."

"A Jew?" They stood wondering. But an angel who had been standing in mid-heaven and reciting, "Blessed be the Lord Who is blessed" said, "I'm his relative, flesh of his flesh."

"And why are you without wings?"

"Because were I to grow wings and feathers, I would cover you, the heaven, the skies and all the world."

And so the fifth band and the sixth and the seventh. When the last band arrived, they began pushing, shoving and tormenting him.

He stood frightened and drove them away.

"Home, home, home—flats full of feathers." He waved his hands and shouting as one shouts at geese and chickens.

"Keep away from me—or you'll endanger your lives."

They all jumped back.

Only one of them, a white, rotund angel whose wings hung limp because of his obesity, held his ground and chattered at him,

"How do we endanger our lives?"

"Say Amen, and get away safely," Ya'ish made bold. "If any angel, even a double or triple angel, even a Seraph, or a Cherub or a heavenly being, flies over me, he will burn to a cinder."

"How now does he burn, if he flies over you?" the angel queried.

"Because I'm made of fire," Ya'ish said in an exaggerated and threatening tone.

"And what if you are made of fire," he said, as if this were the most natural thing.

"It is written, 'The fire of Law is opposite his right hand.' The words of the Torah are like fire and whoever approaches them is burnt."

"Where's it written, why's it written?"

"Do you know any Torah?"

"It is not in the heavens."

Ya'ish saw that they knew nothing of the Torah and he was pleased.

"And I know the entire Torah," he said proudly.

"And in what way are you so different now that you know the Torah?"

He soon realized the bent of the conversation and did not know what he might answer.

He began speaking in order to change the subject.

"What do you do?" he asked. "Where are you going?"

The angel, who was the most loquacious of the group, answered, "Under our Creator's orders."

Ya'ish sweetened his tone, smiled and asked, "How old are you, wingy?"

The other responded somewhat vaguely, "I was born yesterday."

"My chick, I'm the dust under your feet," Ya'ish joked with him, "Let me ask you a question."

"Ask, wingless one, ask."

"What are you, male or female?"

"As you wish."

"I wish you male."

"Good."

"Males are important, more complete, superior. As our Sages said, 'There are three things that man does not desire: Weeds in his crops, vinegar in his wine and a female among his children.'"

The angel let his head rest between his wings. He stood like a dull school boy, pondering the matter over and over again. He said nothing.

"By your leave, may I ask you a question?" Ya'ish once again said gently.

"Ask, wingless one, ask."

"Tell me! What sort of birth did you have?"

The angel looked up at him in astonishment as if Ya'ish had asked him a very difficult question.

"How were you born?" Ya'ish explained.

"I don't know, since I haven't been born as yet, even once."

"You haven't been born? From where do you come?"

"From there." He lifted his wing toward heaven.

"Have you a mother?"

"I don't know."

"Perhaps a bird hatched you?"

"Perhaps."

"What do you eat?"

"What do I eat?" He cast his eyes backward toward his companions and stood confounded like one who had never heard of such a thing.

"Manna?"

"Manna," the angel repeated like a pupil repeats after his teacher.

"Manna. 'And it is like white grain and tastes like a honey wafer.' It is the bread which the angels eat, and is absorbed in all their limbs, as Scripture says. 'Man eats the bread of the mighty.'"

"I don't know."

"Perhaps *matzot?*"

"I don't know anything."

"*Matzot*—the unleavened bread which the Children of Israel ate when they left Egypt."

"I don't understand what you're saying."

"You are an ignoramus, with all due respect. You haven't learned Torah. Our Sages were quite right when they said, 'The Torah was not given to the ministering angels.'"

"If you don't eat, then you don't know Torah?"

"Certainly. Our Sages have said, 'No flour—no Torah.'"

"And have you eaten?"

"Certainly. I'll pull out your feathers and roast you and eat you from head to foot."

After a while they took their leave of him gaily and affectionately. One lifted his wing and the other his thigh and they took off.

Ya'ish remained behind and followed them with his eyes. After a few minutes one of them turned round and glided. In a moment, he dropped and came running to him with spread wings, and beat against his feet.

He was a little angel, soft and white as a gosling, all feathers.

A fluffy, pretty ball of feathers. He had the face of an infant, eyes like the moon and his mouth looked like a rosebud.

Ya'ish bent toward him and passed his hand along his feather-back, squeezing him between his wings. His heart was pounding as if he had turned his hand to sin.

"What's wrong, angel mine," he whispered in an agitated and excited voice. "What's, wrong, my Cherub?"

He seized him, lifted him high and glanced at his body and his glowing brightness. He hugged and fondled him and kissed his face. Then he began to play with him; he would let him fly and catch him, let him fly and catch him.

"O, Light of my Eye!" He threw him upward, crying joyfully.

"Caught!" He grasped him with both hands with delight and affection.

"God bless you!" Again he threw him upward.

"Caught!" He grasped him.

"Be blessed!" He swung him from side to side and cast him ten cubits high.

"Delicious!" He caught him under his wings and his hands were filled with feathers, pleasure and softness.

"Bravo, bravo!" He lifted him above his head and cast him into empty space.

"O my Joseph!" He caught him and pressed him to his heart.

And so the angel would fly several rounds, rise and descend, rise and descend, his face shining and glowing with much joy and frolicking. Until like a bird he lighted upon him and hung on to his chest.

Ya'ish stretched his hand, removed him and cast him below.

"Enough, enough," he said, "Wait a minute. Let me ask you a question."

The angel folded his wings, looked at him and stood still.

"What's your name?" Ya'ish said to him.

He was silent and gave no answer.

"Can't you talk?"

He answered, "I do not know my name."

Ya'ish said to him, "All right. Tell me how you were created...."

What are you like, what do you do and what is God's power within you?"

He answered, "You created me."

Ya'ish stood dumbfounded.

"I...I...When did I create you, how—and with what? Why do you make such false accusations against me?"

He responded, "Don't you fast?"

"Yes, I fast. What then?"

"I was created out of this pious act of yours."

"So—o," Ya'ish concluded and his face beamed.

"So, so, so."

The angel lifted his wings above his head and waved several times.

"They've given you my food and that's why you've become so fat?"

"I was created out of your pious acts, and I am nurtured from them every time you fast."

"That's ve...ve—ry good." Ya'ish nooded his head, smiling with great pleasure.

"Then you're m—ine. You're my son. O my soul, my liver. Let me hug you and kiss you—my angel, my angel son!"

He embraced him and kissed him.

"From now on, my child, you must listen to me and do whatever I command you. You must honor me as you've been bidden to do in the Torah. You do know what the Torah says about honoring your father?"

"What Torah? What honor?"

The angel glanced at him sideways as he stood with his wings dropped to his side and his head turned about.

"Haven't you gone to school? Don't you have a teacher to instruct you?"

"No school and no teacher."

"Next time I'll bring a *Chumash*[1] and teach you the *Shema*, the prayers and the responses."

---

1. *Chumash*: The Five Books of Moses

"The Torah was not given to the angels."

"Aren't you my son?"

"Correct, but I'm an angel."

"But you are my son. It is quite improper that I should have a son who is an ignoramus, God forbid! You are obliged to fulfill my will and God's will. You must learn Torah."

"It is not in the heavens."

"All right, my child." Ya'ish agreed unwillingly, "As you wish and in accordance with the local custom. But you must fulfill the commandment to honor your father. You must obey me and help me in everything necessary."

"Good."

"Not that way. Say, with God's help."

"With God's help."

After some time the angel returned, jumped upon him, clung to his chest and held on to him.

"Please let me go."

"Why do want to leave me?" Ya'ish fondled his hand.

"By your leave, let me go, my time is up." He wriggled and flapped his wings against his chest.

"All right," agreed Ya'ish, "I'll let you go but you must promise to visit me again."

"With God's help."

The angel then spread his wings, circled two or three times and disappeared from sight.

Translated by Ezra Spicehandler

The Lord Have Mercy

S
A Yemenite Story

a'adya Araki didn't on no account consent to volunteer for the Army, like was being expected of every man's son in the prime of his life and all there and without no children. So the members of the Draft Board in Jerusalem, they come and kick him out of his job with the carpenter, where he made his living. Sa'adya, he just stood there and folded up his toolkit and left the shop with a mighty peculiar expression. It was hard to tell, if you know what I mean, whether he was welcoming the Sabbath or taking leave of it, he looked glad on the right, and awful sorry on the left.

His missus, Badra, she saw things the way he did, and she wanted what he wanted.

"Why, man," says she, "y'is d'on'y husban' ah'se got. Is ah gonna give mah honeybunch, mah sweetiepie, mah big buck, to study war? Not on yo' life! Not on yo' lives, damn yo' souls! An' ah don't mean yo' pappies'! Ah'll see 'em dead first! No, suh!"

Now Sa'adya, he made the rounds of all the carpenter shops in town and kept asticking his nose into every corner where he scented a job, but he couldn't smell out a thing, seeing as how he didn't have no work card.— "Has y'got yo' exemption?" they all asks him, like they is singing hymns or a love song.

So he give up trying to make a living, and he goes to work on the missus, to get him a little exemption at home by making her pregnant. Man! he kept at her night and day, astrutting and acourting and atussling her like he was a rooster.

"Ah'se gotta get me a son!" He was sot on that. "Come hell or high water, ah'se gotta have one."

But nothing seems to do him no good, not the day tussling nor the night tussling, and things is looking pretty dark.

So he takes hold of the missus and he totes her to the Yemenite Rabbi, and from the Rabbi to the wise men of the Kurds, and from the Kurds to the Mugrabis, and all the rest of the tribes found in Israel. Says he, if they all can't bring him no help from Heaven, why let it come from the "other place", so long as they helps him!

But! just as he was no damn good to her hisself, so he couldn't get no use for her from all the spelling and charming of them witch doctors. When the Lord He shuts a door, no mere human man ain't going to open it.

From all the worries that was eating him, and from the wolf aprowling at his door, and from it all—he began to pine away, and the meat on his bones it got shriveled and dried up like a carob, and he kept astorming and afretting all day, and his heart was bitter and his mind was cross. The way the world was looking to him, he had no peace, nohow.

"Oh Lawd!" he pours out his troubles, complaining to his Maker. "How come Y'All make dis here trouble on'y fo' me? Why is ah worse'n de udders? Y'All got Kurds, an' Urfals, an' Chalabs, an' all sorts o' queer critters Y'done made fo' Yo' Cre-a-shun, an' dey all gets 'em litters as fast as jackrabbits, an' ah'se d'on'y man cain't git nary a one. Is Y'All doin' hit, God fo'bid, on pu'pose? Why? For what cause? What sin ah done? So dey all kin cotch me an' draf me an' beat de stuffin' out o' me in dis here war? Lawd, Lawd!"

The biggest gripe Sa'adya had in his heart was against his poor wife, and, not once and not twice, he'd jump on her and use hard words, and he'd tell her off.

"What d'hell use ah got fo' ya, if y'is dry an' y'don't do me no good?" he'd yell at her as if he was aiming to swallow her up. "Y'kin bu'n in hell a t'ousan' times, damn yo' soul, y'bitch!"

"Ah ain't dry, an' dere ain't nuthin' wrong wid me." Badra bows herself down, as meek as a lamb, and answers him. "Dis here ain't mah fault. Hit's de Lawd's doin'. If'n He-All wanted hit, we'd done had us a son a'ready…"

"Can't fool me none wid dat high talk! Talk ain't 'nuf! When a hen don't lay no eggs, she goes t'de butcher!"

Right off, when she heard him talking thataway, the tears began to flow.

"Why y'blamin' me?" she clucked through her tears. "Am dis here sometin' ah kin do? Do hit res' on me? Wasn't Sarah, mudder o' Israel, a dry one? An' wasn't Rachel, mudder o' Israel, a dry one too? Till de good Lawd, He blessed 'em, an' sho' 'nuf Abra'm got'm a son when he was ninety-year-old…Jes you wait, ole man. De Lawd has plenty. We-all is still mighty young, we still got time."

"Y'go 'n give dat line o' talk t'de Draf' Board," says Sa'adya, aboiling and apuffing at her. "Dis here chitchat o' yourn ain't doin' me no good. Ah'se gotta git me a son! One way or 'nudder—t'git shet o' dis here draf' !…"

Pretty soon the town got wind of what was going on, and the news was spread around, from neighbor to neighbor, from stonecutter to chipper, from chipper to muler, from muler to porter. So some, they picked themselves up and came to give Sa'adya a load of heavy advice and tell him about all sorts of sure-as-hell-fire remedies; and some, they just came to give him the giggles and sound off to him the kind of stuff that ain't fit to print. The womenfolk too got a kick out of getting fenced into this here chickencoop, and they were kept pretty busy with Badra, telling her sometimes things that helped, and sometimes things that didn't.

"Looky here, Badra gal," they give her a sharp look and say deliberate like. "Mebbe yo' ole man he's weak, he ain't atryin' an' aworkin' 'nuf; mebbe he jes ain't doin' no ridin' an', po' t'ing t'ain't yo' fault nohow."

"What y'all blowin' 'bout?…" says Badra, and her face gets

red as a live coal in a breeze. "He's as healt'y and as hot as dey come! Like a rooster!"

"Well, now, sometime bein' healt'y don' help an' bein' like a rooster don' help," says they, trying to draw her out by talking. "Mebbe his ball-stuff ain't sharp…"

"No, no, no, no!' Badra rocked her body like a water wagtail and put their doubts to rest by her tone and her look. "Sharp 'nuf, sharp 'nuf…Bless de Lawd, de man is healt'y as a stud-hoss. He's all dere an' got what hit takes."

"Den y'try an' git'm t'take ya t'a doctor. De doc kin tell if'n de trouble is his'n or yourn."

"Ai, ai! De Lawd protec' me. How'll ah strip me nekked an' show mah innards 'fore de doctor! Ain't dat a shame?"

"So, who care? Y'be sure o' one t'ing: y'ain't agoin' out from dat dere doctor widout you'se acarryin' twins…"

"So *dat's* hit? *Dat's* hit, y'bitch? A jinx on yo'pappies, y'good-fo'-nuthins! Dat's how y'talkin'?…"

Sa'adya, he had no rest or peace of mind. He ate lots and lots of ginger and coconuts, and eggs that Badra mixed with butter, and all kinds of that there grub as is good for the man-stuff. Everywhere he went he kept apestering people and asking their advice, ahustling and abustling, afretting and afuming, this way and that, looking for a cure, hoping maybe anything could help a little. Now and then he'd get so all-fired jinxed by old man trouble that he'd hop into his house, and stand there before Badra, looking like he couldn't make up his mind, his eyes popping this way and that—like they'd given him a prayer book where "The Lord is My Shepherd" was all mixed up with "The Song of Moses".

"Well, now, ole woman!" says he, and his voice is low. "What am ya feelin' now?"

"De Lawd'll help, ole man." Badra, she drawls and she sighs.

"Dat ain't no answer!" He's boiling over and laces into her with a shout. "Ah'se a-askin' ya: What am y'feelin'? Is we got anythin' yet?"

"Ah still cain't tell.. ."

"Goddam yo' pappy, an' yo' chile-bearin', an' dis here Jewish

Agency an' Draf' Board t'gedder! Dey sh'd all bu'n in hell a t'ousand times! What a Goddam mess dey's made o' mah life!…"

Then he'd jump on Badra, mad as a hornet and plumb out of his mind, and he'd grab her and throw her down on the bed.

"De door…shet de door…" she'd cluck, all crumpled up beneath him, like a hen. "Shame…"

"Shet yo' mout', ya Goddam no-good an' yo' no-good pappy!' he'd huff and he'd puff. "Ah'se agoin' t'kill ya!"

II.

Day by day, this gripe that was eating Sa'adya's heart got stronger, and all this time he couldn't speak with her a word of peace. The least little thing would set him off, and he'd boil over and spill his words out on her in a fit of temper. It didn't help Badra nohow that she'd listen to his scoldings and keep quiet. Contrarywise, her being so soft and humble made him hate and fume at her even more. And he'd already thought some about giving her a divorce, but he was going to wait until they straightened out his case in the Appeals Board, seeing as how he'd sent up an appeal and was pinning all his hopes on them.

This was what he told her once when he was boiling,

"Now looky here, y'bitch, if dem dogs on d'Appeals Bo'd don't let me go, ah pity ya. Ah'se agoin' t'have t'give ya a dee-vorce, an' den y'kin go straight t'hell a t'ousand times. Ah ain't agoin' t'put mah life in no danger 'cause o' you. Hit am all, all yo' fault! If 'n y'da on'y give me a little boy o' gal befo', ah wouldn't be havin' none o' dese here troubles. But ah ain't expec'in' no hope f 'om you. Look't all de toil an' trouble ah done had fo' ya, an' hit ain't done no damn good. Ah'se good as dead a'ready! Ah'se weak as a baby, an' mah knees is shakin'! Damn yo' pappy, y's gotten t'be like a good-fo'-nuthin' mule. Y'pour water in a leaky dam, she keeps on runnin'! Damn yo' soul, ah'se been asweatin' an' adyin' fo' a barrel o' nuthin's!"

Badra, she didn't answer him none. She just shook her bosom, real scared and her eyes apopping, and she whispered,

"Oh Lawd! De Lawd protec' me!…"

But though he gave her the miseries and treated her so all-fired bad, and was fixing in his thoughts to do her dirt, still he never stopped from loving her. That was just his trouble, that his heart was like split in two, and his hating and his loving were getting all mixed up and fighting one another, and he couldn't tell what would be the end, and he didn't know what he would do. When he'd go home and see her face, he couldn't stand her and he'd fret and fume and want to tear her up like a fish, to smash, to kill and destroy. But when he'd go out into the street, right away he'd blame hisself and go crazy as a loon with knowing he'd done wrong, and with wanting her and feeling sorry for her.

"Dere ain't never been no trouble like mine!" He'd shrug his shoulders and get to feeling awful sorry for himself and awondering. "Tain't bad 'nuf dat ah hates her, but ah'se gotta see her side too an' be alovin' her…"

Once he came back home from the street with his heart full and thinking to make things up with her. He found her sitting on the ground and chanting a tune, kind of sad and mournful, over and over, like the childless women in Yemen used to chant at the spring of Rabbi Salim Shabazi, and her eyes were running tears and her thin face was lit up with a brightness a little like a beautiful sunset,

"Fader o' Peace, strengt'en mah heart, an' give what ah'se a'askin'. Ai, help, holy fount'n an' give me a son."

He stood there an looked at her out of the corner of his eye, and it was like a storm passed over in front of him, and he changed from loving her to hating her, and his body shook and he shouted at her,

"Git outa dis here house, y'ugly bitch! Git outa mah sight! Ah'se sick an' ti'ed o' seein' ya, damn yo' soul!"

"What ah done?" She was scared and tried to make up with him. "Ain'tcha mah honeybunch, mah lover boy, de light o' mah eyes, an' ain't all in yo' hands like a no-good she-donkey…"

"Ah'se atellin' ya: 'nuf o' dat!" Sa'adya boiled over and yelled. "Y'd better git on outa here quick, so ah don't see yo' face again! So ah don't feel yo' smell in here no mo'! Ah'se sick o' ya, y'bitch!"

As if that wasn't bad enough, things got even worse. Once

Sa'adya even raised his hand against her and hit her. This was something new and something to wonder at, seeing as how he'd never been like this and never played that game before. Right away, when she saw what he was at, she bent herself low and turned her face and her arms up to him, and her voice was abegging him in a whisper, like she was asking him to keep one of the Commandments,

"Beat me, ole man, so's ah kin make up f 'all mah sins. Mebbe de good Lawd'll have mercy on me, an' mebbe he'll give me a son 'cause o' yo' beatin's. Beat me, beat me, much's ya like. Ah'se all yourn, mah back's yourn, an' dese here arms is yourn..."

Then he controlled hisself and stopped hitting her. He left her and went off to a corner and sat down and put his head between his knees.

Badra stole after him, quiet-like, and sat down, and she kept her eyes on him and shook her head and just mumbled with her lips and kept still. But after a few minutes she began speaking,

"Y'see, ole man, dat y'didn't beat me, after all! You'se a good man, you is, and y'ain't no trouble maker, and y'd be 'shamed t'beat yo' wife...Me, hit don't matter t'me nohow, ah'se ready fo' yo' beatin's. Why, ah'd sho' 'nuf like it if 'n y'd beat me, yo' beatin's feel sweet t'me, but hit's better y'don't do hit. Y'don't want, God fo'bid, de Lawd Protec' us, t'git inta no trouble over me an' do no sinnin' 'fore de Lawd. Better disaway, better. Never min' dat ah keeps quiet an' ah'se ready t'take hit all f 'om ya, even so hit's better disaway, better fo' you. May de Lawd be good t'ya fo' mah sake, so y'don't do somethin' y'll be 'shamed of, an' give d'ole man Debbil chance t'git atcha. Ah'se contented, ah'se contented..."

From then on he took this to heart and didn't raise his hand to her, but only kept lacing into her with his tongue. When the evil spirit got into him he'd take his two fists and beat on his own face and heart, or he'd hit his head against the wall. Except for three or four times when he beat her and she was willing and they both knew it. But those beatings had no sorrow or shame in them, they was a kind of medicine-beatings—seeing as how there was some jokers done give him a tip that he ought to beat her on her middle after he'd atussled her, the way some hits the cow after the bull, to make sure of her seed. So he did the same, and he hit her with all his might, and after every blow he gave her he'd say, over and over again,

"May de good Lawd give us dat we'll sta't bein' f 'uitful an' amul-tip-lyin'! May de good Lawd give us dat we'll sta't bein' f 'uitful an' amul-tip-lyin'!"

Badra, she'd take these beatings from him with love and keep urging him on,

"Mo', mo'! Beat me mo', ole man, mebbe dat ain't 'nuf fo' me..."

III.

The days went and the days came, days of anger and wrath, days of weeping and brawling and troubles. Day by day the little sum of money left from the old days kept shrinking, till Sa'adya, he was kept busy working at how to keep their few pennies together, and they was eating less and less.

This was pretty hard on Sa'adya, and he started getting afraid of the hunger-sickness.

"Name o' God, what'll 'come o' me?" He put the fear of the Lord into hisself and trembled with terror. "Pretty soon ah won't have nuthin' lef ' , an' den we gonna die, t'die! Who kin help us, who'll listen? Nobody knows our trouble, or gives a damn fo' us!"

Badra, she made up her mind to help him and get her some maid-work with the Ashkenazis. But she just didn't know how to tell him about it so he wouldn't get into a fit and spoil her whole plan. She could tell without asking that he wouldn't like the idea of her working for others. He done told her more than once, before and after they was married,

"No, suh! Ah ain't goin' nohow t'have ya gettin' ti'ed aworkin' fo' no strangers. All ah wants is dat y'set at home like a queen, dat y'be dere awaitin' fo' me when ah gets home, an' ah kin be lookin' at you, an' y'kin be lookin' at me..."

So one day she fed him up with black-eyed peas and cornbread, since there was nothing set on his stomach easier and pleased him more than cornbread, and soon as he was asitting there all heavy-like and his hands was hanging loose and his soft side showing, she came over to sit with him.

She took ahold of herself and chose her words carefully and began talking to him real loving-like, and her tongue ran with milk and honey,

"Looky here, ole man, ah wants y't'take hit real easy-like, eatin' an' drinkin' an' strollin', an' ah'll go do some maid-work like ah useta, an' whatever ah make'll be 'nuf fo' us two, wid de Lawd's help. What y'grievin' bout? Why does y'let dem dere no-good Ashkenazis make y'life mis'able an' hunt after ya fo' dis here draf'? How much dey goin' t'pay ya? Six o' seven pounds. Mebbe, mebbe—nine pounds! We don't wan' none o' dat! Y'take yo'sel' out an' stroll, till de time'll pass an' de war'll be t'rough."

Sa'adya, he shook hisself a bit and threw a look at her and inspected her over and sat there awondering. And after some two or three minutes he hopped up on his legs, real spry and chipper, as if she hadn't filled up his belly at all with lots of black-eyed peas and cornbread, and he yelled at her,

"Who's de man in dis here house, me o' you? Mebbe y'd like t'be awearin' de pants here an' let me wear yo' dress, y'ole bitch? Y' wants me t'be awaitin' on de money y'll be agivin' me?…"

For a long while he kept on fretting and fuming at her, and the longer he kept at it the hotter he got. Till he himself felt that he couldn't keep his hands from doing something.

So he picks himself up and starts to leave the house.

"Ah'se agoin' t'de draf'!" He turns to her as he's going out the door. "Ah'se agoin' t'd'Ashkenazis! Be a soldier man! No damn use! 'Nuf o' dat! 'Nuf o' dat, damn yo' soul!"

Boiling with anger, he can't find no rest, so he keeps on the move, shuffling along from street to street and from alley to alley.

"Ah hates her! Ah hates her!" He kept on saying this to himself, practicing the words in anger and in sorrow, repeating them to make them stick. "Ah hates her guts!…Ah'se just gotta give her a dee-vorce, an'get rid o'dis here trouble, ah'se gotta, ah'se gotta!…"

It seemed like the Lord had fixed that day to be one of bitterness and foolishness for Sa'adya, a day when old man Devil was dancing inside him. Dark, without no light. That day he got himself mixed up in a street-fight with Yichye Hamuda ("Loudmouth"), and then a big crowd gathered round and bothered him, and there was anguish and terrors.

This is the way it was. After he'd grown tired out from all his fuming and his troubles and his shuffling, and he wanted to rest—he runs plumb into the business of Yichye Hamuda. This "Loudmouth" meets him in the middle of the street and stands there ajoking at him like he usually does, he being lightheaded by nature, a funny man and a shrewd customer; but nobody pays no attention to his talk, really, though he's always strutting about with all his business, and saying he can tell fortunes and cast out spells, like the witch-doctors.

So that Hamuda, he stops him and says,

"Hi, Sa'adya, how's d'ole woman? She still dry?"

"De Bawd have mercy," says Sa'adya and sighs. "De Lawd have mercy."

"Mebbe she really *dry*," Hamuda winks at him, with a laugh and a fooling in his voice. "Mebbe you'se gotta take her t'de *mikve*-bath an' leave her dere t'ree o' fo' days—mebbe she'll get a little wet dataway..."

"Lemme 'lone!" says Sa'adya without any patience. "We a'ready done hit all."

"Could be, Sa'adya ole boy, dat de good Lawd, He done made *you* dry wid her, an' she ain't de one dat's dry?"

"De Lawd knows. It's all de Lawd's doin'."

"But dere's a cure fo' dis here," says Hamuda, casual like.

"What cure?" says Sa'adya, getting fearful.

"Ah knows dis cure. Ah kin do hit."

"What cure? What cure? Ah swear, y'se gotta tell me. Ah'se awillin' t'give mah eyetoot'."

"Ah kin do de trick real quick." Hamuda takes his time. "Ah'se studied all 'bout dat dere stuff!"

"Ah swear t'God, if ya kin do dis fo' me an' save me—y'll jes 'bout save me f 'om death! Ah'se awillin' t'give ya mah soul, not jes money!"

"Ah ain't a-askin' fo' yo' soul or fo' nuthin'. But ah kin promise ya, word o' honor, dat ah'se a real expert in dis here cure line. Wid de help o' de Lawd, y'll fin' ev't'in' fine an' dandy in a jiffy."

"Ah don't gitcha," says Sa'adya, in a wonderment. "Kin y'give me dis here cure right now?"

"What's de hurry!" Hamuda smooths down his beard, and his eyes is aglistening like two wet olives. "Dis here is agoin' t'take a little time, ole pal. Like de good Book says, T'eve'y t'in' dere am a sea-son, an' a time t'eve'y pu'pose...a time t'em-brace an' a time t'ree-f 'ain from em-bra-cin'. Watch yo'sel'."

"Well, when?"

"Whenever y'wants hit."

"Ah wants hit dis here day," says Sa'adya in a hurry. "Dis here day."

"O.K., smaht boy." Hamuda, he swallows a smile into his moustache. "Y'send yo' ole woman t'me, an' res' easy dat when she leaves me she'll be abelchin' a'ready."

"Abelchin'?" Sa'adya can't follow. "What kin' o' cure is dis y'll be givin' her?"

"F'om de stron' an' f 'om de sweet an' f 'om de goat..."

"Am dis here cure a sure-as-hell-fire one?"

"Oho! Dis cure is de one an' on'y! Ah 'll open her eyes, an' she'll see de mid-night stars. She won't come out from under mah han's widout she's satisfied, so satisfied she'll be abelchin'. Ah ain't like you, pal, dead lazy, a good-fo'-nuthin' stiff..."

When he'd spoke that far, Sa'adya started in ashaking, and he got so angry he wanted to kill him.

"Damn ya, and damn yo' soul, y' rat!" he yelled out loud. "Basta'd! Whoremaster! Dirty mout'!"

"Shame, shame." Hamuda stretched his hands out to him and preached at him a bit. "Y' really is one ungrateful cuss. Here ah was athinkin' o' yo' good, so dey wouldn't be atakin' ya t'de war, an' 'stead o' thankin' me y'starts acussin'."

"Basta'd! Pimp!" Sa'adya grabbed a stone and jumped on him. "'tis an ole goat, damn yo' soul!"

Hamuda, he slipped out of his hands and shook a hot leg, and was ahopping and ajumping and arunning like a deer. Sa'adya, he ran after him, yelling as loud as he could, "Rascal! Scoundrel! Y'is a son-of-a-bitch! Y'is a hell-cat!…"

Right away, all the children in the street was running after them, ahelling and ayelling, and after them came the grownups from the street and the grownups from the yards, and they took hold, and they all got into two gangs, one gang around Hamuda, and another around Sa'adya.

"What's agoin' on?" they all shouted. "What's happened 'atween ya?"

"Kee-razy! He's jes plumb loony!" Hamuda honked like a goose, wiping the sweat from his forehead with his hand, and complained. "What do he want f 'om me? Why do he keep on achasin' a'ter me? Ask him, what he want f 'om me, dis here crazy loon?"

"Y'is a no-good son-of-a-bitch! Scoun-drel!…" Sa'adya, he choked and he fluttered, his face got pale and his eyes popped and his lips trembed. "De t'ings he says t'me, d'ole goat! He's fit fo' de hell-fire! Fo' t'git a fu'nace an' t'row'm in de flames!…It's dogs like 'im brin' wars in de worl', an' den dere's mu'ders an' troubles an' dead sons, all 'cause o' dem dere rascals, damn dar souls! If y'on'y knew de t'ings he done said t'me, y'all'd bu'n'm yo'sel's, y'd mu'der'm!…"

IV.

Now Sa'adya he was tired from all the trouble he done had with his wife, and he felt like a man that has stuffed hisself like a pig till he is so fed up he has no strength, and now he's alooking to just set, doing nothing and resting up a little.

"'It's like de good Book says: Ah'se afindin' de woman more bitter dan death…" he mumbles to hisself, feeling all-fired weary and fed up with Badra, and with a laziness in all his bones.

Even so, when he came to do his usual with her, and she excused herself from it and with good reason, he blew his top at her and wanted to tear her to pieces till she was dead.

But when the time came that she was clean again, he'd be atussling her and rejoicing in her like the day they was married.

Those days he was athinking that this time his work'd not be for nothing in the eyes of the Lord. To make double sure he began being one of the first in the synagogue, every morning and every evening, and he put his mind and heart to it, and he'd say special prayers and "Our Dear Lords" and Hallelujahs, in a loud and weepy voice, and the whole congregation would come to him and bless him, "May de good Lawd hear yo' shouts, an' may He open t'ya de gates o' His mercy"—so that he was pretty sure that his salvation would be coming soon. It was clear as day, plain as the nose on your face, and no ifs or maybes, God forbid and may the Lord protect us.

From then on he didn't think no more of giving Badra a divorce, but he loved her more and more, and he'd be atussling with her from night to night and from day to day.

"Give her a dee-vorce?" he'd be athinking to hisself. "Nohow! Woe is me if d'angels o' Hebben done prayed a'ready dat ah'se gotta do dat ter'ble t'ing. How'll hit be a'ter ah done give her a dee-vorce? How'll ah be acomin' home t'an empty house, widout no Badra in hit? Where'll be her face when she's gone, an' her body all shiny an' bright? Where'll be de fun in her heart an' her talk, an' de way she keep busy all de time 'roun' de house an' fix t'ings jes right? Mah God! Mah God! Ah'se gettin' tetched in de head! Here ah'se jes athinkin' 'bout it-all, 'bout leavin' her, an' ah'se afeelin' loony a'ready! De whole i-dee am plumb crazy. If ah'se agettin' tetched right now, how'll hit be when de Sabbaths'll roll 'round' an' de holy days an' synagogue time. Ah'se athinkin' dat no woman ah aim t'take'd be worth de shoes on her feets. Ah'se been 'roun', an' ah'se got eyes in mah head t'see d'udder womenfolks—ain't none like mah woman! No, sirree! whatever come, ah ain't gonna let d'ole man Debbil git aholt o' me, nohow. Dey say, Hoss-sense is better'n cash. We'se gotta t'ank de Lawd dat He done give us some o' dat dere hoss-sense. What's dat? What kin' o' tomfoolery ah been thinkin' t'do? If 'n ah be gone from her jes one night—ah kick d'ole bucket! Ah bus' a gut! No sirree! Ah be a crazy loon. Ah be a basta'd if 'n ah chase her 'way. Fo' dem dere sons-o'-bitches Ashkenazis wid dar wars, is ah gonna lose mah wife? Betcha life! Dat ain't never gonna happen!'

It wasn't always he was thinking thisaway, but now this and now that: now she's beautiful and now she's ugly, and between times he's sick of them both. Them days, Badra, she keeps ahoping and amoping, and Sa'adya, he keeps asinking into debt to keep body and soul together, just atoiling and amoiling and not knowing what to do.

Then one day he got an invite-card from the Appeals Board asking him to come and lay his case before them. So he went and stood before the three members of the Board, with his heart beating and his lips aquiver.

They began talking thisaway,

"Well, what's your story?"

He took ahold of hisself, and shifted from one leg to the other, fixed his eyes in the ground and then raised them to the Board members, and his lips they got twisted up in a miserable sort of smile, "Gen'l'men...." and he coughed two or three times like the whiskers of the corn done got stuck in his throat. "Gent'l'men, or feller cit-zens, whichever y'like...Whats done got int'y'all? Ain'tcha got nobody else but jes me t'be adraf 'in'? Ain't dere t'ousands o' men fit fo' de draf, but ya gotta be apickin' on poor little me? Jes take a look't me an' see how po'ly ah'se lookin', jes skin-an'-bones. Why, a little ole rifle, she heavier dan ah is. An' it's on'y jes me y'is awantin' t'make a soldier man? Ain'tcha got no better help in dis here war but jes me...?"

From minute to minute his talk got better, and he felt hisself getting stronger.

"Ain'tcha'all afear'd o'de Lawd Almighty?" he complained, and his face was straight and his head high. "Is it me y'all am chasin' a'ter t'get inta dis here draf'? Y'gonna come t'sinnin' 'fore de Lawd 'cause o' me! Ain't hit writ in de good Book, What man am dere dat am fearful an' faint-hearted? let'm go an' ree-rurn t' his house. Ah'se a man what am fearful, ah is. When ah sees two cats afeudin', ah'se afear'd o' dem. What'll ah do if y'all sends me t'dis here front o' de war where t'ousands o' de little guns an' de big guns is ashootin' all 'round'? When ah hears dat, ah be dyin'! 'Nudder t'ing, ah ain't got no chillun t'come after me, an' how y'all athinkin' t'wipe mah name off de face o' d'earf when ah ain't yet kep' de comman'men' t'be f 'uitful an' mul-tip-ly? Mebbe y'all is thinkin' t'dee-stroy de Cre-a-shun, God fo'bid an de Lawd protec' us? What'll y'gonna have t'say on de Day o' Judgment?…Y'all oughta go t'dem as has t'ree or fo' chillun, dem as has a'ready kep' de comman'men' t'be f 'uitful an' mul-tip-ly, an' dis here law was made fo' dem an' not fo' me, seein' as how ah ain't got no chillun. No suh, gen'l'men. Y'all gotta help me t'bring mo' souls inta Israel, so's ah kin work 'gainst de B'itish Gov'men' what ain't lettin' in no im'grants. Sho' 'nuf! Y'all am good Zionist believers, an' y'se gotta help, an' 'specially a man like me what am atryin' wid all mah might. Why, if 'n ah co'd even b'ing in twins eve'y year, ah wouldn't beg off, nohow…"

He spoke fine, real fine, that time and that place, good sense and from the heart, and he got louder and louder and more excited till it was like trumpets blowing.

Now the members of the Board, they had a real good time ali-stening to his speech, and they was winking at each other and laughing. But their hearts was hard, and they didn't see things hisaway.

"That's why," they said. "You've got to be drafted because you have no children. That's the law."

"Whatch'all mean, no chillun?" says he, standing there in a wonderment and looking them in their eyes. "Dey'll be acomin', dey'll be acomin', dey'se a'ready on de way. It's de Lawd's doin'."

"If you'll bring a certificate from a doctor saying that your wife is pregnant we'll give you an exemption."

"Why, ah been a-askin' her an' a-askin' her," says Sa'adya ahumoring them by a tone and a tune and a manner of speaking. "An' she he'sel' still don't know is she on de nest, is she ain't. T' go t'de doc—she ain't willin', fo' shame. But she boun' t'git in de way o'de wimmen, she willin' o' not, nex' day o' nex' week. Soon, ve'y soon…Ah'se a'ready doin' all ah kin. Ah ain't agoin' t'let her 'lone, not fo' a single hour, be sure o' dat. Y'all is good folks, an' y'll do de right t'ing, ah knows dat. An' me too, ah'll do de right t'ing by y'all an', seein' as how ah'se a ca'penter, ah'll make y'all a little chess set like we makes here in Israel, wid all de trimmin's, so'se y'all kin spen' some o' yo' time aplayin' dat dere game, an' den y'll fo'get 'bout me, an' y'all won't be rememberin' me all de time, an' y'all won't be thinkin' o' me fo' dis here draf'…"

But Sa'adya was talking to a stone wall, and they didn't listen and didn't pay him no mind. Finally he left them, all bent and broken, and his eyes was dark, and his knees was aknocking together.

V.

When he came home he let hisself down to the ground and sat like a mourning man with his dead one laying before him.

"What's t'do, ole woman?" says he in a squashed and trembling voice. "Ah'se still in de same ole trouble. Dey's apushin' me plumb inta dis here draf'. Look't how ah'se agettin' bald, here and here. Dey sticks to dar guns, an' you sticks t'yourn, like'n empty stove—no chillun, an' still no chillun. What'll become o' me? De Lawd pity me, Mammy, dat y'ever done bo'n me, t' dis here draf' an' t'dis here great trouble dat ah'se agotten inta. Where'll ah go an' what'll ah do? Dere ain't no mo' hope, no mo' hope in dis life.. ."

"De Lawd'll have mercy," says Badra like always, sighing and standing there, fine and skinny, and her eyes are low and her face is small and sharp, but all lit up like a cloud at twilight.

"What's dis here 'Lawd have mercy' talk o' yourn!" he complains. "We'se adyin', we'se los', ole woman!"

"De Lawd'll have mercy," says Badra again, and she thinks her own thoughts all to herself. "Ah'se even ready now—t'swaller leeches. Ah'se ready."

"What leeches?" says Sa'adya, raising his e'yes to her in a wonderment.

"Whatever happen, ah don't care. If 'n ah live—ah live, an if 'n ah die—ah die. Who care?" says she, bending her head with a sad smile. "On'y jes dat y'll be wid me, ole man…"

"What's dat? What's dat stuff?" Sa'adya gets excited. "How y'talkin'?"

"One o' de Ay-rab womenfolks, ole man," an' she bends her head still further, "she gimme de word dat ah sh'd swaller leeches in d'even'in' o' de night ah goes t' de *mikve* bath fo' mah monthlies. But dis here trea'men's a matter o' life or death. Mebbe de leech, she grab aholt o' mah heart an' choke me, but if she go down deep den ah'se a gonna git us a chile. Who care? Ole man, you hunt up one o' dem leeches an' ah'll swaller her. De Lawd'll have mercy, de Lawd'll have mercy…"

Then a kind of cloud came down and covered up Sa'adya's face, and his eyebrows kissed one another, and it seemed like that very minute he was going to jump on her in his anger. But he didn't jump on her, nohow, and he didn't say a word, but he sat and squeezed his head between his knees, and his back was moving, and his shoulders were shaking.

Translated by I.M. Lask

The Ring and the Canopy

S torks are said to have this characteristic: they build their nest on the roof of a house, but before the Angel of Death enters, they fly away. Just like the storks, Hanina Porat and his wife left their home before evil days came.

All their lives they had lived in Gregorod in Volhynia, at first under the Russians and later under the Poles, and all the traveling they had ever done was to make their way from their home to their shop and back. Here they had been born and married and bore their sons and daughters, grandsons and granddaughters, accreting to a large, ramified family; and they were like two trees, their roots plunging deep into the earth, their foliage rearing to the skies and their branches spreading far and wide.

When the government started oppressing the Jews with heavy taxes and fines, extorting all their money and molesting them in other ways, Hanina no longer felt firm ground underfoot and he decided to go to Eretz Israel. His children and their families, however, would not go along with him; on the contrary, they tried to dissuade him from leaving, but he was adamant. Liquidating his property, he emigrated to Eretz Israel with his wife.

For eight years he lived in Tel Aviv trying to run a business which did not prosper, for he lost more than he earned, and each time he bought and sold merchandise his money dwindled.

In the meantime the war broke out and disaster struck the Jewish people everywhere, more terrible than had ever befallen them throughout the ages.

Weakened by the fears and tensions of the war and by old age, which had crept up on him and rendered him ineffectual, Hanina gave up his business and took his place among the old men sitting in the Beth-Hamidrash. From now on he lived on his meager savings, living out his days aimlessly.

Though the dire misfortunes suffered by the Jewish communities in the Diaspora did not become fully known until after the war, some news did nevertheless come through. Torn between fear and hope and in constant anxiety, Hanina and his wife kept praying to the All-Merciful to spare their children and stand by them in their hour of need.

When the war was over and the news of the extermination of the Jewish people came through, they learned of the destruction of the Gregorod community—all the men, women and children had died horrible deaths, machine-gunned at the brink of the grave-pit, in concentration camps, or in the flames of the incinerators.

Hanina fell ill, prostrated by his terrible grief and by the sight of his wife. Like one demented, she rent her heart uttering shrill, fitful screams, like a swallow before an impending storm, and then, in the agony of her soul, she would fall quivering into a swoon.

For three months Hanina struggled with his illness before he passed away.

II

Desolate and forlorn, the bereaved old woman remained in her lonely house without a single kindred soul in the whole wide world. Alone she sat, crushed under the burden of grief that was too much for her to carry—grief too great for the world to contain, for words to describe and the heart to understand.

Distraught and half-crazed, she would sit nodding her head, her hand clutching her heart. With broken, piercing moans she would tell over the names of her sons and her daughters and their sons and daughters, her seamed face drenched with tears.

She would remember them as they were in the cradle, then in their childhood, she saw them under the marriage canopy and in the bridal chair, the pangs of childbirth, the infants in their arms and the joy that abounded in their homes. Sometimes she would call out to them, speak to each one in turn, as if they all stood alive before her. At times she would blame herself for their death, for not having insisted firmly enough that they come with her to Eretz Israel, for not having expostulated and implored and cried, "Come, leave this place! Do you not feel the hostility of the *goyim,* the malevolence of the enemies all around us!" And at times she would try to persuade herself that they might perhaps still be alive, that the light might yet shine on the darkness which enveloped her and that there was still hope. For it was inconceivable that they were no longer in the world, that she should be alive and not they, that the sun should shine, that the streets should be thronged with happy people strolling with crowing babies, that life should go on as usual—and that they should be no more, particularly they, only they…She felt that one of these days, very soon, now perhaps, they would suddenly come in, fling themselves on her and embrace her in wild joy, every one of them, from the eldest to the youngest.

Her neighbors, old women like herself, came in to sit with her and tried to console her, like Job's three comforters, though they themselves were in a similar plight and bore a similar burden of grief, having been severed from their families and their frail glow of life had been all but extinguished. They would weep with her, urge her to cling to the hope she nurtured, reason with her that her children had possibly managed to escape to Russia, or had survived in the concentration camps or forests, and would surely arrive eventually in Eretz Israel together with all the other immigrants; the mercy of the Eternal One, they said, knew no bounds.

III

The life that is given to man is granted unconditionally. For better or for worse, life pursues its course. That is the way of the Creator.

Once the seven days of mourning were up, the old woman began to be concerned about making a living. She found herself left with very little money. Most of it had been frittered away by the failing business her husband had tried to run and the rest had gone on doctors and medicines during his illness, so that all their savings had dwindled to practically nothing. She still had some jewelery; a gold bracelet, a diamond brooch, three rings set with jewels, a few strings of pearls and some other trinkets, but she did not wish to sell and live on the proceeds. "Let them stay where they are," she said to herself.

She realized that her money would only last her a few months. As she had no one to fall back on—no one took the least interest in what happened to her—she decided to do something about earning a living so as not to be dependent on others. Nor did she delay putting her decision into effect. She bought a small stock of fancy goods and knick-knacks from a wholesaler and went round peddling her wares in the cafés and restaurants.

There were many such peddlars making the rounds of the cafés: they were refugees, survivors of the Holocaust, who came from Germany, Austria, Hungary, Poland, former lawyers and doctors, bankers and financiers, merchants and property-owners, all respectable householders who were past their prime. But the old woman was the most conspicuous among them all. There was something extraordinary about her appearance that singled her out as distinct from the others: she was small and bent, her clothes were faded but clean, she wore a wig awry on her head and earrings dangled from her earlobes; her seamed face, crisscrossed with a web and woof of thousands of wrinkles, bore an expression of deep sorrow, the epitome of Israel's bereavement and widowhood; her pouchy eyes looked bewildered and rather frightened, her drooping mouth was pursed inward, her pointed chin receded sharply. She walked with short, hurried steps, like a baby that had not yet learned to walk properly.

There was something in her gait suggestive of a pigeon walking with its neck bobbing and wings flapping.

Unobtrusively she would go up to the people seated in the café, her purse dangling from one hand and her basket in the other, and ask them to buy something in a timid, halting voice, her tone friendly and suffused with a kind, motherly humility.

The people would look up at her in surprise, which would give way to a tinge of sadness. For a moment their hearts would go out to her, as if they saw their mother standing there, or their grandmother, depending on who or how old they were. With a repressed sigh they would rummage in her basket and extract a bar of soap, a little bottle of eau-de-cologne, a packet of razor blades or some other usable item, and pay her. Occasionally somebody would want to give her an extra shilling or two, which she would not accept. Sometimes people would enter into conversation with her and ask her all about herself: who she was, where she had come from, how long she had been in the country and what had reduced her to her present circumstances, and she would immediately reply in a whisper, her face downcast, her mouth twisted in utter bitterness. In fitful, acrid whispers she would relate all that had befallen her, the wealth and comfort she had once known, the expensive sideboards, the upholstered couches and the large mirrors extending from the floor to the ceiling of her house; she spoke in praise of her sons and daughters, such delicate, refined children, pure and holy souls who—woe to her—had been slaughtered like sheep at the hands of Israel's enemies, and of all the family she was the only one left alive. Her husband had passed away, she told them, but he, Lord be praised, had died a natural death at the hands of Heaven. Concluding her recital with a prayer to the Divine Comforter that He may console Israel, His people, she hastened away jerkily with her pigeon-like gait.

IV

The old woman became absorbed in her trade, which she plied day long from the time she left the synagogue in the morning to the time she entered the synagogue at dusk, day in day out, in the winter rain and in the scorching summer sun.

The memory of her children never for a moment left her, flooding her heart with a constant sorrow and drawing from her an occasional dull, anguished keening, like a seashell that keeps moaning though far from its native sea. They were always before her eyes, at every moment of the day, whether she was plying her trade or idle, lying on her bed at home or at prayer in synagogue, in the street making her rounds of the cafés, they were there wherever she looked. It was as if they had been woven into the very pattern of the world, had merged with all things and had become part of them, and yet had remained distinct. If she happened to look absently at the sky she immediately recalled her children, and when a breeze alleviated the heat of day it put her in mind of them. When the street was thronged with people she would stand watching them, shaking her head despondently as if to say: I have no one among all this crowd. Every time she drank a glass of lemonade to quench her thirst, its taste and coolness would somehow be associated with them, bringing it home to her for the thousandth time that *they* were no more, that *they* would not ever drink again. Everything else she perceived, things connected with living creatures and with inanimate objects, all were associated with her children and constantly reminded her of them.

The passage of time, far from healing her heartbreak, rendered her anguish more acute. From day to day her disaster became more real, more palpable, more overwhelming.

Within a year she had aged terribly; her frame had shrunk, her features had shriveled and her strength was waning. More and more frequently she had to sit down to rest on a chair in front of a café, on a doorstep or on a bench in a park, where young mothers would be taking their little children out for a walk. She would watch the tots frisking about, chasing one another and being chased, yelling at the top of their voices, skipping and jumping, their bright-hued clothes forming a medley of color. She would frequently go up to one or other of the children, stroke their heads and give them a few sweets, her lips mumbling words of endearment. Some of the children would stand staring at her, never having seen such a strange creature in all their short lives, while others would cheekily make faces at her or even fling a handful of sand. Their mothers would scold them and smack their bottoms, but the old woman would try to stop them. They must not hurt their children the least bit, she would tell them—children must be pampered and spoken to gently and lovingly, with patience and kindness, for Jewish children were surrounded by so many enemies, cruel, merciless, murderous Gentiles; even here in Eretz Israel there were *goyim,* with a wicked government to boot, and who knew what evil these haters of Zion were plotting? Blinking in whispered agitation, she would go on and tell them how she had once had children and grandchildren just like these—may they be spared to their mothers for long life—babies and infants, all so beautiful and pure and innocent of sin, and they had died all manner of horrible deaths at the hands of the enemy. She would then unfold her sad tale and tell them of the life of riches and honor she had once led, of the beautiful furniture in her house and the many servants she had kept, of the sons who had made a name for themselves and the daughters she had married off to respectable, honest husbands with her bless-ing and ample dowries; she told them of how she had emigrated to Eretz Israel, and how her sons and daughters would not come with her, afraid of losing trifles and not of afraid losing their all, and in the end the arch-enemy had seized them and flung them and their children into the burning furnace, to the last one.

The women would hear her out, sighing, and reply that they too, just like her, had lost all their families in the Holocaust. Each would say how many of her kin had perished; one was the sole survi-vor of a family of eighty, the other had only two sisters left, but they were kept imprisoned in the "illegal-immigrants" camp in Cyprus by decree of the wicked government, and were unable to join her in Eretz Israel.

In this way they would sit and talk of things that seemed so faraway, as if they were remote episodes from the history of Israel's past among the nations. Yet they themselves were part of this history, their everyday lives were closely interwoven into its minutest detail, and they lived it as did each and every member of the Jewish people.

After a short while, having rested a little, the old woman would pick up her purse and basket and go back to dragging herself from café to café, from table to table and from one person to the other.

V

In the course of time, as she went about peddling her wares, she came to be a familiar figure. People got to know her and her history, and she became a topic of conversation in the cafés. Opinions were divided. Some regarded her as a sort of legend and spoke of her in glowing, lyrical terms, praising her courage and fortitude and attributing to her every human virtue. Others were rather critical, resenting her suffering and grief and toil, her odd manner and the clothes she wore, and above all, the very fact of her existence and everything about her and all she stood for. There were even some who wished to find a solution for her and contemplated placing her in an old age home, where she would no longer bob about among them, a living reproach.

She took no notice of them or what they said and would not agree to be buried away in a home for the aged. She had all she needed, thank God, she said. She had gold and pearls and other precious things, and besides, she was making a living, good or bad; when she earned much she ate her fill and had something left over, and when she earned little she still ate and had something left over, the Lord be praised.

Her peddling trade prospered, in fact, and she earned more than she actually needed, particularly as she lived most sparingly: a loaf of bread, two or three tomatoes, an onion and a handful of greens was all she had each day. Apart from plying her trade, which she did openly, she secretly engaged in charitable deeds, caring for the poor and sharing her bread with them, for that was what she meant when she said that she always had something left over, whether she earned much or little.

Many were the poor people she cared for, sparing no effort. There was the pregnant woman, with children as many as the large and small clusters that hang from the vine, with an insane husband at home and an empty house; there was the wretched woman just after childbirth, emaciated and destitute, with nothing to sustain her; there was the woman abandoned by her husband, ill-tempered and bitter, with a brood of children peeping out from behind her apron, stunted, scrawny and wasted, their bellies swollen, their legs spindly and warped, and their eyes staring from their sockets; there was the old man, hovering on the brink of the grave, who had been discharged from hospital as incurable—a hopeless case; there was the demented old woman babbling in senility, and a host of others.

Simply and unobtrusively she busied herself with their troubles. She neither patronized nor fawned on them; she did not delude them with false hopes or crow over them as do-gooders are wont to do, but did her duty, as if she were one of them.

If one of them thanked her for her kindness and the trouble she was taking she would blink and reply, in her fluttering, halting manner, that she, just like him, was one of Israel's poor and that there was no difference between them. Sometimes she would answer in a different vein and say that she was not doing it for him but for Heaven; in fact she was definitely at an advantage, for she was accumulating a hoard (of good deeds) up above, in a safe place where none could touch it, so that actually she was doing it all for her own benefit.

VI

She kept her jewels stowed away in her cupboard, among her linens, and cherished them like a rare treasure of priceless value. Hanina had refrained from touching them even when he needed them badly, and had left them for her, to support her in her old age till the end of her days. But now she no longer needed them, neither to wear nor to live on, and did not even think of putting them to some charitable purpose, though she was more than once tempted to do so. Frequently her conscience troubled her that such a large fortune, with which such a great deal of charity could be done, should lie there idle and unused. The jewels themselves seemed to cry at her, as it were, clamoring to accomplish their charitable mission, "You have such a large fortune!" they said, "there is such a lot of gold and pearls and jewels with which to support the poor, feed the hungry, clothe the naked and give a new lease of life to the sick, and you let all this good go to waste!" But she managed to resist the urge to sell her jewelery for a long time.

Though a man is enjoined "to be heedful of a light precept as of a grave one, for he knows not the grant of reward for each precept," nonetheless she intended to use her treasure for a good deed of such magnitude as would have a lasting effect, long after she had left the world of the living. Much and long did she ponder over the matter, struggling with her thoughts and the various ideas that came to her mind, but could arrive at no definite conclusion, discarding each new idea in turn.

Time and again she would take her jewels out of the closet, run them through her fingers, gaze at them, now at a diamond brooch, now at a gem-encrusted ring—they still scintillated and sparkled as they had done in her youth—and the rush of memories of that bygone world would come flooding back, a good world permeated with song and laughter, with the happy voices of children and the exultation of youth.

Long would she sit like that, her head bowed, slow tears trickling down her cheeks, lost in her distant memories—some sharply outlined, some dim and elusive. She saw herself as a young girl, before her children were born, and later as the happy mother of many; she saw her husband Hanina, the very lineaments of his face, the kind way he treated her and the manner in which he conducted his daily affairs; she conjured up the memory of each one of her sons and daughters, looks, their behavior, their different natures, each one a world unto himself. There was one of her sons, a man wholly devoted to public welfare and good deeds, who was highly thought of in the community; there was her daughter, a woman chaste and virtuous, pure as the Sabbath loaf as it emerges from the oven, her skillful hands ever plying the needle and loom—the perfect housewife; there was the frail scholar, silent and ascetic, with his dreamy eyes and lofty thoughtful brow, absorbed in his books; there was the lively daughter, witty, intelligent and vivacious, her face aglow with the joy of living, her company and conversation much sought after; then there was the shrewd, practical man of the world, the local bank manager, who was called in to arbitrate in every dispute, his judgment being highly respected; and there was the timid daughter, soft and plump as a downy pillow, with her dimpled chin, her eyes clear as the cloudless skies, her voice soft and pleasing. Thus she remembered them.

And as her sigh-laden memories roved from one child to the other, her tears would course more swiftly and the jewels in her hand would refract a myriad flashing hues, then grow dim; yet one small facet would be caught in a lingering sparkle, like the pure glitter of a lone tear.

VII

As she was making her rounds one day she came to a row of seaside cafés, huddled together like stalls in the market. Gramophones and radios were blaring out the latest song hits, a sacchariferous groaning and sobbing, or a screeching medley of jazz, rising to a deafening, numbing clamor.

Men and women in bathing suits lolled about in pairs or larger groups, refreshing themselves with a glass of cold beer after the rigors of swimming, humming the hit blared out by the gramophone, playing cards intently, or regaling one another with jokes and witticisms. One would make a witty sally, his companion would retort with a barbed jest, and the third would outdo them both with the wittiest remark of all—as Jews are wont to do when they are together, for they are very quick of wit and love to make a show of jesting.

Bowed and shabby, the old woman walked among this lively clatter, proferring her wares to the gay throng. But wherever she went the atmosphere seemed to undergo a subtle change, as if she infected those near her with her humility of spirit, and a brooding air of restraint seemed to set in, shutting out the wild clamor. People looked up at her in surprise or with quickened interest, as if they had just remembered a dream they had had the night before and which had eluded them till that moment. She and they struck a sharp contrast, not merely a contrast of age—of decrepitude set against the flowering of youth—but of two antipodal planes of life, contradictory and incongruous, and for a moment it was not at all clear which was real and which was illusory.

Some of the café crowd, without relinquishing the glasses or playing cards they held in their hands, bought some item or other, to the accompaniment of a jest or a bit of small talk; and she, as was her wont, would unfold the whole story of her life and of the terrible calamity that had befallen her. As if overwhelmed by compassion for these people, she would conclude her tale with words of comfort, calling on the Blessed One to preserve His people, Israel, from all foes and enemies, from all the evils and disasters of this world. With this injunction she would go her way, flapping and swaying, her withered dewlap quivering and her head bobbing up and down as if in silent affirmation.

VIII

Having called at all the seaside cafés, she felt tired and wanted to rest a little. The sea stretched invitingly before her. Going down to the beach, she disencumbered herself of her basket and sat down on the sand.

It was early afternoon, the hottest part of the day, when the sun beat down mercilessly and the beach was deserted. A few wisps of bright cloud streaked the motionless sky. The sea, blue and glinting, a darker reflection of the skies, heaved in a slow swell. The waves came rolling in endless furrows, one after the other, some ponderous and flat, others light and rearing, green or white-capped, breaking against one another in a low, muted rumbling that never ceased. Racing onto the sand they frothed and eddied, piling up on one another in a crescent-shaped tidal flow, branching into numerous little streams that grated among the heaped-up shells and whispered among the bits of green seaweed, and were sucked back by the undertow, leaving behind a hushed soughing and some specks of foam. Out at sea, the sun looked down on its fiery image, like the moonlight cleaving a silvery path through the waters, yet incomparably brighter.

Stooped, weary and shrunken, a limp heap of tatters and wrinkles, the old woman sat gazing at the wide expanse of glittering sea and listening to its endless monologue. Its speech not be rendered in the language of men, but it spoke in a voice that could be heard and understood in the heart, a voice that told of sadness and pain; tears welled up in her eyes and deep sighs racked her frail body.

There seemed to be a kindred feeling between them, the forlorn old woman and the heaving sea. Perhaps it was because the sea is nearer to the heavens than to the earth, for they both gaze upon one another eternally, or perhaps because the sea bears the clear stamp of the might of the Creator, or because of the two tears the Holy One sheds into the great ocean when He recalls the suffering of His children among the nations of the world. Be that as it might, all her bitterness and sense of bereavement surged up within her in a plaintive gush; stretching out her arms to the sea, she bemoaned the fate that had befallen her and her children.

For a long time she sat weeping and moaning, calling to each of her children by name, with a host of endearing fondling terms, the tears coursing down her anguished face, her mouth contorted. After a while she fell silent and sat rocking back and forth, her face clasped in her palms, while the sea lapped at the sand near her feet in an unceasing rhythm, like the human heartbeat.

Gradually her eyes shut, opened and shut, opened and shut, and the whole world seemed to resolve itself into a striation of scenes, of sea and sky, and again of sky and sea. Her limbs went slack and all awareness left her. Gone were the sea and sky, gone were her sons and daughters and all other living creatures that God had created in His world; they were no more, they had never been, they were but a dream, she herself was a dream, this world was a dream, and the sea was but a figment of the dream of this world.

Presently awaking out of her stupor, she looked around her blindly, uncomprehendingly, and for a moment she did not know where she was. But soon she regained possession of her senses and peered across the sea to where the sun's reflection glared white-hot like incandescent molten iron, ringed by a corona of leaping tongues of flame, and throwing out a shower of golden sparks. There was something out there among these golden sparks, rising and falling, swaying from side to side, lost to sight for a moment in the white glare and reappearing. Shading her eyes with her hand, she gazed at this thing in awe and bewilderment, now it looked like a large case, a Holy Ark, now it looked like a Scroll of the Law floating on the water. Inconceivable as this was, she was ready to accept it as some sign. A few moments later, however, she recognized it for what it was—a lad standing on a flat-bottomed boat, his legs apart, paddling with vigorous strokes. But the idea had been planted in her mind and her thoughts, no longer centered on what she saw, reverted to the little fortune she kept hidden away in her closet; she would donate a Scroll of the Law to the synagogue: that was the sign and token she had received from heaven.

IX

Henceforth she neglected her business and started making the rounds of booksellers and vendors of devotional articles, enquiring about a Scroll of the Law and its cost. She also went round to jewelers and goldsmiths to price her jewelery. By dint of much running about from one to the other she learned of their cunning and deceit. They were all the same, out to fleece you as best they could, outdoing one another in ruthlessness; one would merely skin you at one stroke while the other would do so in two. When approached by the old woman, they all sensed what a good thing they could make out of it and sharpened their teeth for the spoils they hoped would be theirs.

Before she made any deal, however, she went to ask the rabbi to advise her what to do with her jewels. The rabbi, who knew her and all that had befallen her, and had also known her late husband, unhesitatingly counseled her to donate a Scroll of the Law. She immediately replied that the Holy One had already given her a sign to this effect, and she told him of the great light she had seen out at sea. The rabbi was very glad, for his counsel was in accord with the sign given by his Maker.

The rabbi set himself to help in this virtuous deed and assigned to her an honest, trustworthy and learned man to deal with the merchants. An assiduous and restless man he was, his body lean and spare (like a poor man in years of famine), his face pure and serene like a Sabbath loaf, his kind eyes a dreamy blue, his earlocks curling up like a drake's tail, his goatlike beard sparse and drooping.

Without delay he plunged himself into his meritorious mission. He rushed from place to place, his eyes ever roving the streets, his mouth buzzing like a busy bee, his face muscles working furiously, and all the time the old woman hopped after him, frantically trying to catch up and never succeeding. And as he rushed through the streets, he would greet one man, wag his beard at another, stop a third and peer at him with a quizzical expression as if to say, "What are you up to?"; stop another and give him a look of devout thanksgiving, catch one man by the arm and fling a hurried question, "What good deed have you done today?" console another with "Don't worry, my brother," and then he would plunge on his way in feverish haste, his beard awry, humming busily to himself. Finally they came to the jewelers and he started bargaining with them.

The haggling with the jewelers was tiresome and long-drawn, but he managed at last to get a good price—two hundred pounds—for her jewels. He sold them all, except for a diamond ring which the old woman decided to keep in case of need. He had previously found a finely wrought Scroll of the Law, rescued from a Jewish congregation in Poland which had been destroyed in the Holocaust, and bought it for one hundred and fifty pounds.

They were both well pleased—she tearfully, and he with thanksgiving for a good deed well done. She wanted to give him some reward for his pains but he refused, for a meritorious deed is its own reward. When she insisted, however he gave in with a sigh, reflecting that even a king in his palace must have some livelihood.

X

She had a craftsman engrave on the handles of the Holy Scroll the names of her sons and daughters, their wives and husbands and children. She bought a length of fine velvet, sea-blue, and had a seamstress sew it into a mantle for the Scroll, and embroider on it, in gold thread, her husband's and her own name as an everlasting memorial. At last the Scroll, after having been examined by a scribe, was brought to her house, resplendently attired in fine cloth and embroidered in gold.

In honor of the occasion she put on her black silk dress, preserved from the time she was a young bride. The dress was somewhat shabby, split here and there at the seams, frayed at the hems and it exuded a strong smell at naphthalene. It was far too big on her, its loose folds hung about her shapelessly and trailed after her on the floor, making her look like a child dressed as a grownup.

A handful of neighbors, old women like herself, came in to congratulate her, wish her well and console her. Overcome with excitement she went from one to the other, her face bearing an expression of childlike sadness, of wonder and resignation, as if to say "Blessed is He, whose world is thus." Partly filled with wonder that it had fallen to her lot to accomplish that for which the whole world was created and without which the whole world was without worth, and partly unable to realize what it all meant, confused by the women's chatter, she hastily and sorrowfully returned their greetings and good wishes.

When all her visitors had gone, she returned to the table where lay the Holy Scroll in an open case and broke into bitter weeping. She buried her face in its velvet mantle, covered it with her kisses, her fingers frantically caressing the names of her children, engraved like scars on the woodwork of the Tree of Life. Long and loud did she mourn, "My children! Look down, O Lord, and see what the Gentiles have done to my children!", and uttered lamentations that might well have been written in the Book of Job or in the Book of Jeremiah, weeping more bitterly than she had ever wept before. And it seemed as if the Holy One wept with her, and the whole of Israel wept with her, and all the generations of man wept with her, till her soul could no longer withstand the anguish and she fell fainting to the ground.

Again and again she stood over the Scroll of the Law, pleading and expostulating with the Holy One Blessed be He, wailing and lamenting. And the tears that flowed from her eyes fell on her name embroidered in gold, sparkling with a fire that illuminated the whole Scroll.

Henceforth she became more and more listless. At times she would stand softly pleading in a humble, beseeching voice, or sit mutely on the edge of her bed, bowed and rocking to and fro, her face shriveled like a dried-out lichen-covered citron, her eyes fixed on the Holy Scroll.

When she lay in bed at night she would see the Scroll of the Law gleaming at her with its gold embroidery, like that golden sea she had seen glittering in the fiery sunlight, with tongues of flame dancing and leaping upward. Sleepless, she would fall to pondering over the miracles and wonders, the prodigious deeds and marvels the Holy One was able to accomplish to restore her children. For hours she would rack her brains, contemplating such impossibilities, chattering to herself, distraught and demented. Sometimes she would unconsciously sing a snatch of melody at dead of night in a crashed, wavering voice, and she imagined she was hearing her sons chanting the chapter of Prophets in the synagogue on the Sabbath. Finally she would fall into a merciful slumber.

XI

She had originally intended to have the Scroll of the Law dedicated to the synagogue on 7th Adar, the anniversary of her husband's death, but later changed her mind and decided to have it brought there immediately, for, she said, "No man knows when he will be called away, particularly an old woman like myself, who is here today and in the grave tomorrow." Consulting the rabbi and the synagogue warden, she agreed to fix the date for the coming New Moon, the first day of Elul.

When the day arrived, she arose at dawn and hastened to the cemetery to prostrate herself on her husband's grave. From there she went to the market and bought basketfuls of meat, fish and wine. With three pious women helping her, she worked all through that day preparing the ceremonial feast.

After the evening prayer, a large multitude assembled at her house. There were clusters of learned men, and a motley crowd of beggars and idlers, lame, blind, hunchbacked and otherwise crippled (eloquently pleading the cause of the Jewish people before their Father in Heaven); after them came the minstrels carrying their instruments: violin, trumpet, flute, drum and cymbals.

They washed their hands in the ritual manner and sat down at the table, with their beards, earlocks and devotional fringes. They set to with a will, munching and gulping with a grunting and puffing, waving their hands and wagging their beards and licking their fingers, commending the meritorious deed and praising the name of the Lord. Between glasses of wine they delivered themselves of wise homiletics, and between each dish they praised their God-fearing hostess and her virtuous works.

After the meal was over they stood up. The warden took the regally attired Scroll out of its case, kissed it devoutly and handed it to the rabbi. The whole throng pressed forward to kiss the Scroll and offer the old woman their felicitations. She stood before them bowed, frail and awkward, her face twitching, her eyes streaming with tears, and her wig gleaming mirror-like in the harsh electric light. In a timid, quavering voice she said,

"May it be His will that you live to see the Scroll of the Law brought to the Temple, which will be rebuilt speedily in our days."

With great pomp and ceremony the procession made its way to the synagogue. The rabbi bore the Scroll under a fluttering canopy, flanked by candle bearers, to the accompaniment of music, singing and rejoicing. The night resounded with the shrilling of the violin, the blasting of the trumpet, the trilling of the flute, the clashing of the cymbals and the thundering of the drum, while the multitude raised their voices in mighty song as they walked through the night, resembling a heavenly host of immortals…

Overwhelmed with awe and the sanctity of the occasion the old woman hobbled after the canopy, with two women supporting her. The candle in her hand trembled and flickered like a golden ear of corn, and her heart quivered as she meditated on the souls of her children who were no doubt accompanying her in the holy procession at this moment.

When they reached the synagogue, all the Scrolls were taken out of the Ark to welcome their newly arrived brother. As on the Feast of the Rejoicing of the Law, they were carried round the synagogue seven times, while the congregation changed psalms. After the rabbi had delivered a homiletical discourse, the band again struck up a merry tune.

All the congregation leaped to their feet, clasped one another by the hand and broke into a lively dance. From moment to moment they grew more spirited, more hectic, as they hopped and skipped, sang and shouted, crouched and sprang; beard waving against earlock, fringes flying against skullcap, they cavorted round in a roisterous circle.

Gayer than all was the man who had helped her purchase the Scroll. With zeal and vigor he danced with all his might till the sole of his shoe came loose. Merrily he capered up to the old woman—his sole flapping, his skullcap pushed back, sweat streaming down his face, his eyes smiling, his beard awry and his fringes flying about—and asked her to do a ritual dance.

The band began to play a merry tune. The crowd pushed back and formed a circle, clapped their hands and sang and the old woman walked into the middle of the ring. Gravely she raised one foot and set it down, made a turn and then another, her dress flapping and her earrings dangling. She then heaved a deep sigh—the epitome of her whole life, as it were—and slowly returned to her place.

The dancing was resumed with renewed vigor and merriment. It went on right through the night, till it was time for *selichot*, the penitential prayers.

XII

Joy comes and goes in one day. The old woman immediately went back to her daily labors, earning the pennies that she gave away as charity.

On the Sabbath she went to the synagogue to hear the portion of the Law read from her own Scroll, and this was a great consolation to her. She had, in fact, stipulated with the synagogue wardens that the first four Sabbaths would be "hers", then the Day of Atonement, the Sabbath following the Feast of Tabernacles, and every third Sabbath after that.

In the second week her strength began to fail and in two or three days she suddenly found herself exhausted and seemed to see the Angel of Death beckoning to her. Again and again she had to take to her bed, but she would not call in a doctor, for she did not wish to deprive the poor people of the money she would have to spend in doctors' fees. In this she followed the injunction of the sages who said: If a man goes to doctor, he may be cured and he may not, but if a man gives to charity, he will certainly be cured. She accordingly added what she would have spent in doctors' fees to the alms she gave and went back to earning a living.

Though she had aged considerably, she was not afraid of death, nor did she even think of it, as if her days were not numbered, as if her life were fixed immutably in time.

The world had always seemed so remote from her, as if it had receded back to the days of the Patriarchs or progressed forward to the days of the Messiah. But now, more than ever, it was immeasurably remote, had dwindled to a minute speck, held nothing for her except for the Holy Scroll she had donated, her acts of charity and her few good deeds that would speak for her when she entered the world to come. She demanded nothing and took nothing for herself in this world, but toiled to give others all she had, and more. Her every thought and yearning were set on the next world, where all her children were. At every moment of the day she thought of them, held converse with them, like a man walking along one bank of a river conversing with a friend on the other bank.

One rainy night she lay in bed unable to fall asleep. Suddenly she heard people shouting and rushing about outside. Getting out of bed, she went over to the window and looked out. People were milling about in the street, shouting like mad at the top of their voices, "We have a State, a State of our own!" In the distance she heard a loudspeaker blaring and crowds rumbling like a stormy sea. For a few moments she stood there uncaring, her mind a blank, moved neither by joy nor by wonder, chewing her tongue absently as an animal chews the cud. Heaving a deep sigh from force of habit, she went back to bed.

XIII

During the conflict with the Arabs her sister's grandson arrived in the country. She did not recognize him at first, having last seen him when he was still an infant, just before she and her husband had left for Palestine. But when he told her who he was, her heart leaped and her limbs trembled violently. She fell on his neck, embracing and kissing him, crying out in an anguish of joy, held his face in her palms and gazed at him, clasped him to her as if he were her own child.

He was a young man with the frail build of a boy and the wizened face of an old man. His back was bent, his skull hairless and there were toothless gaps in his mouth. His eyes were clouded as if with a pall of smoke. They were the eyes of a man who no longer has a single doubt, whom nothing can surprise, the dull eyes of a man for whom everything is clear and certain and inexorable.

He had undergone all the atrocities and barbarities that had befallen the Jewish people in that last decade; they had become part of him, they made up his short life's history, they were still deep-seated in his being. They were the sole substance of his thoughts; they made him withdraw into himself, weary and disgusted with human beings; they rendered him taciturn, silent like a judge in his courtroom, with the whole world on trial. It was a heavy, bitter silence, sullen, dark and withdrawn, yet it implied everything, more than words could ever convey. It spoke of the blood of his father and mother soaking into the ground; of the anguished cry of the Jewish masses as they stood on the brink of the grave pits they were forced to dig for themselves; of the screams of mothers as their children were plucked from their arms to be slaughtered; of infants hurled from rooftops, their blood spattering the ground and the trees; of frenzied young men and women driven naked through snow and icy wind, lashed by their tormentors' whips and torn by ravening dogs, to redden the snow with their blood; of forced labor, starvation and cold under the brutal hand of the oppressor; of bodies bloated with hunger sprawled grotesquely in every house and in every street; of days and nights passed in trembling fear in dark cellars and airless burrows; of those many other diabolical acts of the Gentiles and of the civilized world, too horrible to describe and too hideous to hear.

He sat and told her in fragments of what had befallen the rest of her family, who had perished to the last one. He recounted a little of what he himself had been through and of how he had been saved, and she listened, wringing her hands and weeping bitterly.

Very soon he got up to leave. She tried to persuade him to stay in her house, where she would look after him and provide for him, but he refused: he must go back to the army and fight the war, he said. In vain did she plead with him not to leave her—she was all alone in the world, desolate and forlorn like a discarded pebble; all she had now was him, in whom she saw the faces of her children and heard their voices. When she saw that he could not be prevailed upon to stay and that all her pleas were unavailing, she took out of the closet the ring she had kept behind and held it out to him saying, "This is what I bequeath to you." Gingerly he held it in his fingertips, squinting at it wryly, then pushed it aside, as if it were not made of gold and diamonds, but of some base metal and cheap glass. Thinking that he did not realize its value, she told him how precious the ring was, praised its beauty, and urged him to take it.

His face darkened and his eyes clouded as he saw in his mind's eye all those gold rings, jewels, watches, bracelets, pendants, gold teeth and other spoils heaped in neat piles next to the incinerators.

Again she pressed the ring on him, extolling its virtues, its value, its craftsmanship. After a moment's hesitation he gave her a thin, twisted smile, a grimace of pain, and told her he did not wish to accept her legacy; he had all he needed and more. So saying he walked away, leaving her weeping bitterly as if she were mourning the dead.

XIV

That same day, she took a strip of silk and sewed it into a little pouch, like the kind children are given to keep their Hannuka money in. She then fetched a dribble of ashes, which she filled into the pouch with much sighing and tears and whispering to herself, placed the ring inside and hung it by a thread round her neck. On second thought she unclasped the pouch, removed her earrings with trembling hands and placed them in the pouch, too, and hung it again round her neck. Devoid of the earrings, her face looked smaller, more shrunken, and her eyes were sadder and more bewildered and frightened.

Among the bustling city masses the old woman felt lost and confused. Everyone was jubilant at Israel's victories and walked about confident and proud. Jeeps raced back and forth, armored cars rumbled through the streets with a triumphant roar, Israeli soldiers sang lustily as they stood shoulder to shoulder in trucks. Immigrants arriving from the Diaspora waved their hands through the windows of the buses that carried them from the port to their new homes. Loudspeakers of the different political parties vied with one another in anticipation of the coming elections. Young girls armed with Sten guns stood on guard at barbed wire checkposts and barricades. Boys and girls roamed about in loud, guffawing clusters, free and frolicsome.

Amidst all this tumult the old woman felt wretched and forlorn; she did not belong here, neither in time nor in place. All this jubilation, this joy of deliverance, meant nothing to her. She was insensible to everything but the loss of her children who had perished as martyrs, who had not lived to enjoy all this munificence. She thought of them with a heavy load of anguish in her heart, and choking sobs would ever rack her frail body.

She went about peddling her wares, darting across busy thoroughfares at great peril, her purse dangling from her right arm, her basket in her left, and the ash-filled pouch on her breast. Heaving and pushing her way through the crowds she went from place to place offering her goods. For though Israel had achieved statehood, the way of the world hardly changed: whoever was poor remained poor, the hungry still went hungry, and those who shed tears in secret continued to shed tears—and many were the poor people in Israel who had none to turn to but the mercy of heaven.

XV

Her sister's grandson came back to see her and sat with her for a short time, recounting various details about her children as he had last seen them. He told her he would not be seeing her for some time as his unit was about to try to break through to Jerusalem. He never came back again.

She became ill with worry, her eyes grew dim with weep and anguish, and frequent illness forced her to take to her bed. In a few days, however, she made an effort to get up again and go about her daily business.

It was a fine day, sunny and clear, a day that emanated from the blue skies, as it were, as if a piece of sky had dropped down and flooded the earth with its bright warmth. Hobbling along feebly, she came to a main thoroughfare; Israel soldiers were marching in columns with shouldered arms down the street, watched by crowds that stood pressed together on either pavement. Pushing her way through the crowd, the old woman stood at the curb, swaying, stretching out her arms to each soldier as he went past, mumbling and nodding her head.

A young woman stood near her. Her body somewhat flaccid and over-plump, her face ruddy and blooming, bore the grace of motherhood; there was something about her reminiscent of a flowering landscape, of early autumn scenes and hues. Thinking that the old woman was begging for alms, she took the trouble of explaining to her that this was out of place here. Surprised, the old woman replied that she was no beggar-woman, God forbid, and that she was not asking the soldiers for charity; she was blessing them that the good Lord would lead them to peace and deliver them from all enemies and hostile forces.

The young woman was immediately drawn to her, as if she saw her own grandmother standing before her. It brought back memories of her little home town, scenes of her childhood, and all those dreams and longings that were gone, never to return.

When the army procession was over, the old woman turned to go, but found walking difficult. Her knees giving way and limbs leaden, she stumbled over to a doorstep and sank down, exhausted. After resting a short while she got up to go, but no sooner had she taken a few steps than she again collapsed. The young woman, who had been watching her from a distance, came over to help her and saw her home, holding her by the arm like a mother walking a little child.

On the way, stopping every few paces to rest, the old woman gasped out her life story, jerkily and haltingly. She told her companion about the Scroll of the Law she had donated to the synagogue, about her sister's grandson who had just arrived in the country, who had no sooner escaped from the enemy there, than he went out to fight the enemy here. "Lord of the Universe!", she cried weakly, "how many are Israel's enemies everywhere!" She then told her about the precious ring she had wanted to give him, a ring that was priceless…

"And he didn't want to take it…" she exclaimed in plaintive surprise. Exhausted by this effort she leaned limply on the arm of her companion, panting heavily. She felt as if all her bones were crumbling. With great difficulty they got to her house, where she collapsed on her bed.

"I have arrived…" the old woman muttered in a harsh whisper, her hands lying inert on the sheet. Her lips twisted into a weak smile. "I have arrived to the end of God's works." And she immediately fell asleep.

The young woman leaned over her and looked at her intently. Then she nodded her head contentedly two or three times, as if she saw something rare and pleasing.

A few moments later she slipped out of the house, her face glowing with satisfaction, her eyes thoughtful and a smile of pleased wonderment playing on the red of her lips.

She came back again the next day and found the old woman ill in bed, with a neighbor looking after her. A few days later she found the door locked—the old woman had passed away.

"She has gone to her eternal home," the neighbor-woman told her piously. "May she rest in Paradise, for she was a righteous woman, a very righteous woman…"

Translated by Yosef Schachter

Mulberries! Mulberries!

Avigdor was now Vitia, Vitia Gorelick. He had come to Kiev from a small town nearby. Soon after his arrival he had the good fortune to find work with the government. In those days the government was short of workers since many people were refusing to have anything to do with it.

"You—who are you?" probed the commissar—a tall heavily built man resplendent in French military tunic and Galliley riding breeches, a red star, a revolver and the other trappings of authority on him. "Are you a party member?"

"A student," answered Vitia.

"A sympathizer?" asked the commissar. "Are you a sympathizer?"

Vitia's faint "yes" was swallowed up in a shy smile. And so he was accepted by the government, not after careful consideration, but because of an uncertain smile. He was immediately signed up and given a food ration card. By authority of the government he occupied a room for himself in an apartment whose owner had been dispossessed.

He did his work in the office as ordered. He kept away from

politics. He made no speeches, nor did he express any opinions. Every free hour he spent in his room.

The room was large, full of sunshine, but food was scarce. He had his longings, he felt loneliness and sadness. And he had his dreams. Hundreds of dreams but not one about real things. Between dusk and evening he would take walks in the streets of the city. Sometimes among the passing women he would see one who seemed to have the aura of those he had read about in books, and then in the starlight he would return to his room, hungry and tired and exalted. But whenever he heard the sound of an approaching car he would become upset and hasten to put the light out, afraid of the Cheka. And because of this fear, too, he would avoid the Cheka building both in the daytime and in the evening.

He was content with living in a big city, on his own, alone. This was a start for him. All his past, his parental home, childhood days, boyhood—were all behind him like an evening field hidden in mist. Nothing was now left of all that. He felt certain that something was going to happen to him—something desired, hoped for, marvelous. And yet this hoped-for something—what, he didn't know—caused him disquiet and filled him with foreboding.

Evenings he heard a rustling sound coming from the adjoining room, the sound of light taps, continuous, repetitive. At first he was annoyed by it as it distracted him from the book he was reading or from the poem he was concentrating on writing, but in the end he became used to it. And then suddenly the sound stopped. That again disturbed him, as if the proper order of things was out of joint. The room had changed for him, the quiet was too much; it seemed heavy as if a soft, thick dough were permeating it from wall to wall.

One day, he met a young girl in the hall as she was coming out of the adjoining room and going down the stairs. She glanced at him in passing. At that moment it was as if the sunlight had burst into the hall, making a garden of the stairs.

In a low voice as if talking to herself she said, "Food." He wondered and went right down to the market. There he exchanged a shirt for a small loaf of bread, two tomatoes, two cucumbers, and a handful of black mulberries. As darkness was falling, he knocked at his neighbor's door and brought her his booty. His heart was fluttering, his face was red, and his eyes looked away.

"For me?" She stood there astonished.

"Yes," he answered with difficulty.

Joy shone in her face, in her teeth, in the nostrils of her quivering nose, and especially in her eyes. Her eyes were green, like a cat's.

He immediately turned to leave. She stopped him.

"Please," she said, "come in and eat with me."

She didn't wait, and started at once to prepare the meal.

Eagerly she went to the table taking bites out of the bread and the green cucumber.

"Spring," she called from out of the cucumber that was being crunched between her teeth, "the smell of spring in my mouth."

And she went on about the tomato quavering in her mouth like a violin.

"Oh, how good it is." She closed her eyes. "As if a violin were playing a tune in my mouth."

She was eating, excited and laughing. Her cheeks flushed.

"I was as hungry as a wolf." She kept looking at the remains of the food on the table. "I never imagined I'd be eating tonight."

More than what she said was expressed in her eyes. Her eyes quickened, brightened, bloomed.

"Eat, please," she urged him, "don't let me eat it all up."

She offered him the mulberries.

"Eat, eat."

Between berries she told him what she was doing; she had been studying rhythmics and acting in an experimental studio of the reconstructivist school.

"Oh," he opened his mouth in astonishment.

"What's the matter?" she asked.

"That's it," he said. "I didn't know what the noise in your room was."

"Noise in my room? What did you imagine it was?"

"Something like the sound of nuts being cracked," he replied, "or of a pestle being pounded in a tiny mortar."

She laughed, her teeth all black from the mulberries.

"I was practising."

Now, she went on, her studies were being discontinued for the summer and she was looking for work to support herself. In the beginning she had a little money from home, not much, and she had spent it on one thing or another. From now on even this little was a thing of the past, and ahead of her—nothing. Her parents' fortune was gone; the Bolsheviks had shaken them like a pear tree until all the fruit had fallen to the ground. Her father, she explained to him, had supervised government forests in Polesia and her mother was of a noble family that had come down in the world. She had had to slough off quite a few prejudices before she had drifted here.

She got up and took out of the chest of drawers a picture of a man, middle-aged, with a big moustache, a pipe in his mouth, and a double-barrelled gun slung diagonally across his back.

"My father," she said.

Then she showed him a photograph of her brother, a young man dressed in the uniform of a cavalryman holding a whip lengthwise between his hands.

She raised her arms and pushed her hair back. She looked at him coquettishly, making eyes at him, and asked him who he was. He didn't know what to answer.

"A high school kid," he said, "working for the government."

"Oh," she wondered, "for the government?"

He was lucky, he told her, to have found work the same day he had come to the city.

"They gave it to you because of your father," she guessed with an air of certainty.

"No," he replied, "on the contrary. My father was a simple tradesman. They didn't investigate me; they didn't check up on my origin. They need workers."

"I'm different," she spoke again. "I'm not used to work. I'm not good at anything."

He thought of giving her half his rations, but he didn't have the courage to suggest it to her.

"What's your name?" She raised her eyes and looked at him

"My name?" He blushed as if she had asked him a very difficult question. "My name is Vitia, yes."

"And I'm Katia."

She chattered away now, speaking about her work in the studio, the theory and techniques of bio-mechanics, the doctrine of "whole elements," of "whole emotions," of absolute control over the body.

At his request she demonstrated three or four exercises. Although he didn't understand a thing about the convolutions of hands, feet, and torso, he sat as if under a spell.

"You'll be a ballerina," he half mumbled.

After a while he got up to go. She came after him. As she was walking she pulled aside the blanket of the bed with a swift motion of her hand, revealing about half the sheet. They reached the door. She got ahead of him to the doorway and stood looking at him sideways with a kind of solemnity.

He was at a loss; his eyes wandered, he made a face; and a faint smile played uncertainly about his parted lips.

She slowly backed away, her eyes fixed on him. He bade her a feeble goodnight, and pushing with side and shoulder edged himself out, as if he were moving through a narrow passageway.

II

In a daze he entered his room and sat down on his bed in the dark. His heart was pounding, his feet shook, and his eyes misted with tears about to fall.

He felt hurt, ashamed. He didn't understand.

"What does it mean? What does it mean?" he whispered to himself. "For the sake of a meal, one meal?"

She had intended to degrade herself...like a slut...such a young girl! Wasn't she afraid of the risk? Could it be that she was loose, that she was in the habit of holding herself cheap, perhaps a street-walker?

He went over to the open window and looked out on the green tin roof that the moon was sweeping with its light. He stood there brooding over her, first finding fault with her and then vindicating her. One way or the other, he said to himself, perhaps she was fond of him, or perhaps she wanted to tempt him, or may be it was a momentary impulse, or maybe the revolution was at fault. And perhaps he had made a mistake, nothing had really happened, it was all his imagination.

He struggled hard with himself. He would hurl a heap of accusations at her and then tell himself that he was mixing up the trivial with what was important.

At night he couldn't sleep. Out of the medley of moonlight and darkness Katia would emerge in all her sweetness and loveliness, her face, her eyes, the outline of her body. He remembered her standing in the doorway, her eyes challenging him. He recalled the whiteness of the bedsheet. His heart raced. Sordid thoughts assailed him, excited him, incited him. He wanted to get up, to knock at her door—but he couldn't find his legs.

The next day and the two following days he didn't happen to meet her.

"It's finished—finished," he whispered unhappily.

He saved his rations and put them way for the day she would return. On the fourth day he suddenly met her as she was going up the stairs, a small basket on her arm.

He greeted her. She returned the greeting.

"I was at my friend's," she said, "for grub."

"I have some food for you," he said, lowering his eyes.

She nodded, passed him by, and went on. In the evening they ate together as if nothing had happened. They chatted about art. Vitia read some poems he had written.

"You're a poet," she cried out in a sort of amazed wonder.

"Humph—a poet," he said breaking into laughter. "Blok is a poet...Mayakovsky."

"Mayakovsky is a Bolshevik." Her lips curled in contempt. "How can a poet be a Bolshevik?"

"He can," he answered, "why not?"

"Are you a Bolshevik?" she asked.

"I? No."

"Ah, but here's the proof."

"It proves nothing."

She straightened up and looked at him.

"A curse on them," she said in a whisper, "those horrible…"

"They are like some natural force," he answered, "like the raging sea, like a snow blizzard. Do you remember the blizzard in 'The Captain's Daughter?'"

"That's right," she replied, "Pugatovschina. That's just what it is. It's exactly the same. I first saw it in my father's house. They took everything." He made a grimace. "Confiscated, nationalized everything. They confiscated the sugar factory and it's now standing idle—the cash in the bank—the house and everything in it—swept clean like the steppe—emptied out."

"And we," Katia drew out her words, hesitating to say it, "my father and my brother—I showed you their photographs—were murdered by the Cheka."

"Oh," he whispered terrified

A little later she shook off her memories and again spoke of choreography and its rules, of the new fine arts. Among other things she said she was preoccupied with a ballet, a heroic ballet of vengeance.

"Yes," she spoke emphatically. "Vengeance."

She began telling the story of a highwayman in the forest waiting in ambush for the gentle, delicate girl. He approaches warily with wolf-like leaps. She sees him, becomes alarmed, but is drawn to him as one pulled to the edge of an abyss. Then like an acrobat, he jumps on her, flings her upward and catches her on the back of his shoulder, her leg and hand curled into the curve of an arabesque above her head which he has pushed back. Slowly she drops down resting on his arms as if in a trance. At that moment a young prince appears bearing a shield and a sword. Immediately the two are joined in a tempestuous dance, striking one another, falling and rising.

"In short," she ended, "the prince overcomes the brigand, stamps his foot on him, raises his sword over him."

Vitia was enthusiastic.

"That's marvelous!" He searched for words. "What an idea! Something new! Timely!"

He wanted to do something for her. He found an opening for her in the propaganda department. Katia began working and getting rations from the government—whatever food was available.

They were happy, both of them. He in particular because all his heart's desires were now fulfilled, all those miraculous and secret wishes. Together they ate their bread, together they dreamed their dreams, and together they wandered everywhere. The days were beautiful, as it was early summer; the sun warm, the shade cool. Each day the skies brought back the days of childhood. There was still a smell of lilac in the air, the acacia was in full bloom, the chestnut was raising its candles; all anger and fury had vanished and the world was emptied of all fear.

From time to time they would climb up a green hill within the city limits. There they would sit looking down at the river and its surroundings, the towers and domes of the monasteries and churches, the fields and the forest stretching out to the blue line of the horizon. The times they spent on the hill were idyllic hours, cherished like a well-loved poem, a dream compounded with reality.

They didn't speak about their feelings for one another. The closer they came to each other, the less they spoke; it was all submerged in the depths of their being unsaid. Until one day, without premeditation, he spent the night with her. From that time on the flow of words between them didn't cease. They both spoke endlessly, he with lowered eyes, she looking straight into his. They spoke of love and its many faces. Vows of love were exchanged, reaffirmed; poetic endearments, pledges of tender devotion; sometimes it was all light banter, even a bit of nonsense.

While chaos raged outside and people behaved like beasts to one another, their love gained in strength. No one existed in the world except the two of them. All he could see before his eyes was her face—a rose garden—her ardent lips, her body yielding to his hand, the boundless happiness that was all his. If when lying in bed at night they would sometimes hear the sound of an approaching car, she would shudder, cross herself and whisper in terror, "Vitia, the…"

"It's nothing." He would press her to his heart, his voice would harden. "Be calm."

It was good that she wasn't alone any more. In the past she had lain trembling like a leaf at night, especially winter nights when it was very cold and she couldn't fall asleep.

"Why didn't you come before, in the winter?" she would say sadly. "You would have spared me so many fears."

"I didn't know." Vitia gazed down at her large mouth that was red and moist. "I've been searching for you all my life, yearning for you. My heart was longing for you."

"There can't be anything worse," she said with downcast face, "than to be a young girl, alone, without anyone, and a bourgeois to boot. That's what I am, right? I would lie alone in bed at night curled up under a mountain of old clothes, my fingers swollen and painful, my feet like two icicles, all kinds of nightmarish fears preying on my mind. Here, here they come, they grab hold of me, take me to the Cheka, straight to the head, the terrible Boldariov, Who are you? What's your name? Your father's name? What's your family's name? Ah, really? A chip off the old block, a class enemy! Your father and that bastard of a brother—we've already liquidated them! So you tried to run away, to hide from us? Take her to the wall! Straight to the wall!"

"Katia, poor Katia." Vitia stood before her with helpless hands, his eyes blinking.

"Terrible, terrible," she whispered, "It was as if I were being ripped apart, choked."

"From now on we'll always be together, forever together," he said.

"Only death will part us," she answered.

On one occasion she went beyond all bounds, speaking as no one did in those days, not even a father to his son, not even in utmost secrecy. Her tongue lashed curses down on them; it wouldn't last, the reign of cruel villains that crushed every soul, even to the cradle, and enjoyed shedding blood in the name of equality and justice. Like dogs she would kill them, like dogs. She ended with the words, "The Chekist interrogates and the revolver replies."

She didn't mince words.

III

To Vitia, Katia showed a contrariety of faces; today's face was not like yesterday's; she could be happy and sad, dreamy, radiant, somber, furious—in one individual, a multiplicity.

And he told her so.

She roused herself from her musings and looked at him as if he had suddenly made everything clear to her.

"So," she said, "I'm different. I'm contrary, I'm a mass of contradictions?"

Vitia laughed. "A whole world of contradictions, my whole world."

She stared into space and sat brooding. After a while she looked at him from the side, screwing up her eyes.

"I am not myself?" she, said uncertainly, "perhaps I am, perhaps not."

Chaos was mounting. The Cheka was hard at work crushing the counterrevolution at the roots. Fear of the Cheka pervaded every household, permeated the very air in the light of day, in the dark of night. Bloodshed was the order of the day. People were rotting away, living by stealth, hiding. Food grew scarcer. There was no water in the houses and no electricity. Nor was there any medicine in the hospitals.

Life became more violent every day. Night after night people were seized by the Cheka; in the morning most of them were dead. There was a story current about a certain woman commissar, a pillar of the revolution and of the Cheka, the head of the gang, who with her own hands killed all those condemned to death. Some said she was an old spinster, wrinkled, thin-lipped without eyelashes, and others, that she was a beautiful young girl. Both rumors were equally plausible.

Katia began to show a change. From day to day she changed

more and more. She didn't rush to him any more as in the beginning, and she didn't behave lovingly to him as she had. Sometimes they would quarrel and she would leave him. At other times she kept away from him and would shut the door on him.

Vitia didn't know what had happened to her. He began to think that to her their love wasn't anything unique, but something common, a possession of hers.

He was amazed and troubled and didn't understand.

"Katia," he would begin.

"Well, what?" She was short with him.

He would immediately shrivel up, unable to face her.

They were used to pooling their rations and eating together. One day she brought some fresh fruit and berries. He was delighted, it was a rare treat. Another time she brought some horsemeat. He was surprised at her since this was especially rare. He refused to eat it.

She laughed at him.

"Take your piece," she said.

He refused.

"I can't eat it."

"You'd better get rid of your stinking prejudices."

One day she told him that she had decided to join the party.

He was taken aback. He turned pale.

"How," he stammered, "you with those murderers?"

She pouted and didn't answer.

The same evening she came home with one of the "boys," a curly-haired fellow, dressed in a leather jacket, a revolver on his hip.

Vitia heard them talking and laughing on the other side of the wall. He suffered in anger and pain. Later, however, when she came to him, he curbed himself and said nothing.

The next day the curly-haired fellow returned. Vitia shut his eyes, clenched his fists not to shout out. He fled from the house and walked the streets for hours.

When Katia saw him composed and silent she was seized by anger.

"That's something for you," she said to herself in amazement.

As the days passed she changed completely. Her repasts were

no longer composed of meager rations; they were now full-course meals. Vitia did not join her at the table.

"These aren't meals for decent people," he hinted.

She immediately jumped at him with insults.

"I'm surprised," he said, "you whose father and brother were killed by them are becoming like one of them; they are your friends now."

"Mind your own business," she shouted at him with quivering lips, "Shut your mouth! It's no affair of yours."

She excoriated him now that he had dared speak to her in that way.

"Go to the devil!" She turned her back on him and called after him like an angry fishwife.

It was all over now, past repair. They broke apart. They stopped talking to each other. They didn't even greet one another.

Vitia was overcome by sorrow; he was melancholy and dejected. Katia, however, was euphoric, exhilarated, relaxed. She went out in a new dress and new shoes, her face beaming, her eyes filled with a luminous, laughing blueness.

Not many days passed and she moved from her room.

Vitia was shaken. This was the worst yet of all the troubles that had befallen him. He had never imagined that it would come to this; as if a part of him had been torn out of his very flesh.

Loneliness closed in on him. Bitter thoughts harassed him. Katia's image broke through them, beat against his heart, filled him with sadness and pain. The world had become disenchanted. A day which had been all sunshine had turned out to be a delusion. The revolution had ceased to exist for him—its humdrum reality as well as its terror. Without knowing it, he had forgotten to be afraid.

IV

That night the Cheka came and searched his room. They took him away and threw him into prison.

A few days later he was brought before the Cheka interrogator It was after midnight. The interrogator sat behind his desk in the full panoply of authority: French military tunic, and riding breeches, the revolver before him. He questioned Vitia and wrote down the answers.

Vitia was panic stricken. The examiner tried to put him at ease. He was an educated man. The expression of his face, his fleshy mouth, the bald patch showing through his pale hair suggested an easy-going man.

The questions were routine: name, parents' names, surname, and many similar particulars. After he had covered the entire paper from top to bottom he lifted his eyes and looked straight at him. His eyelids were red with fatigue, his eyes a faded blue.

"Do you know Podbelskaya?" He leaned his head on the palm of his hand.

"Podbelskaya?" He wondered. "Who is she? No, I don't know her."

"Yekatrina Alexeyevna, a young girl."

"Oh," he caught himself, "Katia."

"Well?"

"I know her," he said weakly as a suspicion flashed through his mind.

"Who is she?"

"What do you mean, who is she?" He didn't know what was being asked of him. Hastily he added, "She's an excellent person."

"She's a counter-revolutionary," he contradicted him curtly.

"She's a counter-revolutionary from home and on her own account. What is there between you?"

"I…. I.." He struggled for words.

"You were together, close, inseparable."

He bowed his head and didn't answer.

The interrogator's stare goaded him on as he waited in silence for a reply.

"What is there between you?"

"She left," he said in a broken voice.

"What activity did you participate in? What did you talk about?"

"We didn't do anything." He gave him a frightened side glance. "We were government employees."

"Don't make me lose my patience," he rebuked him.

He put a piece of paper and a pen in front of him.

"Now write," he ordered him.

Vitia sat down on the edge of the chair holding the pen feebly in his hand; he fidgeted restlessly, wrinkling his forehead, his eyes darting frightened glances from side to side.

"What should I write?" He consulted Trotsky whose photograph was hanging on the opposite wall.

"Everything. Your activities, your attitude to the workers' and peasants' soviet, whatever concerns you. Write everything."

He concentrated, bending over the paper.

"I'm a high school kid…"

So he began. He continued, writing about the seven years he had spent in grammar school, his teachers, his schoolfriends, the literary magazine he had edited, the socialist circle that he and his friends had founded, and all the other youthful pastimes he had engaged in.

The interrogator drew the paper to him and examined it.

"What was that circle you founded?" he asked.

"Socialist, of course," Vitia answered with subdued satisfaction.

"Socialist revolutionary?"

"Just socialist. That was in the fifth form."

"It's a lie!" He raised his voice. "Cross that out and write that you are a socialist revolutionary."

"No…I…"

He didn't manage to say what he had in mind before the interrogator jumped up and slapped him twice.

"Cross it out and write fast."

Vitia busied himself with his nose from which thick drops of blood were slowly oozing. He turned his cheek sideways and shook his head to say no.

"Ah.. so.." The interrogator was shocked. He raised his arm and beat and kicked him. "Yes or no? Yes or no?"

The more he raged and beat him the more silent Vitia became turning the cheek that had swelled to the side and shaking his head no.

"I'll murder you," the interrogator screamed shrilly. Finally he returned to his desk, pale and trembling, beads of perspiration showing on his forehead.

"Son of a bitch," he whispered angrily, "I'll show you." He pushed the bell. An armed soldier came in and took Vitia from the room.

Five days later they again look Vitia from the prison and brought him before the Cheka interrogator.

The interrogator was sitting at his desk. In his hands were Vitia's poems, which he was reading. He turned a page and laid it on the desk, took another page and pored over it. He paused between poems, leaning his head on his hand and sitting as if dreaming. Then he read the poem all over again from the beginning, since poetry should be read with the fullest concentration.

"Yes." He spoke decisively.

He raised his eyes and looked genially in Vitia's direction.

"Fine," he said, "you write well, first-rate poetry."

Vitia stood before him like a vagrant; dirty, his hair disheveled, his clothes creased and covered with filth.

"Well now," the interrogator's voice hardened.

Authority emanated from his voice, from his military tunic, from the two straps holding his revolver which crisscrossed his chest.

"Well," he asked softly, "what are we going to do with you?"

He waited a bit and then added,

"I'm surprised: that you, an intelligent man, a poet, when you have to fill out a questionnaire make such a jumble of the devil only knows what."

"I wrote the truth," Vitia replied.

"But what have you here!" the interrogator pointed his finger at the paper before him, speaking slowly as if this were a casual conversation, "that you are a social revolutionary, an unredeemed enemy."

"I am not a social revolutionary," Vitia echoed him as if clinging to his words.

"All right." Bored, the investigator took up his pencil and began to roll it between his fingers. "If you aren't one, then what did you have to do with the workers' and peasants' government? Why did you sneak into a government office?"

"I didn't sneak in," Vitia shuddered.

"You didn't sneak in?" He looked straight into his eyes, "but what else then? You are not an enemy of the people?"

"I came to earn a living."

"What you are saying is absurd. You intended to sabotage the government of the workers and peasants."

Vitia was at a loss for an answer.

"Where do you meet?" The interrogator shouted. "How many are you? Who are you?"

Vitia held out both hands in dumb amazement and didn't say a word.

"Open your mouth and talk!" The interrogator struck the desk with his fist. "Talk."

Seven times they brought him back to the interrogator; each time he was accused of some new crime. The seventh time he returned to the episode of Katia. This Katia, who is she, what is she like, from what sort of family does she come, and what was there between them. And why hadn't he reported her.

He didn't know what to answer.

He said, "We were neighbors."

"Neighbors?" His eyes probed him.

He was silent.

"Only neighbors or more than that?"

He opened his mouth like a hooked fish. He wanted to say something and said nothing.

"Did you help her with food?" the interrogator pressed him.

"Yes, I did," admitted Vitia.

"Did you go to the market and buy her tomatoes, cucumbers, and mulberries...mulberries?"

When Vitia heard this, his hair stood on end. He realized that Katia was here, that she too was in the hands of the Cheka, and that it was from her that his interrogator had heard about the things he had bought.

"She didn't have a thing to eat," he pleaded for Katia, or perhaps for himself.

"You are two of a kind," scowled the interrogator, "cut from from one block."

"She did nothing wrong," Vitia said terrified.

"Aha…she did nothing wrong! You were soulmates, what?" he said, as if this were a punishable crime.

He quickly jumped from his seat and began pacing with big steps.

"Counter-revolutionary!" He stamped his foot, his face a fury, his hands clenched. "Mulberries, mulberries! *Ha*! Speak! Open your mouth and talk! We know everything. Podbelskaya is in our hands."

Vitia turned pale. At last he understood that it wasn't just a matter of mulberries, but something far more serious…a personal enemy, as it were, not a political adversary, but a mortal foe, and perhaps a madman?

The interrogator returned to his place and sat down. He pushed the bell before him on the desk. He smoothed his hair down with both hands and followed Vitia with his eyes until he left the room accompanied by the soldier.

Three days went by. At two past midnight they came to take Vitia from the prison to the Cheka. This time they didn't conduct him to the interrogator's room but led him down the stairs.

"Where to?" he asked.

The soldier attending him did not reply. On the last step the soldier left him and went away.

Vitia felt someone standing behind him.

He turned in panic and cried out,

"Katia!"

At the same moment a loud shot was heard.

He made a half turn backward and fell headlong to the ground.

Translated by Pearl Gordon

He Ordained

I

Every week gives birth to a Sabbath, holy days are born at all times of the year, and a new moon is born every month. As a schoolboy, Asher Radilovsky would bless the new moon joyfully in the presence of the entire assembly at the synagogue, since "in the multitude of people is the king's honor." He danced before the moon, repeating *sholem aleikhem* three times, like a well-practiced old man, and those standing nearby would respond *aleikhem sholem,* and again and again he would exclaim, "May it be a good omen and good fortune for us and all Israel! A good omen and good fortune for us and all Israel! A good omen and good fortune for us and all Israel!" and so on and so forth, to "the ends of the world."

When he grew up, he would sail with the girls in a boat on the river and when the waves danced against the moon, he would raise his voice in the "Internationale," "Volga-Volga," and "Dubinushka," and it was not long before he was caught and arrested.

With the coming of the Revolution he was released from prison. At once, he rushed off to fight against Petlura, and then against Denikin and the Poles. Three times he was wounded and recovered.

During the Spanish war against the fascists he boarded a Soviet boat for Spain and fought there too. When he returned, he completed his studies at the university and married one of the nurses who had taken care of him in the hospital. The match did not flourish. He suffered with her less than a year before they were divorced. Just then the Nazi war broke out. He got himself sent to the armored corps and fought throughout those hard and bitter years. He was one of the first to enter Berlin with the Soviet army.

Returning to Moscow as a hero from the battlefield, he was promptly imprisoned and then exiled to Vorkuta. He did not know why it happened to him, what he had done wrong. He spent years and years at hard labor, until a member of the Polish government, the husband of his younger brother's daughter, plucked him from the mines of Vorkuta and brought him as a Polish citizen to Warsaw. This was due to his native town, Kosnitsa, having become part of Poland after its repartition.

His entire family had vanished. Some had fallen victim to Petlura, some to Denikin, some to the Poles, and others perished in the Nazi gas chambers. The only survivor was his niece, who had been sheltered in a convent and brought up as a Catholic.

He was weary of all that had happened to him, despaired of Communism, of the party leaders and their oppressive rule. He spent a year in Poland, resting and recuperating. Pondering what future course he should follow, he devoted himself to studying French. Poland did not agree with him and he wished to go to France. As special favor, he was allowed to leave by those in power.

In Paris he did not mix with French Communists and did not present himself at the Polish embassy. While still on the train, he had torn up his membership card in the Communist Party.

It was at the house of a Russian newspaper editor, a former Social Revolutionary, that he met Madame Tissaud. She was a French-woman in her forties, a widow, good-looking and pleasant. She taught medieval history and was a devout Catholic.

They met occasionally and became friends. They would discuss social affairs, Communism and democracy, the principles of philosophy, the ferment of modern literature and art. He soaked in every new development, rushed to see every exhibition and play. Four or five times he accompanied her to ancient churches, where she drew his attention to their style and the art works they contained, and explained the arches, the stained-glass windows, the galleries which hung between the columns on the left and on the right, angels, paintings and statues. In passing, she half-knelt before the altar, lighted a candle before the Virgin Mary and lingered in front of a statue of Jesus. Later, when they left, she praised that statue which, she said, was a sixteenth-century masterpiece. Asher Radilovsky was not moved by it and said that Apollo was better looking.

"At any event," he added, "He did not need to be the Son of God to be crucified." Pausing briefly, he then said, "I've seen many like him. Thousands."

Mme. Tissaud, taken aback, glanced at him and looked away.

"Forgive me, madame," he said, alarmed. "I hope I haven't offended you."

One day she asked him about his past. He said, "I've changed. Oh, I've changed a great deal."

She asked to see a picture of him in his youth. He did not have one, but produced from his wallet a small crushed photograph of a man with wild hair, lifeless eyes and a gloomy face encrusted with a week-old beard.

"Who's that?" her hand recoiled.

He looked up and replied indirectly, "Only the leader deserves hard labor."

"Was that you?..." she looked doubtfully from the photograph to him.

"A judge who sentences a criminal to hang should be hanged first," he said in a low voice, half to himself, following his own thoughts.

Before long they were in love with each other. They resolved to marry, but she made it a condition that he convert and marry her in church.

It was a difficult step for him. Not that he cared much for religion, or considered the change a fault; neither the one nor the other. Nevertheless, his heart failed him and he hesitated, being of two minds in the matter.

Mme. Tissaud spoke to him in order to make him feel better and to show her love for him. Not only did she think highly of him, she said, and loved him dearly, but most especially she loved him because he was part of the people of the Son of God. He laughed and murmured, not altogether to the point, that he was a bad Jew, since all he had done in his life had not been for the Jews, nor had he been among them or a part of them.

"Ah," said she, "that confirms it. You do not know yourself nor do you realize this fact."

This sounded strange in his ears, but he hastened to declare to her that he was opposed to all religion, be it spiritual or materialistic, and was equally antagonistic to angels, spirits, demons or popular leaders.

Mme. Tissaud did not agree with him, and said that one did not resemble the other. He did not retort again, but won her over with an amicable smile and good humor.

"It is not necessary," he said, "to prove to a lovely woman something that is above common sense."

He moved from his hotel to one that was nearer the apartment house of Mme. Tissaud. A French publishing house commissioned him to write a book about labor camps and prisons in the Soviet Union. He worked hard at it, the enterprise went well, and he was in good spirits. Now he lacked only a home of his own, a family, a woman to be his companion, to fill his house with light and warmth, eternal love and endless happiness. These matters were close to his heart and he thought about them constantly, all the more so as old age was approaching and he was no longer a young man, being past middle-age, and was fearful of loneliness to come.

As always, he spent much time with Mme. Tissaud. Together they frequented the theater and the cinema and argued about art. Mme. Tissaud was always affectionate, yet now and then she would grow unwontedly thoughtful and sit quietly, seeming detached and distant.

Once, when they had been conversing at length, he asked, "What ails you, Margo? Is there something you are keeping from me? What are you so deep in thought about?"

"It is nothing, my friend," she gazed at him affectionately, with a slight smile that raised her upper lip and revealed her small pearly teeth. "I shall go to church and pray for me and for you."

He accompanied her as far as the church, and then went to a café, where he sat with a glass of beer in front of him. He was thinking that it was unseemly for a good-looking young woman to be kneeling before a skeletal body. It seemed to him to depreciate the woman's dignity, to be an ugly and unthinkable sight.

He put his lips to the glass and sipped his beer.

"Poor Margo," he said.

He repeated, "Poor Margo," by which he meant to say that all her sorrows and inner struggles were caused by none but himself. He, to whom religion meant nothing, who had freed himself from the precepts and observed none of them! What did he care about that small matter of the church? What held him back? What prohibition barred him?

After a while he left the café. It was an autumn evening. Clouds formed in the heavens. The moon sailed from cloud to cloud, hid itself, and then reappeared. He recollected an incident from his childhood, when the first fourteen days of the month had gone by and still the moon was unseen. His father, fearing that the night might pass and he would not be able to bless the new moon, walked from window to window, his eyes searching anxiously. Suddenly the heavens cleared and moonlight shone upon the earth, and he hurriedly rose and said the blessing. Then the sky clouded over again, and the family rejoiced.

Asher Radilovsky strove to recall the blessing of the new moon but it escaped him. This troubled him and his mind struggled to pull together some scraps and snatches, "The heavens and all the host thereof...the moon and the stars that Thou...that Thou..."

II

Many years have passed since that autumn night. Asher Radilovsky has become a God-fearing Jew, careful in the observance of all the precepts, the major and the minor alike. His wife Marguerite helped in every way. At first, she married him in a secular ceremony, at city hall, but later she willingly became espoused to him in the synagogue, according to the Laws of Moses and Israel.

"It is more seemly thus," she said.

As she put it, the only true Christians are the Jews, for they are persecuted everywhere, and the poor crowded synagogue where her husband prayed was a better place for the worship of God than the grandest churches in the city.

She took pride in her husband, who recollected the lessons of his youth and taught the Talmud to many, to such as professors, rabbis and priests. A kinsman of hers, Father Mercadieux, was extremely fond of him and was a regular visitor at their house, and always shared their Passover *seder* and their Purim feast.

When the American astronauts who landed on the moon recited the psalm that is said before the blessing of the new moon, it shook Asher Radilovsky to the core. When they came to "When I consider Thy heavens, the work of Thy fingers, the moon and the stars which Thou hast ordained," his eyes filled with tears.

"Margo," he said in a tremulous, choking whisper, "you remember that autumn night?—that was the start..."

Some time later his students came to see him, rabbis, priests and ordinary scholars. The conversation came around to the moon, which is home to no living creatures.

Said one, "Why did the Almighty trouble to create a world that is utterly desolate?"

Said another, "Why did the Almighty trouble to create a populous world?"

Said a third, "But is that the only empty world? Surely there exist hundreds of thousands of empty worlds."

Said a fourth, "Might there not be many populous worlds too?"

Asher Radilovsky shook himself, for he had been drifting into an old man's doze, stood up, pressed his arm against his breast and sang the *Adon Olam*, "Master of the Universe."

Later, they all left save Father Mercadieux. Asher Radilovsky paced back and forth in the room, singing, "And He was and He is and He will be in glory. And He is one and there is none like Him."

Father Mercadieux stopped him and questioned him about some of the more obscure passages in the hymn, to which he responded with translation and explication.

"Do you understand, my friend," he said, "do you under-stand?...Christianity is a religion unto itself, limited and small. That is to say, it is provincial, accepted in a world with the outlook of a child's mind. There are many worlds, worlds without end, a vast multitude of them, quite unrelated to the idea of Christianity. Aye, so it is. Neither the idea, nor a shred of significance...*Adon Olam*, the Master of the Universe, He is the creator.... Do you understand?.... Not merely of this globe, this one droplet.... A Master of all the cosmos, of this entire vast and terrible universe!"

"Let's not get carried away," replied Father Mercadieux with a gentle smile.

But Asher Radilovsky did not heed the priest's words and did not notice when he left. He kept pacing back and forth and singing again and again, "And He was and He is..."

Marguerite came in, meaning to ask what had caused Father Mercadieux to depart with such a gloomy countenance. She stood and watched him, her shrunken face puzzled, her white hair gleaming like fresh snow.

"What song is it you are singing, my friend?" she asked.

He told her the meaning of the hymn.

"What is man that Thou art mindful of him, and the son of man that thou Thinkest of him?"

He rested his head on her shoulders and the tears streamed from his eyes. "Forgive me. They are an old man's tears. We have aged, dear heart, we have aged..."

Translated by Yael Lotan

Thunder

The two of them, Marusia and Pesach Gafni, did not suit each other, neither their character nor their style, nor did their views concur. Marusia was firm in her views and Pesach Gafni stubbornly held to his; her arguments were "but of course" and his were "but perhaps," she in a vexed disputative tone and he in one of inner complaint. Not a day passed without their becoming plaintiff and defendant. At times they leaped into strife and meted out to each other eye for eye, and at times they restrained themselves and walked about sullen and fuming, not speaking their thoughts, one not yielding and the other not pardoning. Such were their ups and downs all their days. The older they got the more the anger grew. It grew especially from the time Pesach Gafni was pensioned off and started spending most of the day at home. The affairs of the house were decided by Marusia, and Pesach Gafni was ignored and left idle, like a man dismissed. A pensioner in a double sense.

In March Marusia went to Tiberias. This was her custom every year: to go and bathe in the hot springs at Tiberias. Pesach Gafni didn't go, and stayed at home. This, he said, was his Tiberias.

These were days of both rain and sunshine. The sun stayed out and the rain came and went; the rain left and the sun reappeared. Pesach Gafni was happy. His mind was at ease and he was pleased with himself, like one who has paid off a debt and knows peace. In the morning he made himself coffee and read a newspaper at leisure, at noon he ate with relish a dish he had cooked. In the afternoon he lay down and slept a lot. Then he and a friend told each other things, or he played chess at the pensioners' club. In the evening he listened to the radio or wrote letters to his sons in America, all of whom were famous professors—to them and to their wives and children. He wrote at length, and lightly, with much sharpness and good humor. His sons knew that their old man's wit still had an edge to it. From time to time Marusia telephoned from Tiberias, and in an affectionate tone gave either advice or orders: do this and don't do that. Yes. As she said. He'd do this and he wouldn't do that. Agreed. Very good. Everything in the world suited him.

One night he awoke from his sleep. Earlier he had gone to bed and read a book until slumber had snatched him. At midnight he awoke. It was dark in the house. A great heap of darkness. Dread descended upon him. Not the dread that comes from a bad dream, for nothing had appeared to him, but a dark blank dread, buried in the heart, the dread of death.

He wanted to turn on a light. He confused the right-hand wall with the left-hand wall and his hand roved groping in the darkness, not finding the place where the lamp was. He jerked himself half off his bed and bumped into either the wall or the wardrobe. He fell on his back and lay there. Sweat poured from his body and his hair stood on end. The pressure mounted and stifled him in the throat.

From outside came the sound of the rain that had just started falling. By the knocking of the rain on the shutters of the window he aimed for the place where the lamp was and turned on the light. But the dread didn't evaporate. On the contrary, the light proclaimed it further and made it a reality. Yes. It was a certainty. No certainty was greater than this one. His course was done. The end.

He sprang from his bed and went into the living room. He walked to the window and listened to the singing of the rain in the drainpipe.

"It's a good rain," he said. "It does its work well."

The rain and its work didn't pacify him. He moved away and wandered into the kitchen and out of the cupboard took a light cake. He didn't enjoy it in the slightest. He spread out his fingertips and the cake fell from them. He thought of telephoning Tiberias, to Marusia. What use would Marusia be to him? Marusia, uncompassionate, sad and bitter…domineering! His hour had come. An old man, full of days.

In his heaviness he walked slowly, step after step. He stopped abruptly, casting down his eyes and put his mind to the similarity he felt to what Tolstoy had described in "The Memoirs of a Madman". He remembered the body of the tale but not how it ended, not what had made the dread go away, and not only that—even a great joy that had come. No, no. This wasn't something to be learned by analogy. Nonsense. Nonsense inside and out! Tolstoy had deceived him, had cheated himself.

The dread didn't leave him. Old, old. His years had run out, he was declining into the shadow of death. He dragged his feet back to his bed, and lay down. He turned his mind to several matters, lay there in a mist of vagueness, repeated a poem by Lermontov inside his mouth. He found no rest—his mouth and heart seemed poles apart.

He started trying to clear his mind, telling himself, ,"So, nonsense. A new discovery you've made ! This is the measure of all men." That was it. Yes. Yes. He was about to die. The end of all men is to die. He'd be laid out, like this, in his shroud, with two lighted candles at his head, his face waxen, his lips blue, his eyes shut and Marusia standing before him, her swollen eyes dripping tears…

He shuddered, feeling his soul shrinking within him, lamenting in this light which was substantial, which was exposing, malicious. He reached out his hand and put out the light. The darkness mingled with his body and swallowed him. Loneliness came over him and made his load even heavier. It seemed he was cast off in the world, alone and deserted, abandoned to the sentence of death that had been passed upon him. The darkness was bad and the light was not good, and the stillness was oppressive, a stillness as of dying and of after death.

The rain grew stronger and drove down rapidly, mightily. A torrent of rain. Thunder rolled from afar and came and beat on the rooftop as if the sky had burst upon it, filling the house with the noise and din of childhood. At that moment his loneliness vanished and with it the mourning in the heart.

"Ha!"—he exclaimed, and sat bolt upright, placed a hand on top of his head to cover it and whispered the blessing, "He Whose power and Whose might fill the world."

Translated by Richard Flantz

Ecce Homo

Buffalmacco left his friend Del Saggio's place in high spirits, his eyes foggy from the wine that he had drunk. He saw a man approaching, stopped to look at him, and suddenly it was though a cloud had passed and the sky had turned bright.

He went up to the man and, his face full of wonderment, saying, "Who are you?"

The man answered him, "My name is Alessandro, and I'm on my way from a place which I had to leave."

"*Ma va!*" Buffalmacco exclaimed, delighted with him. "Then we're birds of a feather! Come along with me."

Alessandro thought that Buffalmacco had latched on to him thinking he was someone else, and refused to go along.

"Come on!" Buffalmacco insisted. "Don't be stubborn. By order of His Holiness the Pope!"

Alessandro held his ground.

"Listen to me! Nobody has ever been sorry that he listened to me," Buffalmacco said reassuringly. "I am the famous Buffalmacco. Giotto and then some. At my place you will find food and drink to your heart's content."

Alessandro stood there, pondering.

"I'm not letting you out of my hands," persisted Buffalmacco. "Oh, no! Heaven itself has sent you to me. You're a veritable messenger from Heaven."

He fastened his arm about Alessandro and the two of them staggered along, weaving from side to side as they went. At last they reached Buffalmacco's place, an old house leaning to one side, dry as an old shard, its shutters faded and rotted with age.

The three pupils sensed the approach of their master, and began fussing about, this one sweeping the floor—raising the dust to the very rafters, another pinning up canvas for a picture, the third applying himself diligently to the painting which his master has assigned him to finish.

Buffalmacco came into the house cursing, ,"So, you've been shooting dice, have you, you pack of sluggards? A bloody plague on you!"

Alessandro's eyes swept over the chaos in the house: paintings, sketches, old domestic utensils and paint-soiled rags scattered everywhere.

"Sit down," said Buffalmacco. "Something to wet the throat?"

"Yes."

Buffalmacco let out a yell, "Olivetta! Where are you, you old witch? Set the table!"

An old serving woman, with smiling eyes and disheveled gray hair, came in and set the table.

"A pitcher of wine!" bellowed Buffalmacco.

He clutched the pupil who was sweeping the floor and threw him down. Then he went up to the picture to examine the work of the other student.

"*Merda!*" He gave him a box on the ears, snatched the brush from his hand, and ran it over all that the student had done. "To scratch your belly, that's all you know, not how to paint!"

Then he sat down with Alessandro, and the two of them attacked the delicious meat and excellent wine with gusto.

When they had finished eating and drinking, Buffalmacco rose from the table.

"It's time," he said to his pupils. "Have you ground some pigments? Well, grind some more! Quickly!"

He took Alessandro and dressed him in a blue silken robe that fell in voluminous folds. He showed him how to sit, how to raise his eyes. Then he took the brush that his pupil brought him and began painting Alessandro's likeness on the canvas. His three pupils stood behind him, watching.

As he worked, Buffalmacco praised himself, proclaiming that, had Dante not been exiled, he would have now put him into his Divine Comedy along with Guido, Cimabue and Giotto.

"But never mind, I will paint you as Apelles painted Alexander the Great."

He paused between strokes to gaze for a while on Alessandro's face. He resumed his work and said, "Just as Apelles completed the portrait of Alexander, his horse saw it and neighed. The animal thought that he was looking at Alexander in the flesh, not at his likeness."

For three days Buffalmacco painted Alessandro, then he paid him generously and dismissed him.

It was the figure of Jesus that he had painted. Now he had only to find someone resembling Judas Iscariot, so that he might fulfill the agreement between him and Pope Boniface. The Pope had commissioned him to paint Jesus and Judas Iscariot engaged in affectionate, intimate conversation.

In Florence word got around that Buffalmacco had painted a Jesus such as no painter before him had done, not even Giotto, and that it deserved to be placed in a church for worshippers to kneel before it. But Buffalmacco hid the painting, saying that it was of little worth and quite insignificant, and, besides, that he had already painted a picture of Aphrodite over it.

Buffalmacco was a renowned artist in his day, and his frescoes and paintings were to be found in all the churches and monasteries of Tuscany. He was well aware of the power of his brush, but found no pleasure in all those godly images on the cross, or in the shabby saints with their mortified, decrepit faces. He would have liked to see the world in the light of life, not of death. If he had his way, he said, he would paint the Mother of God naked, he would reveal to the eyes of the world the majestic beauty of her breasts and all the other charms and delights of her body so that all people should be drawn to her radiance. But he had to content himself with modeling her after the visage of Concettina, a very lovely woman whom he drew to his bed at night from time to time, and then he would boast that he had lain with the Mother of God.

Many of his pictures bearing the image of Concettina were hung in churches and people prayed to them.

"Many a Concettina," he jested "has been done away with by the people who lit sooty candles under her nose."

He would philosophize over a glass of wine, asserting that art was nothing but the artist's imagination. There was a widely held theory, he said, that it was not Medea who murdered her children but the Corinthians, and that it was Euripides who invented the whole story of Colchis. It appears, then, that invention triumphs over truth. And the same goes for Concettina and the Mother of God.

Buffalmacco was a *bon vivant,* a joker and a wencher, a glutton and a drunkard, who delighted in the content of the cooking pot and the jug. That's just how he was. He and his friends—artists all—would gather at Mazzo Del Saggio's and think up all kinds of pranks and sly tricks. There is the incident of the pig which they stole from their friend Calendrino, salted and ate together with him; on another occasion, they cast a spell on Calendrino to make him invisible. And there is the story of how Buffalmacco beguiled some nuns by telling them that he needed a pitcher of wine for a pigment to redden the figures which he was painting on the walls of their church; and, of course, he promptly proceeded to swallow the wine. There is also the incident of the townsfolk who refused to pay him for a mural that he had painted of the Mother of God holding the Holy Infant in her arms. What did he do but transform the babe into a bear cub! Such were the pranks that he played and that is how he carried on for many years until he reached middle age and began to think of settling down.

There was a girl in the town who had captured his heart, Maria

Cecilia was her name, and he pursued her affectionately with such names as Nymph, Venus, Psyche. At first he tried to lead her astray by the tale that love could be won not by mere words but by acts alone. She laughed in his face flinging "Concettina!" at him. He pretended not to hear, and kept on flooding her with flattery. She turned her back on him and went off. But, in the end, she yielded and married him.

Before the year was out she bore him a son, and in another year produced a daughter. She tried to turn him into a solid, staid, citizen, but he was too much for her. Once Buffalmacco, always Buffalmacco! Maria Cecilia kept conceiving and delivering, conceiving and delivering, filling out, thickening and overflowing on all sides. Now Buffalmacco no longer called her Venus or Nymph but shrieked Hecate, Bellona, Cerberus, Fury, or just plain hell-hag, at her.

One day he fled from the house into a tavern. There he found a man sitting over a glass of wine. It was the sort of man the world were best rid of, an embittered person of evil and violence. He sat down with him.

"Who and what are you? he asked.

The man did not reply but took the glass and emptied it in a single gulp.

"Two glasses of wine!" Buffalmacco called out into the space of the tavern.

The waiter instantly brought two brimming glasses.

"What have you been up to?" asked Buffalmacco.

The man lifted his glass and drank.

"Do you belong to the Blacks or the Whites?" Buffalmacco kept prodding him.

"I am Popolo Minuto," the man answered evasively.

Buffalmacco studied him and decided that he was a partisan neither of the Pope nor of Colonna, but most likely a highwayman. At once he remembered Judas Iscariot, who had been in the back of his mind all these years, and now here was Judas Iscariot right before him, as large as life, a Judas Iscariot without compare.

Buffalmacco took his glass and drank.

"Come home with me," he said to the man. "At my home you

will find a loaf of bread, a hot meal and all the wine that you can drink."

The man smiled slyly out of the corner of his mouth.

"You're a painter?" he asked.

"The greatest of them all!" Buffalmacco said, proudly blowing out his cheeks.

"One can see that you're a great one," the man answered.

Buffalmacco clapped him on the back and pulled him up.

"Let's go!" he shouted.

He took the man and brought him home. There he started to rummage among the piles of pictures and sheets of paper that were heaped on top of each other throughout the house, until he found the picture of Jesus. Turning his back on the man, he began to paint him, glancing at him now and then as he painted.

For three days he toiled over the man. When the three days were over, he paid him his wages and thrust him away.

"Begone, Judas!" he growled at him.

The man ignored him and his scolding, and just stood there, gazing at the picture.

Suddenly he bent down and knelt before the image of Jesus.

"I.... I..." he said in faltering tones, as he spread his arms out toward Jesus. "This is me. Alessandro..."

Buffalmacco looked from Jesus to the man and from the man to Jesus.

"Me... this is me..." cried the man, beating his hands together, genuflecting again and again. "Me...Alessandro..."

Translated by Batyah Abbady

About the Editor

Dan Miron is the Leonard Kaye Professor of Hebrew Literature at Columbia University and Chair of the Department of Hebrew Literature at the Hebrew University of Jerusalem. A prolific scholar, critic and editor, Dr. Miron has established himself over the past three decades as the leading authority on Hebrew literature. His influential books (more than twenty, in both Hebrew and English) study most of the prominent Hebrew and Yiddish authors, fiction writers and poets since the revival of Hebrew literature in the nineteenth century. As an editor-scholar, he is responsible for some of the most important "collected writing" projects published in Hebrew from the previous century (Bialik's poems, Gnessin's stories, and many more). His latest book, *From the Worm a Butterfly Emerges*, is a spellbinding examination of the life and work of young Nathan Alterman.

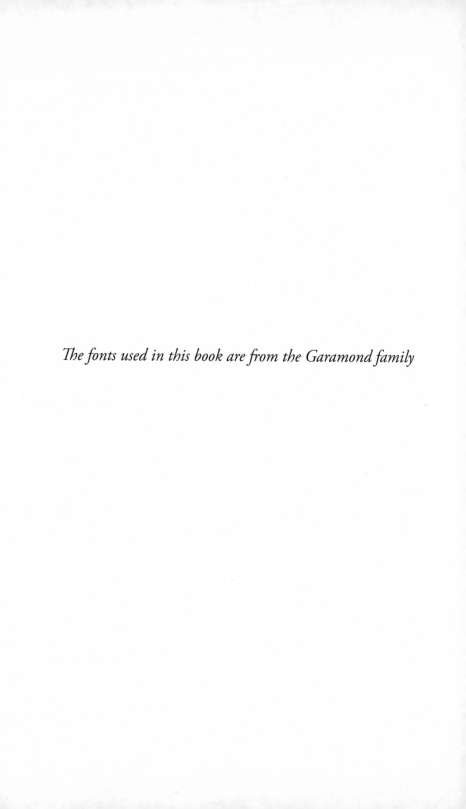

The fonts used in this book are from the Garamond family

The Toby Press publishes fine writing, available
at leading bookstores everywhere. For more
information, please visit www.tobypress.com